The Loveless Child

Elsie Mason is the pen name of Paul Magrs.

Paul was born in Jarrow in 1969 and brought up in the North East of England. Since 1995, he has published fiction in many different genres – literary magical realism, Gothic mystery, science fiction, crime and young adult. He lectured in Creative Writing for many years at both the University of East Anglia and at Manchester Metropolitan University.

In 2019, he published his book on writing, *The Novel Inside You*. In 2020, Snow Books republished his Brenda and Effie Mystery series of novels. In 2021, Harper Collins published his book of cartoons, *The Panda, the Cat and the Dreadful Teddy*. In 2022, he won the Crime Writers' Association prize for best short story of the year.

Whichever genre he has worked in, he has always written about working-class women from the north. In many ways, historical and romantic saga fiction was the first genre he was aware of, as a child, when he eavesdropped on his female relatives telling tales around the kitchen table in South Shields.

Taking on a female pen name has been wonderfully liberating: he has loved writing as Elsie.

He writes and lives in Manchester with Jeremy and Bernard Socks.

The Loveless Child

Elsie Mason

ORION

First published in Great Britain in 2025 by Orion Fiction,
an imprint of The Orion Publishing Group Ltd.
Carmelite House, 50 Victoria Embankment
London EC4Y 0DZ

The authorised representative in the EEA is Hachette Ireland,
8 Castlecourt Centre, Castleknock Road, Castleknock, Dublin 15, D15 XTP3,
Republic of Ireland (email: info@hbgi.ie)

An Hachette UK Company

3 5 7 9 10 8 6 4 2

Copyright © Paul Magrs 2025

The moral right of Paul Magrs to be identified as
the author of this work has been asserted in accordance
with the Copyright, Designs and Patents Act of 1988.

All rights reserved. No part of this publication may be
reproduced, stored in a retrieval system, or transmitted
in any form or by any means, electronic, mechanical,
photocopying, recording, or otherwise, without the
prior permission of both the copyright owner and the
above publisher of this book.

All the characters in this book are fictitious, and any resemblance
to actual persons, living or dead, is purely coincidental.

A CIP catalogue record for this book is
available from the British Library.

ISBN (Mass Market Paperback) 9781398709003
ISBN (eBook) 9781398709010
ISBN (Audio) 9781398721098

Typeset by Born Group
Printed and bound in Great Britain by Clays Ltd, Elcograf S.p.A.

www.orionbooks.co.uk

Dedicated to the Masons and the Magrsies.
I showed you all.

Chapter One

Life was always going on around her, but Minnie Minton never really felt like she was fully a part of it. Life was exciting, wonderful, dizzying. Sometimes, it could be alarming and dangerous, especially here at the heart of the Sixteen Streets, where there was always some kind of drama going on. Still, Minnie Minton felt like she was left out of things.

Take this evening, for example. There was a celebration going on at the Robin Hood public bar at the top of Frederick Street, where all of Minnie's family and friends lived. There were boys back from the Front on leave and they were being welcomed home for a little while. Why, you could hear the noise from the pub all the way over here. On the other side of the street, where Minnie was working at the fish bar, the heated hullabaloo could still be heard. How she longed to be part of that gathering, singing along to the old songs at the piano, maybe having a dance or a cuddle with someone.

She flushed even to think of that. How silly of her. Who would want to cuddle Minnie Minton? At twenty-seven, she was more homely-looking than ever. She was moon-faced and ever so slightly boss-eyed. This was the less-than-kind way her best friend Junie had once put it. Junie, who was blonde and slim and beautiful, had a sharp way with words. 'Your face is sort of puddingy, Minnie. That's what I'd call it. Your eyes are like currants in a big doughy bun.'

She knew that Junie didn't really set out to hurt her feelings. It was just the way she was. She felt that she could talk any old how to her best friend in all the world and there would never be any hard feelings. How could there be? Minnie adored Junie and always had, ever since the first day the blonde girl had arrived here in the Sixteen Streets.

How long ago was that? By, it was years ago. It was well before the war started, wasn't it? Junie was only sixteen when she pitched up here – as the long-lost daughter of the landlady of the Robin Hood. Minnie herself had only been seventeen, and she had felt much, much younger beside the self-possessed and sophisticated Junie.

All that time ago. Why, it seemed a whole different world. The world as it was before this damned war. It had been a poor time and they'd all been hard up of course, but at least there was no danger. It was a relatively carefree world. There hadn't been death raining down from the skies when the Luftwaffe came roaring overhead like demons from hell. People had never had to sit all night sheltering deep underground as the bombs went off. Mind, hiding under the ground in the deep, damp shelters was preferable to the alternative. Everyone in South Shields knew of someone who had been killed or made homeless by the air raids. Everyone Minnie knew had been brushed by the shadow of death.

She shivered and shook herself out of her gloomy thoughts. There was work to do. She still had fish to fry and chips to cut and customers to serve before her night's work was over. A whole night manning the hot counter at 'Swetty' Betty's fish bar could be exhausting, but Minnie was determined to finish up here and shoot over to the Robin Hood. She wanted to get there in time for last orders, so that she could see what all the fuss was about over there tonight.

Her mother was beaming at her endless queue of customers, wrapping their suppers in reams of greaseproof paper and pages of the *Gazette*. 'You'll let me nip off early for last orders, won't you, Mam?' Minnie asked.

Betty Minton scowled at her daughter. 'Eeeh, Minnie. You're a hopeless article. What do you want over there with that lot? They don't want you hanging round them all the time. Them Farleys and the Sturrocks and all of them. They just laugh at you behind your back, you know. You'll never fit in with that crowd.'

Minnie felt her face grow hot. 'That's not true,' she gasped. She realised she was answering back in front of customers, but she didn't care. 'They're all good friends of mine.'

Her mother tutted. 'None of you lot are bairns anymore. You're not going out to play with your pals. Why, they're all courting and getting married, all those Farley boys and what-have-you. Even that Tom Farley has gone and got himself married, I hear. Some lass from down Norfolk. She's come up here to live. They're all just about spoken for, all the lads round here.' Betty Minton laughed and shook her head so that her fleshy wattles shook. 'There's no use hanging round all them lads, Minnie. You've not caught yourself one yet, and I doubt that you ever will.'

Minnie frowned. 'I'm not after catching myself a lad,' she said in a small voice. 'But they're all my friends, all the lads and lasses round here, and even if they're grown up now, and getting married and settled . . . why, I still like to keep up with what's happening with them all. It's important to me.'

Her mother sighed, wrapping up four fish suppers for portly Mr Chesney, who lived right at the bottom of Frederick Street with his three grown-up daughters. That little, pink-faced man with the ginger tash had his overcoat buttoned right up to the neck against the autumn cold and he looked just as amused by Minnie's silly chuntering as her mother was. 'Mr

Chesney,' Swetty Betty appealed to him. 'You've brought up three daughters. Why, you've done so very successfully, and as a widower, too. You've done a fine job and all three girls are a credit to you. What do you reckon to my one, eh? What do you have to say about this useless article?' Betty waved dismissively at Minnie, who was dusting silvery fillets in flour and blushing furiously.

But portly Mr Chesney from number one Frederick Street was a kindly parent. He was much kindlier than Betty Minton. 'Ah, she's a fine girl, your Minnie. I always thought so, Mrs Minton. She's worth ten of the more flashy ones round here. You'll see one day, Mrs Minton. You'll see what a treasure she is.'

Then he paid for his family's supper and shuffled out with a swift nod at them both. Betty Minton stared open-mouthed at his departing back, and Minnie allowed herself a small grin of delight at the compliment. She wanted to shout: 'See, Mother? Not everyone thinks I'm hopeless.'

By the time Minnie was over the road and pushing her way into the crowded saloon bar, it was almost too late to order a drink. She caught the landlady's eye just before the old ship's bell was rung to signal the end of another busy night.

The room was stuffy, smoky and dark with the blackout curtains down. It felt rather stifling after the cool night air out on Frederick Street.

'Minnie, you'll be wanting a stout?' landlady Cathy Sturrock asked her.

As the drink was plonked down on the polished wooden bar, Minnie grinned. It was lovely to feel welcomed and at home here, at the heart of their community. Well, so she should feel at home. She had worked here, behind this very bar, for several years, from being nothing but a nipper. She had spent about as much time working at this bar as she had at Swetty Betty's.

The dark stout with its creamy froth tasted deliciously bitter. It slaked her parched throat after hours of working in the damp steam of her mother's shop. 'Eeeh, that's lovely that,' she beamed at Cathy. 'Thank you for waiting for me.'

Cathy nodded and jangled the bell that had hung for decades above the bar. 'That's time now, lads and lasses,' she bellowed. 'I'll not be telling you all again.'

The pub started to clear almost at once. At one time, the job had been harder, with Cathy and her loyal barmaids having to scoot the drinkers out into the street. With the war on, however, people were keen to get safely home at night. They didn't dally so much in the unlit streets.

'What's all the fuss about tonight?' Minnie asked her older friend. She looked at Cathy and for the first time saw that the landlady was looking her age. The fine wrinkles around her eyes had deepened. She had lines down the sides of her mouth, too. How old was she now? Forty-something or so? She was still fine-looking, of course, and glamorous in her off-the-shoulder frock. She always wore deep green or red, to accentuate her long auburn hair. There was no hint of that wonderful colour becoming duller, Minnie thought admiringly. Then, the thought struck her: why, maybe Cathy actually dyed her hair that colour these days? Might she be giving nature a little helping hand? The rumour was that she had taken up with a much younger man, so maybe she felt the need to keep herself as young and fresh as she could . . . ?

'Oh, it's just been the whole Farley clan. They've all been in, bar Tony, who's still away. But all the rest of them. Ma Ada and all her brood. She looked pleased as punch to have them all about her: Beryl and that new lass Irene, and her Tom and Sam . . . and Bob, of course.' She faltered oddly and looked over Minnie's shoulder at the departing drinkers as she said Bob's name. Her pot man, Bob. He had worked in the pub for several years. He was thirty now and Cathy's junior by quite some years. But if the tales Minnie had heard were true, Bob Farley the pot man was doing more than fixing up the barrels and seeing to Cathy's beer cellar . . .

Not that Minnie relished gossip, of course. Idle tittle-tattle wasn't the kind of thing that should be encouraged. But all the same, Minnie loved it when some juicy titbit came her way.

'So I've missed out on seeing all the Farleys, then?' Minnie frowned and disappointedly sipped her stout. The Farleys were the most boisterous and popular family round here. There was always a good kerfuffle of drama when they were about, especially when they were gathered in large numbers.

'They went home about half an hour since,' said Cathy. 'But there's someone here you might like to catch up with. Someone I know would like to see you. The pair of you haven't seen each other in goodness knows how long.'

Minnie's eyes lit up and in a flash she guessed the truth. 'You mean *Junie*? Are you saying that your Junie is back in town . . .?'

Chapter Two

Junie was indeed back in town. She was supping her gin in the inglenook of the fire, at a table that had been called the Women's Table ever since Cathy had started working in the pub.

'She fetched up just this morning, out of the blue,' Cathy shrugged happily, waving a damp cloth in the direction of her errant daughter. 'I imagine she'll be glad to see you again, Minnie. She seems ever so down in the dumps. I've tried, but there's no reaching her. She won't tell me what the matter is.'

'Oh . . .' Minnie was quivering with alertness and excitement as she took her drink over to greet her friend. Here was the turn-up she had been waiting for. For some reason, she had been expecting something like this all day. Something out of the ordinary. And here it was. Her oldest friend. 'Junie . . .?' she said, feeling almost shy.

The girl turned away from studying the ebbing flames and considered Minnie coolly. As the old friends' eyes locked, Minnie managed to stop herself from gasping in surprise. Why, there was something different about Junie. What was it, though? Her features were arranged just the same. She was just as bonny as ever. Yet her expression in that moment made Minnie feel like she had a scar or some disfigurement: the alteration was as marked as that. There was something pinched about her. Her nose was sharper, her mouth was pursed in a particular way. Yes, she seemed sharper altogether, as if she could taste something bitter.

'Oh, it's you,' Junie sighed, rolling her eyes. 'I should have known you'd be over as soon as you heard I was back.'

Minnie didn't like to hurt her feelings by telling her that she'd had no idea of her return. She knew that, tough as she was, Junie's feelings could be quite easily hurt. 'What are you doing back? They said you were down south, down Manchester way. You were doing voluntary service work and being trained, that's what your mam said. I thought you were ever so brave . . .'

Junie sipped her drink and gave a sour smile. 'Yes, that didn't work out so well. I tried to get trained up for a few things. War work, you know. I thought they could use my skills. I thought I could be of some use.' She shrugged.

Minnie giggled. 'Some were putting it about that . . . well, since you'd gone off so suddenly and quietly, they were even whispering that you were doing hush-hush work. They were saying that you'd become a spy.'

Junie looked cross. 'Minnie Minton, you're as bloody gormless as ever, aren't you? What do they tell you about loose talk, eh? What's the matter with you, woman?'

Minnie clamped a hand over her mouth and squealed. 'Eeeh, have I said something wrong? I'm always saying the wrong thing. My mother goes mad with me. She says I've never grown up nor changed since I was a bairn.'

At this, Junie smiled a little. 'Well, I'm glad to hear that, actually. Everything's changed so much for the worse. The world's got worse in every way. I'm glad to hear that Minnie Minton is just the same as she ever was.'

This simple statement made Minnie happier than she had been for weeks. She sat down at the Women's Table with her old friend, just about glowing with pleasure. 'I'm sorry I said that everyone was saying you were a spy, Junie. You're right – that's the kind of information that could be dangerous if it fell into enemy hands.' Minnie cast suspicious glances to her left and right at the mostly empty bar room and this made Junie laugh out loud.

'It's all right. I'm really not a spy. Do you think they would have taken me? I don't think so,' she chuckled to herself. 'I was firefighting for a bit – what do you think of that? I was working in Stockport and South Manchester. When there were raids, I was zooming around dark streets on the back of a truck.'

Minnie was amazed by this. 'How wonderful. I'd never dare do that.' She glugged her milk stout. 'But how come you were down there? All that way down south? Wouldn't it have been better to be here, among the folk you know?'

'Folk here?' Junie sighed. 'As you'll remember, they're not really my people. I don't belong here like you do, Minnie. You with a mam and a dad and all your lot. Who've I got?'

'You've got your mam,' Minnie pointed out, glancing back at the bar, where Cathy Sturrock was single-handedly cleaning up and preparing to finish for the night. 'She thinks the world of you.'

'Aye, I suppose she does,' said Junie. 'But that's a complicated story, as you know. We've had our ups and downs.'

'I do remember,' Minnie nodded. There had been more than ups and downs! There'd been war on between mother and daughter in the past. How on earth were the two of them still talking? How had Cathy ever forgiven her daughter for some of the stunts she'd pulled in the past? Sometimes, Minnie found it hard to believe that Cathy and Junie still got along at all, given some of the things that had gone on. Eeeh, but Minnie knew it all! All the twists and turns in the women's relationship. She couldn't help stopping for a moment to reflect on how much of that story she had been privy to, back in the old days when she and Junie had been in their teens. Junie had told her everything, it seemed – too much, sometimes! Why, they had been inseparable back then. There was nothing happened to Junie that Minnie hadn't known about straight away. This huge gulf had opened up between them in the past ten years. It was more than the gulf caused by the war.

'There was a fella, down in Manchester,' Junie said, lowering her voice. 'I was involved with someone. That's why I was living there. I had a whole different life.'

'Oh,' said Minnie. 'What's he like? Where is he now?'

Junie drained her glass. 'I've no idea. He whistled off some time around Easter. Said he was nipping out for fags and he never came back. It was no loss, really. He was no good. He . . . he used to thump me. When he didn't get his own way.'

Minnie gasped and drew closer. 'Oh, Junie . . .'

'We lived in proper squalor. We had this little room upstairs in this old tart's house. It was a terraced row, just like here, but not so nice. It was dingy and awful. Oh Minnie, I used to cry every night and wonder what I'd done with my life. What was I doing there?'

The larger, slightly older girl inched forward, longing to take hold of her friend and cuddle her. 'But you should have known that you could come back home any time. You should just have come straight back home. You'd always be welcome at your mam's, surely.'

As if this was her cue, Cathy Sturrock was suddenly standing beside them with her hands on her hips. 'Come on, lasses. It's time I locked up. If you want to carry on gassing, you'll have to come over to number twenty-one. I'll get a brew on. Are you coming over, Minnie?'

Minnie Minton had never been known to turn down an invite. She handed her drained glass to the landlady and beamed. 'I'd love a cup of tea, thanks.'

*

That night, they sat up very late by the smudgy lamplight, with the blackout curtains drawn tight against the dark. Cathy was worn to a frazzle, she said, after all the day's excitements. She brewed them a large pot of tea and sat them at the parlour table. 'I'll make my excuses and say goodnight,' she smiled at the girls. 'And I'll leave you two to catch up with each other.'

'Thank you very much, Mrs Sturrock,' Minnie said, and Cathy hurried off upstairs, the light of the lamp she carried bobbing down the hall as she went.

'It must be good though, being back here with your mam, after everything,' Minnie said to Junie.

Junie gasped. 'Are you kidding? She's gone crazy.'

'What? What do you mean?'

'My mother. Carrying on like she is. At the age she is.'

'How do you mean, carrying on?'

Junie narrowed her sharp, canny eyes at her friend. 'I reckon you know exactly what I'm on about, Minnie Minton. You're not so daft that you don't keep up with all the gossip.'

Minnie shook her head. 'Well, obviously, working at the fish shop, you hear all kinds of things. But I pay no heed. Like you say, loose talk and everything. I don't spread tittle-tattle.'

Junie looked sceptical at this. 'Oh aye, of course. But I'm betting you that you've heard what they're telling about my bloomin' mother. I bet you know all about that.'

'Maybe,' Minnie said, blushing. 'Though I'm sure there's no truth in it.'

'Oh really?' Junie burst out. 'Well, I'm telling you that I caught them. I caught the pair of them – *at it*. Round here.'

Minnie's eyes just about shot out of her head. 'At what? Who . . .?'

'My mother and her fancy man. That young bloke. That daft bloke who does the barrels and pots. Bob Farley.'

'He was round here, was he?'

'In the morning light,' Junie nodded. 'I let myself in with my own key. I thought I'd surprise her. Coming home unannounced. Well, I more than surprised her, the old besom. I just about gave her a heart attack. Her and her pot man.'

'Junie, I'm sure you must have got it wrong. These things are just malicious rumours. I don't think anything's really going on . . . Come on, he can't be her fancy man. He's only a little bit older than what we are . . .'

Junie hissed at her, 'She was in her slip. He was in his shirtsleeves. Minnie . . . they had been at it in the daytime. I could just tell. There was guilt in the air. They were looking guilty as sin.'

Minnie bit her lip. 'He's married as well, isn't he? To Megan. She's right bonny, too. Megan Farley, who lives over at number thirteen with the rest of the Farleys.'

'My mother's a brazen hussy,' Junie said. 'I can hardly believe it. Well, just wait till I tell Megan what's been going on round here. She's no softy and she's no fool. She'll rip my mother's face off when she hears the truth. There'll be hell to pay.'

'Oh, but, Junie, why would you tell Megan? Why would you mix things up and make them worse? This is the kind of thing you used to do. Aren't you too old to go making mischief now?'

Junie laughed at this. 'What? Mischief? Is that what you'd call it?'

'Yes, I would, Junie. You caused a lot of misery and upset back in the day. You know that. And all because you thought your mother deserved it. You thought she deserved to suffer. But here you go again – mixing things up! Why would you do that?'

Junie's eyes flashed at Minnie's daring to criticise her. 'Why would I mix things up?' She looked at Minnie furiously, as if she thought Minnie had clear forgotten who it was she was talking to. Minnie's commonsensical kindness was reviving in her that old desire to cause trouble. 'Because it's *fun*, that's why,' she said with relish. 'And, by hell, that mother of mine deserves to suffer, so she does.'

Chapter Three

She couldn't mean it though, could she? Minnie shook her head fervently and blew on her chapped hands to keep them warm. Even Junie couldn't be so malicious as to want to deliberately stir up trouble? Not for her own mother. Surely not.

Ah, but Junie had always had a vengeful side. Minnie was remembering some of the awful things she'd been responsible for when they were both nothing but lasses. And, going by her demeanour last night, she was nothing if not worse nowadays. The rough life she had lived in recent years had made her even more bitter and resentful.

The next morning, early on, when it was still frosty in the backyards of the darker side of Frederick Street, Minnie was perched on the cold seat of the outside privy. She was thinking it all over.

She couldn't help liking Junie. The blonde girl could be as bitter and resentful as she wanted to, but Minnie would always like her. More than that. No need to mince words in the privacy of her own thoughts. Minnie *loved* Junie and she had done since the very first time she'd clapped eyes on her. That first time when Junie had come waltzing into the Robin Hood – all dolled up – for a reunion with her long-lost mammy. Minnie could recall all the effort Cathy had gone to, putting on a special party to welcome her estranged lass to the street. She had been baking savouries and cakes for days to make a delicious spread. And then Minnie could remember how scornful Junie had been. Standing there in her smart travelling costume and clutching her luggage. She had looked like she had come right down in the world and hated the sight of the place she had landed.

Ah, that was back then though, and so much had happened since. So many twists in fortunes and changes of allegiances. Why, back then, Cathy's horrid old hunchback husband had still been alive. The old man – Noel – who'd bequeathed Cathy both the house and the pub. Minnie hadn't thought about him for ages. She had banished him out of her head since the day he'd been found dead from a bad fall down the stairs at number twenty-one. She could still summon up the ghostly scent of his acidulous and smoky breath, steaming down the back of her neck as he berated her behind the bar at the Robin Hood. Horrible old man. And yet . . . Junie had somehow bonded with him, hadn't she? She had called him 'Daddy', even though he was nothing of the sort. Of course, Junie had done this just to drive her poor mother to despair. She did it just to rile her up.

That was the kind of person Junie was. She caused trouble for no reason. She brewed it up out of the air. She made bother where there was no bother before. And now she was back to do it all over again.

Minnie finished up in the privy, glad to pull her warm clothes up again and over her thighs and bum. She felt like her flesh was turning mottled and blue with the cold. As she got up to go, just before she pulled the rusted chain, she realised she could hear someone crying. They were doing it ever so softly, trying to make no noise at all.

'Hello?' Junie called.

'Oh,' came a woman's voice. The sobbing stopped and there was a sudden embarrassed pause of silence. 'S-sorry.'

Minnie frowned, realising that whoever it was must be sat on the lavatory pan on the other side of the wall. They were using the privy at number thirteen. One of the Farley clan were sitting in there, having a quiet cry to themselves. 'Are you all right?' Minnie called out.

'Oh yes, I'm fine,' said a shaky voice. It was a younger woman's voice. Minnie tried to work out who it must be. She thought about all of the Farleys, listing them in her head. Ma Ada, Beryl, Megan, Sam, Tom, Tony, Bob . . . and the new lass from Norfolk. What was she called, again? By, there were hordes of them living in that house. It was no bigger than Minnie's own home. Mind, in the old days, when all her siblings and the adopted kids had been living at home, the Minton place had been pretty full, too. It had been like a nest of baby mice, she remembered her da' telling the vicar. Where did all the bloody kids even come from? 'If you don't know by now, Mr Minton,' the priest had chuckled, 'then I'm not going to explain it to you.'

The sobbing started again, through the whitewashed wall. From being round there at Christmas and other dos, Minnie knew that the Farleys' outside lav was absolutely spotless. Ma Ada wouldn't have it any other way. It was very unlike the stinking, mouldy hellhole where Minnie was currently installed. Now that really was something to make you cry. With all the work that needed to be done every day, there never seemed to be enough time to keep their house nicely enough. The Minton house was known for its shabbiness and air of dereliction and dirtiness. They lived with it quite happily, her ma and da. Dirt was a sign of life, her ma always said.

'Please don't tell anyone you heard me crying like this,' said the voice in a funny accent.

Minnie frowned as she listened, and she was touched by the desperate pleading in the voice. 'Oh, you're the girl from Norfolk. You've only been here a little while. And they've got you crying already.'

'I don't want any of them to see or to know. I'm not really upset, I'm . . .' She was off sobbing again.

'You're just lonely and missing your family, and this place is so strange and full of funny people,' Minnie added, with a flash of understanding.

'That's right,' said the girl. 'That's exactly it.'

'I'm Minnie,' said Minnie. 'I live next door. Don't be upset. You'll soon find your place here, I'm sure. What's your name?'

'Irene,' said the new girl. 'Are you the ones who have the fish shop at the top of the street?'

'That's us,' Minnie said proudly. 'Now, come on. Stop your crying and wipe your face, Irene Farley. Then I'll see you on the street out front and we can meet each other properly.'

So that's exactly what they did. Some minutes later, Minnie met the rather pink-faced new girl outside their adjoining houses and they leaned on the front walls outside the bow windows and introduced themselves properly.

'You've married their Tom,' Minnie gasped, putting it all together. She studied the new girl, with her cocoa brown hair and her slightly crooked teeth which she covered with a hand unconsciously as she spoke. She was no raving beauty – like Junie – but to Minnie she looked nice and kind, and she had lovely, attractive eyes. Her skin was beautiful, too. Soft and pink, like someone brought up on healthy living in the countryside. She was much taller than Minnie, and Minnie guessed that they probably looked rather comical stood side by side, like a music hall comedy act. 'Oh, you're lucky to nab Tom.' Minnie beamed at her new pal. 'Everyone's loved Tom for years. He's such a gentleman. He's kind of like the dad round at theirs, with his older brother away so much at the Front and their real dad long gone. Tom's become the one they all look up to. He's a proper, lovely fella.'

Irene flushed with pleasure and pride. 'We met in Lincoln. I was working on the land there and he was on the airbase. We met at dances and he always stood out to me. He was more reserved, less showy and noisy, unlike the rest of them. A bit more like me, I suppose. I never liked anyone making a fuss and showing off. We just sort of fell in with each other.'

Minnie sighed. 'Oh, a proper romance.'

Irene nodded. 'A daft time to go falling in love, maybe. What with the whole world going to pot. Everything is mad these days, isn't it?'

Minnie shook her head at this. 'Oooh, no, I think it's a lovely time to fall in love. It's all about hope, isn't it? Making plans for the future. Because we know the future is still going to be there, don't we? Even though it's dangerous and horrible now sometimes, we do know that it's going to be all right in the future. We have to hope that way, don't we?'

Without even realising it, Irene rubbed her own rounded tummy through her cotton frock. 'Yes, we do,' she said thoughtfully, and Minnie guessed at once what she was thinking about. The poor lass was up the tub, wasn't she? To Minnie's expert eye, that was a bun in the oven, and no mistake. Irene was covering it up for now, was she? Maybe it was a secret from the rest of the Farley clan? How long had she even been married to Tom? Minnie was trying to work it out . . .

'I'm glad to make another new friend here,' Irene told Minnie. 'The Farleys are lovely to me. Well, most of them. But it's nice to see someone else. Someone from outside of their family.'

Minnie chuckled. 'We're all one big happy family here on Frederick Street, hinny. Everyone is in and out of each other's houses all the time. Everyone knows all about each other's business.'

Irene blushed even deeper at this. 'Oh dear,' she said. 'It'll all take some getting used to, being here.'

They were interrupted then by the front door of number fifteen flying open. All of a sudden, Minnie's brother, Derek, was standing there in his hobnailed boots and his donkey jacket. He was a great galoot of a fella, and Minnie adored him. He was her last brother left at home, with the other four off at the various fronts they'd been sent to in order to fight. Derek had wonky feet, according to the doctors, and he was spared all of that carry-on. He hated being reminded of that fact and longed to join up and be sent off to battle like his siblings. He was one big bridling mass of dark energy and frustration, glowering at Minnie and her new friend as they budged out of his way.

'Are you off to the biscuit factory then, our Derek?' Minnie asked him.

'What do you think?' he growled in a voice deeper than Tyne Dock itself. He stomped past them both and was off down the cobbled street.

'Bring us back some misshapes then,' Minnie called after him. 'Bring us some funny-shaped rejects.'

He snarled back over his shoulder at her: '*You're* a funny-shaped reject, Minnie Minton. That's just what you bloody well are.'

Minnie fell about laughing at her brother's rough jest, but, eeeeh, she knew it was true. She knew exactly how true it was.

Chapter Four

Junie couldn't help holding her mother in contempt. It was awful, but it was true.

This time, she had been prepared to give Cathy another chance. She needed her help, she needed her mam's love to fall back on, and so she had been ready to forget about the past and make a new start. But now Junie wasn't so sure. Cathy was still a blousy, common piece of work, just like she'd always been.

Junie repressed a shudder at her memory of the time she had first arrived here in the Sixteen Streets. Only sixteen, and used to rather better standards than were enjoyed round these parts, Junie Carmichael had been raised by her Aunty Linda on a small farm by the coast in Northumberland. For most of her life, she had believed that her strict aunt was her mother. Linda had been a rather cold and remote person, divorced after only a year from her doctor husband and happy living on her farm at the extreme edge of a neglected private estate. As Junie had matured into a young woman, the two of them had clashed again and again. Their temperaments were so different. Junie could hardly believe that this person was her mother, and one day, during a heated row, the truth came out: she wasn't her real mother after all.

'What?' Junie had gasped, the wind taken out of her sails. All thoughts fled from her mind and her teenage anger drained out of her. Her whole young life had been changed forever in that instant and she was appalled to see that the furious Linda took pleasure in that. 'What do you mean, Mummy?'

The older woman's face had twitched with irritation as she'd explained, 'Your real mother abandoned you here on my doorstep. She never gave a fig for you. Remember Cathy? Remember the young woman who used to come and see you occasionally when you were little? When you were nothing but a baby? She would come and dandle you on her knee and cuddle you. She would be crying the whole time. Her whole life was one great mass of regrets. She was lucky I even let her come inside to see you for those few early times. All she did was confuse and upset you . . . Don't you remember her, Junie?'

And then, when Junie had thought back on the inchoate memories of her early life . . . why yes, there was a jumble of feelings and memories to do with a woman who cried. She had very soft, long auburn hair Junie would catch in her infant fists, so different to the brittle, grey hair Linda kept pragmatically short. 'That was my . . . mother . . .?' Junie had sobbed, all at once remembering green eyes welling up with tears. Those tears had fallen on her. The woman had wept all over her when Junie was a toddler and it had been confusing and strange and horrible, especially when there was a row and Junie was snatched out of the woman's hands. The young woman had been chased from the farmhouse. There had been an awful, awful scene.

Of course, Linda soon regretted telling Junie the truth. Her bitter anger evaporated when she saw how the tale took her daughter. Junie went cold and hard. She stared at Linda in horror. 'You aren't who I thought you were. I don't belong to you. I never belonged to you.'

For days after that, they had returned to the argument and gone through its twists and turns again and again. They used a million words when it all really boiled down to a handful. I don't belong here. I never did. I still want you here. I should never have told you. But you did. It's too late now. This explains everything.

'I've never fitted in here. I don't belong here.'

'Then go to your mother. Go to the big city. Go and find out where that harlot ended up.'

The big city indeed. Junie could have laughed herself sick at the thought of it. Her aunt's words had filled her imagination with ridiculous ideas of a bright, sophisticated city with big houses and glamourous people. Like something out of an old novel. As if she would find her mother living in the lap of luxury and she would be so glad to be reunited with her Junie.

Aunty Linda had realised she was on the brink of being left alone. 'No, no, I never meant any of it . . .'

But it was too late. Junie had wanted to know where her real mammy lived. How would she find her? And then, from the chest of drawers in her room, Linda had produced a wadded pile of envelopes. They had been roughly tied together with string, and they dated back sixteen years. 'What are these?' Junie had asked with dread, smoothing down the crumpled envelopes.

'She would have confused you. She would have twisted your mind . . .' Linda had said stiffly, furiously.

'These are letters, cards . . . going back years . . .' Junie had gasped and then stared at her aunt. 'You kept them from me. You never let me know the truth.'

'She would have been a bad influence on you . . .' Linda had said, unbending.

Later, when Junie arrived in South Shields, having written ahead to tell Cathy she was on her way, she had been horrified to find the life her true mother lived. It wasn't a rich and sophisticated world she lived in. South Shields wasn't a city of bright lights and excitements. The place Junie had arrived in was really – to her eyes – no better than a slum. The serried ranks of smoky streets and tumbledown houses were packed so tightly, it made her feel claustrophobic. The cobbles were slimy with horse dung and slops. As soon as she set her dainty feet down in the Sixteen Streets, Junie had wanted to turn tail and flee all the way back home to Northumberland, where everything was wild and fresh and natural.

Junie could remember only too well her feeling of revulsion as she had entered the poky, foetid atmosphere of the Robin Hood public bar. She had recoiled when she saw the cast of gurning grotesques that surrounded her slatternly mother each and every day.

And her mother . . . This woman in a dress that showed her shoulders and her breasts so obviously. With her hair up in that style like some dreadful courtesan. Imagine belonging to such a person, every fibre of her being . . .

Ah, but it had been worse than that, hadn't it? Sixteen-year-old Junie had stepped into that den of iniquity, making herself feel much bolder than she actually was. All dressed up in her finest outfit. All prepared to embrace her true mother and be welcomed into this fold – however hideous it might be. But right at that moment – surrounded by all these rough denizens of the infamous Sixteen Streets – Junie had been betrayed.

Her own mother had disavowed her. 'Here is my long-lost *niece*,' she'd said. 'I am her aunt. Her Aunt Cathy. Junie here has come to live with me and her Uncle Noel.'

At that moment, Junie's already broken heart had split into further irreparable shards.

What was wrong with her?

Did no one truly want her to belong to them?

Was no one really her mother?

She went cold and hard inside on that night. No matter how warm the welcomes and no matter how carefully they had tried to look after her, Junie had never really recovered from that moment. It was yet another betrayal, simple as that.

Oh, in later times her mother had tried to explain. She hadn't wanted to go too far, too fast. She didn't want to take it for granted that Junie didn't mind the truth being told. She had been playing it carefully.

But deep in her heart, Junie had felt betrayed. She had run to her mother and her mother hadn't claimed her. She had held her at arm's length.

The coldness that came over her still hadn't left Junie, even ten years later and more. If she cared to dwell on it, she could probably put every mistake and every bad choice in her life down to that single earth-shattering moment.

I could probably blame Cathy for every rotten thing that's ever happened to me, Junie thought, waking up that morning after her reunion with the lumpen, hopeless, devoted Minnie Minton. She woke up thick-headed and groaning in the sunny room filled with Victoriana that had once belonged to old Theresa Sturrock. *Here I am, back in the heart of the Sixteen Streets*, she thought miserably, *and I just have to make the best of it*.

Well, it was better than the mucky, straitened circumstances she had faced in Levenshulme, in South Manchester. At least here she could force everyone to dance attendance on her. They were all beholden to her: her mother, Minnie and others. She was known here, and she knew just how to wrap them all around her little finger . . .

She would just have to put up with them, that was all. These people she had tried to escape from and forget about. She would just have to tolerate their cloying affections.

There was a knock at her bedroom door. In came her mother

with a steaming breakfast tray. 'Look. I saved the bacon for you. I made you a bacon sandwich, Junie. Just how you used to like them. It's a whole week's ration. And the last of the sugar in your tea. I remember just how sweet you like it.'

'I do, I do.' Junie forced herself to smile as she sat up in the lacey sheets and her nest of pillows. 'Oh, Mam. I'm sorry if I've been grumpy and out of sorts since I arrived back. It's just . . . it's all taken it out of me. The things I had to face in Manchester. That awful man. The place he had us living in. And the things I saw when we were fighting fires.' She shuddered and began sobbing.

Cathy put down the tray hurriedly and hugged her daughter to her bosom.

'Oh, you poor, brave girl,' Cathy told her. 'But you're back home now. You're where you belong, Junie. I'm going to look after you. Everything is going to be all right from now on. Everything is going to be wonderful.'

Junie felt herself swamped in her mother's embrace. *Oh, it's going to be wonderful, is it? she thought. We'll see about that, Mammy. We'll just have to see.*

Chapter Five

Derek Minton was a brute, according to all the lasses down at the biscuit factory. He was twenty-one now, but he'd already racked up five years doing every job he could, from the packing room to the bakehouse. His pan-shovel hands were made of asbestos by now, and it was no bother to him, carrying the great big burning hot trays to and from the ovens. He clomped around in those shiny black boots of his and all the women would watch in admiring, wary silence.

Of course, he was one of the Minton clan, so they all knew he was rough as guts. He came from a sprawling family who were always causing bother, though that had all lessened since the hostilities started and most of his siblings had been sent away. They were using all their aggression and surplus energy in the cause of king and country.

Everyone knew that Derek's feet were wrong somehow and he was exempt. This drove him furious, for he hated the thought of anyone looking at him, seeing a fit and healthy bloke and wondering why he wasn't away fighting. Anyone who niggled at him would get thumped. A man of few words, he didn't have time to argue with anyone. He just put his head down and got on with his work.

Today, at the biscuit factory at the bottom of Frederick Street, he was aware that he was being paid extra attention by his supervisor, Faith Chesney, eldest of the Chesney sisters. As they took their break out in the breezy open air, smoking by the back wall, she was staring at him. Up and down. She was looking at him appraisingly, like she'd never really noticed him before. Oh, but she was a snooty piece, Faith Chesney. Just because they had a bit of cash stashed away, the Chesneys. They still lived on Frederick Street, didn't they? They still had to work at the factory. What made her so special then, looking down her pointed nose at him as they both smoked and waited for the mid-morning hooter to sound. What business was he of hers?

'Derek Minton,' she said, purringly, like she'd been studying the women in the films. Who did she think she was being today? Marlene Dietrich? Derek snorted in secret laughter at her pretentious ways. 'You're a dark one,' she remarked, still staring at him.

He opened his bait box early. He was starving. What had his mother put in his stotty cake today? He frowned. Cold chips. Cold chips again.

'Are you listening to me, Derek Minton?' asked Faith Chesney. 'I'm your immediate superior, don't you know.'

He nodded and took a huge bite of his cold chip sandwich. It was disgusting, but the morning's work so far had made him ravenous.

'You have to do just what I say,' Faith told him. Christ, she was milking this. How long since her dad had promoted her? A week? She'd barely been here a month. She was younger than Derek by a year or two as well. She'd been in the year below him in junior school; he could picture her now. Her and her two younger sisters, all three of them nightmares in pigtails. They had clamoured around him noisily, after his attention. He never understood why. He always thought they were horrible, skinny creatures, even if they thought a lot of themselves. The

Chesney sisters carried with them an air of tragedy, having lost their mother when they were young. They had been brought up by their dad and everyone's hearts had gone out to them. The Chesney girls were awful, though, Derek knew this of old. Motherless or not, they were horrible girls. They had always ragged him something rotten and now he felt himself at the mercy of the oldest and the worst of them: Faith.

'Just leave me to my bait in peace,' he growled at her.

'What are you eating, Derek?' she asked, snidely.

'You can see what it is.'

'Is it cold chips again? Greasy cold chips from Swetty Betty's fish bar?'

'Yes. Don't call me mam "Swetty Betty".'

'That's what it says on the sign above her shop.'

'That's what vandals put up there.' It was true: no matter how many times the graffiti was obliterated by a fresh coat of whitewash, someone would get up there in the middle of the night. They would scrawl 'Swetty' back in the space. In all these years, no one had ever spelled the word correctly.

Derek carried on chomping at his greasy stotty bread.

'You're a dark horse,' Faith said and he stiffened slightly. He knew what was coming next. 'Aren't you? That's just what you are. You're a proper dark horse.'

'Am I?'

She dropped her tab end on the concrete and stepped on it. 'We always thought you was black, to be honest. Me and my sisters used to speculate. We'd stare at you and say, *Is he a gypsy? Is he an Arab? No one else in his family is as dark as that.*'

Derek studiously stared at the remains of his early lunch. Great hanks of bread and potato were twisting in his gut. He didn't say a word.

'Ah, come on, you can tell me,' Faith said to him. 'You must know the truth. You should be glad I'm interested. You should be glad of the attention. Come on, tell me. What are you, really? Why do you look much darker than the rest of your clan?'

He crumpled up the greaseproof paper that his mam had wrapped his sarnie in. He slammed his tin bait box shut and stood up, carefully brushing down his overalls and getting all the yard dust off them. He didn't say a word to Faith Chesney.

'Ah, come on, Derek. Don't be like that,' she called after him. 'I haven't said anything bad, have I? I haven't called you names. Now, come on, lad, don't be touchy. You have to do what I say, don't you? I'm your superior, aren't I?'

She followed him back into the steaming heat of the bakehouse. He was furious and confused, all at the same time. She was being mean as ever, but there was something else in her voice. There was a challenging note that was almost . . . flirtatious. He hated it. He wanted nothing to do with her. There wasn't a picking on her, the skinny witch. She had no allure for him.

But she followed him round all afternoon as he went about work he was so accustomed to that he could have done it in his sleep. She just wouldn't leave him alone.

After work, after a day that seemed about three months long, Derek traipsed up the steep cobbles of Frederick Street. The hooters were sounding and the billowing aroma of biscuits floated up into the early-evening skies. Unfortunately, Derek felt completely indifferent to the scent of Wights Biscuits. To him, they were cloyingly sweet. Still, he had with him a small paper sack of cheap misshapes for his daft sister Minnie, just as requested.

She squealed when he gave them to her. She was at the dining table with their mam. 'You look shattered, son,' said his dad, hunched over in his chair by the range. His dad was rubbing his bony hands together, trying to warm them through. His circulation was so bad, he looked blue all over, even though he wouldn't have moved from the fireside all day. Everyone knew that the Mintons' father was incurably ill, though no one ever really said what it was that was wrong with him. He'd been ill since Derek was a boy. He'd been sat, rubbing his hands warm like this, for as long as Derek could remember.

Derek kissed his mam's cheek, his sister's and then his dad's. They were a rough lot, the Mintons, as everyone said. Their house was mucky and all, but they were devoted to each other, the lot of them. If you listened to how they were, beneath all the rough talk and grumbling, you would hear how they really felt about each other. They were a family who had more than enough love to go round. It was why they'd taken in so many orphaned and abandoned kids over the years. Their extended family was huge.

'Your dad's right, pet,' Betty Minton told her youngest son. 'Now, don't let them take advantage of you, what with you being one of the few strong fellas about the place. They've got you labouring like a dray horse.'

'I don't mind that,' he frowned, taking the huge mug of tea that Minnie had poured for him. 'Work's OK. Takes my mind off everything. I like using my muscles.' He put his massive hands down on the table. They looked so scarred and work-worn, his mother's heart flinched at the sight of them. She felt both protective and proud of her youngest and – if she was honest – dearest lad.

'Take him out for a pint,' Betty commanded her husband. 'Go on, Dad. You've not shifted your stumps all day. I'm not doing supper till late. Minnie will help me open the shop. You two get up the hill to the Robin Hood and have a pint or two.'

Minnie muttered a bit about how she'd love to go to the pub, given half a chance, and her mother elbowed her. 'Tush, you lazy mare. Your brother's need is greater than yours. You've got tatties to chop.'

'Thanks, Ma,' Derek smiled and watched his dad achingly, creakingly, stoop to tie up his shoes and reach for his jacket.

'Ooh, see if Junie's in the pub,' Minnie told her brother. 'I bet she's in there tonight. Maybe her mam'll have her working behind the bar again.'

Derek frowned. 'Who? Not that lass from next door with the big teeth? The one you were standing out front with this morning?'

Minnie shook her head. 'No, that's Irene. You're hopeless, Derek. You can't keep up with everyone.'

'All you lasses are the same,' he shrugged, just to aggravate her.

'Oh, you'll know Junie when you see her. You were only a little bairn when she was here last. But she's the most glamorous person who's ever walked down Frederick Street. She really is.'

Their dad wheezed painfully in the doorway and laughed at her. 'Don't say that in front of your mother. You'll hurt her feelings. Your mam's the most glamorous doll on our street, hinny. And she always was.'

There was a loud croak of laughter from Betty Minton at this. She bundled up her apron and hurled it at her stooped old man. 'Hadaway with yer,' she cackled.

Off he went with Derek, drawing strength from the presence of his great big lad by his side as they headed up the road to the pub. It delighted Harry Minton to be dwarfed by his wonderful sons. He felt like he had his own invincible army around him, even with most of them away at the Front.

'Are you sure you're OK, lad?' he asked, just before they went into the noisy saloon.

'I'm grand, Dada,' Derek told him.

'Well, let's go in and have a look at this bonny lass of Minnie's then, shall we?' His dad chuckled. 'Let's see what she's like.'

In they went, into all the noise and smoke, and that was how Derek met Junie.

Chapter Six

Years later, people would ask her what had drawn her to Derek in the first place. What made him stand out in that busy bar on that very ordinary weekday night during the war? Once she was even asked, 'Was it love at first sight, Junie?'

The thing was, Junie was so cynical and hardened by life that no one would ever have suspected she would believe in a thing as daft-sounding as love at first sight. She was unsentimental, pragmatic, toughened by everything life had doled out to her. And yet . . . when it came to Derek, she was different. When she was asked about their first meeting, she would smile and laugh and her eyes would light up.

Oh yes, she would say, it was love at first sight. It was something special, at any rate. First of all, she fancied the arse off him. She saw him walk up with his skinny little father in tow and he took up so much space at that little wooden bar. His hands went down on the beer-sodden surface and it was like he was laying claim to the whole place. Not aggressively, not even territorially. It was just that he took up so much space and lesser men found themselves shrinking back, drawing away from him, the way cats would cautiously withdraw from a great big tom ambling its way down the alley.

Junie – who was helping her mam out behind the beer pumps that night – found that she was staring at him unashamedly. His jaw was black with an early shadow of beard. His brows were constantly frowning and his eyes were deep-set and seemed mysterious to Junie. She felt her throat constrict and go all parched, just like one of the pumps when the barrel ran dry. *Who is this bloke?* she heard herself wondering. *Why've I never seen this one before?*

'Ah, that's the youngest of the Minton lads,' Cathy told her round the back room, once they'd been served their pints. Junie had been notably quiet as she took their money. Her mother was amused by her strange attitude. 'He's your pal Minnie's brother. Only, when you were last here, he wasn't of an age to go drinking in pubs.'

'So he's one of the Minton clan,' Junie frowned, peeping round the corner of the slop room at the crowded bar. Derek had taken his dad to sit by the fire, and they'd found stools beside the Women's Table, where Ma Ada was holding court and psychic Winnie was watching everything that was going on. 'How old is he, then?'

'Just twenty-one. They put some money behind the bar for his birthday in March. His ma gave him the key of the door and they all sang and got him drunk. I remember thinking that he'd grown into the bonniest of that whole family. Though it must be said, they're not a bonny-looking family.'

'How come he's not at the Front? Is he on leave?'

'Funny feet, they say.' Cathy watched her daughter filing all this information away. 'Well, I've never seen you take such an interest in a lad before, my lass. He's too young for you, don't you think? You're twenty-six now, hinny. You're like an old lady to him. An old maid.'

Junie's eyes flashed with anger, and Cathy was glad to see that her spirit was returning to her. 'Hardly. Old maid like hell!'

Cathy laughed at this. 'Eeeh, you make me laugh. You remind me of how I was.'

Junie pulled a face. 'Well, you'd know all about carrying on with younger fellas, wouldn't you, Mother?'

Instantly, Cathy's face went red. Her blush went right down to her breastbone and her barmaid's cleavage. 'Hey, now . . .' she murmured. 'You've no call to get personal. I mean, there's nothing going on like that. There's nothing scandalous about . . .'

'About what?' Junie smirked. 'About you and your pot man, Bob?'

Cathy wasn't going to discuss this now. She glared at her daughter. 'There's nothing wrong in any of it. There's no scandal. Keep your mucky thoughts to yourself, lass.'

Junie just smiled at her. 'Very well, Mother.'

'I mean it, lass. Don't you go spreading gossip and causing trouble. Bob is a very pure, simple kind of lad. He doesn't need bother in his life . . .'

'I understand,' Junie smirked and went swanning off into the saloon of the Robin Hood. Now she had regained her composure, she was ready to face the crowd again. She was prepared to go over to those stools in front of the fire and introduce herself properly to that lovely-looking bloke.

And she loved leaving her mother standing there in the slops room, feeling awkward and provoked.

Junie, surging forward through the crowded bar, felt that she had returned to herself. She felt like she was at the height of her seductive powers, in her absolute prime. It was just the right moment for her to meet the love of her life.

Harry Minton sat supping quietly, contentedly, enjoying the warmth of the flames. He was enjoying listening to his lad burble on about that day at the biscuit factory. The old man loved tales of the factory, since it was the place he'd worked for most of his life, too, before his health had failed him. Back then, there'd been less of the fancy machines they had now and, as he was keen to tell Derek, the work had been much more manual and more difficult. The end results were just the same, however: fancy, colourful tins of gingernuts and custard creams, sent out all over the world for folk everywhere to dunk in their tea. The continuity between the generations made Harry feel proud.

'So they've got all three of Chesney's young lasses working there now?' he asked Derek.

'Aye, they've been put straight into jobs that they're bloody useless at.'

'You mustn't be awful about them,' Harry said. 'They've had a proper tragic life.'

Derek shrugged and wiped a moustache of beer foam off his lip with his sleeve. 'They'll want for nothing though, won't they? They'll have all the money they need – thanks to their old grandad.'

'Hey, lad, don't go all bitter and envious. You must never look at other people's lives with greed in your soul.'

'It's not greed, Da . . . it's just . . . well, it's all so unfair, in't it? Why do some folk get an easy life? And why do others have to work their bollocks off every day just to get by?'

His father chuckled at his coarseness. 'That's just the way of the world, son. Unfairness is a fact of life. And remember – yes, those skinny Chesney lasses may have all the advantages that come with having a grandad who owns the factory they work in, but they haven't got a mammy, have they? They lost her before they were even old enough to know what a loss she was to them. Eeeh, and by, she was a smashing lass, Mary Wight. She had the softest, kindest, most loving nature. It was bloody cruel, the way she went. It was the cruellest thing I ever saw. Now, those lasses were robbed of her, so I don't blame their dad, or their grandad, for spoiling them a little. I don't blame them at all.'

This was the longest speech Derek had heard his da make in weeks and he stared in surprise at him as Harry swigged down the dregs of his pint.

'I never knew you cared so much about those awful girls,' Derek said. 'Cos all of that's true, but I still think they're hoity-toity little madams.'

Father and son laughed at this. Harry joshed him, saying, 'You should propose to that oldest one. She's clearly after your attention, son. Get her to marry you. You'd be quids in. You'd be heir to the biscuit-factory fortune, then.'

Derek scowled at the very thought. 'Nae bloody fear. Now, are you wanting another pint?'

All at once, Junie was standing beside them. She popped up like the fairy in *The Wizard of Oz*. 'Can I get you the same again, fellas . . .?'

Later, they would all laugh at the very idea of Junie appearing in a flash like Glinda the Good. Derek would tease her. 'You're more like the Wicked Witch of the North, hinny.'

Just then, Derek was looking up at her with a strange expression. 'Aye, two more of these, thanks, pet.' Then he blinked and stared at her for longer than necessary. 'What do they call you, then?'

She beamed at him broadly. 'I'm Junie. And I believe your name is Derek Minton, is it not . . .?'

Harry Minton always said he knew in that precise moment what was going on. He watched his son stop scowling for the first time in his whole life. Derek went from carping on those Chesney girls and being his usual grumpy self to falling head over proverbial heels for Junie Sturrock. It all happened in a split second. The old Derek was gone, he was lost forever, and a new man was sitting in his place.

There was never going to be any going back.

Chapter Seven

Minnie was delighted for them, of course. He was her lovely brother and she wanted to see him as happy as he could be. If being happy with the most lovely-looking girl in the Sixteen Streets was his fate, then Minnie Minton was all for it.

Like everyone else, she stood back, holding her breath in awe and amazement as the young couple started courting.

'How'd you like that?' Betty Minton cried, more than once, out loud to her queue at the fish bar. 'Our little lad – not so little now, of course. And him so gloomy and sullen all his life. Why, look at him now . . .'

Everyone had to agree: it was quite the transformation. He simply couldn't help himself. Derek was actually frowning less. As the weeks of autumn deepened and grew colder, the warmest thing on Frederick Street was his smile when he was with Junie. 'She just makes me happy,' he shrugged.

Courting meant dances at the Alhambra, the Albert Hall and the community hall. It meant sipping ersatz coffee at Franchino's ice-cream parlour. It meant long walks in all weathers along the seafront. They walked the length of the beaches that were tangled with barbed wire, and from the cliffs they watched the waves come crashing in from abroad.

They never said much to each other. That was something that people remarked on when they observed the young lovers for any amount of time. Not for them the excited, inane chatter of most courting couples. There was a quietness between them that was almost solemn.

'Well, you could knock me down with a bloody feather,' Harry Minton declared, shaking his head. 'Our Derek. I've never seen him like this. I reckon that Junie Sturrock has made a man out of him. Don't you think so, Mother . . .?'

Harry was sitting in his usual chair by the stove and Betty was busy ironing all the shirts for the coming week. She gasped at the scandal of Harry's words. 'Eeeh, don't be crude, Dad,' she frowned. She didn't like to think about things like extramarital carrying-on. It was wrong, and that was all there was to it. 'Our Derek's a good lad. She won't have led him into bad ways.'

Harry grunted and returned to knocking out and refilling his old pipe. He could see what was going on, no fear. Derek was clearly getting what Harry's generation used to call 'his oats'. Somehow, Derek and Junie were finding the time and the privacy to do what came naturally. And really, good luck to them, thought Harry. He didn't have any moralistic qualms when it came to the physical side of things. Let them enjoy their lives. There was a war on, wasn't there? People had to find a way to make life worth living, even in the face of awful disaster.

'I think they make a good pair,' Harry told his wife.

'Aye, we'll see.' Betty pursed her lips because she had her doubts about Junie. She thought she was two-faced and hard, which she was.

That evening at the counter of Swetty Betty's, during a lull in service, Betty said as much to her daughter. Knowing that Minnie knew Junie very well, she was checking her out. She was keen to know Minnie's true opinion of the match.

But Minnie was uncharacteristically guarded. 'Oh, Junie's a lovely person. And you can see how she's bringing our Derek out of his shell . . .'

Betty knew when she was being fobbed off. 'Aye, but there's more to it, isn't there? And there's more to her, isn't there? You've known her well since you were a bairn. She's a complicated character, isn't she?'

Minnie laughed at this. 'You can say that again.'

They were interrupted then by a delegation from the Farley household. Beryl and Megan came in, bringing with them a swirl of cold night air and dead leaves. Beryl was slightly older, in her late twenties, and Megan was the more glamorous. Both were from the biscuit factory. There was a scent of winter spice in the air already, Minnie thought. Both girls were dressed up in their woollen coats and mufflers, rubbing their hands to get warm. They ordered three fish suppers, to be carefully divided between everyone at number thirteen.

'Also, if you've got a fish head or two for our Lucky,' Beryl pleaded. 'Poor old puss is getting old these days. It takes him all night to suck the goodness out of a single head, and he lies there all night with it between his paws like he's been given a prize.'

They all laughed at this, thinking of old Ma Ada's queer, hairless pet, and as Minnie saw to their order, she was haunted by the image of the cat lying with the fragment of fish caught protectively between his paws. The staring eyes and hopeless grin of the fish haunted her. She scooped around in the scrap buckets till she found a suitable one. That was their Derek, wasn't it? Caught between the paws of Junie Sturrock. She could retract her claws and seem gentle and sweet . . . Minnie frowned at her runaway imagination. Was Junie really toying with her new boyfriend? Was Derek truly at her mercy like that? Minnie shook her head of this awful thought. Junie was less dreadful and cruel these days. She wasn't like she used to be. And Derek – was he really as helpless as that?

Minnie knew, though, that she had perceived the truth. Derek was in thrall to Junie, just like Minnie herself had once been. Not any more, of course. Minnie had broken off that fond, foolish affection. It had been childish, immature and . . . well, it was just what the whole world would say it was: unnatural. The kind of thing that no one ever really talked about out loud, just in whispers. Something the Bible was against. Something that the whole world frowned upon. Minnie felt that she had had a narrow escape from where her own nature had tried to lead her, that's how she saw it now. It was something that needed to be nipped in the bud. But oh . . . she recognised that look on her brother's face. He was *mesmerised* by Junie.

'How's everything at number thirteen then?' asked Swetty Betty Minton, avid for the gossip as usual.

Megan – never satisfied with anything – scowled at her. 'Completely overcrowded. We're sleeping three to a bed round there.'

Beryl laughed at her. 'Ah, don't exaggerate.' There was always something so warm and reliable about that girl, Betty thought. Good on her for snagging the most handsome of the Farley lads. 'It's fine and cosy round there. We're lucky to have each other. Thanks for asking, Mrs Minton.'

The fish and chips came sizzling out of the deep golden oil and Betty swaddled them quickly in paper. 'You give your old ma my best regards, and I'll hope to see her at the Robin Hood this Friday for dominoes and a catch-up.'

Megan Farley frowned at the mention of the pub. 'I'm not going over there to be served by that trollop,' she muttered.

They all stared at her. 'Beg your pardon?' Betty said.

'That old Cathy Sturrock,' Megan growled. 'She's a trollop. I don't know why more people haven't seen through her before.

She cracks on like she's queen of the street, waltzing round the place. She's an awful old piece, if you ask me.'

Beryl tried to make light of her remarks. 'I'm not sure anyone did ask you for your opinion, Megan.'

Minnie didn't like to hear her old friend, employer and champion maligned publicly in this way. 'Cathy Sturrock has always been very good to me, Megan.'

The way Megan looked at Minnie made Minnie feel like she was beneath Megan's consideration. Like she was less than a person to her and her opinion didn't count. Megan simply rolled her eyes. 'I think she's an old bitch. Like many round here.'

Betty eyed her sharply. 'Well, you know, if you're not liking it round here, Megan, no one's making you stay. You can whistle back off to . . . Where was it your people come from? Hartlepool? You can always go back to Hartlepool.'

Megan snatched up the tightly bound fish suppers and snapped at her: 'Do you know what? Someday I might just do that. There's bugger all for me here.'

'Not even your lovely husband, Bob?' Betty asked.

'Him!' Megan cried nastily and stormed out into the street.

Beryl shrugged apologetically and followed her out.

Betty turned to her daughter and said, very philosophically: 'Some people are just never happy. You'll find that as you grow older. They think too much, or they want too much. They're never satisfied. The thing to be is a bit daft, just like you are, hinny.'

The next day. Minnie had some precious time off work. She went to the old town library to swap over books for her whole household. A tricky job, but she knew what her mother and father would favour, and she would be happy with whatever they would enjoy. Three thick novels would last them a fortnight and the books were crucial on these long and sometimes sleepless nights. The cardboard-covered library tomes went with them – along with flasks of tea and heavy blankets – on the nights they trooped out to the air-raid shelter at the back of the town hall.

After the library, she popped into Franchino's ice-cream parlour, which was just across the road. Its green and pink signage was familiar and welcoming, as was the steamy air and the scent of coffee as she passed through the heavy glass and silver doors.

Minnie was surprised to see her new friend, the Norfolk girl Irene Farley, working behind the counter. 'Hey, they've got you a job here,' she grinned and, at once, Irene's hand flew up self-consciously to mask her own smile.

'Aye, not only do I have to earn my keep at the biscuit factory, but they've got me slaving here as well.' Irene laughed, but there was no bitterness or complaint in her tone. She looked as if she relished being of use and liked being this busy. It suited her, too. She was flushed and fresh-faced. She looked a picture in her clean overalls and her funny paper hat. Quickly, she made chicory coffee for them both and took her break sitting in a booth at the back of the parlour.

'So . . . that's your brother finding love now,' Irene said. 'Why, everyone seems to be pairing off these days. What about you, Minnie? Is there a lad somewhere for you?'

Minnie felt a flash of irritation. Who was this new girl to quiz her like that? Why, Irene hardly knew her. Ahh, she was just being friendly, wasn't she? That was all. Irene's mind was idling over questions of love because she was missing her own fella, who was off at his airbase somewhere.

Minnie said, 'I don't think there's anyone special for me. I'm going to be an old spinster all my life.'

'There's someone for everyone,' Irene said. 'You'll just have to wait and see. Someone like you . . . why, it would be a waste of a good, loving nature if you were left on your own.'

Minnie's round eyes widened at this. 'Do you really think so?'

Irene nodded and sipped her coffee. 'I think you've got a lot to give. Someone will be very lucky one day.'

'Aye,' Minnie chuckled. 'One day, maybe.'

Chapter Eight

As time went on, Minnie realised she was feeling more left out than ever. Of course she was glad about her brother and her one-time best friend doing whatever they were doing. They were courting very publicly and everyone could see how happy they were. Oh, but they were exclusive with their time and their attention.

'They only have eyes for each other. And that's as it should be,' crowed Minnie's mam, hefting the scraps out of the deep-fat fryer. Upset as she was, Minnie found herself salivating at the sight of all the glistening batter scraps. She took a punnet of them, blew on them to cool them down and gobbled them up at once.

She was putting on weight, too. She felt miserable and heavy and found that she was sighing all the time.

Even her new friend next door, Irene at number thirteen – she who'd been so glad of the attention and company at first – well, even she was proving a bit elusive now. She was working two jobs, sure enough, but now she was getting all excited because her fella Tom was coming home on leave. They were going to have an early Christmas, she said. The brightness and excitement in her face was infectious and Minnie was pleased for her, but she did feel left out, too. There was lots of noise and kerfuffle from next door in the Farley household and Minnie wished she belonged to them round there.

Instead, her own home seemed rather dull and dreary. Everything smelled of chip fat and batter. It always had, she supposed, but now Minnie was extra conscious of the fact.

There were snow storms early that winter, and the cold winds came blowing over the cliffs from the North Sea. The inhabitants of the Sixteen Streets used up their coal rations, banking up their small fires and feeding the ranges. They sat by the hearts of their houses and tried to keep warm as best they could.

Minnie reflected grimly that she had no other human being to keep her warm. Everyone she knew had someone to cuddle up to.

The sirens went off occasionally, often in the middle of the night. This triggered a mass exodus to the shelters and – God forgive her – but Minnie even enjoyed these nocturnal trips under the old marketplace. It was company and camaraderie, wasn't it? Everyone trudging along with their few necessary items to see them through the night. Blankets and pillows and books. Once, to try to help out, she had offered to smuggle Ma Ada's frightened cat, Lucky, under her jumper with her into the shelter, but she had been rumbled by the warden and forced to set him free.

In the shelters as the noise from above started up, they sang all the songs they could think of. They sat on rough wooden benches side by side, crammed like preserves in a scullery pantry. The dull, endless explosions were somewhere far away. Maybe further up the coast. Sunderland, perhaps? They sang as if songs could keep the Luftwaffe at bay. Minnie started them all off singing the songs from *The Wizard of Oz* – which had been her favourite movie from right before the war began. She knew all the words to all the songs and didn't mind making a show of herself, getting up and doing the actions, doing all the voices. They all laughed at her squawking, screeching voice, but she didn't mind. Just for once, she liked them all looking at her as she performed her heart out.

'She's a card, your Minnie, ain't she?' Ma Ada leaned across and told Betty Minton.

'She certainly is,' Betty grinned, and Minnie was pleased to see her mam looking proud of her and not embarrassed.

'She could be on the stage,' Ma Ada said.

'Or in the zoo,' added Sam, her youngest lad. Well, he was in disgrace for something or other anyway, so he got short shrift from his mother.

On that particular night in the shelters, Minnie was sent to get the family flask filled up with tea by the volunteers and she was startled to bump into Bella Franchino doing exactly the same thing. The glamorous girl from the ice-cream parlour looked flustered and confused at being yelled at. 'Shouldn't you be in a shelter at Seahouses? You lot live over that way, don't you? Not here in the Sixteen Streets. Not anymore.'

Bella had fond memories of when her family lived over this way, on Jackson Street. In many ways, it had been nicer than living in the big house by the sea where they had lived for the last ten or twelve years. There had certainly been fewer money problems when they lived in a smaller place round here.

'I was at the Robin Hood tonight,' Bella told her. 'I was supposed to be having a nice time, but I got into a bit of a scene with that pal of yours, Junie . . .' Bella rolled her eyes. 'You know what she's like. She's insufferable now that she's started going out with your brother. She thinks she's the bee's knees.'

'She always did,' Minnie said, feeling like a betrayer for saying it. The two girls stood on wooden duckboards in a puddly alleyway, lights flickering around them, hugging their warm flasks of tea to their chests. 'What was the scene about?'

'Something and nothing, same as everything with Junie. She can blow anything out of all proportion and cause trouble.'

'Don't I know it.' Minnie sighed, thrilled at gossiping like this.

'Well, we sat there at the Women's Table and I was wishing I'd never sat down with her, because straight away she was pointing at poor Bob, the pot man. Well, you know he's a bit daft and soft, don't you? He got banged on the head when he was a bairn. Fell onto the fire surround when he was hit by his da'.'

Minnie nodded sorrowfully. 'I do indeed. I remember all the drama.'

'So Junie's going on about how slow and gormless he is and everything. Then she's saying – "Just watch. Watch how he is with my mother, with Cathy. Look at the two of them carrying on." And I told her – don't be daft, Junie. She's old enough to be his mother, and he's married anyway. Don't go mixing up bother when there's nothing there. And do you know what she said to me?'

Minnie was agog at all of this. The noise from above ground was getting fiercer. The lights were crackling and cutting out for seconds at a time. The cries of alarm from their fellow denizens of the underworld were becoming louder by the second, but Minnie was hooked completely on Bella's breathless tale. 'What did Junie say to you . . .?'

'She said – "I know just what's going on. I've seen them. I've seen the pair of them in flagrante. My mother and that daft bloke. And do you know what I'm going to do?" She said: "I'm going to tell his wife Megan that they're having a ding-dong. I'm going to dob him in the shite."'

'I've been worried that she would do that,' Minnie muttered.

'And also – Junie said – "I'm going to report him to the military police, that bloke. He should be at the Front with all the rest of them. There's nothing wrong with him. Look how he carries beer barrels around," she said. And then she said – "Look how he's messing about with my mucky old tart of a mother."'

'Eeeh,' said Minnie. 'That's awful. Is that what she called her own mam?'

'She did, an' all. She's got no respect for anyone, that Junie. She was always the same, from the day she first turned up here.' Bella looked Minnie up and down. 'Mind, you were always her best pal, weren't you? You could never see anything wrong with her.'

Minnie bit her lip. Yes, she'd always adored Junie. Her own strange thoughts and desires had made her blind to Junie's many faults. She could admit that to herself now. Minnie could see that she had wilfully blocked out the many signs of her beloved's cruelty. She had hoped and prayed that Junie would settle down and start to be less bitter and angry. And in recent years, it seemed that those hopes had come true. Junie was less abrasive and vengeful. On the whole, anyway. But then Minnie would hear things like this! Fancy bad-mouthing her own mother like that and promising to stir up trouble! It made Minnie feel cross that she'd defended Junie so much over the years. She had struggled so hard to see the good in her. Yet here Junie was, still being dreadful. Minnie opened her mouth and found herself saying something that felt almost treacherous. 'I think I've gone off Junie since she's come back to the Sixteen Streets. I think she might just be as bad as ever.'

Even in the dark tunnel, in all the noise, Bella intuited that Minnie was feeling lonely and left out these days. 'Listen, come to ours. If we get through this night, that is. If we're all here tomorrow . . . come to Seahouses. Come and visit us there. You haven't seen us all in ages. Mam'll be glad to see you again, and the lads, and Nonna . . .'

Minnie beamed at this invite. 'I will. Thank you, I will.'

*

The next day dawned with palls of smoke hanging over the bombsites. It hadn't just been Sunderland that had been hit. A factory had gone up in North Shields, and a row of houses somewhere near the middle of the town.

The all-clear sounded and it seemed like hardly any time passed before the morning klaxons went, summoning the workers to the docks and the factory buildings. The skies were wintry pink and blue, marred only by the greasy smoke.

Minnie was up early, chewing on a hank of bread and dripping in the scullery and taunting her brother. He was sullen this morning. 'By, I think being in love is making you worse than ever. When you're not with your Junie, you're gruffer than you ever were.'

'I'm not in love,' he growled at Minnie. His dark expression was enough to warn her against ragging him too much. He clearly had a thick head this morning. She couldn't help herself, though.

'I hear your Junie was being a pain in the pub last night. Bella Franchino was telling me about it. She was mixing up trouble and gossiping the whole time.'

Derek sneered at his sister. 'Like you'd never gossip or stir up bother, eh?'

'I certainly wouldn't,' Minnie gasped. 'I'm not like Junie. She does that kind of thing for fun.'

Derek glared at her. 'You don't know her. You cracked on you were friends all that time, but you really don't know what Junie is like at all.'

Oh dear, Minnie thought. *She's got to him. She's got him wrapped round her little finger, just like she does to everyone.*

There was a spark of anger in Minnie. Deep down, almost hidden. But it burned there all the same. She was furious with

Junie. She always would be. Was furious the right word? It felt like fury. It was a strong, passionate feeling, hidden away from sight. It was rare that Minnie ever really considered it. She knew that it was all bound up with the way she used to feel about Junie. It was easier, perhaps safer, to think about it as fury. But it was better, in the end, to keep it all tucked away. She couldn't really afford to let herself have strong feelings about anything. She must push them all down and overcome them.

'I'm going out for the day,' she told her ma and da, swanking a bit as she tied on her headscarf. 'I've been invited to Seahouses by Bella. I'm visiting friends who live in their posh house by the sea.'

'Ooh, listen to her,' Betty Minton cackled. 'Popular at last, are you, Minnie? Well, off you go, pet. You'll not be missed round here today.'

Off Minnie shuffled, into the frosty morning streets. She'd catch the trolley bus on Ocean Road and be there in time for morning coffee. Bella had promised her real coffee, made from beans. Her dad had hidden some precious sacks away in the cellar before the war. Minnie hurried along the cold streets and she felt like she could already taste that deliciously genuine coffee.

Chapter Nine

It was snowing heavily by the time Minnie arrived on the street where the Franchino family lived. It had been a while since she had visited, and she was amazed all over again at the size of their wonderful red-bricked house by the sea. It had what they called gabled windows and attic rooms and everything. Bella had a bedroom up at the top that was like a princess's turret, Minnie thought. She even had a dressing room to herself, with loads of frocks stashed away. Well, she was very glamorous, wasn't she? Just like her mama, Sofia was, too.

There must be a lot of cash in ice cream and coffee, Minnie thought to herself, enjoying the soft, cool tickle of snowflakes falling on her face. She remembered her mam grumbling about this: how come them Franchinos get to buy a big house like that just from ice cream? And us Mintons with our fish bar are still here in the Sixteen Streets?

Minnie's da' had simply laughed at her chuntering. 'Would you ever move away from Frederick Street, you daft old boot? Would you leave these Sixteen Streets? Really?'

Betty had been forced to think about this and her own answer surprised her. 'Why no, of course I wouldn't. Not for all the fancy houses in the world.'

'Exactly,' Harry Minton had nodded. 'It might be a bit poky and old-fashioned round here. It might not have changed much since my great-great-grandad's time – not really – but when you belong here, it's a bad idea to move away. I've known many that have tried over the years, and they've had hard luck afterwards. They've found it difficult to start somewhere anew.'

Her parents' voices accompanied Minnie as she hurried up the front garden of the Franchino homestead. Their beautiful gardens had been ploughed over the summer before last and turned into a working vegetable garden, with everything set out neatly in serried ranks. Of course, this time of year, there was little to be seen but churned-up earth, all covered in frost. Minnie understood that it was the old Nonna who had taken charge of this whole operation. She had always enjoyed shuffling about, tending and growing things, but since the war started, she had filled up every available corner of the garden with vines and roots and leafy stuff. She was a marvel at her age, Bella always said.

It was the fearsome Nonna who answered the door to Minnie's knock. She was a tiny, shrivelled woman draped in black, clutching her silver-topped cane. 'Ah, Minnie Minton,' she scowled, and Minnie was gratified to be remembered. 'Come into the kitchen.'

The Franchino kitchen was very modern and advanced, with all kinds of machines and labour-saving devices. The air was fragrant with freshly brewed coffee and baking bread. Here, Minnie found Bella's mother, Sofia, who had once been her fellow barmaid some years ago at the Robin Hood. Sofia had become rather plump since the last time Minnie had seen her. She had had a third child, somewhat later than the others. Little Carlo was now at school. Minnie tried to tot up exactly how old he was.

Sofia did her best to seem flustered and annoyed at having a houseful of young people – Bella in her mid-twenties, Marco no longer a teen and little Carlo, too. Not to mention the old Nonna still going strong. Minnie knew that Sofia's irritation was all an act, however. Sofia thrived on having a large family to look after.

Bella joined them, smiling warmly as they gathered at the kitchen table for the promised proper coffee. Three generations of Franchino women sat down with Minnie, keen to hear her updates and all the gossip from Frederick Street.

She quickly filled them in on her brother's courtship of Junie Sturrock and how Junie seemed more headstrong and spiteful than ever.

Bella nodded firmly. 'From what she said to me, she seems intent on stirring up trouble for her own mother.'

'Ah, poor Cathy.' Sofia shook her head. 'She's let her life be blighted by that little madam. All because she felt so guilty for abandoning her when she was a little one. Not that Cathy had any choice, mind you. She was tricked by her wicked aunty. But still Cathy feels terribly guilty and beholden to Junie.' The look on Sofia's face made it clear that she had no love for Cathy's daughter. 'Eeeh, and I'll never forget the state that Junie got the pub into, and the mess she made of Cathy's house. That time when Cathy was away in Naples with me, having a rare, well-deserved holiday. That girl ruined everything for her out of sheer spite.'

'It was the old man, as well,' Nonna piped up. 'Cathy's dreadful old husband. May he rest in peace. He was a right old bugger, too.'

'That's true,' Sofia sighed. 'Cathy's not had it easy.' A fierce light came into her eyes. 'Remember when old Noel Sturrock claimed he had a paper that signed all our business over to him? When he said my Tonio had gambled everything away to him in a game of cards. And we thought he was going to own everything of ours, lock, stock and barrel?'

'That was a terrible time,' Bella said.

'We were very fortunate that he died just about that time,' said Nonna, pursing her lips pensively. 'What good fortune that was, indeed.'

'Good for us, and good for Cathy, too,' Sofia said. 'Everyone's life was improved by old Noel's terrible death. How awful that was. But better, in the end, for everyone around him.'

There was a respectful lull in the conversation and then Minnie, feeling brave, dared to ask something that had niggled at her for a while. 'How come you and Cathy aren't as close as you once were, Sofia? You used to be best friends, didn't you? Way back, before the war. Back when we all worked at the Robin Hood together. Why, you went off to Naples together and had a marvellous time, didn't you? You were inseparable back then.'

Sofia's dimpled smile was fond and reflective. She patted her tied-up hair. It was still as jet black and glossy as it had been back in her thirties. She looked fleetingly regretful. 'I suppose time always moves on and it rushes us this way and that. Friendships have their seasons, I believe. We all change and move on, I guess . . .'

'No,' barked the old Nonna loudly. She struck the pine table with her clawed hands. 'Damn your friendships and their seasons. That is wrong. So wrong. Why, I believe friendships and loyalty are *forever*. All of this chopping and changing is very modern. Where I come from, you are loyal to your people always. You would kill for them.'

Sofia and Bella laughed at this. 'We aren't in the dark ages now, Mama,' Sofia chuckled.

'Then more fool you,' said Nonna crossly. 'You make me spit with anger. Why, you hear that your old friend is being given trouble and the mad runaround by her evil daughter and you could not care less. You simply say that it is all her fault.'

'Oh Nonna,' Bella smiled. 'No one is saying that Junie is evil . . . that's a terrible thing to say.'

Minnie looked at the old woman and something in her expression made her shiver just then.

'There is just something bad about that girl,' the old woman said. 'There is a shard of ice in her heart. That is what evil really is, you know. When people let ice touch their heart.'

'What about ice cream?' said Sofia, trying to lighten the mood.

'You are frivolous,' shouted her ancient mother.

'No, I meant it. I've got a little batch. A rare little batch I've mixed up. It's in the freezer box.' She beamed at Minnie. 'You wouldn't say no to *Fior di latte*, would you, pet?'

Minnie loved being with the Franchinos. She stayed all day, and it was like a small holiday. When the father of the family, Tonio, came home from the ice-cream parlour, he kissed both her cheeks and told her that she was more beautiful than ever. 'Ha. Rubbish,' she laughed, grinning at him.

Tonio had always had a soft spot for Minnie. She was the kindest and brightest of all the friends Bella had made. She always seemed rather downtrodden to him.

'Come and see the cellar,' he urged. 'Come and see all the preserves and dried goods and the bottles of limoncello and wine.'

When she saw the ranks of bottles and jars stored deep in the Franchino cellar, Minnie couldn't help gasping. 'Why, you could live down here for a year.'

Tonio insisted that she take a bottle of the Nonna's homemade lemon liqueur home with her. Minnie knew from experience that it was sugary, delicious and lethally strong. 'It will be lovely for Christmas for you,' Tonio told her, patting her rounded shoulder. He wrinkled his nose slightly. The girl really did smell of chip fat, bless her.

'Well,' she told them all. 'I'd best be catching the trolley bus back to the Sixteen Streets. It's been lovely to see you all again.' The women had spent the entire day in idle gossip, and it had done them the world of good.

'Now I feel like I know everything that has been happening on Frederick Street,' Sofia laughed. 'I know all about the Farleys and the Sturrocks and the Mintons . . . and everyone else down that way.'

'But you must promise to come and see us in person,' Minnie told her. 'I'm sure Cathy would be glad to see you. Come at Christmastime at least. It isn't long now. There'll be the usual Christmas Eve gathering at the pub. Please say you'll at least come for that.'

Bella hugged her. 'Of course we will. We'll all be there for that.'

'I wish I could invite you round to number fifteen,' Minnie sighed. 'But there's not room for you all and the place is like a midden all the time. It's hardly the place to entertain anyway . . .' She thought about her mother's washing, eternally hanging from racks in the back parlour. Her faded combinations were always steaming gently in the heat from the range. The posh front parlour was too chilly and old-fashioned to have anyone round to sit in, too. It was hopeless, trying to think of how to reciprocate the Franchinos, hospitality. Minnie would just have to rely on the Robin Hood. 'And you, too, Nonna,' she told the old woman respectfully. 'I hope you'll come to see us again in the Sixteen Streets.'

'Of course,' Nonna cried dramatically. 'I'm the only one who remembers where us lot really belong. We'll be there to see you, Minnie. We'll see you on Christmas Eve.'

For some reason she didn't quite understand, a vague feeling of sadness accompanied Minnie home on the trolley bus. As the tram clanked along the lines on the White Leas, she watched the huge skies darkening and the snow coming down in billowing flurries. Why was she so sad? Why did everything feel so bittersweet to the usually upbeat Minnie Minton?

She hugged the parcel, wrapped in beautiful bright blue tissue paper, that Tonio had given her. She had limoncello, a jar of pickled onions and a small packet of dark, ground coffee. She clutched it all to her chest, along with her gas mask in its cardboard box at the end of its strap. It was her friends' togetherness that had made her feel so tender, wasn't it? They had touched her heart just by being there, all together, and welcoming her like that. The Franchino clan treated her like a normal person: one that was worthy of respect. They didn't see her as a simpleton or a workhorse or a pitiable case.

It was the glimpse of happiness that made Winnie feel sad. She hugged the sugary wine and the pickles to her chest as the trolley bus swerved up Ocean Road and she thought: *I need to find my own way to be happy. Next year will be* my *year. I must see to it. I must find the right way and step out of my dull life and become the woman I'm supposed to be.*

Somehow.

Chapter Ten

Cathy decorated the interior of the Robin Hood with great glossy branches of holly and fir. She enlisted Junie to help her and they went off one day on the trolley bus into the countryside and brought back swags of greenery, getting some very odd looks on the way.

There was something wonderfully Christmassy in the air: a spicy scent and a nip of frost. For the Farleys at number thirteen, the season had started early, with their Tom coming home for a few days at the beginning of December. They had their big meals and celebrations and gift-swapping earlier, and when they came into the pub, they brought the spirit of the season with them. Songs were sung and kisses were bestowed and everyone felt a little lighter in their hearts for a while.

Cathy kept a benign, watchful eye on the new Farley girl, Tom's bride, Irene. Word was about that the lass was pregnant, so she had a lot on her plate, what with getting used to a new place. It was good to see that Beryl, her older sister-in-law, was taking good care of her. Cathy went to drink with them at the Women's Table, telling a few tales about the place and explaining how life worked here in the Sixteen Streets. Cathy marvelled at her own ability to sound like a seasoned resident of South Shields. Of course, in many ways that's what she was.

Next year she'd have been here – what? – twenty-four years. Was that right? It hardly seemed possible. She felt very much like the same girl who'd pitched up here with hardly any possessions to her name. The same girl who had been missing her secret daughter terribly and who had no idea what to do with her life.

Cathy strongly believed in helping others out. Having had to rely on people like Theresa Sturrock when she first came here, she knew just how important a helping hand could be. Irene Farley was a nice young woman and deserved all the help she could get. The major fly in the ointment for her was her younger sister-in-law, Megan, who had decided that she couldn't stand the sight of the new girl. There was a strange antagonism between the pair of them. All she knew was that Megan was a proper little madam, who didn't deserve to be married to the almost saintly Bob, and so it was easy to take Irene's side against her.

She explained some of this to Junie, who stood at the bar with her, skilfully helping out on the busy nights leading up to Christmas.

'Ha,' Junie laughed. 'There's another reason why you don't care for Megan.'

Her mother frowned at her mocking tone. 'And what's that, pray tell?' Cathy bit her lip, knowing that she was straying onto thin ice here.

Junie didn't beat around the bush. 'You and her fella, that's why. You've got a soft spot for her bloke, Bob. Your pot man.'

Cathy shushed her crossly. 'Keep your voice down, lady. You'll have the whole bloomin' bar listening in to my business. They gossip enough about me as it is.' It was true, Cathy was often the source of speculation, even in her own pub. Just this afternoon, she had been amused to hear Beryl spinning a completely erroneous tale about how Cathy belonged to some grand family in Northumberland, and how she'd been banished because she'd fallen in love with an Irish docker. How had Beryl come up with such stuff? That kind of legend-spinning amused Cathy, but this other stuff from Junie was quite different. It was the kind of gossip that could really damage lives. She didn't like the fact that her daughter was turning into a troublemaker. Cathy was just going to have to brave it out. No, no, there was nothing going on. Junie, you're wrong. Shut up about it. Keep your gob shut. But she knew her daughter was terrible when she got a bit of gossip between her teeth. Cathy asserted: 'There's nothing going on between me and Bob. That's a ridiculous thing to suggest. Why, he's about fifteen years younger than me . . .'

Junie arched her delicate eyebrow. 'I know what I've seen. He's stayed round ours. You've been up to hanky-panky, the pair of you.'

Cathy felt her face grow hot. What had Junie actually seen? Had she really seen Bob at their house? She must have. Junie was sneaking around and spying on her own mam. It made Cathy feel horrible and dirty, her daughter speaking to her like this. 'You'd do well to keep your gob shut, madam. That Megan Farley wouldn't take kindly to such tittle-tattle.'

Junie gave a ghost of a smirk. She turned back to pulling pints and didn't say another word about it. Cathy returned to welcoming everyone and playing the part of the glamorous and warm-hearted landlady. But she had to admit it to herself – she was getting so that she really didn't trust her own daughter. It had taken so long to regain any kind of trust at all for Junie. The peace they had arrived at felt so hard-won. Now Cathy was starting to wonder whether she might have been foolish in letting her daughter back into her life again, after all the things she'd done. Maybe Junie hadn't actually changed at all?

*

Christmas crept ever closer and, even with the planes going overhead and the daily reports of death and misery coming in from all over the world, the residents of the Sixteen Streets were determined to enjoy themselves. Paper decorations were made, ancient baubles and ornaments were brought out of sideboards and put proudly on display. Geese and chickens were in short supply, and there was a flurry of illegal trade going on. Someone got hold of a box of oranges down at the docks and smuggled them away, to be sold surreptitiously, one at a time. It would be a poorer and leaner Christmas than any other, in some ways, but that only made everyone more determined to have a smashing time.

Irene had a dreadful fall down the stairs at number thirteen. There was a kerfuffle as all the women swept into action. Had she lost the baby? Would she be all right? Cathy and Minnie and Betty and Winnie: all went hurrying round to see that she was OK. The new lass sat up, white-faced and worried-looking, in her bed. The doctor had been to see her and listened to her belly. All would be well, he declared, but she must take proper bed rest.

Why had she fallen down the stairs like that? Well, it all came out that someone had foolishly left an old fur tippet lying out on the staircase. She had trodden on its slick pelt and come a cropper. Then it was discovered that Megan had been the one to do something that careless, and immediately it was suspected that she had done it on purpose.

'Why, you could have killed the lass,' gasped Ma Ada. 'She could have broken her back. She might have lost the bairn.'

There was an unholy row at number thirteen, right before Christmas, over the saga of the deadly tippet. Next door, Betty had a glass beaker pressed up to the wall so she could hear all the details. 'What are they saying, Ma?' gasped Minnie, avid for the particulars.

Harry sat shaking his head at his women. 'You're so bloody nebby,' he told them. 'Fancy getting a kick out of other folks' misery.'

'Getting a kick, by hang!' thundered his wife. 'I'm concerned for them. It sounds like the bloody war's broken out in their back parlour next door. That Megan and Ma Ada are screaming at each other like I've never heard them.' She passed the glass to her daughter. 'Just listen to the language. Eeeh, it's shocking.'

Minnie listened and was amazed to hear the women screeching at each other like hellcats. Well, that Megan was always acting up. This kind of row was bound to break out, sooner or later. Suddenly, there was another voice. A man's voice. He was roaring at them. He sounded both commanding and furious.

Betty heard him even without holding a glass to the wall. 'Who's that? Is that Bob? Is quiet, gentle Bob joining in with the shouting now?'

Harry Minton nodded to himself. Yes, they could do with a fella shouting at them. Those women needed telling to shut up, they did. Christ, if they could just have some peace, the lot of them. There was just too much going on these days, he thought. Even without the bloody war. It was war round these doors every day, even without the flamin' Germans.

Bob went knocking on Cathy Sturrock's door late that night. He was a blubbering mess of tears. 'What's the matter, man?' she cried, panicked by the sight of him. 'Whatever's happened, lad?'

He hugged her closely, and she felt suddenly conscious that they were standing on her doorstep, where anyone might see them.

'Here, come inside,' she said, drawing him into her hallway, careful not to let light spill out into the street.

'I *h-hit* her,' he sobbed when he had calmed down enough to get his words out. 'I'm no better than my own father Billy was. He used to bray my ma.'

'I remember, Bob . . .' Cathy found she was holding him tightly, trying to make it better for him. He was shaking in her arms. 'You hit Megan?'

'I slapped her in the face. I would never do such a thing. I . . . I just . . . I panicked. She and my mother were fighting and they were out of control. They were fighting because Irene nearly lost her bairn and it was all Megan's fault. I couldn't stand them screaming and hissing at each other, so I went in there and yelled at them, but they wouldn't listen. And so I . . . I slapped her. She went quiet just like that. She stared at me like she'd never seen me before.'

'Oh Bob,' Cathy said. 'You should never have hit a woman . . .'

'I didn't have any control. This feeling . . . just burst out of me. It had been building up.'

'Where is she now?'

'She went. She upped and went. She never said another word. She just went. I think . . . I th-think she's left me, Cathy.'

Cathy hugged him close. She didn't say another word. She let instinct guide her and led him wordlessly up the stairs and into her bedroom. He was unresisting and completely passive. His sobbing subsided, but he didn't even seem to realise where he was or what they were doing. He stood in the honey-coloured lamplight beside Cathy's bed and he let her undress him. She pulled off his workday togs and when he was naked, she stood back and admired him frankly. Then she lay him down in her bed. 'Just go to sleep, Bob,' she told him gently. 'I'll take care of you.'

'All right,' he said.

She tucked him in and slipped downstairs to make some warm milk for them both.

Junie was in the scullery. Of course she knew what was going on. She raised that ironic eyebrow of hers once more. 'Nothing going on, eh Mother?' she laughed.

Cathy warned her: 'You just keep your nose to yourself, my girl. You've got complications of your own to take care of.'

'Complications?' Junie frowned. 'Why, there's nothing at all complicated about my love life. It's the simplest, most straightforward, most wonderful of love stories. There's nothing twisted or peculiar or clandestine about it. Derek and I are extremely happy.'

Cathy was in no mood for her daughter's taunts. 'Well, bully for you, Junie. Bully for bloody you.'

Chapter Eleven

'Are you all right in there, hinny?' It was surely Irene in the other privy again. Minnie was sitting in the darkness of the lavatory at number fifteen and she recognised the sobbing coming through the brick wall. 'Irene?'

'Aye, it's me,' said the Norfolk girl.

'Are you feeling bad?' Minnie remembered the tumble Irene was said to have taken down the stairs, and her belly went cold at the thought of it. 'You're OK, aren't you?'

'Aye, aye, I'm . . .' There was a horrible retching noise and Minnie realised that her friend was being sick into next door's immaculate toilet bowl.

'Oh, I'm sorry, Irene,' said Minnie, feeling like she was intruding.

There was a pause while Irene's nausea subsided. 'Oh, it's all right. I'm just not feeling my best lately. With Tom going away again, and the fall, and the baby and all . . .'

'The baby's all right though, isn't it?'

'Oh yes. The doctor's been out and all's well, thank goodness.'

'Here, let's meet outside and talk over the wall,' Minnie suggested. 'I'm finished up here.' There was a strange kind of intimacy in their lavatory chats, Minnie thought.

Moments later, they were in the frosty backyards, leaning over the wall and gabbing to each other.

'I bet you're pleased that Megan's whizzed off and ran away. Was she really responsible for you falling down the stairs?'

A shadow crossed over Irene's pale face. 'I'd rather give her the benefit of the doubt and assume she dropped that fur stole by accident. And I never wanted to see her hit like that, by Bob of all people. He was so angry at her. Now everyone's worried about where she might have run to, and what's become of her.'

Minnie pursed her lips and tried to summon up some pity for the honey-blonde girl from next door. The truth was, Megan had always terrified her. 'I bet she's gone back to her family in Hartlepool.'

'Poor Bob's been roaming the streets, calling after her, like she's a dog that's gone missing . . .'

Minnie shook her head. 'He's never had much sense . . .'

'And the latest thing is . . . he's had his calling-up papers at last. They're late, but as Ma Ada says, they must be low on choices by now. They're even taking the ones who are a bit slow. She was in tears, poor old thing. "They're going to take all my lads off me," she was saying.'

Minnie nodded. 'Yes, we heard another drama going on, through the back parlour wall. You've had some awful trouble round yours recently.'

'We have indeed,' said Irene. 'I don't really have the heart for Christmas coming up. I feel like we already had it once, while Tom was here. The Christmas spirit has completely gone out of me.'

Minnie perked up. 'Oh, I'm looking forward to it,' she couldn't help herself grinning. 'We've got ourselves a chicken. And Derek's asked Junie to be his guest at our table for the day.'

'That'll be nice for you all,' Irene said, though she didn't sound that enthusiastic. She was wary of Junie. 'Does that mean Cathy's going to be sat at number twenty-one by herself all day?'

'I hadn't thought of that . . .'

'Perhaps we'd better ask her to ours,' Irene mused.

'Oh. Are you coming to the Robin Hood on Christmas Eve?' Minnie asked her new friend. 'You haven't had a Christmas here yet, have you? This is traditional, and even the war hasn't stopped the whole street getting together on Christmas Eve.'

'I believe we are going to be there,' Irene said, though in her heart she knew it couldn't be the same as the nights when Tom was home. At least she had the bairn to think of, and the curious thought that this time next year the baby would be actually here at last: a person in their own right.

'I'm glad to hear it. Now I'd best go and help my mother,' Minnie said. 'She's getting out all the fancy crockery and plates and everything, ready for Christmas Day. Everything needs scrubbing. Only the best for Junie, apparently. Only the best for my mother's future daughter-in-law.'

Irene's eyebrows went up. 'Are they that serious then, her and your Derek?'

'They seem to be,' Minnie said, with a shrug and an unreadable expression on her face. Then she shivered, said a quick goodbye and hurried back into the warm house.

Christmas Eve brought thicker snow, which froze and made getting up and down the sloping streets a hazard. It was so cold that the air seemed to sparkle and freeze right before your face. Minnie didn't dash around so much buying last-minute presents as she had in other years. This year, money was tighter and there was less to choose from in the shops, anyway. She had found an antique cameo brooch for her mam on a market stall back in the autumn, and a cigarette case for her dad. It had someone else's initials engraved on it, but he'd never mind that.

Minnie actually found herself feeling excited for Christmas. The year had been a hard one, in so many ways. She was looking forward to a few days away from the fish fryers and letting her hair down a little. She was also – she had to be honest with herself – actually looking forward to having Junie round for Christmas Day. Yes, things were complicated. Yes, she bridled with all kinds of unspoken thoughts about Junie. Yes, it was never very easy when she thought about what Junie was really like. But, at the same time, Minnie still loved to be around her. She felt different and better and more like herself when she was in Junie's presence. Now it had been a little while since she had spent much time with her oldest friend. Since he had started walking out with her, Derek had been taking up all her time. Any spare hours the two of them could get they spent together.

'The lovebirds,' Betty sighed happily when she thought of them, or when she caught a fleeting glimpse of the courting pair. Derek so dark and quiet and secretive. Junie bright and colourful in her expensive clothes. 'Eeh, she always insists on looking her best and dressing up, doesn't she? She's a credit to him.' Betty looked Minnie up and down. 'I wish you dressed yourself better, though, our Minnie. You've never made much of an effort, have you?'

Minnie flushed crossly. What was the point when everything ended up reeking of chip fat? But she never answered her mother back. It was never worth fighting with Swetty Betty. It wasn't unheard of to get a clattering from her mother. She could lash out with those ham hock arms of hers and fetch you a hefty slap.

'Maybe I'll dress up for tonight, then,' Minnie grinned at her. 'For going to the Robin Hood. Maybe I'll get my glad rags on.'

'You do that, lass,' her dad encouraged her, beaming at her from his usual place by the stove.

*

'Bella. You're here . . .' Minnie was delighted that the first person she saw in the crowded saloon bar was her friend.

The Robin Hood was already packed to the rafters at barely eight o'clock on Christmas Eve. Aunty Martha was settled at her usual place in front of the battered piano and was vamping gamely through a selection of Christmas carols. The regulars were singing along lustily and helping themselves to punch from a vast salver that had been set up on a table with some fish paste sandwiches and sausage rolls.

'What's in the punch?' Minnie grinned.

Bella had no idea. 'It's lethal. I think Cathy must have tossed in half-bottles of every kind of spirit and liqueur she had left mouldering on her shelves. It has the funniest taste, too . . .'

This reminded Minnie to check with Cathy that she wasn't going to be on her own tomorrow; to see that she was indeed going to spend the day with the Farleys. Minnie hated the idea of the landlady – who did so much to bring everyone together – sitting on her own.

'My whole family's come down here tonight, apart from the bairns, of course,' Bella said. She ushered Minnie over to a table, where Sofia, Tonio and the old Nonna were sipping glasses of the queer punch and looking rather tipsy.

'Happy Christmas to you, pet,' Sofia told her. 'I hope next year will bring you everything you're wanting.'

Minnie laughed out loud at this. 'I don't think that's likely, but I'll settle for health and a certain amount of happiness, thanks. Let's not get carried away.'

Her one-time fellow barmaid looked philosophical all of a sudden. 'I think in this day and age we might as well wish for the moon,' Sofia said. 'I feel like we're praying all the time for the world to be all right. For the war to end and for everyone to be safe. We might as well pray for everything we can think of, mightn't we?' She touched Minnie's face fondly. 'And I wish you all the happiness in the world, Minnie. I really do.'

Everyone was quite drunk, Minnie realised. It wasn't like Sofia to be quite so sentimental and open about her feelings. She was quite a practical, quiet person, really. Now her husband was up on his feet and singing as he stood next to Martha at the piano. He warbled away like an Italian opera singer, all grand gestures. His voice cracked here and there as he gave them 'The Holly and the Ivy', and everyone joined in to help him out.

Even Minnie found herself singing along, and she hated her voice. It was croaky and horrible when she tried to raise it in song. Back at school, the teacher had once stopped everyone mid-hymn, listened frowningly to Minnie doing her best solo and then asked her to simply mime in future. 'Just open and close your mouth, Minnie Minton. Simply pretend to be joining in.' All the kids had laughed at this and Minnie had laughed, too, trying hard not to let them see how much this had hurt her.

In some ways, it was how she had gone about her whole life, wasn't it? Opening and closing her mouth, and only pretending to join in with everyone. Her whole life had been a case of miming along.

She shook her head and sang out loud tonight. She didn't care if she was off-key or croaky. Let them hear her terrible voice. It was Christmas and she was with a whole lot of folk who she really cared about. The curious punch that Cathy had mixed was starting to taste a bit more palatable and a feeling of warmth and goodwill was spreading right through her whole body.

She turned to see her mother and father coming into the bar, bringing Derek and Junie with them. *We're all together*, Minnie thought gladly. *Here we are, all together, and there's nothing more important than that, is there? That's the most important thing of all. We're here in the same place and things are just as they should be.* It was enough for her. It would just always have to be enough.

Chapter Twelve

At the end of the evening, Minnie stayed back to help Cathy out. People jumped up woozily, happy to hurry home before midnight. They bustled into the unlit, frosty streets, automatically lowering their voices as they went outside. It was as if they thought the Luftwaffe might hear them, creeping home from the pub.

Minnie could see that Cathy would have to cope with the mess on her own. Junie had cleared off much earlier, without any thought of her mother and all the dirty glasses left out on every table.

'Thank you, Minnie, you're a marvel,' Cathy smiled wearily at her. 'Remember, you can have a job back here at the Robin Hood any time you like.'

Minnie reflected that that might not be such a bad idea. Perhaps she could do fewer hours slaving over the fish bar? It might do wonders for her and ma's relations if they were in each other's hair a bit less.

As Minnie clinked tankards and glasses together onto trays and took them through to the back, she exchanged happy farewells with the Franchino clan. They had stayed until the very end of the evening, which was very gratifying to see. Bella was helping her red-faced dad into his coat and hat, and the pair of them were laughing in a daft, carefree way. The old Nonna was in her shapeless black sheepskin coat, tapping her cane on the floorboards impatiently. 'All this way to walk home,' she grumbled. 'You'll kill me with all this dashing about. I'll be dead on Christmas morning, and then how glad will you be?'

Minnie realised that Sofia had taken her old dear friend Cathy aside. She was hugging the landlady in her arms and rocking her inside a warm embrace. At the sight of this, Minnie felt her heart glow happily. Why, the two women hadn't been so close in years and years.

'We just sort of drifted apart a bit,' was all that Cathy would ever say, with a sigh that went all the way down to her boots. They'd had the conversation again only very recently. 'It was down to that husband of mine, Noel Sturrock . . . he played Tonio at cards even though he knew Tonio was a hopeless case who would gamble away every last penny he owned. Well, Noel took advantage of that and suddenly he was telling the Franchinos that he'd won their business off them. He claimed he now owned everything of theirs – overnight. It was an awful time. Nothing to do with me, but that kind of thing can really taint friendships, you know.'

'But Sophia would never have imagined you'd mean them any harm,' Minnie had protested, like she did each time this curious topic recurred. 'She would know it had nothing to do with you.'

'Now old Noel is long dead,' Cathy had curtailed the discussion. 'He was dead before he could make any more trouble. And – to be honest – we all breathed a great sigh of relief. He was never a happy soul in himself, and couldn't let anyone else be happy, either. I assume he's gone to a better place.'

'Aye, maybe,' Minnie had said doubtfully.

'But things were never really the same between myself and Sofia . . .' Cathy had sighed. 'And then the war started and life went off in a different direction.' She'd shrugged. 'It's just the ways of these things, I'm afraid.'

Minnie still thought it was a great shame, and it delighted her to see the old friends cuddling like this at the very end of Christmas Eve. Why, she remembered all the palaver and fuss that time when Cathy and Sofia upped sticks and went off abroad for a holiday to Italy. When had that been? Over ten years ago, surely? They had gone off to Naples, spending every last hoarded penny they had and scandalising everyone hereabouts with the suddenness and the expense of it all. Minnie could remember Sofia talking about that handsome suitor of hers – Mario, wasn't it? In his faded black fedora and the blue-black five o'clock shadow on his chin. Fancy that. The two women swanning off to the continent, then coming back with tales of exotic food and amazing old buildings and scary moments and idyllic beaches.

It had all sounded like a different world to Minnie. Back then, she had been an impressionable seventeen-year-old. It had been hard for her to fathom the distances the two women had travelled, there and back. Of course, these days, with local lads off in Europe and Africa and who knows where else, the whole world had shrunk to a much, much smaller place. How terrible that thought was, though. The world had become smaller because of the war.

Minnie dunked glasses in the warm soapy water round the back and swished them around. When she peered round the corner, she found she was eavesdropping on Cathy and Sofia. She didn't mean to pick up every word, but somehow she did. She didn't make a habit of gleaning everyone's goings-on, but that was the way things often worked out.

'I need to ask you,' Sofia was saying, her voice sounding more urgent than Minnie had expected.

'Ask me anything,' Cathy grinned, looking glad that she had her friend back again and they had seemingly bridged the gap between them.

'Money's tight,' Sofia said. 'Well, it is for everyone these days, of course. But the ice-cream parlour isn't bringing in what it should. How could it, when supplies are so poor?'

Cathy was nodding. 'Yes, of course.'

'So . . .' Sofia said, casting a backward glance to her mother and husband, busily fastening up their bulky coats and preparing for the off. 'I will need that thing that I left in your care when we came back from Naples all those years ago. Remember?'

Cathy stared at her friend. Her mouth fell open in surprise. The colour seemed to drain out of her face. 'Oh . . .'

Sofia's expression sharpened. 'You . . . you do still have it, don't you, Cathy?' She clutched her friend's hand. 'Please tell me . . . tell me yes. You've looked after it, haven't you?'

Cathy struggled to allay her fears. 'Of course. Why, of course I have. I knew just how much it meant to your Mario as a family heirloom. And I knew how important it was to you, as a gift from him . . .'

Sofia clucked her tongue. 'I never wanted it. I never asked for it. If Tonio or my mama had known Mario had tried to give me his ring, there would have been an unholy row.'

'I know, I know . . .' Cathy nodded. 'And that's why you gave it to me for safekeeping, ten or more years ago.' Cathy could still picture herself and Sofia, sitting on that clunky old diesel train as it pulled through the lush green valleys of Italy. She could see Sofia taking the ancient velvet box out of her sack of provisions for the journey, opening it and gasping. She could still see the diamond ring, glittering like crazy in the morning sunlight. Mario had slipped it into her possession. It was the most foolish and romantic gesture both women had ever known. 'Of course. Why, of course I have looked after it,' Cathy assured her.

Sofia smiled and tears touched her eyes with relief. She hugged her friend again. 'Oh, thank God for that. I had worried that . . . Well, I don't know what I was so worried about. Of course I can trust you. One of my very oldest friends. My best friend. Oh, thank you, thank you, Cathy. One day soon I might need to ask for it back . . . I might need the money. Things are that desperate . . .'

'Oh. Surely not . . .' Cathy said.

Sofia nodded. 'I haven't heard from Mario for years. With the war and all . . . Why, he might well be dead. He gave me the ring and now I think I might need to cash it in . . .'

Cathy nodded as Sofia relinquished her grip on her at last. 'Oh . . .' she sighed, and from the corner of the bar, Minnie saw that the landlady was looking ashen and sick.

Sofia shrugged on her coat and bade them goodbye. She gathered her tipsy family around her and prepared for the moonlit walk home to Seahouses. 'Merry Christmas. Merry Christmas, all . . .' the Franchinos called out as they left.

Cathy stood alone, hanging onto the brass rail of the bar. For a moment, she looked as if she was going to faint.

Minnie set down her tray and ran to her. 'Whatever's the matter?'

Cathy let Minnie help her to a chair. 'Did you hear any of that?' she asked sharply, knowing exactly what a nosy parker Minnie was.

'I did, yes,' Minnie admitted. 'Something about a ring. Left in your possession for safekeeping. Otherwise there would have been bother.' She gasped with realisation. 'Does that mean Mario proposed to Sofia when you were all on holiday?'

'Aye, but that was a long time ago, and he's over there, in an enemy country. My God, he might even be dead. But none of that matters now.' Cathy's voice sounded bitter. 'What matters is this damned diamond ring that Sofia reckons she might well need giving back quite soon.'

Minnie frowned. 'So? You can just give it back to her, can't you?' She looked at Cathy and was horrified to see a bleak, guilty expression on the older woman's face.

'No,' said Cathy Sturrock. 'No, I can't.'

After she locked the front door of the Robin Hood and waved Minnie off home, Cathy hurried up the cobbled lane to her own front door.

She was swearing and cursing under her breath all the way. In her shock, she had told Minnie Minton far too much. That lass wasn't to be trusted with important secrets. Surely Cathy had learned that much by now? But in her desperation, Cathy had spilled out some of the truth about the ring and then she'd had to beg Minnie to make sure she kept her big trap absolutely shut.

'Of course, of course,' vowed the moon-faced girl. Cathy knew that it wasn't as simple as that. Minnie might mean well, and she might set out to keep quiet about certain, important things, but there was no way she could be relied upon. Cathy had made a mistake. She groaned as she let herself into her own dark, still hallway at midnight on Christmas Eve. Why, she had made many mistakes. So many mistakes.

She laughed bleakly. She had made an impossible number of mistakes in her lifetime.

Strange how so many of those mistakes revolved around her daughter, Junie.

Yes, it was *Junie* who had the ring. It was Junie who had stolen it, wasn't it? And stupidly, *stupidly*, Cathy had let that fact go. She had pretended it had never happened, just for the sake of hanging onto her daughter's love. Maybe Cathy had been naive to forgive her daughter the theft. Maybe she had brushed it under the carpet too easily. But after almost losing her daughter's love so early on, and working so hard to earn it back, Cathy hadn't been able to blame Junie forever. She had to forgive her. She had to keep forgiving her, whatever stunts she pulled. Even stealing expensive things. Even disappearing for years on end and not being in touch. Cathy knew she had allowed Junie to twist her round her little finger.

What an idiot I've been, Cathy cursed herself and hurried up the stairs.

She'd confront her. She'd ask her for it back. She would tell her: I know you went through my things in my room when you were only sixteen, and you stole that precious ring. What did you do with it, Junie? I can't believe I ever let you get away with such a thing . . .

Yes, it was late and Junie was already in bed. It was Christmas and maybe not the best time to go opening up old family wounds. But Cathy was cross and exhausted and her head was reeling. She hammered loudly on Junie's bedroom door. 'Junie. Junie, wake up . . . I need to ask you something . . .'

She thrust open the bedroom door.

'Are you awake in there? Are you listening to me, my girl?'

Junie was awake and she wasn't alone. She was lying there in the naked arms of Derek Minton, and the two of them sat up looking furious. How dare Cathy interrupt them like this? How dare she come flying in and shouting the odds?

'Mother . . .' gasped Junie, more angry than ashamed.

Cathy stood there frozen in horror. 'You're a *thief* . . . and a *jezebel* . . .' she accused her daughter.

Chapter Thirteen

Junie brought wonderful gifts. Well-chosen, beautiful, but not so expensive that they embarrassed their recipients. A headscarf in jewel colours for Betty. 'Oh, now that's marvellous. For when I haven't washed me hair and I'm nipping out to the shop.' A tie for Harry, who became very formal and proud as he knotted it round his pressed shirt collar. For Minnie she brought American silk stockings, which astonished mother and daughter with how sheer and slippery they felt. They were luxurious to the touch. 'I'm not at liberty to say where I procured such items,' Junie warned them all, and everybody laughed.

She brought Derek argyle woollen socks and he smiled at her like she had given him the crown jewels.

The fire was roaring in the grate and there were carols on the radio. Christmas was off to a good start at number fifteen, and everyone was glad. Junie was proving to be a guest. She had even produced a small crate of oranges, all deliciously scented and wrapped in twists of bright paper. It seemed like years since any of them had smelled fresh fruit.

'Let's crack open the sherry right now,' Betty Minton cried at half past ten in the morning. 'I really feel as if we're properly celebrating this year.' She patted Junie's cheek. 'And that's because of you, my lass. You're a lovely addition to this family of ours, you really are.'

Minnie felt herself blushing at her mother's presumption, as did Junie, but she hid it better. The two girls caught each other's eyes and Minnie couldn't help feeling that she was letting her mixed feelings and her secret longings show, just for a brief second, before she looked away again. She had the feeling – as she had from the very first time that they'd met – that Junie could read everything that was written in her heart. The connection between them was as fierce as ever. It was bliss – and torture – spending Christmas with Junie, Minnie thought. And maybe secretly she even wished that Junie would catch a glimpse of the longing in her face. She wished that Junie would see what was in her heart. Maybe, maybe, she even dared to hope.

'Come and help with this flamin' chicken,' Minnie's ma commanded her. Already, Betty was making a muck of the dinner. She was used to frying everything in batter, at the highest possible temperature, and all the subtleties of cookery were lost on her. Luckily, Minnie knew just what to do, fetching the bird out of the oven and carefully basting it in its own juices until the skin was golden brown and everyone's stomachs grumbled with the lovely aroma.

Soon, Minnie was doling out her own presents to her family, and her parents were chuffed as muck – or so they said – with the bargain antiques she had found for them on Shields market. She presented her brother with some cufflinks that he admired gruffly and then she turned to Junie. 'This is for you,' she said almost shyly. 'It's nothing as fancy as those lovely stockings you gave me,' and once more Minnie flushed red as she looked her friend in the eye. Silk stockings. They were so intimate, it made her feel peculiar even to talk about them. She was used to workaday clothes and practical things. Silk against her skin would feel shockingly sensual.

'Oh, what's this? Help. A book.' Junie crumpled the tissue paper into a fist and produced a small, shagreen-covered hardback book. 'I'm not much of a reader, you know.'

Betty gave an embarrassed laugh. 'What's she given you, then? A Bible? Eeh, our Minnie. She mustn't have known what to get you, hinny.'

Junie leafed impatiently through the flimsy, onion-skin pages. 'It's a really old one. It looks like poems.'

'It *is* poems,' said Minnie stiffly, and now she was feeling foolish with everyone's eyes upon her. They were making her feel that a small book of love poems was the most ridiculous present anyone could have given Junie. 'It's John Donne and Keats and Shakespeare. Beautiful poems that I thought you might—'

Junie wrinkled her nose. 'School stuff.'

'Love poems,' Betty cackled. 'Aye, that'll be because you're in love. Minnie's bought you love poems because you and our Derek are so lovey-dovey these days.'

Minnie was appalled to see her brother scowling at her, as if she was taking the mickey out of him. 'No, no, no . . .' she said. 'I just thought . . . it was such a beautiful little book, lying alone on the market stall . . . I thought Junie might like it.'

'Eeeh, that's our Minnie,' her da' laughed. 'She buys all her presents off one of the old junk stalls. She always has done. It's all dead people's stuff there, you know. But she thinks it's all treasure, bless her.'

'Dead people's stuff . . .' Junie gasped, holding the small green book at arm's length. She put it down on the sideboard as if it was covered in grave mould.

Minnie was kicking herself. Of course, it was a very stupid present to give Junie. It was only inside Minnie's head that Junie was the kind of girl who would appreciate such a gift.

The book stayed on the sideboard, beside the carriage clock, and it was days later that Minnie realised it was still there.

*

They drank sherry and then port during the dinner that Minnie served up alone. Her mother became quite giddy as she sat quaffing tumblers of strong drink at the head of the table. Junie sat beside Derek and became demure and quiet as she tucked into the food that Minnie had prepared, accepting only the most ladylike portions of the white meat and the crispy roast potatoes. Harry grew bumptious, urging her to eat more: 'You could do with more flesh on those bones. A fella likes a woman with some meat on her, don't he, Derek?'

Derek stared at his father and Betty cracked out laughing. 'Eeeh, listen to that mucky devil. Don't you listen to a word of it, Junie. I think you've got a smashing figure, I do. Not like our Minnie. She's like me – like a giant baked potato.'

Out came the whisky and the ginger wine, and the ersatz Christmas pudding which had been steaming for hours in its muslin wrap. Minnie found it easier to concentrate on the food than to listen to her mother and father showing off, and her friend simpering all the while, pretending to be such a fancy lady.

Minnie escaped in the early afternoon to sit on the privy and smoke a cigarette. She had left her parents dozing tipsily in their chairs and all the washing-up dumped in the stone sink. With a bit of luck, maybe Junie would take the hint and start cleaning up, but she doubted it. Junie was acting like a princess today, and she wasn't about to stop yet.

'Oh,' Minnie gasped, as she stepped out of the outhouse loo to find Junie standing waiting for her.

'Give me a cigarette,' her friend demanded. 'My head's absolutely banging.'

The two friends smoked, leaning against the side wall of the yard. Minnie knew that Junie was angry, just from the stiff way she was stood and the way she sucked in the smoke. 'A-are you not enjoying Christmas at ours then?' Minnie asked her.

'What?' Junie frowned, as if she could hardly remember where she was, or what she was meant to be doing. 'Oh, it's OK, I suppose. Your parents are making an effort at least. You've got a face like a smacked behind, mind. Why's that? Are you jealous?'

'Jealous?' Minnie winced. 'What of?'

'All the attention I'm getting from them all,' Junie said, with a laugh. 'I'm like the daughter they never knew they had.'

Minnie shook her head sorrowfully. 'No, no. Not at all. I'm really glad you're here with us, Junie. I always am so, so glad to see you. You already know that.'

Junie pulled a face. 'Aye, well. I'm lucky to have somewhere to go, really. Just about anywhere would be better than home with my mother today.'

'Why's that?' asked Minnie.

Junie didn't feel like explaining everything just now. As it happened, she still felt foolish and embarrassed after being discovered romping between the sheets with Derek last night. Usually, she would have brazened it out. Whatever her mother saw, it was her own damned fault for bursting in without knocking like that. What the hell had she been thinking of? But, no . . . actually . . . Junie was mortified by the memory of her mother's crazy, pale face at the bottom of her bed in the early hours. She looked like she had gone mad. And what was all that rubbish she'd been spouting about a ring? A missing, stolen ring. A diamond ring.

It took a little while for the penny to drop, after Derek had hurriedly dressed and dashed home again. And it was some time after Cathy had left her alone, that Junie had realised what all this business over the ring was about.

'You took it, didn't you?' Cathy had squawked. 'You went through all my things and you stole it away.'

Aye, Junie could have told her mother, I did as well. You guessed it all right. And something else. Something else that she didn't dare confess to yet. Junie had sold that ring, years back. Down in Manchester. When she was desperate for cash, she had taken the Italian heirloom to a dealer in Didsbury and got herself a terrible price. Even at the time, she knew she was being ripped off. But that was desperation for you. Surely her mother would understand that?

Well, it was all too late now, anyway. The money was long spent and gone. The precious ring was irrecoverable.

Junie shook her head and laughed bitterly. 'Fancy buying me a stupid little book,' she said. 'Love poems, indeed. What do I want with rubbish like that?'

Minnie was spared from having to dredge her feelings to come up with an answer to that. She knew she would have to sound jocular and unhurt, but instead there came an interruption from over the wall. There was a voice coming from the yard at the back of number thirteen.

'Eeeh, is that Junie and Minnie out there?' asked this familiar voice. It was Irene Farley, who had come out from some air in the middle of the Farley family Christmas.

'Happy Christmas, Irene,' Minnie told her, smiling.

Irene put an upturned bucket by the wall and stood on it so she could see both girls. 'A happy Christmas to both of you, too,' she said. 'Eeh, but Junie Sturrock . . . what on earth have you been up to? Your mother's been ragin' round here, about you and all your carry-on. She's been playing war about you.'

Junie huffed and demanded another cigarette off Minnie. 'I couldn't care less. That old cow can get stuffed. She can be lonely on her own in her old age for all I care. I'm moving out of there. It'd kill me to carry on living with her.'

Irene and Minnie both stared at her. 'What? But she'd be so upset,' chided Irene.

'Well, *good*,' said Junie.

'But where will you live . . .?' Minnie asked her.

Chapter Fourteen

It felt as if Junie was taking over everything. Once upon a time, Minnie would have been delighted by the idea of all that was going on lately, but now she wasn't so sure. Life had become much more complex in the Minton household.

Her mam was clear about one thing above all else: 'There's to be no carrying on. Not under my roof. This is a decent, godly house and if I get wind of anything untoward, then the arrangement is off, do you hear me?'

She was thundering this at her son, first thing in the morning on the day after Boxing Day. Christmas was over and done with for the year. There was no dragging it out for the Minton clan. Now it was back down to ordinary life and trying to work out how they could let Junie move in without there being an almighty scandal.

Junie was adamant she could not return to her mother's house.

'It's ridiculous, really,' Betty Minton scowled. 'All those rooms over there. Cathy Sturrock has got that huge house all to herself, plus the rooms above her flaming pub. And yet her daughter still has to come over here to move in with us.' Betty only aired these complaints to Minnie, as they slaved over the potato peeling in the afternoon. She was nicer than nice to Junie's face, of course.

'You don't have to let her live with us,' Minnie shrugged, letting an expert ribbon uncurl under her nimble fingers. She could peel a tatty in one long strip in less time than it took to exhale a bored-sounding sigh.

'I thought she was your pal,' Betty cried. 'And she's in real need, too. Her mother's turned right against her, by all accounts.'

Minnie pulled a face. 'Well, yes, she's my pal and I love her to bits, of course. But I'm not blind to her faults. Junie causes bother wherever she goes, and I imagine Cathy has very good reasons for this row.'

'So you think I'm daft for saying yes she can move in with us?'

Minnie shrugged and tossed another finished tatty into the bucket. 'Far be it from me to tell you what to do, Mother.'

By now, Betty was kicking herself for being so soft. She had been much too full of the Christmas spirit when Junie and Derek had floated their suggestion. 'She'll be what? She'll be homeless? Never. Never in this world. That Cathy Sturrock would chuck out her own bairn at Christmas? That's monstrous. Why, you must move in with us, lass. We'll find room here. Why, our house was always the place where all the waifs and strays came to live, wasn't it, Harry? Why, aye lass, you must move in here.'

Junie had looked triumphant. 'Derek, will you help me move a few things across from number twenty-one? We'll do it while my mother's out. I'll watch for her leaving . . .'

Then had come Betty's putting her foot down about what she called 'funny business'. She didn't want folk of the Sixteen Streets to start saying she was allowing his son and his girlfriend to cohabit, or whatever they might call it. 'This is no house of sin,' Betty had glowered at them.

Junie had made herself look horrified. 'The very thought. Why, Derek and I are content to wait for that kind of thing until we are united as man and wife in the sight of the Lord.'

This mention of being united as man and wife was news to everyone. Betty's eyes had lit up at once. Harry had looked confused and Derek's expression had grown even darker and more perturbed. 'What?' he'd said.

'All in due course,' Junie had said calmly. 'One thing at a time.'

'Oh . . .' Betty had sighed. 'I had no idea that the two of you were . . . engaged.'

'Well, we aren't . . .' Derek had muttered.

'We're as good as,' Junie had put in quickly. 'I have made my feelings quite clear, and that should be enough. I want to be a part of this family, Mrs Minton. I want to become Junie Minton as soon as I possibly can.'

And with that, the wily Junie had invited herself into their family and their home. Drinks were drunk, toasts were given, and everyone had felt very pleased. Only Derek looked like he had misgivings and Minnie was thwarted with mixed feelings, but that was nothing new.

*

The day after Boxing Day saw Junie and Derek trekking back and forth between the Sturrock and the Minton households, bearing armfuls of bags and boxes, all while Cathy was out at work. 'She'll get such a shock when she realises I've gone for good,' Junie grinned. 'That'll serve the old bitch right.'

'Are you sure, though?' Derek asked her, lumbering under a heap of ratty cases filled with immaculate garments. 'Is this really what you want? Do you really want to hurt your mam?'

'Oh yes, of course it is,' Junie told him. 'And to be nearer to you, too, Derek. I'll be near you every single day.'

Then had come Betty Minton's declaration that the downstairs front parlour was to be turned into a little bedroom for the new house guest.

Junie let her displeasure show. 'The downstairs front parlour?' she frowned.

'It will be really lovely for you,' Betty said. 'All our nicest things are in there, and we only ever use it for best. We'll make the settee up into a comfy bed for you and you can put all your things in the cupboard under the stairs in the hall.'

Junie didn't like the sound of any of this, but she struggled to be polite and look agreeable. 'Won't it be a bit chilly downstairs at night?'

'Why, no, pet,' Betty said firmly. 'You'll be as snug as a bug, I promise you.'

Junie hadn't looked at all mollified. Derek simply shrugged his shoulders at his intended. He knew just how strong-willed his mother was. There was simply no getting round her. Junie was just going to have to learn.

Minnie sat with her on the dusty, old-fashioned settee in what was to be her new bedroom. 'I never knew when I was well off,' Junie whispered to her. 'Just think of that beautiful bedroom I had at number twenty-one. All full of Grandma Sturrock's lovely old things. It was so cosy. This place . . . it smells . . . *fusty.*'

Minnie wasn't about to indulge her any further. 'You've made your choice, hinny. You've left home again and there's no going back.'

'Home?' Junie sneered. 'What home did I ever have? My mother abandoned me as a bairn. I never truly had a place or a family I belonged to.'

Minnie squeezed her arm. 'Well, it seems like you belong to the Mintons, now.'

Minnie and Betty were stewing over all these developments in the early evening, just ahead of opening the fish bar. After all the heavy, rich food of Christmas, they were sure there'd be a queue outside Betty's come six o'clock, with everyone craving a fish supper.

'Do you really think they'll marry?' Betty asked Minnie. 'I'm not sure our Derek seems quite so smitten now that she's moving in.'

'Maybe we should ask old Winnie to read the tea leaves?' Minnie suggested, nodding at the door, where Winnie was first in the chip queue, along with Ma Ada. The pair looked frazzled after a couple of day of Christmas festivities. 'Perhaps we should get her to tell us what the future has in store?'

'No thanks,' Betty frowned. 'She never comes out with anything good. Right, now . . . open the door.'

The rest of the evening went by in a blur of fragrant steam and shovelfuls of golden scraps. They never asked Winnie for her pronouncements about the future, but they did hear a lot about everyone else's busy Christmases. There had been a row at the Chesney house between the three grown-up sisters. Something about their inheritance from their granda' who owned the biscuit factory. By, they were always fighting, those girls. And it just proved that a bit of money was always the cause of bother. Apparently, the neighbours could hear the fighting right across the road, which was quite something in a street where there had been – by all accounts – quite a lot of drama throughout Christmas Day.

'I think there's more goes on in Frederick Street than in all the other fifteen streets put together,' Betty opined as the rush hour waned.

'You just say that because that's where we are, and that's what we hear about,' Minnie said sensibly.

Betty wouldn't be deterred, helping herself to a punnet of hot chips during a lull in the service. 'No, I definitely think that we're special here. We just have more life in us than most places.'

'That's one way of putting it.' Minnie rolled her eyes. Then she realised that her mother was studying her. 'What is it? Is my slip showing? Have I got a mark on my face?' She rubbed at her face with her pinny.

'No, I was just thinking,' Betty told her. 'You're a good daughter, really. Sometimes I don't give you enough credit for that. Seeing Junie run away from her own mother this week . . . well, it's given me pause for thought.'

Just half an hour since, Ma Ada had been leaning across the fish bar, telling them just how anguished and distraught Cathy Sturrock had been, finding that her only daughter had done a moonlight flit. Junie, it seemed, had got the reaction that she was after from her mother.

'Well, thanks, Mam,' Minnie smiled. She wasn't used to her mother coming out with nice things like this.

'You've slaved away in this place with me for years and you hardly ever complain. When have I ever asked you what you want to do? When have I taken your feelings into consideration, eh?' Betty seemed to be in a strangely philosophical and emotional mood. Perhaps seeing Junie leave her mother in the lurch really had made her think about her own relationship with her daughter. 'I've taken you for granted, hinny.'

'Oh no, not really,' Minnie rebuffed her. 'I don't mind working here . . .' But she did. When she thought about it, she'd much rather not be shovelling up chips and battered fillets. This place had put her off fish suppers for life, which was a shame when you thought about it.

'Well, see here, I've got an idea,' said her mother. And then she told her daughter what it was. It was so simple and elegant, it was perfect. Also, it was funny. It made Minnie smile. Oh, the poetic justice of it. Ah, it was a great idea.

'But . . . are you sure?' Minnie asked her ma.

'Oh yes, I am,' she nodded vigorously. 'That Junie will have to pay her way, won't she? She's not occupying my best front parlour free of charge, is she? She'll have to do some work. And I'll soon have her trained up. A clever lass like that, she'll soon learn the ropes. Why, if you can do it, Minnie, then surely she can? It's only working in a fish bar after all, isn't it?'

Minnie grinned at her mother. Junie Sturrock, working here? Up to her ears in grease and batter? What would she say when Betty suggested it? Why, she'd hit the roof. She'd go crackers.

Minnie could hardly wait. 'When will you tell her?'

'Tonight,' Betty nodded decisively. 'I'll tell her when we get in tonight. Why, I'm sure she'll be glad to pay her way.'

'I'm sure she will,' Minnie smiled.

Chapter Fifteen

The old year finished with everyone switching about. That's how it felt. At number thirteen, there was kerfuffle when Megan turned up on their doorstep at Christmas. She looked like the prodigal daughter, and word went round that her own family in Hartlepool had refused to take her back in. Luckily, the generous-hearted Ma Ada swept her back into the bosom of her family.

Over at the Robin Hood, Cathy was very sceptical about this. 'To me, that lass looks like she's up the spout. And, if I know anything, it isn't poor Bob's. So, in that case, whose is it?'

Minnie listened to all this kind of gossip with her ears wide open, agog. 'Have you heard anything from Bob?' she asked the mithered landlady.

'He can't write letters, so he's not a great one for keeping in touch,' Cathy shrugged. 'So we'll need to find a new pot man, as well as a new barmaid.' She sighed deeply and looked faintly panicked. 'All my staff have vanished at the same time.'

Bob had been called up just before Christmas: summonsed to barracks for training, somewhere down Durham way. The officials had caught up with him at last, even though he was a few grades short of the optimum specimens they were after. 'Poor Bob,' Minnie smiled sadly. Inwardly, she felt awfully guilty. She had known! She had known all about it! Now she found herself trying to hide the fact that she knew all about Junie capriciously contacting the army board to alert them to Bob. 'He can lug those beer barrels about. So why can't the yellow-belly fight, eh?' Junie had said spitefully, within Minnie's hearing. And maybe there was some truth in that. The other fellas had to fight, didn't they? They went to war for king and country. Bob was slow, but he was strong, wasn't he? Maybe there was something in what Junie was saying and it was right that Bob should be sent away. Minnie wrestled with her conscience. She knew she always gravitated to seeing things Junie's way.

'Aye, poor Bob,' Cathy said, sitting heavily at the bar to polish the pumps. 'He won't do very well in the army. He's a soft-hearted soul who's been battered and bruised by everyone, all his life.'

Minnie knew that Cathy loved her pot man, fifteen years younger or no. Even if she hadn't heard the rumours, then she would have heard it in Cathy's voice.

'So here I am, on my flamin' tod,' Cathy burst out ruefully. 'What do you think of that, Minnie Minton? What the hell have I done to wind up lonely at New Year?'

'I don't know.' Minnie bit her lip. 'I think you've been good to your Junie all these years. You've given her all the chances . . .'

Cathy's face darkened at the mention of her daughter. The image of that precious stolen ring was haunting her. What on earth was she going to say to Sofia Franchino? Any day now, her old friend was going to come asking for that priceless heirloom back, and what the devil was Cathy going to tell her? Oh, I lost that years and years ago. My daughter swiped it and there's no chance now of ever getting it back . . .

She would have to think of something to say to Sofia. There would be hell to pay. There would be another war on.

'You look like you've got the cares of the world on your shoulders,' Minnie told her.

'Why, it wasn't the nicest Christmas, even though the Farleys did their best to make me feel welcome. It became awkward when Megan turned up, all covered in snow and begging for shelter. I didn't stick around for long after that.'

'Why do the bad ones get all the best treatment?' Minnie gasped. 'Well, I don't mean bad exactly. But I mean . . . the pushy ones, the loud ones, the ones who grab, grab, grab everything that they want . . .'

Cathy smiled sadly at her. 'Like my lass, you mean?'

'I suppose I do.'

'And how have things been over your way since she moved in?'

Minnie's mouth quirked into a naughty smile. 'I shouldn't laugh, but . . . she's not finding my mother the pushover she might have thought she was.'

Cathy cracked out laughing. 'I should think not. No one puts one over on Swetty Betty. It's time that Junie learned that not everyone's as soft as her own daft mother.'

Minnie pressed her hands over her mouth to stop herself from laughing. 'I can't hold this in any longer . . . but we had a right scene last night. My mam told Junie straight out. At the dinner table. Junie was already in a bad mood because of sleeping in the front room and it being chilly and damp. But then my mam tells her: "We've decided that the best way for you to pay your bed and board is if you come and work with me – at the fish bar."'

'What . . .?' Cathy threw back her dark red tresses of hair and laughed wholeheartedly for the first time in days. 'She's going to make my Junie work in the chip shop?'

'Oh yes, Mam's quite determined. "It's only fair," she cried and you should have seen your Junie's face. Thunderstruck, she looked. All she could do was cry out in this high-pitched voice, "The fish bar? Swetty Betty's?" Well, that made my mam grow mad and red in the face all at once. You know how she hates anyone calling it that. "It's a most respectable trade," she bellowed. "And you, my lass, if you're entering this family like you reckon you are, will be joining me with immediate effect."'

Cathy's eyes widened. 'Did she really say it like that?'

'Oh yes, my mother can be quite formidable when she wants.'

Cathy hooted with laughter. 'Oh, poor Junie. That poor little lass. My heart goes out to her, but she's brought all this on herself. It'll do her good to do a bit of hard work and not get treated like a princess. I've always treated her too soft . . .'

'Any road,' Minnie said, suddenly businesslike. 'So then, my mother has solved a whole set of problems for all of us, hasn't she?'

'How do you mean, hinny?'

'Well, Junie's presence at the chip shop has freed my time up, hasn't it? I can come back here and work at the pub with you. It'll be like the good old days, won't it? I'd love to come back to the Robin Hood – if you'll have me, that is?'

So that was how they faced New Year's Eve, in a pub still covered in stolen greenery and small, glimmering candles. New Year felt more hopeful and convivial than Cathy had expected it to. She and Minnie formed a tight unit, dispensing drinks with easy, practised skill and chattering along to all of the regulars as they came to drown their sorrows over the passing year and to tentatively toast their hopes for the one that was yet to arrive.

Music played, and the same old traditional songs were sung. Miraculously, there were no fights or punch-ups, and it seemed that even the three feisty Chesney sisters from down the hill had patched things up and made some peace. There was talk of them pooling their inheritance and opening a shop together, somewhere on Westoe Road.

New things, Cathy thought. New hopes and dreams and new ideas. Even in the midst of war, with all the ever-present threats hanging over them, and even with all those men away from home, there was still room for wondrous new thoughts and hopes. Like Irene Farley over there, looking green around the gills after a couple of drinks, her belly showing much more prominently of late. New life. In the thick of death and disaster, there was always new signs of life to cling to.

They counted down the midnight hour and everyone stood and grasped each other's arms and sang, Auld Lang Syne, while Aunty Martha banged out the well-known tune.

Faces came and went, Cathy thought. Some old faces stayed the same for many years and others went away too soon. Some came back after long absences and were changed for the worse or the better. The cast of characters shifted and blurred over time, and Cathy had been here long enough now to see how it all worked. Yes, there were changes good and bad. There were high points and low points. There were terrible things that happened, unforgettably horrible things. People could be nasty to each other and life itself could be bitterly cruel. Over the years, though, Cathy had learned this simple fact again and again: that life went on. Whatever happened to the individuals involved, the mass of mankind still kept getting up in the morning and they got on with their own particular lives.

It would all still be going on long after Cathy Sturrock had clanged her final last-orders bell and locked the bar up for the night. She found this thought reassuring at the end of her New Year's Eve shindig. Life went on and she'd carry on enjoying it as best she could. Even the tricky bits. Even the bits where she had to knuckle down and scrape through. Even the bits where she had to tell lies to her best friend . . .

No, she'd not think about the missing ring and the Franchinos tonight. Not tonight. As the bar emptied and her revellers started straggling home, she poured a final nightcap for herself and her new-old barmaid Minnie.

'Ooh, brandy, lovely,' Minnie grinned wearily. She smacked her lips on the precious spirit. 'It's been so wonderful tonight, Cathy. Much nicer than shovelling hot chips. Eeeh, I wonder how your Junie got on with my old mam tonight? I half-expected to see them here, after the chip shop closed, drowning their sorrows and joining in with the singing. Maybe they've had a big falling-out already?'

'If they have, I'm sure we'll hear about it soon enough,' said Cathy. 'Now, come on, help me toast 1943, eh? Let's give it our solemn blessing and hope for the very best for everyone. Let's pray with all our hearts, shall we? A better year for everyone.'

'Aye,' Minnie said enthusiastically, holding up her shining glass. 'Let's make it a better year for everyone.'

They clinked glasses and downed their heady, amber drinks and then Cathy poured them another.

The new year – 1943 – had begun, but despite the barmaids' most fervent wishes and prayers, it was a year that didn't start well at all. It was a year that started with the most awful tragedy.

Chapter Sixteen

Early in January, the coldest night in living memory, the bombers came again. It was a sparklingly clear black night. It was beautiful, but by now everyone knew that that clarity could be deadly. On the frozen, clear nights, the pilots could see the harbour down below as they zoomed through the cloudless air and they knew where to drop their bombs to cause maximum damage.

The docks were bombed that night, and the noise was ferocious. Even deep under the frozen-solid black clay, the denizens of the Sixteen Streets could hear the wanton destruction up above. 'It's like all the devils out of hell,' wept old Mrs Stevenson from down the far end of Frederick Street. 'They've come out to play and we've taken their places in the bowels of the earth.'

Ma Ada sat pursing her lips and frowning at such melodramatic talk. She was worried about her family. Especially Irene, who was finding the night in the shelter even more uncomfortable than usual. She was worried about Megan – who was also pregnant with a grandchild belonging to the Farley clan. Ma Ada had dashed out of the house without both her family Bible and her cat, and she was missing both fiercely as the night went by so slowly and noisily.

'Oh, this is hateful,' sighed Junie, squashed on a wooden bench between Derek and his mother. She wrinkled her nose at the stale smell of so many people in close confinement, and the showers of dust and soil that would occasionally come raining down on their heads. 'I'd rather take my chances up there than cower down here.'

'Nay,' grumbled Harry Minton. 'They're too close tonight, lass.' His face looked ashen and bleak. He was concentrating on the muffled sounds from above. He had never heard the bombing sound this close. Could it be that they were all going to clamber out tomorrow morning and find their beloved Frederick Street gone? Blasted out of all existence? And what then? Where would they go? They would all just have to join the world's endless, shuffling queue of the homeless and the dispossessed.

Minnie Minton tried to keep her spirits up, and those of her friends and neighbours around her. Truth be told, up until tonight, she had found such periods of enforced captivity and sheltering almost enjoyable. No, enjoyable wasn't the correct word. She had found them neighbourly and convivial. If they had to sit, suspended and frozen with panic and fear, she would rather do it surrounded by her close neighbours, even if they didn't all quite see eye to eye.

She was looking out for Cathy Sturrock. Where was the landlady tonight? Surely she hadn't stayed at home, ignoring the warnings and the sirens? There was no one else living in her house to urge her to leave her bed. What if she'd simply turned over and blocked up her ears?

The night rolled on and they sipped anxious cups of tea and chattered about anything they could think of to take their minds off the danger from above. As the noise of the bombs subsided and grew more distant, it even became possible to succumb to tiredness and doze . . .

*

The next day, they emerged into a frosty world of smoke and smouldering wreckage. For a heart-stopping moment, it looked as if Frederick Street had been hit, but it was Harton Street, two streets across, that had taken a direct shelling. Three houses had been blasted out of existence, leaving only a hole in the ground and exposed walls, dingily papered and tattered. It looked like a grotesque doll's house, open to the world.

Frederick Street was mercifully untouched, and its occupants uttered heartfelt prayers as they staggered back home in their pyjamas and overcoats. Ma Ada suppressed a sob of relief as she saw her house standing safely there, intact. The idea of returning home and finding it gone sent horrors through her.

But everyone she knew and cared about was safe this morning, weren't they? Harton Street wasn't far away, though, and there were plenty of familiar faces who lived there. Death and destruction were coming closer every time . . .

Everyone returned to their homes and tried to get on with their day as best they could. All the while, the jungle drums were going, and the whispers were winding around the backyards, over the fences, through the sculleries. The women were passing on the news of who had been hit and where had been destroyed in the night. There was talk of Seahouses and the coast. When the bombers left, at the end of their deadly mission, they often discarded their leftover ammunition. They took potluck and threw down the final missiles at the last bit of land they saw. Apparently last night it had been the community who lived by the coast in Seahouses who had borne the brunt.

Irene Farley caught the whisper of this news and couldn't stop herself getting on the tram to go and see for herself. She was like a woman possessed, heavy, lumbering and vulnerable as she staggered through streets strewn with debris. She saw awful sights as she travelled through the town. There were burning pits with shooting flames where houses used to be.

Firefighters were doing the best they could and they didn't need panicked young women getting in the way.

Had Minnie heard the same whispers, she would have done the same thing. She would have gone to see what Irene went to see that day, and it would have been her dashing into that cul-de-sac in Seahouses, coming face to face with the inferno that had once been the Franchino home.

Irene fell to her knees in the street before the terrible sight. She couldn't believe what she was seeing. That whole grand house had been blasted into smithereens, into non-existence. All that was left was a great burning hole in the ground and savage crimson flames leaping skywards. The men were trying to dampen them down, to stop the cellars from burning. It was a horrible sight because Irene knew that it was a charnel house. She knew that the entire Franchino clan would have been down there, in the deep cellars of their home, with their preserves and carefully stocked dried goods. They would have been clinging together as the bomb noises grew closer and closer. They would have all gone up together in a flash. Sofia, Tonio, the old Nonna and the two boys. And Bella. Bella would be gone, too.

It was almost too much to take in. Irene's mind felt like it was caving in, giving up and blacking out under the weight of such terrible news.

Minnie heard the tale from various sources during that day, but it was almost a full day later before she heard from Irene herself what it had been like. The two of them were having one of their more or less regular confabs over the back of the garden wall between number thirteen and fifteen Frederick Street.

Irene still looked white with shock as she described coming face to face with what remained of the Franchino house.

Minnie sobbed as she listened to the details and tried to comprehend what it must have been like for them all. 'But they wouldn't have known anything about it, would they? They would have just been there and then gone in a split second, wouldn't they?'

To be quite honest, Irene wasn't quite so sure. Seeing the scale and the ferocity of the flames, she had had a visceral and terrible sense of what it must have been like. There were no two ways about it. It was a hideous fate that the poor Franchinos had met. 'After everything they had been through. All that life. All those years and hopes and everything . . .' Irene shook her head.

'B-but Bella . . .' Minnie urged her, gripping the frosty wall. 'Bella survived? You said . . . you said she was l-lucky . . .? She wasn't even there that night . . .?'

Irene nodded. 'Yes, yes, it was a fluke. A lucky fluke that she wasn't at home. All her life, she's going to feel like it was a blessing . . . and a curse, I imagine.' Irene pressed her hand over her mouth, in her usual self-conscious gesture, as if she had said too much; as if she had uttered her secret thoughts.

Minnie cottoned on quickly. 'Yes, because she's bound to feel so guilty at being . . . the only . . . the only survivor . . .' Minnie's mind boggled at the thought. Fancy being the only one left out of her lovely big family. Why, Bella had grown up surrounded by people, by all their love and wonderful support. She was confident in the world because she was so sure of them all. What must she feel like now? It beggared belief. Minnie's mind felt puny and hopeless and it shrank from trying to empathise with the Italian girl. 'Where was she? How was she not home?'

'She was with those friends of hers. Mavis, who works at Franchino's with us, that pale girl with the raspy voice.'

'Oh, yes,' Minnie nodded. 'That one who goes on a bit daft?'

'Well, she lives in a house in the rough end with her brother Arthur, though how the two of them can afford a house of their own I've never understood. They had Bella there for the night and they had too much black-market brandy, apparently, and fortunately Bella fell asleep round there.' Irene took out her hanky and blew her nose loudly. She was still producing black soot from her neb after her odyssey through the blazing wasteland. 'It was the saving of her. That delinquent night's drinking preserved her life. Now the poor lass will have to live with the guilt of that all her life.'

'Eeeh,' said Minnie. 'We must help her. We must be the best friends we can be to her . . .'

'Yes, we must,' Irene agreed. 'You must have known them all your life, the Franchinos?'

'Aye, ever since they lived in Taylor Street, the next one over. I worked with Sofia at the Robin Hood when I was just a lass. She was Cathy Sturrock's best mate . . . I wonder if anyone's told Cathy yet? She'll be heartbroken, too, by this . . .'

'It's an awful, awful business,' Irene sighed. 'I keep thinking of that last time I saw them all, down the pub on Christmas Eve. We were all together there. Who's to know, eh? Who's to know when the last time will be? You're all together one minute and the next . . . someone's gone for good . . .'

Chapter Seventeen

Cathy put on her stoutest shoes and her good, heavy coat. It was pouring down today. It was as if the heavens had opened up to douse the burning embers of South Shields and put them out. Greyness arched over the town and every surface seemed to run with cold, silvery water.

Even a sudden freezing snap would be preferable to this endless mizzle.

Cathy slammed the front door on her empty house and set off at a brisk pace down Frederick Street. She pulled up the collar of her coat so that no one would notice her or speak with her. She couldn't bear it if anyone stopped her to speak today.

Several days had passed since the night of the bombing raid and the deaths of the Franchinos. Cathy was still having some difficulty taking it in, though she had received accounts from both Irene and Minnie of seeing the burning pit where their home had once been. The knowledge of that loss seemed to run off the surface of her mind like the rainwater running off the oily cobbles underfoot.

Where was she going today? She hardly knew. She just had to get out of her own four walls, where she was alone with no one to talk to, no one to look after, no one to console her.

What a state to get herself into. She felt like she was going to break down at any moment. She was holding her breath and her guts felt like they had wrenched themselves into a sailor's knot inside her belly. Never had she felt such profound, physical grief before.

Why, she'd never felt like this about any actual relatives in her life. Not even her husband. Why, especially not her bloody husband. She had been much too young to know anything about the demise of her parents. Then there was her young lover, Christopher. He had died in the Great War, and had they been lovers, really? Childhood friends who, spurred on by circumstance and desperation, had gone that little bit too far. Junie was the result and Christopher had never lived long enough to see her. Cathy had been much too focused on how to survive and how to cling onto her daughter to mourn him too much. That sounded harsh now that she thought about it. But that life and those people seemed like they belonged to another century now. She honestly hadn't thought about Christopher and his aristocratic family for years and years. Oh, but wouldn't bloody Junie love to know more about those familial roots? Cathy laughed bitterly to herself at this stray thought.

She turned down Westoe Road towards the grand, dark edifice of the church. Ah, there were missing buildings down here, by the docks. Chimneys and warehouses had been obliterated since the last time she'd walked here. All that remained was dark rubble and a lingering reek of smoke.

What was going to happen to them all? Was the whole world going to end up as smoking ruins? Was that the ultimate end to all of this? Both sides would just keep banging and smashing away at each other, until they had run out of all the ammunition and firepower they could lay their hands upon? By then, the whole world and everything in it would be destroyed beyond all recognition. Is that what it was all about? Was that what it was for? It was as if men – and yes, it was always men behind this – had decided that the world had failed somehow, deeply, fundamentally. The slate had to be scrubbed clean and it would eventually be time to start again.

Grief coursed through Cathy's body uncontrollably and she felt a storm rising up through her chest, making her want to scream. She could run into the church perhaps. The doors would be open, surely. This was exactly what it was for, wasn't it? To offer solace and succour to a soul like hers. But the church had never really been her way. All that solemnity and hypocrisy, as she saw it. What could they do for her today? What kind of sense could they make out of anything?

Her friends were dead. They had been blown to smithereens. There was nothing at all left of them, by all reports. Her friend, Sofia. The beautiful, smiling, clear-skinned girl. Cathy could still picture her, lying beside her on the white sugary sands in Naples. When was that? Ten years ago. Neither of them were young lasses, even back then, and now, in retrospect, they seemed carefree and happy. All they'd had to worry about was men falling in love with them, and having to choose . . .

Ah, it had never been quite as simple as that. Life had always thrown up strange complications, but that time in the early thirties seemed much more preferable to this day. Today, Cathy felt like she was living in hell.

She marched herself down Fowler Street, passing dreary shops whose windows held signs telling her what was and wasn't available today. Everything was dark and empty and there were queues of unhappy-looking souls outside. It was getting harder and harder to gather together the basic necessities of life. What was the point? Why work so hard to scrape it all together and keep it going when it could all be gone in a flash anyway?

Honestly, Cathy wasn't even sure that she knew anymore.

The worst thing about it for Cathy – and this was where her mind flinched away from the darkness – was that she actually felt *relieved*.

Oh, that was like getting a punch in the gut. She almost doubled over, winded at the impact of this awful realisation. Awful, awful. She rounded the corner into the main drag of desolate shops. She hurried into the marketplace, where stalls were setting up with their meagre wares. She needed to keep moving, to stop her mind from ticking over.

But now the thought was there. Yes, relief. Her horror was tinged with relief, and she was so ashamed of herself for feeling like this.

And why? She shook her head, but still the thoughts churned on.

Why, because now that Sofia was gone, she was off the hook, wasn't she? Cathy would never have to explain, never make excuses. Now there would be no one to come asking about that missing ring. She would never have to explain to her best friend that she had let her down so badly. She had let Junie steal that precious heirloom. Cathy was in the clear now.

Oh, but what a dreadful thing to be thinking. Only a few days since the Franchinos had died. Now she thought about them in that cellar again, surrounded by all the bottles of wine and jars of pickles and jams that the old Nonna and Tonio had stored down there. Crouching, alert, terrified. Too near to the surface. With nowhere near the protection that the public shelters provided. What on earth were they doing down there, thinking they were safe? Cathy pictured them clinging to each other. The two younger lads grabbing hold of their mother, the old woman cringing with her gnarled hands over her face. Tonio staring at the floorboards above like they had become their only sky and realising there was nothing at all he could do to protect his loved ones.

Had they even had time to say anything to each other? It was too cruel even to think about. Had they screamed, all together? Or had it all been too fast?

Cathy kept walking faster, faster. She tried to drum these pictures out of her head. What good was it doing her or anyone to think about these things? They were gone. Her friends were gone forever.

Honestly, she would have given anything for Sofia to be alive again. She wouldn't have minded having to explain about that ring. It wouldn't matter. She would love to be able to have that conversation. The idea of mere material things being the only problem they had. The very idea that money was the thing that caused all the bother. Nothing was bigger and more final than death. Now it was too late to talk about anything at all.

She stopped abruptly at the top of Ocean Road, surprised to see that there were lights on in Franchino's ice-cream parlour. It clearly wasn't open, nor would she expect it to be. But there was someone inside. She shivered at the thought of some spectral presence lurking behind that glass-and-chrome frontage.

Cathy knocked at the door.

'Yes . . .?' It was Mavis, the small, sickly-looking girl who worked with all the lasses at the biscuit factory. She stood protectively in the doorway, squinting up at Cathy. She explained that she and her brother Arthur were sitting with Bella, the only surviving Franchino family member. They were trying to figure out what she should do next. They had brought her to the most familiar place in the world and made her coffee with her father's beloved espresso machine.

Cathy followed Mavis into the parlour and came face to face with Bella, who was hollow-eyed and washed out. She looked as if she had aged twenty years overnight. The girl stood up and fell into Cathy's arms. 'There, there, pet,' Cathy sobbed, stroking her hair. All the thwarted maternal feelings Cathy had ever felt welling up inside her came pouring out at that moment. All the love that her own Junie had ever spurned was here for Bella Franchino right now. The warmth of Cathy's embrace was almost unbearably overwhelming for the Italian girl.

'What am I going to do without them?' Bella asked her mama's best friend.

'You'll go on,' Cathy told her sternly and warmly. 'Do you hear me, hinny? We have no choice about these things. People can be taken from us with an instant's notice. They are here and then they are gone. We are lucky – yes, lucky – that we all lived in the same place at the same time for a little while and that we loved one another. But nothing can be taken for granted. Nothing will go on forever. And those of us who are left have to carry on and do the best we can to make our lives as good as they can be. That's what we owe to those who can't be here anymore. Do you hear me, lass? That's how it has to be.'

Bella nodded and sobbed and clung to the landlady, knowing that she was right. Knowing that Cathy had lost and found love in her life, against all the odds. Cathy knew what she was talking about and somehow she had found the strength to be articulate and to spell it out for Bella's sake.

Hearing the truth about life and how to live was all very well, but it didn't make it any easier. Nothing would come easy just yet. But, nevertheless, life had to go on.

Chapter Eighteen

Perhaps it was true that the new year, 1943, grew better as it went on, at least for the folk of the Sixteen Streets. In the wider world, in the theatre of war, it was decidedly worse, with conflicts becoming bloodier and more embittered. The whole mess looked more and more difficult to back down from. The world seemed as if it would never be free from the Nazi menace. The idea of everything returning to normal, and peace returning to the land, seemed absolutely impossible. Everyone became hardened, inured to the endless raids and explosions.

On Frederick Street, there were many developments as winter turned to spring and brightened by degrees into a mercifully warm summer. Bob Farley went missing from his barracks and was hunted by the military police for a while. This caused ructions for his family and heartache for Cathy Sturrock. His wife, Megan, gave birth during an air raid, deep in the bunkers, to a healthy baby boy. Another baby at number thirteen Frederick Street. He joined Irene's prized bairn, Marlene, who she'd given birth to down in Norfolk while visiting her parents. Now Ma Ada's house was packed to the rafters again and cacophonous with baby noise, just as it had been years ago. Next door, Betty Minton would roll her eyes and complain at all the hullabaloo coming through the thin walls, but she didn't mind it really. Secretly, she was longing for grandchildren of her own, and she would eye her Derek and his Junie speculatively.

Junie was still in the front parlour on a makeshift bed. She was still cross about it, but it was better than going home to her mother Cathy again. No, the breach between Junie and Cathy looked set to last, and the two of them averted their eyes from each other when they passed in the street. All the women nearabouts said that it was a shame, two women carrying on like that when there was a war on. But still they couldn't make their peace: the division between them ran much too deep.

As the year went on, everyone was still mourning the Franchino clan. There was a wake and various ad hoc memorials with bottles of limoncello brought out of storage and toasts drunk to that vivid, unforgettable family. Everyone tried to remember the exact taste of Tonio's strong coffee before the war, when he could still get the beans imported, and also that piquant sweetness of the home-made ice cream he called his own family speciality. It seemed like none of these things would ever come back again, and that the ice-cream parlour was lost forever as a social hub and meeting place for the denizens of the Sixteen Streets.

For weeks and months, Bella Franchino was in mourning. She was the guest of siblings Mavis and Arthur, in their slipshod house in the rough end of town. She tidied and cleaned for them in a mechanical way, making the best of her new surroundings and turning the Kendricks's home into a little paradise, for which they were both grateful. It took a long while for Bella to come back to life, however. The loss of her parents, her grandmother and her brothers in one fell swoop was almost too much for her mind to take. A darkness settled over her for several months and it took ages for it to not clear exactly, but to relent slightly. The dark cloud receded enough to allow Bella to return to life. When she did, she found that her loyal friends – Mavis, Arthur and Irene principally – had cleaned and decorated Franchino's ice-cream parlour for her. They had made it ready for a grand reopening and she had broken down with tears of gratitude when she saw just what they had done.

The ice-cream parlour and coffee shop opened again, and it was as if a beloved heartbeat grew a little stronger and a bit more confident. The pulse of the community's lifeblood became a bit healthier and more determined that day. Bella knew that her parents would have approved of her taking on their mantle and continuing in their absence. She knew that she was doing the right thing as she moved into the tiny flat above Franchino's on Ocean Road and tried to make a new life for herself.

Everything seemed to be changing in 1943. All the old relationships and arrangements were shifting slightly. There were surprises – such as dowdy, plain little Mavis Kendricks suddenly going around with handsome Sam Farley, the youngest of Ma Ada's boys. And then they were getting married. It was hardly to be believed. Since when did that wayward, happy-go-lucky lad ever spare a glance for the palest and oddest-looking of all the biscuit factory girls?

Well, you just couldn't guess about love and all that carry-on. That's what Minnie Minton decided. People ended up in the oddest relationships and sometimes it was the least likely of them that seemed to stick. Why, look at her brother Derek and Junie Sturrock. Junie was the brightest of anyone Minnie had ever met – how on earth could she settle for the dour and taciturn Derek? And yet she seemed so content in his company. She would sit there, darning and sewing in the evening. She was almost demure. This seemed almost shocking to Minnie, who was still amazed that she was living under the same roof as her long-beloved girl.

All the same, Minnie felt left out. Her various friends had an awful lot going on in their lives that year, and Minnie couldn't help but feel pushed out.

'It's always the same,' said her mother Betty sagely. 'Everyone gets paired off, and then the babies start coming. All the old friendships get thrown into disarray for a while. You won't see hide nor hair of certain folk for ages, not until they're wanting something from you. It's the whirligig of life, Minnie. You have to cling on hard, otherwise you get flung off and no one even notices.' She looked at her poor, crumpled, moon-faced daughter with sympathy. 'I think you've already fallen off the merry-go-round, haven't you, hinny?'

'I reckon I have,' Minnie smiled, and didn't feel as sorry for herself as she might have. Everyone else really did seem as if they were on some kind of endless fairground ride. They were sleepless, like Irene Farley, with screaming bairns waking at all hours. They were pale and zombie-like from exhaustion at their factory jobs. Their nerves were shattered by the war. Minnie felt better than that. She had only herself to worry about. She could handle her job at the Robin Hood easily, and Cathy found that she could rely on Minnie more and more. Why, with Bob away like he was, Minnie found that she could even do the lifting work of the pot man. She had no bother shouldering the casks of ale that the brewery man brought on his cart. Minnie grew strong and more resilient than she'd ever known she'd have to be.

Who cares if no one wanted her? She thrust out her undistinguished chin defiantly. She really didn't care if she was left on the shelf and no one loved her or wanted to cherish her. That was all soft stuff anyway. When you went soft, someone was bound to hurt you.

She felt her mother studying her carefully. It was as if that bluff, hearty woman was still sensitive enough to see what her daughter was thinking. Betty could read Minnie's heart through the layers of self-protection. 'Ah, now . . . don't go hard, Minnie. Don't close up your heart. Don't turn your back on the world.'

Minnie would shrug. 'I don't know what you're talking about, Ma. I'm all right. I'm always all right, aren't I?'

Grudgingly, her mother would accept this, but she knew that Minnie kept her secret, loving heart buried very deeply these days. And maybe that was just as well . . .?

Before the year was out, Derek and Junie were married. It wasn't a big affair like some of the weddings round there. Even with a war on, some people liked to make a big fuss and cram as many people as they could into Saint Jude's. The Minton family were more modest than that and kept it small, with a quick service at the town hall, with Minnie and Irene Farley as witnesses, then pie and peas at the chop house on Fowler Street. Everyone wore their best clothes and gave their most sincere best wishes to the bride and groom.

Even Minnie felt happy to see them wed at last. Why, surely they were made for each other – her brother and her oldest friend.

'Well, what about this for a honeymoon, eh?' Junie laughed, sitting at number thirteen in her home-made wedding dress. It was a rather matronly affair, Minnie had thought, disappointed: a cut-down, restitched item that she'd picked up from a market stall. Very unlike her Junie, who had arrived here all those years ago like an immaculate model. She'd been like a mannequin out of Paris or somewhere. 'Are you listening to me?' Junie frowned darkly at Minnie. 'You're not even paying attention while I'm complaining and upset, are you?'

'Hmm?' Minnie smiled, glad that these days she didn't take Junie's savage moods so seriously. Because Minnie cared less, because her hopes had been defeated, Junie had seemingly lost the power to hurt Minnie's feelings anymore. And that was good.

'What's that, pet?' Minnie smiled fondly. They were pie-eyed on sherry in the back parlour of number fifteen on Junie's wedding day.

'I'm saying – my bloody honeymoon, what is it? Am I going somewhere fancy and gorgeous like I always dreamed about? Is it going to be like a movie?' She laughed raucously, looking rather wild and disordered suddenly. 'No. I get to go all the way upstairs, don't I? I get to leave the freezing best front room and migrate upstairs to Derek's room. Legitimately, at last. That's the only bloody trip I'm goin' on for my flamin' honeymoon.'

Minnie widened her eyes. 'Legitimately . . . ? Are you saying, our Junie, that you've been up there already to his room? Are you saying that you've snuck up there when no one even knew?'

Junie laughed out loud at her rather innocent friend. 'What do you think, Minnie? Have I ever let anyone dictate to me what I can and can't do? I always get round other people's silly rules, don't I?'

Minnie was staring at her lovely face and for the first time it really hit her: *Junie is my sister, now.*

Then there was a clattering at the front door and Betty Minton was calling out: 'Yoo-hoo! Oh, Junie. Come and see who's come over to say hello. Come and see who wants to see you on your wedding day.'

All at once, Junie tensed up with fury. Minnie was startled by the savage look on her face. 'No, I won't see her,' she said in a cold voice.

'Here she is,' cried Betty warmly, leading Cathy Sturrock into the back parlour. 'Here's your mam. Your mam's come over to congratulate you on marrying our Derek. Isn't that lovely? There's no bad blood now, is there? Everyone's happy again, now . . .?'

Cathy stood there in the doorway of the messy back parlour, overdressed in some mothy old fur like she hadn't already missed the ceremony. 'My Junie,' she said tearfully and held open her arms.

Chapter Nineteen

'My mother . . . my bloody mother . . .'

Junie was bitter the next day, following her so-called honeymoon. Betty had expected her to be blushing and content. Having been inducted into the mysteries and the beauties of married love, Junie ought to have been quite different to how she was today. Betty remembered her own wedding night – oh, so many years before. Hadn't she found herself full of bliss and wonderment after her first night in the matrimonial bed with Harry?

Well, maybe not. Maybe it hadn't been that way; she romanticised such things now. But still, she didn't remember ever being in the stinking mood that Junie was in right now. Surely that wasn't the way anyone was after their wedding day?

Junie clattered about the house, raging and fuming.

'Your mother only came across to make peace with you, hinny,' Betty tried to mollify her new daughter-in-law. 'After that breach between you and your falling-out. She wanted to get things sorted out and I don't blame her. After the Franchinos and everything . . . well, life's too short, isn't it?'

Junie glared at her mother-in-law. She stood there tying and pinning up her blonde hair in front of the back-parlour mirror. Then she tied on a headscarf, ready for work at Swetty

Betty's. 'You don't know what she's like,' she hissed at Betty. 'Everyone round here thinks she's a wonderful woman. None of you have tried being related to the selfish old cow.'

'Oh, no, hey now, stop,' Betty cried. 'You shouldn't speak badly of her.'

'She abandoned me. She left me as a baby in the wilds of Northumberland.'

Betty's mouth squinched up and her eyes narrowed. She'd never quite heard the full story of Junie's beginnings and she was rather eager to hear it straight from the horse's mouth. 'Well, maybe you should tell me about it. Tell me the whole thing as we work.' She cast a glance at the clock on the wall. 'It's time we were next door peeling tatties, lass.'

This was something else making Junie livid on the day after her so-called wedding day: she had to go back to work the very next day, to that vile place, shovelling chips.

'All right,' she smiled at her new mother, trying her hardest to look happier than she was. Junie knew the value of keeping the people she needed on her side.

Meanwhile, Minnie was glad to keep the chip fat out of her clothes and her hair. She was more than happy to scurry over to the Robin Hood to work at the bar with Junie's mother.

Cathy was in a strange, distracted mood as they worked that evening. 'She only pretended to welcome me over there yesterday. She didn't want to show herself up in front of your parents. I know my Junie.'

Minnie knew that the landlady was right. 'It'll all be old water under the bridge, or whatever the phrase is,' she shrugged, giving the tables a quick polish before the doors opened. 'Junie needs you. You're her mam. She'll settle down.'

'Maybe,' Cathy sighed. 'You know, I think I've done everything wrong when it comes to my daughter. Perhaps I should have fought harder to keep her, when my Aunty Linda tricked me and took her off me? Perhaps I should have stolen her away and fought tooth and nail?'

Minnie shook her head. She knew there was no point in questioning the past, years after the event. What was done was done, surely? 'Nay, Cathy . . .'

'And then when she came here, as a teen, off her own bat. She was looking for her mammy, wasn't she? She seemed so confident and smart. And what did I do? I tried to cover up my own disgrace, didn't I? I told everyone she was my niece. She must have felt like I was shamed by her. That lass must have felt so rejected by me . . .'

Minnie kept her mouth shut and simply listened. She knew it was all true, though. She had been Junie's closest friend right from day one, upon her arrival in the Sixteen Streets, and she knew very well that everything Cathy was saying now was true. Junie had been so upset. She had been horrified that her mother wouldn't acknowledge her in public on that first day here.

Oh, but she had done so pretty soon afterwards. She adstarted telling people the tragic tale of how she had been separated from her own bairn. But the betrayal had been there and then on that first night, when Cathy had declared to the whole pub and welcoming committee that Junie was nothing more than her beloved niece. It was like poison had entered Junie's veins at that very moment. Her warm blood had chilled in that instant. Yes, yes, it was only then that Junie's nature had started to canker and go bad. Surely before that she had been wonderful, a loving, innocent girl. But that moment of betrayal had made her feel loveless and hopeless. And yes, Minnie could understand how that could make a chill enter into your very soul.

'I can see from your expression that you're thinking the same as me,' Cathy told Minnie. 'You've been her friend all this time. She must tell you everything.'

'She's told me some things,' Minnie said, careful not to get too drawn in. 'But then she was away for so long as well, wasn't she? Down south in Manchester. Well, none of us know what her life was like down there . . .'

Cathy nodded. 'She told me she was a firefighter during the first couple of years of the war. She was hanging on the back of the fire wagon with all the buckets and hoses.'

'It doesn't sound much like the Junie we know,' Minnie smiled.

'And I think there were a couple of unsuitable men she got herself involved with, too,' Cathy frowned. 'She's never told me much about what went on, but it didn't sound a very happy experience . . .'

Minnie was surveying the saloon bar, happy to see everything spick and span and ready to welcome their first patrons of the evening. She moved to unbolt the door. 'She came back here, didn't she? She'd had enough of her life down in Manchester and so she came back home to where the people know her. She came back to the Sixteen Streets because you are here, Cathy, and you're her mam. You must remember that, whatever she says and however she pulls her face. You're her beacon here. Underneath everything, she loves you. And whatever she does, whatever stunts she pulls – however bad they get – we still love her, don't we? We really do, don't we? We let her get away with it all . . .' Minnie was wondering aloud and surprising herself by voicing her thoughts like this. As she went on, she realised that her epiphany was coloured a little by her own self-doubting. She blinked and looked at Cathy.

Cathy looked surprised at Minnie's sudden passion and articulacy. 'By heck, Minnie Minton, you're a deep one, aren't you? You're thinking all the time, aren't you? Even if you don't always say what's going on in your head.'

Minnie nodded and threw open the saloon-bar door to let in the early-evening drinkers. 'Yes, I do think about things a lot,' she smiled.

Minnie found herself drifting back again and again to the marketplace off Fowler Street. She was drawn to the stall where she had picked up most of last year's Christmas presents. They hadn't been antiques, exactly – but that cameo brooch and the cigarette case had found a certain favour with her mam and dad. She also knew that Junie had bought her second-hand wedding outfit from the girl who ran that little stall of jumble.

The girl was called Susan, and she was a little younger than Minnie. She had short, curly hair that was covered up most of the time by a succession of daft-looking hats, which she also sold on her stall. It was cold standing there all day, and she tended to dance and jig about on the spot as she watched people browse through her wares.

'You live on our street,' Minnie said accusingly, the day she realised that she recognised Susan's face. 'You're one of the three sisters who live right down at the bottom of Frederick Street.'

Susan smiled warmly at her. 'Yes, I've seen you about, too. I know everyone's face in town, but I find it hard to put a name to them sometimes. I'm Susan Chesney.' She held out her little hand very formally for Minnie to shake. Every finger had a clunky, vintage ring on it. It was all costume jewellery, but it looked very impressive. She looked to Minnie like a girl playing dress-up in her mama's jewels. Now that Minnie studied her, it seemed like her whole outfit had been put together from some ancient dressing-up box. She had on layers of extraordinary fabrics and outdated garments. There was something almost piratical about her, presiding over her boxes of glittering junk in that dowdy, damp marketplace. She caught Minnie's eye – and her imagination.

'I'm Minnie Minton . . .' Minnie began.

'I know.' Susan clicked her fingers. 'From the fish bar. Your mam's Swetty Betty, isn't she?'

'I'm not there anymore, I'm behind the bar at the Robin Hood.'

Susan rolled her eyes. 'My dad won't let me go in there. Nor my two sisters. He says it's too rough for us. It's all rough men and all sorts of types. He said we're not to set foot over the door. Only on special occasions.'

'Ah, nonsense,' Minnie laughed. She was picturing that funny little Mr Chesney with his ginger tash and long overcoat. Why, he was so very protective of his three daughters, wasn't he? Word had it that he treated them like three princesses and did all he could to protect them from the wild world. Word also had it that the three darling princesses fought and howled like banshees and gave him the runaround . . .

'I'm very glad to meet you at last, anyhow, Minnie Minton,' Susan smiled at her.

'Well, I've been at this stall before,' Minnie told her. 'I picked up some smashing gifts here for last Christmas. It must have been one of your sisters I met.'

Susan nodded. 'Yes, Faith or Hope. I'd have remembered serving you if I'd been here.'

Minnie felt obscurely flattered by this. Why would she stand out? Why would Susan remember her? Then she said, 'Wait, your sisters are called Faith and Hope? Why aren't you called Charity, then?'

Susan shrugged. 'My dad lost his nerve, I think. Or his religion. I don't know which. But I got the only sensible name in the whole family, that's all I know. His name's Wilberforce, can you believe it?'

Minnie laughed, because she couldn't think of a sillier name for that little man. Still, she remembered that he had been kind to her personally, in the past, saying nice things about her within her mother's hearing. Wilberforce Chesney wasn't so bad, even if he had tried to keep his three daughters away from everyone else on their street.

'I really love the things you sell on your stall,' Minnie told her new friend.

Susan's eyes lit up. 'Just you wait, then. For we're going to have a shop. An actual shop. Can you believe it?'

'A shop,' Minnie echoed. 'But all the shops are dark and they don't have much to sell. No one can afford to buy things. Isn't it a terrible time to open a shop?'

Susan shook her head enthusiastically. 'It's our dream,' she said, grinning, as if that made everything possible. 'You'll come, won't you? You'll come and be one of our first customers, Minnie Minton?'

'Of course,' Minnie promised to this eccentric, beguiling youngest sister. 'I'm sure it'll be wonderful.'

'We're going to sell fancy goods,' Susan told her.

Minnie felt like she'd never heard of anything more wonderfully exotic.

'And we're going to call it Mary's Shop, after our poor, late mother.'

Minnie remembered: this was the other thing that she knew about the three Chesney sisters who lived at the bottom of the lane. They fought like hell, and they had lost their mam at a very early age. Poor Susan here had grown up motherless. In that instant, Minnie's heart went out to her.

'I love the idea of your shop,' Minnie told her.

Chapter Twenty

Junie lost her first bairn during an air raid.

She didn't talk about it much afterwards. It was something she kept quiet about for the rest of her life. What was the point of dwelling on it? Nothing could bring that first, longed-for babby back. Nothing could ever be the same, no matter how many healthy babies she had later on. That first, bitter disappointment cut right into her heart. It would never leave her, that silent fury. It was a resentment that dwarfed anything she had previously felt and, what was worse, it was like everything in her life had led up to that moment. *Of course I don't deserve happiness*, she thought. *Of course I need to be punished like this: in the worst way possible.*

Her family drew around her and looked after her, assuring Junie that none of it was her fault or anything she had done wrong. The women cosseted and cooed. The men brooded and hardly knew what to say. It was a terrible business, all in all. They had all been with her in the dank, wormy tunnels of the air-raid shelter when she'd started complaining of pains and then gasping with the cramps as the light flickered and dimmed. The all-too familiar noises of bombs dropping up on the surface rang in their ears as they clustered round Junie and her body went into horrible, uncontrollable spasms.

So early, much too early. Her whole body was rejecting the baby. It was wrenching and rioting and rebelling and doing its best to expel the foreign matter.

'There is absolutely no reason that a young, healthy girl like you can't conceive again,' said Doctor Palmer later, calmly and phlegmatically. 'This was a terrible aberration. It was most unfortunate, but life, my dear, simply has to go on.'

It was all very well for that wrinkled old bugger to chunter on like this. Sitting at her bedside like an old troll with bushy hairs coming out of his nose and ears. He treated her as just another case, just another sad failed mother, in a career when he'd seen this kind of thing over and over. To him, it was nothing. Just a rejection, a mild mishap. She'd go on and on and be fine in the end. She'd have the children she wanted, but this first one simply hadn't worked out. Doctor Palmer took the money that Betty Minton gave him for coming out to the house to check Junie over, and off he went.

'See?' her mother-in-law fussed over her, plumping up the pillows and leaning too close. Junie wrinkled her nose. Everything smelled so stale and fusty. Something had heightened her senses, making everything too sharp. Lying here in her room at number fifteen, she felt nauseous and short of breath. Betty Minton was still prattling on. 'So the doctor thinks you're gonna be fine, hinny. This awful thing won't spoil your chances. There'll be lots and lots of bairns for you and Derek. You'll build all the family you want.'

These were pathetic platitudes and Junie wasn't minded to hear them right now. 'I won't want any more. I don't even want to try. I'm not going through this again.'

'Oh. Oh. You mustn't talk like that,' gasped Betty, glancing about as if God himself was listening at her shoulder and might take heed. She went to fetch a cold, damp flannel and started pressing it on the girl's face. She still had a slight fever, but it was to quieten her down as much as anything. Junie pulled a face at the mildewy smell of the cloth. Betty was saying: 'I know it was terrible, when it happened. And worse because everyone was there and it was dark and noisy. You must have been terrified, hinny.'

'I was.'

'But you're safe now, and you're healthy.'

'I don't care,' Junie said bleakly. 'I . . . I felt my baby *die* inside of me. Can you even imagine what that felt like?'

Betty teared up and looked away, swallowing hard. She took a moment before she looked Junie in the eye again. Then she was even more determined than ever to reach her. She offered her the only thing she could think of. 'I-I had the same thing happen, you know. I never talk about this. But I lost two of my own. There was one before our Minnie and one after. It was very like what happened to you. They were quite far on and it was brutal. It was frightening and it never leaves you, the memory of that . . .'

Junie pulled the foisty rag off her face and stared at her mother-in-law. 'I never knew that. You never said.'

'Many of the women you meet . . . on this street, in this whole town . . . why, most of the women you know will have experienced what you've just been through. And we have to carry on, pet. We have to put these things behind us, terrible though that sounds. We won't ever forget, but we do have to stay strong. Stronger than men ever have to be.'

Junie allowed herself to be tucked up in her bed by old Ma Minton and she tried to rest, letting her words stew over in her head. For a moment, she had shared a fellow feeling with another person. She knew just how Betty must have felt and the two women were closer in that instant than ever before. Junie thought about this.

But, no. It couldn't be the same. No one – not even Betty Minton – could have felt as awful as this and then been able to carry on. No one had ever felt as badly as Junie did now. How dare that old woman intrude upon Junie's suffering with her own past? As if she knew at all how Junie felt. She was just poking her old nose into Junie's business.

Junie just wanted leaving alone. She wanted it all to stop. She didn't ever want to go through anything like this again.

Derek took it hard, of course. He got himself royally drunk at the Robin Hood, several nights in a row, right in front of everyone. At first, they understood his need to seek solace in temporary oblivion like this. He and Junie were a lovely young couple. Why, they had every right to expect to bring up their bairns safely and healthily. It was the bombs dropping, they'd scared her. They'd started the bairn up much too early, frightening it to death in its mother's womb.

'It was a little lass,' Derek said as he slumped at the bar, supping whisky he didn't even like the taste of. He just relished the way it burned all the way down to his gullet: it felt like a cleansing fire inside of himself. 'I . . . saw her. I was allowed to have a look at the little lass before they wrapped her up and bore her away.'

Somehow, that had felt an even worse sight. Worse than all the blood and mess and everything. The wrapping up of the child and the covering of her tiny, still face. They'd bundled her up like a brown paper parcel that had to be sent off somewhere. They had taken his and Junie's baby away.

Minnie topped up her brother's whisky and listened to him as he stood at the bar. She had never heard him talk so much in years. Not since they were little kids playing together and they had been inseparable.

'Drink as much as you like,' she told her brother during those nights of his at the Robin Hood. 'If it blots it all out, then it's doing some good.' Secretly, Minnie hated hearing all the details. What he'd just said about seeing his daughter's body and seeing her face get covered up with an old sack cloth: it made her belly grow cold with horror. Her niece! It was her niece, as well. The thought just occurred to her. That small, cold body was Minnie's flesh and blood, too, and she had a connection. She had to be strong and be there for her brother, though. She knew she had to listen to him. She knew this was her duty. Someone had to listen to him, didn't they? She was sure Junie couldn't, and his mother wouldn't, and surely his father would be a hopeless audience for this kind of thing.

Minnie had been there, down in the tunnels, when Junie began getting her pains and then her screams started up. She had helped her friend to the Red Cross women and their tiny, tidy sickbay, hidden away in the shelter. They'd had births here before. They'd even had births in the middle of air raids before. Why, wasn't that just how Megan at number thirteen had had her baby delivered, not so long ago?

But everyone had realised that this was too early for Junie's bairn. It soon became apparent that she was losing it early.

It was a shocking night and the details were scored on Minnie's memory forever. How Junie had clung to her – and how they'd had to wrench her fingers off her before they took her away into the sickbay.

'I'm so sorry,' she kept telling her brother, just as she would tell Junie, whenever the girl would consent to see her. 'I'm so sorry this has happened to you.'

But Derek was deep in his cups by now. She kept pouring the Scotch and he kept downing it, like there was no tomorrow.

Cathy said, 'Don't let him get paralytic, Minnie . . . that won't help.'

Cathy was watching this whole scene with mute disapproval. She herself had been over to number fifteen but had been rebuffed by Betty. Junie didn't want to see her mam. 'What?'

Cathy had cried. 'Surely I'm the very person she should be needing right now?'

But she wasn't, and the shutters came down against Cathy. She was relegated to being the responsible adult watching the bereaved Derek drink himself daft.

They ended up having to carry the unconscious fella home. It took four of them to bear his dead weight. At the sight of her wrecked son, Betty was all in a flap. 'Oh, what use is he to anyone, in a state like this?'

'Leave him be, Mother,' Harry Minton told his wife sadly. 'It's all grief. Whichever way people get to express it, and this is his. Let him get on with it.'

They settled Derek under a rug in the best front parlour, where he grumbled and cried out in his sleep through the rest of the night.

Harry asked his daughter as she made them a midnight brew in the scullery: 'How are you, lass? You've had a shock, too, in all of this.'

'Me?' Minnie asked, surprised to be asked by anyone how she was. But of course her dad had. He was the one who'd always kept an eye on her. Even when she thought no one cared and no one noticed anything she did. He was the one, she realised, who always took an interest in her. 'I'm fine, of course. It's been awful for all of us.'

He accepted the mug of tea she gave him. 'Eeeh, I wish we had more sugar to put in it,' he smiled sadly. 'We could all do with some sugar to calm our nerves.'

Father and daughter clinked their tea mugs together in a silent toast. 'What are we toasting?' Minnie asked him.

'Better times,' her dad told her firmly. 'They're coming, you know. It may not seem like it right now . . . but better times are on their way. You'll see, hinny. You'll see.'

Chapter Twenty-One

By the time the war ended, Junie and Derek were starting their family at last. While the whole of Frederick Street was out throwing a VE Day party on the cobbles, Junie was confined to her room upstairs. Her strenuous roars and screeches could be heard even as the revellers tried to block her out.

Looking back, Minnie thought, their party tables weren't exactly groaning with festive fayre. However, everyone on their street had provided a little bit to eat or drink. There was a pooling of baking supplies to make as many cakes as possible, and an army of women buttered bread continuously throughout the day to make fish-paste sandwiches. The fruit punch was somewhat watery and the jellies looked pale, but really no one cared very much. The important thing was that they were celebrating together, those that still could, now that the long war was over at last.

'I can't even take it in, can you?' Minnie gabbled away brightly to Cathy Sturrock, as the two of them manhandled chairs and tables out of the pub and into the street. The pub furniture looked scratched and battered in the strong daylight.

'Me neither,' Cathy admitted, and it was true that she had the look of a creature who had been hibernating the whole winter long. She blinked in the bright sunshine and paused to tie back her auburn hair.

Cathy kept looking up at the upstairs windows of number fifteen as they worked with linen tablecloths and napkins. No one questioned the need to bring all their best tableware out into the street for the occasion. Cathy's thoughts were elsewhere the whole time though. She looked worried to death every time another cry of laboured pain came from Junie's window.

'I wish they'd let me go up there to be with her,' Cathy fretted.

Of course Junie wouldn't allow that to happen, Minnie smiled. The two women had settled into a less fractious relationship in this past year or two, but there was no way Junie would let her mother see her all vulnerable, in pain and distress.

Minnie smiled encouragingly at Cathy, urging her to work and put aside her worries. In her scullery at number twenty-one, Cathy had been making pies and sausage rolls all night long, using the best black-market pork that money could buy. She had lost none of her magic touch with pastry, cakes and fancies and this was the first opportunity in a while to demonstrate her skills.

'There'll be so many people here,' Minnie grinned, watching them start to arrive early. You could hardly hold them back. The party was getting underway even before all the tables and chairs were out. 'Imagine – all of Frederick Street all together for once.' They had had so many years of skulking about, seeking safety and hurrying into boltholes. The only time they had ever gathered in large numbers during the hostilities was when they had all been underground, sheltering from falling bombs.

'And every single one of the Sixteen Streets will be having their own parties,' Cathy smiled. 'Though that rough lot down Jackson Street probably won't make the effort. They'll be sending their bairns round to nick goodies from our tables, I shouldn't wonder.'

The old rivalries between different streets hardly mattered any more. Everyone was just so pleased to still be here: to have seen it all through to the end. For the past weeks and months, it had felt like a whole lot of anguished waiting and delays. It had been a period of bated breath and crossed fingers and hardly daring to hope against hope . . . and then, eventually, had come the longed-for announcement. The war was over. At last, at last, peace was here and life could return to something like normality.

Not straight away, of course. Everything couldn't snap back immediately to how it had been, back in 1939. Of course it couldn't. That seemed like a different country, now. Too much had changed, too much had been destroyed. Every corner of the world had been indelibly touched by the vile spectre of this conflict and everything was in disarray. No one would ever forget what they had been through during these years.

However, for now, the weary and heartsick people were deciding that they were going to celebrate – as best they could. They were going to celebrate with all their hearts. In South Shields, at least, everyone was delighted by that fact.

Now here came Aunty Martha in her best pre-war frock and the hat she wore to weddings, helping to shunt the Robin Hood's upright piano out into the street. Old Mr Chesney was bustling up the lane, brandishing his violin. He astonished everyone by being able to play it like an angel. His three daughters – Faith, Hope and Susan – came up the street after him, dancing a jig on the cobbles while Minnie clapped time for them. Even the tall, solemn, horse-faced Faith was swirling her skirts about as she danced to the fiddler's tune.

This was the signal for the start of the celebrations proper. Even though only half the food was out and the chairs were still being dragged out of all the houses, the music had begun and so the revelry was underway. Aunty Martha supped her usual pint of ale in her genteel way and played them all the songs they knew so well. There was an added novelty of the music and the singing being out of doors. It added a strange timbre to the cacophony, as if it had been set free from the confines of indoors. As Minnie put it to her friend Irene Farley, 'I feel like we're all in a Gracie Fields picture, dancing about out in the street.'

Irene was carrying the youngest Farley bairn and holding her toddler by the hand. The two children were staring solemnly at all the adults carrying on in such strange, unaccustomed ways. Irene couldn't help laughing out loud at Minnie's description of the whole place turning into a daft musical comedy of the type they often saw at the Savoy. The funniest part of it was her mother-in-law, the diminutive Ma Ada, suddenly in a pre-war fancy get-up including a fur stole, hitching up her skirt to dance next to Mr Chesney and his fiddle. She was usually so dignified, even after a few drinks. But here she was – the queen of the Farley clan – kicking up her feet in broad daylight. And she'd not even taken a single drink yet.

'I just wish all the lads were here, to see all this,' Irene sighed, hitching the little boy up and hugging him more firmly. 'They'd love to see everyone going mad like this.'

'They would, wouldn't they?' Minnie smiled. She knew that Irene was talking about her own fella, Tom, and her brother-in-law, Bob, but she was also referring to Minnie's older brothers and all the other men in Frederick Street who were still God knows where, scattered all over the world. How many weeks or even months might it be before they found their way, straggling back home to Shields? And then, of course, there were the others: those who, like the oldest Farley boy, Tony, would never be coming back home.

Beryl, Tony's widow, was out on the doorstep with them now, looking glamorous and determined to put a brave face on it all. Her man had gone down to the bottom of the sea two years earlier, somewhere off the coast of North Africa.

The news of this had shocked the whole street for quite some time: the four Farley boys were popular and well-known in the area. What had Tony boasted to Beryl, the first night they had met? 'We are famous round here. Everyone knows the Farleys.' That made him sound more boastful than he was, when he was just as sweet-natured and kind as the rest of the Farley lads.

Eeeh, but Minnie was growing sentimental about her neighbours and peers and her brothers, as she thought about them and sipped the foam off her pint of stout. She waved at Susan, who was still dancing to her father's merry Irish tune. That girl from the market stall had been the best thing in Minnie's life during the past year, the last year of the war. Only a few weeks after the two of them had become firm friends, Susan had asked Minnie to come and join her, Saturday and Tuesday afternoons, working on the market stall, selling her junk and whatnots with her. She could have her pick of all the new jumble coming in and maybe make a few bob, as well. Minnie had been delighted to join her and gloried in the friendship that grew between the two of them. Susan was bright, enthusiastic and dressed eccentrically in a bizarre, ever-changing collection of hand-me-downs, but she had been the saving of Minnie. Her friendship and her ragbag market stall gave Minnie something to focus on that wasn't Junie and Derek. It was much healthier – everyone thought – that Minnie was making friends with the girl from further down the street.

'Come and dance, Minnie . . .' Susan called to her.

'But I can't dance for toffee. Everyone will laugh at me.' But it hardly seemed to matter at all. Not on Victory in Europe Day. Today it didn't matter one jot what you looked like or how daft you carried on. Everyone was dancing their cares away. They stamped their feet and twirled around giddily. The rooftops and chimneys around them were set to spinning in the brilliant sunshine. The war was over and their worries and their sorrows were at an end.

'Minnie. Our Minnie . . .!'

There came a pause in the music and laughter and through it could be heard the breathless cries of Betty Minton, struggling out of their house. Her pinny and her sleeves were wet and her hair was straggling down. She cut an alarming figure on Frederick Street and the revellers drew back in alarm when they realised she had blood all down her front.

'Mam . . .?' Minnie, realising what was going on, dashed over to hear the news.

'She's had a little girl, Minnie,' Betty panted, doubling over with a stitch. 'The doctor's just delivered her safe and well. Mother and daughter are doing splendidly. Now, where's our Derek, eh? Who's gonna tell him? Which of us is gonna tell him that he's a daddy now?' Swetty Betty was determined that it was going to be her, so she bulldozed her way through the partying crowd towards the Robin Hood, where Derek would be no doubt nervously sitting with his father, Harry.

'What do you think of that, then?' Irene Farley beamed at Minnie. 'Another baby in the street. And I shouldn't doubt, there'll be lots more to come in the months ahead, too, as all the fellas get back.' She laughed and then covered up her mouth as she realised how crude this might sound. 'Hey, Minnie – you're an aunty now. Have you thought of that? You're somebody's aunty.'

Minnie's face lit up like the whole of the broad harbour when the sun came over the horizon. 'Why, I am, aren't I? I'm somebody's aunty.' And, all at once, that seemed like a wonderful thing to be.

Chapter Twenty-Two

Minnie and her mother were sitting in the back parlour one morning towards the end of June. They had all the recent newspapers out on the table, poring over articles and photographs to do with VE Day all over the world. 'Here, what about this one of the crowds in Trafalgar Square?' Betty said, getting busy with her nail scissors. 'And here's old Winston giving his speech . . . saying it was our nation's greatest day . . .'

They had a glue pot and brushes and a large scrapbook they had bought from WH Smith. It was Minnie's idea to turn all their war clippings into an album that they could look at in future years. It was for the next generation, too – which, for the moment, consisted only of Junie's newborn daughter, Ivy. The young ones would be able to see everything that their family had had to go through during the war.

'What about this picture of Hitler?' Minnie asked. 'And the story from when they reported he'd shot himself in his bunker?'

'I don't think so.' Betty pulled a face. 'I think our scrapbook shouldn't be morbid. We shouldn't collect all the tales to do with death and destruction . . .'

Minnie smiled. It was a scrapbook about war. How on earth were they going to leave out death and destruction?

Her mother went on, 'I think we should fill all the pages with happy pictures of everyone celebrating and dancing and going mad in the streets. I think that would be nicest to look back upon.'

'I think we should have things to remind us what it was like to cower in the underground shelters, waiting for our number to come up,' Minnie said. 'That's what the younger ones will need to be told about. And the men going away and never coming back.'

Her mother didn't seem too sure about that. 'The likes of little Ivy are going to grow up in a better world, where war is a thing of the past. They won't want to hear about the awful things we've had to go through, and why should they? People sacrificed everything – some sacrificed their lives – so that Ivy and all the bairns could live a better life in a more peaceful world. They won't want telling about all this gloomy, morbid stuff.'

For a strange moment, Minnie felt herself imagining these cut-up newspapers and this half-filled scrapbook shoved to the back of the dresser. It would lie in one of the drawers, right at the back, under layers of old Christmas cards, forgotten balls of wool, official papers and school reports. The clippings would grow yellow and brittle, the glue would desiccate and turn to dust. Would all of them forget what it was like to go through these past few years together? Would all the most harrowing details just get buried at the backs of their minds? Minnie felt sometimes as if she'd like to forget what it had been like to live through the war. But then Ma Ada from next door had told her that it was all very well wanting to live in peace, but it was a crime to try to forget.

Ma Ada had told her: 'The younger people have to know about it all. They have to understand it all; the reasons why it happened and what was done. Just so they can ensure that it never happens again.' Later on, Minnie found herself repeating these wise sentiments to her mother, Betty.

Her mother studied the determined set of her jaw. 'Of course it will never happen again, hinny. The world has learned its lesson, I think. No one will go hurrying into war any time soon, believe you me.'

'But Japan's still at war with us,' Minnie pointed out. 'It isn't all finished yet.'

Betty waved her concerns away, as if the Far East was just too distant for her to be bothered about. 'You're splitting hairs, Minnie. The war's over and thank God we'll never see its like again. Now we have to be happy and move on. Let's just cut out the nice, happy pictures and stick them in the book. I thought that was the plan.'

'All right, Mam,' Minnie conceded defeat, and the two worked quietly with the scissors and glue pot as the radio hummed with gentle music.

'Oh, look at these pictures of the Princesses,' Betty cooed and started snipping carefully around their edges.

The new baby was an angel, everyone could agree about that. No one had ever seen a more peaceful and beautifully behaved baby. She stared up adorably from her baby basket when friends and relatives came to see her. Her eyes were huge, like something off a character in a Disney cartoon, and her fat little fists reached up to clutch at everyone as if she wanted to hug them.

One by one, the locals trooped round to meet the newest arrival on Frederick Street, and they tucked silver coins behind her lace pillow for good luck. When Junie felt well enough, she went out with the old pram that they had managed to get for a decent price from the market, and up and down the Sixteen Streets she went like a one-woman parade. She was sore from stitches for weeks after the birth, but as the summer warmed up, she loved to get out, showing off her bairn.

'That pram bloody jingles with coins.' Harry Minton laughed. 'You can hear her coming a mile off. I think she only goes out to gather spending money.'

'Ah, don't,' Betty frowned at him. 'She's proud of that bairn. Look at her face. I've never seen Junie so happy.'

There was definitely a glow about Junie, Minnie thought. She seemed well-rested and pleased with herself. No wonder she looked relaxed, mind. It was Betty and Minnie who were doing all the heavy and dirty work when it came to the bairn. There was a pan of stinking nappies in the scullery and somehow it had become Minnie's job to scrub the bliddy things till they were shining white. Junie seemed to glide serenely through the days, with the baby clasped to her bosom or lying sweetly in the jangling pram.

'Ah, you can't complain,' her mother warned Minnie. 'I can see you dote on that baby. You're more than happy to help out.'

Ruefully, Minnie conceded that she was. The few minutes she was allowed to dandle Ivy on her lap each day were enough for her.

'It's all good practice for you, too,' Betty said, as she folded knitted baby clothes into tidy little piles. 'One day you'll have all this coming to you, remember. You'll have bairns of your own to look after.'

'I don't think so, Mam,' Minnie smiled.

'Eeeh, lass,' sighed her mother. 'Where's your gumption? Where's your hope? You can't give up so early on yourself. You're only . . . what are you? Thirty years old! Buck your ideas up, lass.'

Minnie had always hated talks like this. Nowadays – since the end of hostilities – her mother was forever looking to the future, and she'd started up with this kind of talk again. 'I'm happy as I am,' Minnie told her.

'No, you're not,' Betty said. 'You need a young chap. You need bringing out of yourself. You need happiness and a family of your own. What's going to happen? Young Junie and Ivy and Derek are going to move out sooner or later. They'll get a place of their own when they can. Why, it's only natural. And you'll be stuck here with your ma and da and we'll be two old fogeys. When your older brothers get back, they won't be staying round here long, either. You can't just moulder here with us. Is that what you want? To spend your life looking after two old people in the house you grew up in?'

Minnie helped her mother folding up the clean baby things. 'As I say, I'm happy as I am.'

One thing that Minnie was less than happy about was having to return to work at Swetty Betty's to help her mam. Obviously Junie had had to give up helping some time ago – to her own great relief. Minnie went back to automatically peeling tatties and battering fillets. She was so used to the work that it hardly took any brainpower at all. She wandered through those steamy, greasy evenings like she was in a trance. She ate chips every day and sighed when she saw that she was piling on the pounds.

But she was thinking and she was listening. She found time to really mull over the things that people said to her. Like one or two folk had noted over the years: she seemed daft, but she wasn't. She was deep, actually, was Minnie Minton.

Still, she did as many hours at the Robin Hood as she could. That was better work because at least she could spend time talking with people. She preferred the conversation of men to that of women, she found. Even when blotto on beer, they talked about things she was more interested in. The world at large. Government and politics. The men in the pub loved to talk about the many problems that the world's leaders now faced with a world left in chaos by the war. This was much more to her liking than talk of dirty nappies and knitting.

'Putting the world to rights,' Cathy Sturrock laughingly put it.

'Why not?' Minnie fired back. 'Someone has to. Someone has to be interested.'

Cathy raised an eyebrow at the heat in her barmaid's tone. This was at the end of the night, as the two wearily collected up smeary, empty glasses. 'What's bugging you?'

Minnie shook her head crossly. 'Oh, I'm all right. I'm just fed up with everything being so narrow and hand-to-mouth. At home, all they ever talk about is washing and cleaning and eating and feeding and all that dreary stuff. If I try to get them talking about . . . oh, I don't know . . . anything that's not about something right on our bloomin' doorstep, they look at me like I'm crackers.'

Cathy nodded like she understood, but she didn't really. Her own concerns had narrowed down in recent weeks. Where once she'd listen to the radiogram to keep up with the progress of the war, now she was content to limit her world to these few streets by the docks. She hung on every bit of news emerging from number fifteen concerning her new and wonderful granddaughter, and she counted the days until her missing pot man Bob would return. Aside from that, Cathy was interested in very little else.

'Everyone is very caught up in their own lives recently,' said Minnie. 'It's like everyone's world has shrunk and they're only concerned about themselves, their own happiness.'

Cathy shrugged. 'Maybe that's just normal life? I can't remember properly . . . but isn't that what normal life is like? When there's not a war on? Isn't finding a way to be happy just the whole point?'

Minnie sat down heavily at the Women's Table, watching the dwindling fire in the grate. 'Yes, yes, I suppose it is.'

Cathy patted her shoulder and said, sounding suddenly wise: 'You'll find your own happiness, pet. I promise you. One day you'll find your way.'

Chapter Twenty-Three

She was living her life surrounded by other people's cast-offs. That was a self-pitying way of thinking about it, but Minnie couldn't help seeing it that way sometimes. On very rainy days, she felt like this, when she was looking after the market stall for Susan, and she was trying her best not to let the stock get damp. She would think: *Here I am, guarding a load of old woollens and musty old coats and frocks.* Keeping them tidily folded was a palaver, too, after the local women had rummaged through and left the whole lot in a right old state.

It wasn't quite the glamorous job in retail that she might have imagined. It was cold and damp and sometimes quite lonely.

But then, other times, Susan would join her there and those days would be quite different. The younger one would keep up a constant stream of nonsensical chatter and Minnie would enjoy every moment of their time together. Susan was still dressing in her odd assemblages of ill-suiting outfits, salvaged from the second-hand goods that arrived as stock. She was so different to her older sisters, Faith and Hope, who always seemed so prim and grown-up to Minnie. There was something childlike and vivacious about Susan that never failed to touch Minnie's heart. Even the dreariest days of manning the stall in the market were enlivened by the thought that Susan could arrive at any moment to help her out.

All of this was good distraction for Minnie. She was glad to have a life that lay beyond the confines of Frederick Street and her usual places of work. She felt worn ragged by juggling her three different jobs and miffed that even their combined income barely made up one decent wage. Still, it was good that she was kept occupied most of the time. It kept her mind from dwelling on things and feeling dissatisfied with her lot.

She turned thirty-one as the year ripened towards autumn and there was a muted celebration in the Robin Hood. 'You're an old lady, nearly,' Junie laughed at her, looking just as bright and youthful as ever. 'Why, I must have known you almost half your life, have I?'

'Not quite,' Minnie smiled. But it was true that the two of them had shared a lot of life together. Minnie would think back to the awkward girl she had been as a teenager, falling under Junie's spell and following her around in those first few months. She had never seen anyone as lovely or as neat and ladylike as Junie. It was like the muck in the air and on the streets could never actually stick to her. She simply glided through life, that was how it seemed to Minnie.

Though, now, Junie had come down to earth with a bump. She was living in the real world these days, right at the heart of the Minton household, and Minnie was far less inclined to idealise her. At number fifteen, they were all living cheek by jowl, and even though Ivy was a very well-behaved baby, her endless demands had them all running ragged.

There was also something curious going on with Derek. He was restless and dissatisfied these days, according to Junie.

'Wants to better himself, doesn't he?' she smiled, draining her half-pint of stout as she talked with Minnie on that birthday night. 'Which I'm quite glad about. If he gets himself a better job, well then maybe he'll put some proper thought into us finding ourselves a home of our own, away from you lot.'

This cut Minnie to the quick, and she flinched at the very thought of Junie, Derek and Ivy moving away from Frederick Street. 'What? He'd leave the biscuit factory? What would he do? What could he do?'

'You don't have much faith in your brother,' Junie laughed, raising her eyebrows. 'There's more to his talents than just working in that bakehouse. He's sick of it there. Says the smell of biscuits turns his stomach.'

Minnie was shocked. Everyone she knew who worked at the factory seemed set for life. They were more than happy to labour for the rest of their days under the benevolently watchful eye of Mr Wight. It wasn't slave labour, like some of those places could be. He paid a fair wage and the work wasn't too bad, according to the lasses that Minnie knew who worked there – Irene and Mavis and the rest of them.

'Well, what does he want to do, then?' Minnie asked Junie.

'He only told me recently. It's been his ambition for years, but he's never really told anyone . . .'

Minnie felt left out, once again, to hear that her brother had a secret ambition she had no idea about. How far they had grown apart. 'What is it . . .?'

Junie looked as if she wanted to laugh. 'He's like a little boy. You'll laugh when I tell you. But he wants to drive a tram. That's all he wants. He wants to be a tram driver.'

'Oh,' Minnie gasped. 'Is that so impossible? It doesn't seem such a crazy and impossible thing to want to do . . .'

Her friend shrugged carelessly. 'I'm off to the bar. Do you want the same again, birthday girl?'

'Erm, yes please. Is he doing anything about it? Is he applying to be taken on?'

Her sister-in-law sighed irritably. 'You know what he's like. Won't push himself, will he? He's like your dad, content to sit in the quiet and get on with the same old things. Doesn't like to draw attention to himself. I don't suppose he'll do anything about this dream of his.'

Off she went to the bar, squeezing through the gathered drinkers and smiling at people she knew. She cut such a fine, elegant figure that Minnie couldn't help but admire her, even while she felt irked by her attitude. Why, Derek was her fella. Shouldn't she be more supportive? Couldn't she do more to stand by him and help him push himself forward? And when she had compared Derek to his dad and said that they both held themselves back, content to sit on their laurels, why . . . Minnie had felt a stab of rebellion against Junie.

Later that evening, she said to Junie: 'You shouldn't pick fault with my brother, or my dad.' She felt brave, jutting out her chin at her friend.

'Oh yes?' smiled Junie, amused by this small rebellion.

'Yes, you're acting like a few months of belonging to our family has earned you the right to criticise them like this. You must really think you know everything about us all.'

Junie shrugged. 'I do, really.'

Minnie said, 'You don't see anything but our faults and limitations.'

Junie smirked.

'You don't know anything really, Junie.' Minnie was flushed and cross. 'You don't know anything about other people. You're too bound up in yourself.'

All at once, Minnie felt like she had overstepped the mark. She watched Junie's expression change to one of hurt. 'T-too bound up in myself?' Junie gasped. Seeing that stung expression of hers made Minnie feel guilty.

Oh, that was an awful way to think about her oldest and best friend, Minnie thought. It was betrayal almost.

'I'm sorry, Junie. I didn't mean it. You're not selfish like that, you're really not.'

Junie pursed her lips. 'Yes, well. It wouldn't hurt *you* to think about how you might help your brother. It's your responsibility, too, you know. We should all be helping him.'

Minnie was abashed. She turned her thoughts away from criticising her friend and towards helping her brother find a way to make his dream come good.

'I know who can help,' cried Susan the next day as they stood together at the second-hand stall. They were both drinking mugfuls of vegetable soup she had made at home and brought in a vacuum flask. It was delicious and spicy and Minnie could feel the warmth going right through her, all the way down to her sheepskin boots.

'Go on . . .?' smiled Minnie. She had only just brought up the subject of her brother and his secret longing to drive a tram, and Susan had considered the matter for only a few seconds before snapping her fingers.

'Arthur Kendricks, that's who.' Susan beamed at her friend from under the shapeless felt hat she was sporting today. It looked comical and fetching at the same time. 'Arthur who buys stuff from us sometimes. You know Arthur, he stands out a mile. He was in ENSA in the war. He's Mavis's brother and still lives with her and Sam.'

'Oh, Arthur,' Minnie nodded, knowing him well enough by sight and to say hello to. He was so flamboyant and loud she often felt abashed in his presence. He was quite often in the queue at Swetty Betty's when he was up round their way, visiting the Farley clan, for instance, and he'd actually get the whole fish queue singing along with him doing some daft song.

It was the same in the shelters when he'd been back on leave. 'He's a natural-born entertainer, our Arthur,' his whey-faced sister Mavis was known to say. ENSA had been the making of him, everyone seemed to agree. Whereas before, as a younger man, he had stuck out in the town as decidedly odd, everyone agreed that joining the entertainment corps and being abroad had made a man of him. He had found his vocation in life.

'He's working as a clippie on the trams these days,' Susan told Minnie. 'That's the latest I've heard. He's doing it till he finds the right break in showbiz.'

'Oh, I see,' said Minnie. She pictured the tall, elegant figure of Arthur all done up in a uniform and hat, wielding one of those machines that the tickets came out of. During the war, all the clippies had been lasses, of course, standing in for the men who were away, just as they had done in so many walks of life. Now that the men were returning from active service – like Arthur had from ENSA – the jobs were returning to the fellas. 'Do you really think he could help our Derek, then?'

'I don't see why not,' Susan shrugged. 'Surely he could mention his name, or find out for him what he needs to do to apply?'

Minnie tried to picture her brother driving a tram. When she did, he was grinning and looking far happier than she had ever seen him. Yes, it was a good thing, she thought, to help people along when they had a dream. They were lucky to know what it was that could make them happy. She resolved to do everything she could to help her brother. 'How do we talk with Arthur, then?' she asked. 'I must admit, he rather intimidates me. He's such a live wire.'

'Oh no, he's a real sweetheart,' Susan told her. 'He's been so good to his sister and that husband of hers. I think he'll go far, actually. He's got real talent. At the moment he's just getting by, but one day he'll be famous, I promise you.' She chuckled to herself. 'You should see him singing on the tram. He gets all the old biddies singing along with him. They do all the old songs together as the tram rattles along the seafront.'

'Well, we should catch the tram and see him,' Minnie suggested. 'And then I can tell him about our Derek. But will you come with me, Susan? Otherwise I'll feel rather shy . . .'

Susan beamed at her through the drizzle and from under her second-hand hat. 'Let's do it tomorrow then. It's a date,' she promised.

Chapter Twenty-Four

Junie and her baby were bonded more closely than anyone could have expected. Even Junie herself, in the past, would never have thought herself as all that maternal. Yes, she wanted bairns, of course. That was just a normal, inevitable part of life for her. But she could never have foreseen how the baby's arrival would affect her. Junie doted on Ivy to an extent she found almost frightening.

The emotions that swirled through her in those early days after the war's finish were intense. It was as if the person she had been before was being scrubbed away, bit by bit, and she was getting replaced by someone calmer, sweeter, nicer. Junie looked back on her earlier spiteful and self-obsessed nature and was ashamed.

'This is it,' nodded Ma Ada from next door wisely, one day when Junie was round showing off her bairn. 'Now you've started to live for someone else. You're not just concerned with your own shallow needs.'

Junie had been drawn to Ma Ada to seek her advice, as the self-proclaimed most maternal and wise person in all of Frederick Street. She wanted to understand better these raging emotions in her head and the way they threw everything into question.

'It's all natural, hinny,' Ma Ada cackled as they sat together over a pot of pitch-dark tea. 'You've become a mammy and your life will never be the same. That little bundle in your arms? You'd kill for her, wouldn't you? You'd fight like a lioness for her. Well, that's how I felt about all of my lads, even though I'm the size I am and as feeble as this.'

Junie smiled, because Ma Ada was a formidable presence who had never struck her as the least bit feeble. Junie said, 'But it's everything I ever cared about, too . . . it seems now like none of those things matter. Even my mother. I used to resent her so much for dumping me and running away. Now . . . now I don't even care. It's all forgotten.'

'Is it?' Ma Ada fixed her with a gimlet eye. 'Is it forgiven as well as forgotten, hmm? Then you should tell her that. You've made Cathy suffer all these years, you know, with your determination to punish her.'

Junie's face hardened in an instant and she hugged her baby to her, kissing her gossamer hair. 'I'm surprised to hear you defending Cathy, to be honest. I'd have thought you'd feel more ambivalent about her.'

Ma Ada cooed softly like an old bird on her nest. 'You'd think so, would you? And why's that?'

'Because of the scandal of her and your Bob, that's why.' Junie made her voice sound high and appalled. 'Everyone knows that they've been carrying on for ages. What's he, twenty years younger? And his wife, living over here at your place, having his baby at the same time. Why, I'd have thought you'd hate my mother for causing such ructions.'

Ma Ada, sighing heavily, lumbered to the scullery and started going through her pantry to see what could be made for supper tonight. Supplies were low, she grunted to herself. The bloomin' war might be over, but the rationing was still in force. The shortages seemed worse than ever.

Junie followed her into the gloomy scullery, hugging her daughter to her. 'Well, aren't I right?'

Ma Ada's tone turned harsh. 'No, you're not, love. You're very wrong.'

'Oh?' Junie blinked, surprised at the anger in the old woman's tone.

'Your mother has more love for my Bob than Megan ever did. Now, my son's a simple soul. He's like a sunflower because he moves his face to look at the sun to drink in its rays. Do you see what I mean? Without even thinking about it, he moved away to where there was more love, and that was with your mother. And I've known Cathy since the time of the Spanish flu. If there's anyone more honest and loving on this street, then I've yet to meet her.'

'I see,' frowned Junie. 'So the shame of it doesn't bother you?'

'Shame?' cried Ma Ada. 'What shame? There's no bliddy shame in love, is there? Not in real love. Why should there be?' She tutted and shook her head, her eyes flicking over the meagre provisions on her shelves. 'You'd do well to draw closer to people like your mam, and our Bob, and I'll tell you who else – your friend Minnie. Those are people you shouldn't be gossiping about and looking at with shame. You could learn from them, hinny. You could learn more about opening your heart from them.'

Junie said, 'Do I need to be learning how to open my heart?'

'Aye, lass, you do. You've been a sniping, spiteful lass for years, you know. You've caused quite a lot of heartache round here. But . . .' and here the old woman wagged a gnarled finger at her, 'I think you're learning. I think that lovely mite in your arms is teaching you at last to be a nicer person.'

To be a nicer person. Junie tossed her head furiously once she was out the front door of number thirteen and back on the street. How dare that fat old bag accuse her of being spiteful in the past! And what was the other word? Sniping. Spiteful and sniping. Who the hell did she think she was, pronouncing her judgement on people like that? Singing the praises of Junie's mam, of all people.

Junie put the bairn in the pram and jingled her way down the steep slope of Frederick Street, feeling cross with herself for letting Ma Ada patronise her like that. Open her heart, indeed. She didn't need to do any such thing. She loved her baby and who else did she need to love? Who else did she need to make herself vulnerable to? Why, no one really, did she? It did no good to make yourself too soft.

At the bottom of the street, she turned left past the imposing gates of the biscuit factory, breathing in the delicious aroma of the bakehouse. 'That's where your dada works,' she told Ivy, who was lying on her back and smiling placidly at the sky. Junie tucked her blankets more firmly around her. There was a proper autumnal nip in the air.

She found herself wandering along Westoe Road and eventually into town to take the air and to peer into shop windows. There was nothing wrong with window shopping. Not that there was much to see these days. Not yet. It would be some while before the fancy clothes started appearing in windows and on mannequins again. At the moment, everything was still a bit utilitarian and drab. But even when nice things did start to come back, what were Junie's chances of being able to afford them? Perhaps it was time that she firmly bid adieu to the idea of having nice clothes and expensive things. Hers was going to be a life where she had to settle for less flashy clothes and showing off. Her life was going to be dedicated to her family instead.

She still had all of her old clothes, of course. With a few adjustments, they could be made to keep up with the shifts in style, maybe. Thinner collars, higher waists, that kind of thing. Minnie was a dab hand with her Singer sewing machine, wasn't she? And she would do anything to please Junie.

I must keep my figure, though, Junie thought. *I must do everything I can to keep the size and shape I am. Even if we end up having as many bairns as Derek says he wants us to have.*

There was a shop on Fowler Street that looked as if it was having a refitting. Brown paper covered some of the windows and it looked like someone had been having a clear-out inside. As far as she remembered, the place had been a fruit and veg shop previously – a dark, cavernous place that had smelled of damp, crumbly soil. Now there were lights on and there was some bloke up a ladder painting the sign at the front.

'What's this place going to sell, then?' she asked the thin, horse-faced woman in a pinafore who was smoking on the front step.

Faith Chesney seemed startled for a moment to be addressed by this girl with a pram and she smiled stiffly. 'Oh. You caught me in a reverie. I was imagining how it will all look when it's finished at last. It seems a long way off yet.'

Junie narrowed her eyes at the woman's lofty tone. She seemed a proper spinster type, Junie thought, taking against her at once. 'It's nice to see something new coming along. Something to cheer us all up.'

The eldest of the Chesney girls gave her a wintry smile. 'Well, that's to be hoped for. But it still looks like a bomb-site in there, and my sisters seem intent on turning the place into a bazaar or a rummage sale. Whereas I have rather finer ambitions for the place.'

'Do you, indeed?' Junie said, feeling slightly miffed that this skinny woman hadn't shown the least bit of interest in cooing over her baby. Why, everyone else made a right fuss of Ivy. Everyone wanted to pick her up and put a piece of silver in her warm palm. But this long streak hadn't shown the slightest shred of interest.

'We've at least decided what we're going to call this place,' said Faith. 'It's to be named after our late, lamented mother. "Mary's Shop" is the name we have settled on.'

Now Junie couldn't help but be impressed. She was reminded of the fancy shops in the old town of Marwick in Northumberland, where she had been brought up. 'Selling what, exactly?'

Faith waved her cigarette end in the air. 'Fancy goods, lovely things. Luxury items.'

'Luxury items?' Junie burst out. 'Round here? Are you sure? Won't you go bust?'

'Indeed we will not.' Faith looked at her beadily. 'I think people are craving nicer things. Luxurious items. People will want to spoil themselves.'

'Who'll have the money, though?' Junie asked, though inside her heart was leaping at the woman's words. She knew that her own soul was yearning and chiming in with everything that Faith had said.

'We'll just have to have faith that people will come,' Faith smiled thinly. 'People will save up their money or they'll come from further afield. But I am sure that everyone will relish having bright, new, shiny things to look at. Don't you think?'

'Oh yes . . .' Junie sighed. 'Oh yes, I do.'

Chapter Twenty-Five

Minnie and Susan flung themselves into the tram at the stop beside South Marine Park. They only just managed to get themselves on board before it jolted and took off again on the seafront route.

'There's Arthur, look. There he is.' Susan nodded at the tall, elegant figure with the ticket machine at the front of the lower deck. He was busy talking with the women there, looking rather stern in his dark militaristic outfit. All at once, he seemed forbidding and off-putting to Minnie. She had come here to find out how to get a job for her brother, but now she could feel her nerve failing her. 'Oh, don't worry,' Susan urged her, as she noticed her hesitation. 'Arthur is the loveliest chap. He only looks rather fierce sometimes. It's all an act.'

He operated his clippie machine very expertly with one hand, holding the metal rail with the other as he made change and cranked out tickets for the cheerful old ladies. The sun shone through the spotless windows of the tram and Minnie couldn't be sure but thought he might have put a russet rinse in his hair. It had a certain reddish glow in the sunlight.

'I'm scared of him,' Minnie admitted to her friend.

'Don't be. Just smile at him when he gives you your ticket and we'll get him chatting. He loves to talk, does Arthur.'

Then, all of a sudden, he was singing. He was doing a song from the big film from earlier that year, *Meet Me in St. Louis*. It was a giddy, carefree number that had taken place on a tram much like this one, all 'clang clang clang' and 'zing zing zing'. Arthur dashed up and down the narrow aisle, clinging onto the railing above and singing at the top of his voice. And what a voice he had! Resonant and clear as a bell. High and pure one moment, then rich as dark Bournville chocolate the next. All the old dears on the bus were clapping their hands and warbling along.

'There's his sister Mavis,' Susan told Minnie. 'The deaf one, joining in loudly. With the very fine hair and the toddler in her lap.'

Minnie nodded, recognising Mavis from her visits next door to the Farleys.

When Arthur swept up to them with his ticket machine, Susan asked for two returns all the way to Seahouses and back. 'Out for the day because the sun's out, eh?' Arthur grinned at her. 'Who's your friend?'

'You know Minnie Minton,' Susan told him. 'She helps me on the stall these days.'

'I haven't been to your stall for a good rummage in ages,' he snapped. His voice was so loud, Minnie thought. It was nasal and braying, and the way he said things, it was just like a comic on the music hall stage. 'I shall have to come and have a look at your wares. She's familiar though, this one.' He was studying Minnie very closely as he cranked the handle of his clippie machine.

'I work in the fish bar at the top of Frederick Street,' Minnie said shyly, mumbling into her coat collar. 'That's where you might know me from.'

Arthur clicked his fingers sharply. 'Swetty Betty's. You're the nice lass from in there. Are you her daughter? Eeeh, Swetty

Betty is a mardy old wife, isn't she? Always so red in the face. And how come you're not in there so much these days? They've got that blonde piece in there now. She's bonny, but she wears an expression that could curdle milk.'

Minnie's heart leapt up in rebellious laughter. 'Junie. That's our Junie.'

'Well, you can tell she hates working there,' Arthur chuckled. 'And don't you also work at the Robin Hood, hinny? By, you get around, don't you?'

'I do,' Minnie said proudly.

'She wants to ask you a favour, Arthur,' Susan put in, over the clanking noise of the wheels.

'Oh, she does, does she?' Arthur smiled. 'Well, you'll have to wait for my break before asking. You can see how busy I am with this rowdy lot of passengers . . .'

Then, having given them their change, he swept off and got the old biddies singing once more.

Two hours later, they were crammed into a booth at the back of Franchino's ice-cream parlour. The tram had taken them right along the coast and back again several times over, and Arthur had let the girls ride back and forth on just the one ticket.

Now his shift was over and he declared that he was 'absolutely shattered, dear. My God, working these trams is harder than being in Burma. The bliddy natives were friendlier there, I can tell you that for nowt.'

Irene Farley was working the gleaming chrome coffee machine at the front of the café, with her hair pinned up and a bright new apron tied around her thickening waist.

'Eeeh, she's never up the tub again, is she?' Arthur muttered under his breath. 'Why, she's busy enough with that devil-spawn toddler of hers, Marlene, and she's got Megan's kid to look after, too, since Megan did her latest moonlight flit.'

Minnie gasped at this. 'Megan's done another flit?'

He nodded solemnly. 'Oh, yes. She took all her things and left a note, saying she was leaving her bairn to be brought up by Irene – and off she went. Some say she's gone to the Côte d'Azur, but then she was spotted in Seaton Carew.'

Minnie was aghast. How did Arthur know more gossip about her neighbours than she did?

'Arthur gets to know everything,' Susan told Minnie, smiling at her befuddled expression. She had a funny look on her face as she watched her friends interacting. She seemed to be enjoying introducing them.

Irene Farley brought their coffee in clear glass cups and saucers.

'Ooh, new crockery,' Arthur commented. 'And isn't it true, Irene? That bloomin' Megan leaving her bairn in your care and doing a runner?'

Irene nodded frowningly and then noticed Minnie sitting there. 'Oh. Hello, there. We don't see you in here very often.'

Minnie didn't say that she didn't often have the spare money to waste on expensive coffees and ice creams. Money was tight at number fifteen. She just smiled at Irene and thought how funny it was to have a conversation with her that wasn't over the backyard wall or through the bricks of the privy.

'Minnie's got a question for you, Arthur,' Susan said, yanking off her shapeless hat and fluffing up her finger-waved hair. 'She needs your help.'

'Ha. Everyone always needs my help,' Arthur said. 'Did I tell you about what it was like in Burma? I was only supposed to be there to sing a few songs and gladden everyone's hearts. But the things I ended up having to do. I was the bravest and the most capable man for miles around, you see. It's a terrible curse. And then, once, you see, there was this runaway elephant who'd gone mad in the marketplace.'

'A mad elephant,' gasped Minnie.

'Oh, he was running amok.' Arthur rolled his eyes and brought a slim box of Sobranie cigarettes out of his uniform pocket. They were glamorous black and gold-tipped cigarettes and he took one out for himself and lit it dramatically. 'And guess who was called upon to shoot him between the eyes before he killed anyone?'

Susan butted in. 'Arthur, we don't need to hear your elephant story now . . .'

'Did you shoot him, then?' Minnie said.

His eyes narrowed and his expression darkened as he puffed out a plume of blue smoke. 'Well, I grabbed my rifle from the office and ran down to the marketplace and before I knew it, I had two thousand men after me, swarming down the street, wanting to see me shoot this elephant. Then, as we got to the market, we found the bodies. Trampled bodies in the sticky mud. The crazy elephant had got them in his murderous rampage.'

Minnie was hooked. 'What did you do, Arthur?'

'Well . . .' he hunched forward. 'I . . .'

'Enough of the elephant,' Susan cried. 'Arthur, can you get Derek a job at your depot?'

He glared at her and refused to be derailed. 'Well, I came charging round the corner with all these fellas at my back and they were all shouting my name. Then I was face to face with this huge bloomin' monster. You've never seen anything like it. Big as my tram, it was. Bigger. And it was as mad as bliddy hell. The heat and the chains had got to it, poor dear. And it had just flipped and gone doolally. Well, I looked into that poor nellie's eyes and I thought: Eeeh, you and me, chuck. We're both in places we don't want to be. I knew he wasn't going to calm down and go easy, that elephant. I was going to have to put him out of his awful misery.'

Minnie was holding her breath. 'Did you? Did you actually shoot him?'

Arthur took a long drag of his cigarette. 'All the men were yelling at me. Well, the locals were half-starved to death. All they could see was a nice big feast in the offing.'

Minnie was shocked. 'They'd eat an elephant?'

'They were already running up with their pails and knives. They were slavering at the thought of a barbecue that night.'

'Oh, Arthur,' Susan tutted. 'This is an awful story. Look, what are Minnie's brother Derek's chances of getting in at the tram company?'

'Go on,' Minnie urged him. 'Did you kill him?'

'It looked like I'd have no choice,' Arthur said in a tight voice, reliving the moment vividly. 'All those men looking at me. Chanting and shouting. It was the weight of expectation, you see. And then the elephant looked back at me. This great big beautiful beast with wrinkled legs and wrinkled everything. His great big ancient eyes looked straight into mine. And do you know what?'

Minnie's voice came out in a whisper. 'What?'

'I raised up that rifle and I was going to squeeze the trigger and let him have it right between the eyes. It would have been the easiest and kindest thing, all round.'

'And . . .?' Minnie gasped.

'I . . . I *sang* to him instead. I sang a lullaby. He blinked at me like he couldn't believe it. None of the men could believe it, either. They all went dead quiet. I carried on singing and I put down my gun. The elephant just stared and stared at me, listening with those great big ears of his. And do you know what? He calmed right down. All the fearsome anger went out of him. I could see it just draining away as he listened to me sing.'

Minnie gawped at Arthur. 'That's amazing. That's so wonderful.'

He shrugged modestly. 'Well, it's a natural-born talent. What can I say? If the trams go out of business, I could always join the circus, couldn't I?'

Minnie beamed at him, with hero worship in her eyes.

'Well?' Susan broke in impatiently. 'What about her brother? Can you get him work at your depot?'

Arthur blinked, as if he was emerging from a trance. 'What? That dark, handsome fella? Married to blonde Junie? Him?' He pulled a face and nodded firmly. 'Why, aye. They're crying out for new trainees down our place. Let me put a word in for him. They'll listen to me.'

Then he toasted them both with his cooling coffee and, to her shock, Minnie felt herself falling in love.

Chapter Twenty-Six

A letter came for Derek two weeks later and its arrival caused a stir at number fifteen.

'Why do you get special treatment?' his wife gasped as he read out the contents. It was a very polite request from the head of the tram company that he attend an interview.

Derek was dumbfounded but delighted. 'I don't know,' he grinned.

'Eeeh, it must be providence,' Betty Minton cackled, cradling their baby with one hefty arm and clearing the breakfast things with the other. 'The Lord moves in mysterious ways.'

'The Lord doesn't run a tram company,' snapped Junie. 'Someone's gone and sorted this out for you. You're so lucky.'

'I am, aren't I?' Derek read the letter again, frowning as he checked if he'd misread it. No, it was all there in black type. They especially wanted him to come and meet them and talk about a position in their firm. 'But who'd do such a thing?'

Minnie kept her gob shut through this whole exchange, but she was buzzing with excitement. It was a good feeling, sorting things out for people secretly.

*

Later that day at the fish bar, Junie was looking less happy than her mother-in-law thought she ought to. 'Aren't you glad for our Derek, then?'

'He just gets good fortune landing in his lap,' Junie shrugged, scraping away at the mouldy tatties. She was a good deal less expert at these tasks than Minnie had been. 'I know he's your son and all, but isn't it maddening, the way he just stumbles through life?'

Betty smiled tightly. 'It's just the way the Minton men are, hinny, and now that you're part of the family you just have to get used to it. But, yes, actually – a hundred years ago, or whatever it was – when I married Harry, he used to make me go bananas. He had no drive, no gumption. He was content to let things fall into his lap.'

They worked in thoughtful silence for a while, preparing all the chips. 'I'm not complaining,' Junie said at last. 'I know I sound as if I am, but I'm not really. You Mintons have been so good to me. And I love Derek to bits. You know that.'

Betty surprised her by putting down the fish she was filleting and coming out to put her arms around her. It was a mammoth and fragrant cuddle she gave her daughter-in-law. 'I know what you're feeling, pet. You're disappointed, aren't you? It's the feeling of . . . is this *it*? Is this all there is to my life? You love your fella and of course you love your beautiful babby, but now you're looking at your life and thinking – this is everything, now.'

Junie nodded tearfully.

'It's natural,' Betty said in a motherly, understanding tone. 'Everyone feels like you do some time in their life. Now, come on, let's get these flamin' fillets battered.'

Junie wasn't so sure about what Betty had told her. Everyone felt this raging dissatisfaction like she did? Why didn't they all go out of their minds, then? Why were they all so content to just go about their ordinary banal tasks and live in their little houses and do their dreary day-to-day jobs?

She wasn't sure what she wanted, but it wasn't just this. Everything bored her so horribly. Even her baby.

Oh, wasn't that an awful thing to admit to, even inside her own head? Her baby was boring. She couldn't be bothered with all the noise and mess. She was glad to leave as much of that as she could to those willing dupes, Betty and Minnie. Let Minnie stew those mucky nappies about in the boiling water and then wring them through the mangle in the yard.

'Has anything really changed?' Junie was saying loudly that night at the Robin Hood. She'd had two brown ales and she was sitting at the Women's Table, where there was a fire burning for the first time that autumn. 'Do you think? After everything? Does it really feel any different to you?'

She was sitting with a few of the younger women from Frederick Street: Minnie, Beryl and Irene. It was a funny thing: the Women's Table had long been the preserve of the women belonging to Cathy's generation – Ma Ada, Winnie and poor Sofia Franchino. With the passing of the years, it had been gradually colonised by this younger set. The changeover of the generations was seamless, though some of the older women did still come over to take their places by the fire some nights, when they could drag themselves away from their own comfy hearths.

'I don't get what you're talking about,' Beryl spoke up, sounding almost tentative as she queried Junie. That one was known to have a temper, and these days she seemed extra spiky. Tonight, Junie was flushed and hard-faced, as if she was spoiling for a fight. 'Do you mean since the war ended?'

'Yes, of course I do,' snapped Junie. 'Nothing's changed for us, has it? You still can't get the things you want. There's still a queue a mile long out of the butcher's and we're all still on flamin' ration books, aren't we? There's hardly anything worth looking at in the shops. I'm still in my drab old ragamuffin clothes . . .'

The other women looked at her sceptically. If there was one thing Junie definitely wasn't, it was a drab ragamuffin. She still looked wonderfully stylish in one of her outfits from before the war, expertly adjusted for her by Minnie. It was a burnt-orange jacket with a dyed brown rabbit-fur trim and a matching skirt. To the rest of the women, Junie always looked like a film star.

Irene was shaking her head and looking serious. 'I don't think you can say that, Junie, love. Of course our lives are different and better. The bombs aren't raining down, are they? That madman Hitler and all his wicked cronies are dead. And our fellas are back from the Front, aren't they? That's more than most of us dreamed about . . .' As she spoke, she reached out instinctively to take Beryl's hand. Beryl sat there and merely let Irene squeeze her fingers. Of course, Beryl's fella Tony hadn't come back from the Front. His bones lay right at the bottom of the sea. But Junie was oblivious to hurting Beryl's feelings as she stampeded on with her rhetoric.

'But what was it all for, anyway?' Junie said. 'Our lives are no better, are they? They're worse, in fact.'

Minnie was staring at her oldest friend in amazement. 'They'd be a hell of lot worse if we hadn't gone to war. How would you feel about being under the Third Reich?'

Junie shrugged dramatically. 'Oh, I don't know. Would it be any worse? Would we be any the wiser? We might have been able to get decent clothes . . .'

'Eeeh, wash your mouth out,' Beryl said, in a hushed voice. 'Fancy saying stuff like that. It's . . . it's treason!'

'Oh, hadaway, Beryl,' Junie laughed. 'There's no such thing as treason anymore. We won, didn't we? Apparently we won the war.'

'It's disrespectful, at any rate,' Beryl snapped. 'To those who made the greatest sacrifice.'

Junie rolled her eyes, as if bored with Beryl's seriousness. 'I'm going to the bar. Does anyone want another?'

They all did, and she was glad that they all had to thank her for buying them a treat. Silly witches, she thought as she pushed through the crowd of drinkers at the bar. They all felt so superior because their fellas had gone to war. Unlike her Derek, she thought. And she admitted it to herself: yes, she'd be happy if her Derek had been in the army and had seen service. It felt a bit cowardly and hopeless, his spending the war making bloody biscuits like he had.

'Junie,' her mother Cathy said warily in greeting. 'How are you? How's my grandbairn?'

'Two brown ales and two milk stouts,' Junie said. 'That grandbairn of yours is all anyone's interested in. They ask after me, but they don't really care. I'm just surplus to everything. I don't hardly exist anymore.'

'You've got the blues,' her mother said.

'Yes, I suppose I have,' Junie frowned. She watched her mother pouring glasses of beer and thought: *Aye, Mother, and you're looking older*. For the first time in ages, she really looked at Cathy and noticed the thickening of her waist and the careworn look about her eyes. That young lover of hers was making her look and carry on older. Shouldn't he have been making her feel young again?

'Aren't you happy living with the Mintons, then?' Cathy asked, and the look in her eyes showed she was daring to hope. 'You know, you'd be very welcome to move back into number twenty-one. I could help looking after the baby and all . . .'

Junie considered it for a second. There would be more room. She'd be away from Minnie and Betty and all their endless chuntering on. There was talk lately of the older brothers coming back soon and taking up even more space. Junie had never even met them before: they'd be strangers to her. Cathy's would be a nicer house with more space and her mother was so keen to be on Junie's good side these days, she could lean on her a bit harder, maybe. But would her mother help with the bairn as much as Betty did? Was her mother even capable of looking after a baby? Junie didn't even know. All she knew was that she had run away from her own baby, all those years ago.

'Well, think about it. If you and Derek and Ivy came to live with me, it would give the Mintons a bit of a breather. It can't be easy, all you lot crammed under that one roof.'

'Everything smells of fish and chips and nappies,' Junie sighed.

'Come and live with me,' Cathy said. 'Come home to live with your mammy.'

Junie put all of the drinks on a brass tray and smiled as her mother waved away the coins she tried to pay with. 'On the house,' Cathy said. 'Just think about it.'

'I will,' Junie nodded and returned to the Women's Table, where the laughter was suddenly raucous and Irene was covering her mouth with both hands and tears of mirth rolled down her cheeks. What were they talking about now, the daft lot? They were never happier than when they were laughing about silly things, about things that hardly mattered. Why, it was how they got through their days of drudgery, wasn't it?

But Junie wanted more. Junie had always wanted more than everybody else.

Chapter Twenty-Seven

Junie stopped by the emporium on Fowler Street several times to see how the Chesney sisters were getting on with their plans. Faith was businesslike and brisk, Hope was chattier and was delighted to fuss over the baby. Absent as she often was, the youngest sister, Susan, was still running their market stall for them.

'She'll have to give that up when we open the shop,' Faith opined. 'It will be all hands to the deck.'

'Ahh,' sighed the soft-hearted Hope. 'She loves her market stall, too. It'll be a shame to see her give it up.'

'What about our Minnie?' Junie asked. 'She helps out on her stall, doesn't she? Those two are thick as thieves these days. I've seen them at that stall, laughing fit to burst, messing on all day.'

'Messing on?' Faith frowned.

'Oh, they're great pals, laughing all the time,' Junie said. She wasn't sure why, but she felt a stab of irritation at the thought of Minnie being best mates with some other girl. Not that she wanted Minnie following *her* around constantly, like she used to, but it made her feel strange seeing Minnie run around after someone else. 'Will you let Minnie work here, then? When you get your fancy emporium up and running?'

The Chesney sisters had, on this chilly morning, let Junie bring her pram into the shop itself to see the progress they had made. She was suitably impressed with the fresh woodwork and the bright lick of yellow paint that the place had been given.

'Why, it's almost ready for opening,' she said, looking around at the bare shelves and the shining glass-topped counter.

'Yes, yes, almost,' Faith nodded with satisfaction. 'We just need to organise our deliveries and our stock.'

They're like little lasses merely playing at shops, Junie thought to herself. By, they must have some money behind them in order to play like this. Anyone else couldn't have afforded to pay the lease and spend so long dithering about with the details. Anyone else would have had to open the place right away and start selling stuff. They had their factory-owning grandfather behind them, supporting them financially and indulging them in everything they wanted to do. How wonderful that must be, Junie thought. What did she have? Just a flaky old barmaid for a mother, and a stinky fish shop on the other side. Other folk seemed to have all the luck.

'Will you let Minnie have a job here?' she asked again.

'I don't think so,' Faith said. 'I'm not sure she's the right type.'

Now Junie saw her chance. 'What about me? Surely I'm more the type that you want. I could work here. I could fancy myself standing at that counter, all dressed up and talking to customers.'

Faith and Hope exchanged a wry glance. 'We'll have to see,' Faith said stiffly.

'We'll be in touch,' Hope smiled.

Junie left, pushing the pram with a new zest and a spring in her step, convinced that they were going to give her just what she wanted. Fancy goods, she thought happily. That's what they were going to sell there, apparently. Junie could just see herself, all dressed up among the fancy goods.

*

Junie stopped by Franchino's for a coffee and so that all the regulars could get a look at her beautiful bairn. As ever, Ivy was behaving immaculately. There wasn't a peep out of her.

Bella Franchino touched the baby's warm cheek gently and exclaimed, 'Was there ever a better baby than this? She's angelic.'

'That's what they all say,' Junie smiled proudly and glanced about at the pastel interior of the ice-cream parlour to see if there was anyone she knew here. Bella was being helped out today by that pale and wispy woman Mavis, who Junie always found rather irritating. She brought coffee to her table and cooed over Ivy in her scratchy voice. She was deaf, or least partially so, Junie remembered, and that was why her voice came out rather distorted and loud, and she stared intently at your lips while you spoke.

'Ahh, isn't she lovely? Eeeh, I can't imagine how proud you must be.' Mavis stood by Junie's table like she wasn't intending to move. 'You know I had a little one, don't you? Ah, but I lost him, didn't I? He was only a couple of weeks old. Sam says he was too good for this world, that was the problem. He looked about him, at all the world's troubles, and our little Artie couldn't help himself flying back up to heaven.'

Junie looked up at the young woman's sorrowful face and she felt a twinge of pity for her. The weird sing-song quality to her voice as she told her awful story, it was almost as if she had learned it by rote, like a nursery rhyme. It was something to ease her wounded heart, Junie could tell, but to her it made things worse. It made Mavis seem like an overgrown child who hardly understood what had happened to her.

'I didn't know you'd lost your baby,' Junie told her. 'I'm very sorry. It must have been awful for you. I . . . know what that feels like.'

'Ahh, well,' Mavis shrugged. 'It was before the war ended. Everyone seemed to be losing their loved ones, all over the place. Hardly a day went by without terrible news coming in. And it was in the middle of all the horror and everything that our little Artie decided that he'd just slip away again. It was like this world was just too much for him.'

Unbidden tears filled Junie's eyes. All at once, they were really stinging. She surprised herself with this reaction. She hardly even knew daft Mavis. Why was she responding as strongly as this? Of course. She was thinking about her own lost bairn.

'Ah, hey, now,' Mavis croaked, noticing the tears and pulling a crumpled paper hanky out of her pinny. 'Now, don't be getting upset on my account, hinny. I've been dealing with the sorrow in my own way. You needn't worry yourself, pet. Look, you've got your own lovely baby – and she's so bonny, isn't she? Hey, hey, your make-up's getting spoiled.'

Mavis's mumbled words made Junie feel even worse. She was being so kind to her. Impossibly kind. Mavis was thinking about Junie's feelings – it was absurd. Mavis had lost everything, and she could still think about Junie's feelings. She really was as daft as everyone said she was.

Mavis was saying, 'Of course I've got lots of people around me. That's the main thing. My Sam has been as strong as Marsden Rock. And then my brother Arthur came back from Burma. He lives with us and he's a tonic in himself. It was him that we named Artie after, of course.'

'W-will you have another baby?' Junie asked her.

Mavis frowned and fiddled with the clunky hearing aid she had attached to one ear. 'What? Oh? Oh . . . I don't know. I don't think so. They said at the time, when I had Artie . . . I'm very narrow in the hip region. I'm quite boyish in shape, the midwife said. And after Artie there were complications, and they aren't so sure I can carry again.'

Junie stared at her sorrowfully and let her pick up Ivy for a few moments, hugging her close, breathing in her beautiful baby scent. Mavis whirled her about and admired the ivory shawl that Minnie had embroidered for her.

'Oh, you're so, so lucky,' Mavis told her and put the baby back into the pram. Then she went off to work the coffee machine once more and Junie patted away her tears.

By teatime, Junie was back home again, having pushed the pram up the hill to the Sixteen Streets. It was good exercise she was getting, pushing that pram around the town. She collapsed into her father-in-law's chair by the warm range and let Betty Minton take the baby and give the lass her feed. Mashed-up apple sauce had Ivy smacking her tiny pink lips like a kitten.

Junie watched her mother-in-law and basked in the heat of the glowing cinders. 'You Mintons have been very good to us.'

'Nonsense,' Betty smiled. 'You're blood now, you are. And this one, too. You've done my heart good, being here. You've brought life into this house that was so quiet for years.'

'The thing is,' Junie steeled herself to break the news. 'I'm thinking that we ought to move out.'

Betty almost dropped the bairn in surprise. 'You what, pet?'

'My mother, over the road . . . well, I think she's keen to make up for all the disappointments I've had in life and the times that she's let me down. She was never any kind of mother to me, so she wants to be a better granny to this one here.'

Betty said in a dull tone: 'I don't follow you, love.'

Junie spelled it out: 'She's asked us to move over there. To number twenty-one. There's more room than there is here. It's a bigger house and there's only her . . . and Bob. We'd be more comfortable over there.'

There was a gasp in Betty's voice, like she was wounded. 'More comfortable? What's wrong with this place? Is it dirty? Is it cold? Have we not been welcoming enough?'

'No, no . . .' Junie burst out. 'It's nothing like that. Of course it's not. You and Harry have been marvellous. We couldn't have got along without your help . . .'

'Well, yes,' Betty said. 'So what's wrong with continuing in the way we are, eh? We've all got used to each other, haven't we? We're all happy, aren't we?' She was cuddling the baby closer and closer, somewhat protectively. Junie was alarmed that she was going to squeeze all the life out of the mite with her big, hefty arms.

'I just think . . .' Junie began.

'You just think *nothing*,' Betty broke in. 'Life is always spoiled by people thinking too much. Just count your flamin' blessings and stop thinking about where you might be better off.'

'It's just that my mother suggested it, the other night in the pub,' Junie said hopelessly. 'And I thought it might be a good idea. To give you and Harry a bit of space again, and some quiet, and some time on your own . . .'

'No!' Betty cried out. 'No, no, no. What do we want peace and quiet for? What do we need space for? Those lads of mine, they're getting settled elsewhere. We're happy as we are. Don't you see? This little one is the best thing that's happened to us in years and years. You can't . . . you can't just . . . take her away from us.' Now the older woman was sobbing brokenly and trying to cover it up.

Junie was appalled at this display of emotion. She said, 'I'm sorry, I . . . I just . . .'

Betty said, 'I don't want to hear any more about it. You're staying here. You belong here with us, under our roof.'

Betty was being ridiculous, Junie thought, with a flare of annoyance. She felt anger rising up in her breast. Who did the silly woman think she was? Dictating to Junie like this, where she could and couldn't live? And it all had nothing to do with Junie anyway, did it? It wasn't her who Betty wanted. It was the baby. Betty was clutching the baby to her like something precious she'd stolen and wasn't prepared to let go.

'Give Ivy back to me,' Junie said in a sharp voice. 'I'll finish her feed.'

Reluctantly, muttering to herself, Betty passed the calm baby back. 'I don't want to hear any more nonsense,' Betty warned. 'What does our Derek have to say about all of this, eh? Doesn't he get a say in all your plans?'

Junie had to admit that she hadn't asked Derek about it yet. She hadn't even consulted him.

'Ha. Why, there you go then,' Betty tutted and shook her head. 'He'll put his foot down. He'll have none of this. He won't want to leave his mam's house. You'll see, lady. You'll see that it won't be so easy for you to get your own way. Not this time.'

With that, Betty Minton shuffled off to her scullery to get on with cooking the tea, and Junie watched her go, feeling appalled. 'I'm like a prisoner here . . .' she realised.

Chapter Twenty-Eight

Minnie went to the tram depot to have a talk with Derek, and to plead with him not to move away from home. It was impossible talking in the house, what with everyone around. There was no chance for her to get her brother on his own.

'Bloomin' Junie,' she muttered to herself, as she yomped her way across town. 'Causing bother again. Why can't she just leave things as they are?'

There was a proper nip in the air, too, today. Minnie was wearing a muffler that Irene next door had knitted for her — a rather lumpy article dyed green with what smelled like seaweed. All the same, Minnie had been touched by the birthday gift. It was the nicest thing she'd been given by anyone that year.

'He's out on training, love,' said the man at the depot, a huge man with terrible brown teeth, smoking in the front office and consulting a clipboard. 'He's out all day, I'm afraid.'

Minnie swore under her breath. 'I was just hoping to catch him, so's I could have a word . . .'

'Maybe leave him a message?' the man shrugged.

Minnie shook her head. She should never have come haring out like this on spec. It was her mam's idea. Betty was rattled and cross. She had been in a right state when she'd cornered Minnie this morning. 'You've got a morning off, haven't you?

Go and see him at work. Tell him it's no good. He can't – they can't – go moving out of here. Tell them it will break my bliddy heart.'

Minnie had tried to mollify her mother. 'But even if they do, it'll only be over the road. It's not like it'll be miles away . . .'

Her mother had looked shocked. 'I'm surprised by your attitude. Won't it break your heart, too, if they move in with Cathy? Won't you miss them terribly? That little babby? She belongs to us. She belongs to this house.'

To be fair, Minnie had mixed feelings about that. She knew very well that Cathy had a bigger house and room to spare. But still, she could see how upset her mother was. Betty rarely let herself get emotional like this. 'All right, Mam, all right,' Minnie had sighed, and got herself ready to dash out to the depot.

'If our Derek would listen to anyone, it'd be you,' Betty had said. 'You two were always so close. I reckon that Junie bullies him, you know. Have you noticed? She's always telling him what to do . . .'

Now here Minnie was, standing in the entrance to the cavernous depot at the end of the tramlines. It was an oily, dark-smelling place where the staff were bustling busily about, all dressed in their tidy dark uniforms with the red trim. She could quite fancy herself working in a place like this. Not that she didn't have enough little jobs, all at the same time.

Just as she was turning to leave, thinking the whole trip out here a waste of her time, she bumped into Arthur. 'Ooh, mind out, missus,' he jibed her with a laugh. 'What are you doing here, Minnie Minton?'

Arthur looked tired to her. He'd clearly just finished a morning shift clipping tickets and rolling around all the streets of South Shields. His face was pale and his hair under his cap was unwashed. He looked to Minnie like he'd been up all the previous night. From what she could gather from mutual friends, the garrulous Arthur tended to burn the candle at both ends. 'Oh, hello there,' Minnie said to him, and prepared to dash off. She always felt abashed and almost shy in Arthur's gregarious presence.

'Hold your horses, lady,' he called out and hurried after her as she tried to leave. 'I'd like a word with you. Here, let me catch up.'

'Oh, all right,' sighed Minnie, and the two left the depot together. He linked arms with her brusquely, giving her no choice in the matter, and they marched back into town as a duo. Minnie was less irked by that than she might have imagined. 'I tried to see our Derek, but they're training him to drive . . .'

'Don't you live in the same house?' Arthur frowned. 'How peculiar of you.' He walked very quickly, and Minnie was breathless keeping up with him.

'I couldn't really talk about it at home,' she gasped. 'Not much privacy.'

'I see,' mused Arthur. 'So it was something you didn't want the glamorous Junie to hear. What's your brother up to behind her back, eh?'

'Nothing,' Minnie burst out.

'In that case, what terrible thing is Junie up to? I can see that she's no good, just by looking at her.'

'It's not like that,' Minnie protested. 'It isn't something scandalous . . .'

Arthur cracked out laughing. 'You lot who live in the Sixteen Streets, you've always got something going on. There's always bother or summat happening. Tell me what it is this time.'

Minnie amazed herself by explaining the whole business of Junie wanting to move in with her mam over the road and how Betty was up in arms about it all.

'Oh dear,' Arthur said, lighting up one of his exotic cocktail cigarettes. 'Want one?'

Minnie almost choked on the strange article. 'Where do you get these?'

'There's a little man on the market who gets them for me. Maybe those Chesney sisters will stock cocktail cigarettes in their fancy emporium when it opens.' He eyed the coughing Minnie up and down. 'Will you be working there with them, do you think? Or are you only good enough for their market stall?'

'I-I don't really know,' wheezed Minnie. 'I've told their Susan that I'd really love to serve in their shop.'

'They must be quids in on account of their grandad,' Arthur said. 'Him who owns the biscuit factory. He's always given them everything because of their ma' dying young. Though I can't understand why their da' never got them somewhere nicer to live. Somewhere fancier than number one Frederick Street. But hey ho, what do I know about what goes on in people's lives?'

Minnie burst out, 'There's nothing wrong with living on Frederick Street. It's a proper community. Everyone looking out for each other. You should be so lucky.'

Arthur pulled a face. 'You sound just like Sam Farley. That's all we hear about, me and Mavis. Well, me and my sister weren't lucky enough to grow up in the bosom of a warm community like that. Do you know what happened to us?'

Minnie shook her head, though actually she had heard all the stories and rumours.

'We were out on the streets. We were like street rats when we were kids. We were taken in by all kinds of people. We were living off scraps and almost died of the cold. So you were lucky, living where you did, even if your whole house does smell of fish and chips.'

'It does not!' Minnie said hotly.

'It does, you know,' said Arthur. 'And so do you, pet. Now look, this is my street. Are you coming in for a cuppa or what?'

Minnie blinked, astonished at how far they had walked in such a short space of time. They were on a run-down street called Tudor Avenue in what Minnie's mum – who certainly was no snob – would have called the rougher part of town. There were derelict lots and bombed-out remains. All at once, Minnie remembered how there had been a bomb that landed near here on the day of the funeral of old Ma Johnson, who was the queen of the criminal family who lived round here. The horses had been killed and the hearse overturned and the coffin had fallen on Mavis, hadn't it? Wasn't that the tale that spread like wildfire round the town? Trust that daft Mavis to get herself caught up in disaster like that.

'Didn't a coffin fall on your sister on this road?' Minnie asked Arthur.

'Kind of,' he said. 'She was clonked on the head by a startled horse and that's how she went deaf, poor thing. And she was so upset – she said the worst thing about it was that she'd never hear me singing again. Of course, it's started to come back to her a little. She can hear better than she could at first.' He stopped abruptly in front of a battered, paint-flaking door. 'Are you coming in, then?'

As it happened, Minnie was dying for a cup of tea.

They perched at the melamine kitchen table and Minnie sat there, amazed by the sheer disarray and muckiness of the place. 'Don't mind the mess,' Arthur slurped his tea. 'You see, all three of us are much too busy to do any housework. We've got all these jobs and we're hardly ever in. And when I'm not working on the trams, I'm trying to get my showbiz career back up and running.'

'Showbiz!' Minnie gasped.

'Oh yes, you just watch.' He waved his black cigarette about elaborately. 'I want to be in films, cabaret, theatre, everything.

You'll see. This time next year – or maybe the year after – I will be huge.'

Minnie beamed at him. She was warming to him and becoming a bit less intimidated by all his carrying on. He wasn't really as fierce and loud as he pretended to be. That was all a bit of silly bravado: that was what she was beginning to realise.

'I think I've chosen you to be my new pal, Minnie Minton,' he told her suddenly. 'I've had my eye on you for a while.'

'W-what . . .?' She was unsure what he was leading to with this, and her guard went back up at once.

'Us two, we're both at loose ends, aren't we? You've been dropped by your Junie since she got married and had a bairn. And my Mavis, well, things haven't been the same since she married Sam and I went away to Burma. It's hard to pick up the old threads of relationships again, don't you find?'

'I do,' Minnie agreed, and sipped her tea. Arthur had splashed a measure of whisky into her teacup and it was warming her right through. 'Oh, I do indeed.'

When she thought about it, she did feel somewhat lonesome these days. Yes, she'd made pals with lovely Susan on the market stall, but that was only two days a week and those Chesney sisters were a little unit on their own. They never really mixed with people outside their house. And Irene had her kids and her husband, and Beryl was never really a close friend to her. Perhaps Arthur was right? Perhaps both he and her were going about like lost souls, all lonely and abandoned by everyone else?

'They're all pairing up,' she said. 'It's like at a dance when they put the last number on, isn't it? And everyone gets all lovey-dovey.' She sighed and shuddered. 'I make a fast retreat whenever that happens. I always have done. I go and sit at the sidelines.'

'Hmmm,' said Arthur. 'Why is that, Minnie? Why are you on the sidelines like that?'

She pulled a sullen face. 'I don't know. I'm just not the type to go all lovey-dovey and dance around kissing some fella in front of everyone. It always seems daft to me.'

Arthur was studying her very carefully. 'I think we're of the same tribe, you and me, Minnie Minton.'

Oh help, she thought. *What's he on about? Is he going to start proposing things and trying to kiss me now?* Part of her was appalled at herself, that she had simply followed this fella into his house and put herself at his mercy. The other part of her was thrilled. What was going to happen? Arthur was very handsome of course, though she had never imagined that he was the type to start kissing lasses. All of a sudden, she wanted to laugh. But when she looked at him, he was deadly serious. 'What's up?' she asked. 'What's the matter?'

All at once, he beamed at her. His smile lit up the whole dingy kitchen. 'Come dancing with me, Minnie. Tomorrow night at the Albert Hall on Fowler Street. What do you say? Will you come out and play?'

Chapter Twenty-Nine

'Eeeh!' Betty Minton kept explaining. 'Wonders will never cease. Our Minnie's got herself a lad. She's gannin' out with a lad on Saturday night.'

Minnie couldn't get her mother to see sense, or to shut up.

All Friday night at Swetty Betty's, her mother was crowing from the shiny counter at her customers: 'Isn't it lovely? Our Minnie is gannin' courtin' at last.'

To be fair, everyone who came to the fish bar seemed very interested in the fact that young Minnie had snagged herself a fella at long last. She had never seemed all that bothered about such things before. The assumption was that Minnie was too homely-looking or too timid, or she just wasn't the type to go running after blokes. She was the kind of lass who'd grow old at home and be happy doing so. A proper spinster type, that's what she was – already thirty-one, they said – and she'd be happy to look after her mam and dad when they started ailing. More than happy, surely. Aye, there was a recognised type like that and Minnie fitted right into that certain groove. She was a lass who would stay at home.

Except . . . 'Wonders will never cease! Can you believe it?' cried her mother at all and sundry as Minnie parcelled up their chips, blushing furiously.

'Mam, man,' she tried to tell her in the rare lulls in the evening. 'I'm not courting. Arthur isn't going to be my boyfriend. It isn't even a proper date . . .'

'Ha!' Betty cracked out laughing. 'You're going dancing at the Albert Hall together. On Saturday night when there's a band on. What else would you call it, eh?' She shook her head and laughed. 'Eeeh, you need to grow up, our Minnie. You go on like a little lass. I've kept you sheltered all these years and you're proper naïve, aren't you? Can't you see? A fella has asked you out. You. You're going on a date, you are.'

'I'm not.' Minnie shook her head steadfastly. 'It's just Arthur. He reckons I could do with a laugh, some fun . . . He offered to take me out because he thinks I need a nice time.'

'Well, there you are!' Betty chuckled. 'What more need I say?'

'But it's Arthur,' Minnie cried out in exasperation. 'Don't you see? He's not like the other lads. He isn't the same. This can't be a proper date, can it?'

All at once, her mother's expression darkened. Her sparkling eyes dimmed and they narrowed at Minnie's words. 'What's that supposed to mean?'

'He's . . . he's . . . not like other blokes,' Minnie struggled. 'You know . . .'

'I'm sure I don't know what you mean,' said her mother stiffly. 'And I'm sure he wouldn't appreciate hearing you talk like this behind his back. Why, that fella has been good enough to ask you out to go dancing. He's asked you out when no one else has ever done so in all these years. God knows, I've prayed that someone would. My heart ached for you, Minnie Minton, and your being left out of everything by all the young'uns round here.'

Minnie looked away. 'I've been happy as I am,' she mumbled.

'And here comes this nice bloke. He's so polite, he dresses immaculately, and he's got a polite tongue in his head. So what do you do? You spread the same awful tittle-tattle about him that all the worst gossips do. You listen to their slander and lies. Eeeh, you should be ashamed, our Minnie. Taking heed of sheer wickedness like that.' Having said her piece, Betty went back to flouring haddock fillets at the back of the shop. 'Now, hinny, have you thought about what you're going to wear?'

Junie's outfits from when she was pregnant would fit Minnie now, it was decided. Minnie herself had let them out, putting a bit of give into the seams so that Junie could still look stylish even while she was up the duff. Firstly, however, Minnie had to tell her why she wanted to dress up.

'You're going out?' Junie gasped on Saturday morning, with her bairn on her knee, sitting by the range. 'You are?'

'Aye, to the dance,' Minnie said, and she couldn't help sounding a tinge smug.

'Who with?'

Minnie told her.

Junie burst out laughing. 'Him?! That . . . fairy?'

Betty heard this from the scullery and came dashing in. 'Now, don't you start, lady. I've heard enough slanderous and salacious gossip about this lad of our Minnie's.'

'He's not my lad . . .' Minnie sighed.

Betty was raving: 'Just because a fella takes time and care with his appearance and talks politely and isn't a bliddy caveman . . . that doesn't mean nowt, right? Do you hear me, Junie? It means nowt.'

Junie stared at her mother-in-law. 'But . . . but . . . everyone knows what Arthur is. It stands out a mile . . .'

'Rubbish,' Betty shouted, brandishing the eggy spatula she'd just been using. 'How would you like it if everyone believed all the horrible things they said about you, eh? How would you like it if we gave those things credence?'

Junie gasped. 'Well, what do they say about me?' Unconsciously, she covered up her baby's ears.

'Aye, wouldn't you like to know,' growled Betty. Ever since Junie had declared her intention of moving back out to her mother's house and taking Ivy and Derek with her, Betty had found it hard to talk nicely to the spoiled madam. 'See? Gossip's a nasty thing. It can ruin folks' lives. I remember a pal of mine, when I was just a lass. Alan, they called him. Chucked himself off the cliffs, didn't he? He was only nineteen and it was all 'cause of the things they said about him. Things like you're saying about this Arthur fella. Now, you mustn't. It's wickedness.'

Junie rolled her eyes at Betty's melodrama. 'Ha'way, Minnie. We'll go and look through my outfits I wore when I was fat. You might pick out something to suit you . . .'

Up in the bedroom that Junie shared with Derek, the two girls had an open-hearted chat like they hadn't had in years. As Junie went through the large, Victorian wardrobe she had inherited from Betty's mother, she was telling Minnie: 'I wasn't trying to be nasty downstairs. Whatever your mother thinks.'

'I know that, Junie,' Minnie said.

'It's just that I'd never want to see you getting hurt.'

'I know,' said Minnie, her eyes on the lovely outfits that Junie flicked through. Why, imagine her wearing something of Junie's. Imagine looking glamorous like she did. A little bit of excitement was starting to stir round in Minnie's guts that morning. She was picturing herself dancing at the Albert Hall, all dolled up. And why shouldn't she? Why should she always be on the sidelines?

'I know you're not daft, and you're not as naïve as everyone thinks you are,' said Junie. 'But don't go pinning your hopes on someone wrong.'

'Hmm?' Minnie was still in her reverie, staring at the jewel-coloured fabrics. She gasped when Junie pulled out a flowered summer dress she remembered working on very late at night, hunched over her Singer sewing machine. It was cream and sprigged with lilac flowers. 'Oh, that would be lovely.' She could just picture how it swirled about Junie's neatly shaped knees. Why, if it made Minnie look even half as elegant, she would stand out wonderfully at the dance hall. 'What are you saying, pet?'

'Arthur is . . . Arthur . . . Well, everyone knows what Arthur is. He even dares to joke about it, even though it could get him in trouble.'

Minnie shrugged. 'I don't care about any of that. Besides, that's just his carrying on. That's all just showbiz. It's like a music hall act. That's what he wants to do, you know? He told me. He wants to go on the stage. He's going to be famous, he says, by this time next year.'

Junie tutted. 'Well, I'll believe that when I see it. Whoever got famous coming from South Shields? I always knew he had ideas above his station. He goes about like he's already famous.'

'That's right, he does,' Minnie smiled. 'I was actually quite nervous around him. Wary. He's so confident and loud. He makes a joke out of everything. But then . . . he talked to me so nicely, Junie. He took me under his wing. He said that we are both alike . . .'

'Fellas,' Junie scowled. 'They're all the same. They'd say anything to get you doing what they want. I don't understand what Arthur wants with you. Clearly he can't fancy you . . .'

Minnie gasped. 'What?' She sounded cut to the quick.

'Now, don't take on. Don't be offended. But even you must see that to anyone normal looking on . . . you'd both make a pretty odd couple . . .?'

Minnie clamped her mouth shut and didn't trust herself to reply.

'Don't sulk, Minnie pet,' Junie said. 'I've got your best interests at heart. I'm your best friend, aren't I? And, to me, you're just not the courting type. And neither is Arthur flamin' Kendricks.'

'Doesn't matter,' said Minnie stiffly. 'We're going out dancing anyway. Tonight. Can I borrow this dress?'

'Aye, you may,' Junie told her sweetly. 'And I hope he treats you just like a lady.'

Arthur came to the front door and knocked at seven o'clock that night. He was dressed in a navy blue suit with wide collars and an immaculately pressed cream shirt.

'You look a right bobby-dazzler,' he told Minnie as she stood shyly for inspection in the back parlour. Like a miracle, Junie's cream and purple summer dress clung to her perfectly, making her look curvaceous and bold. Junie had even helped set her hair nicely, in close-cropped curls around her beaming, well-scrubbed face. ('No make-up,' Junie had warned. 'You're best going for the natural look, I think.')

Betty, Harry, Derek and Junie all stared at the elegant and gobby individual who had come to squire their lass about the town. Betty was gabbling nervously the whole time, as if Arthur really was someone famous who was gracing their home with his presence. 'We all thought – wonders will never cease! Our Minnie is such a homebody. She's always working on Saturday night, or, if she's not, she's sat round here hunched over that sewing machine. She's a good worker, you see. She's always been a good worker.'

Minnie looked embarrassed at the way her mother went chuntering on. She watched on as the two most important men in her life warily shook hands with the dashing Arthur.

'How's your training going?' Arthur asked Derek, his eyes twinkling merrily.

'Aye, champion,' Derek muttered.

'Enjoying the thrill of the open road, are you?' Arthur grinned.

'It's not exactly the open road,' Derek shrugged. 'But, aye, I'm loving it. It's good.'

'Derek's got ambition,' Junie put in proudly. 'We've got our hearts set on bettering ourselves. We're going in for one of the new posh houses that they're building on the new estates. What about that, eh?'

Everyone looked at Junie, because this was the first that anyone had heard of it.

'I thought you were moving in with your mother?' Betty glared at her daughter-in-law.

'That's an interim measure,' Junie declared. 'But we've got our hearts set on bigger and better things, haven't we, Derek?'

He sat back down in his chair. 'Aye, we have, lass, aye.'

Harry was fixing Arthur with a challenging look. 'Just you take good care of our Minnie, Arthur Kendricks. Just you treat her like the princess she is.' Harry's voice quavered oddly as he stood there, looking rather shambolic in his saggy cardigan and his slippers. There was a fierceness in his voice as he told Arthur: 'She's the best one of us, you know. She's very precious to us, is our Minnie.'

Arthur gave a theatrical bow and promised Minnie's dad, 'I will treat her like she's made of Lalique glass, Mr Minton.'

'And have her back by midnight, an' all,' Harry added.

Minnie beamed happily at her dad's overprotectiveness and also at the gallantry of Arthur. She allowed herself to be swept up and escorted to the front door, knowing that everyone's eyes were on her.

As it turned out, the dancing didn't finish till almost two in the morning.

Chapter Thirty

In later years, Minnie would marvel at how that night shaped their lives. It was only a night at the dance, at the Albert Hall, where the band played so loudly the floorboards seemed to shake and rattle underfoot all night long. People were stamping and jumping and going crackers. Were they all going mad? Everyone was red, sweat streaming down their faces. The band was playing some hectic jazzy number that seemed to have far too many beats in the bar.

'It's mad in here,' she shouted at Arthur, who was grinning at all the noisy hullabaloo.

'Oh Minnie Minton,' he said. 'You don't get out much, do you, lovey?'

It was quite true that she didn't. When everyone else was dancing and jitterbugging and doing all this stuff, she was generally shovelling hot golden chips or pulling dark pints of ale. She was used to being the server and definitely not the one out having fun.

'Come and dance,' he told her, pushing through the crowd, elbowing and jostling his way through, just like he had every right to be here.

And why not? Minnie thought. *Why, we both have every right to be here, don't we? We're young, same as everyone else. Youngish, at any rate.*

There was an almost feverish excitement in the air. More and more servicemen were coming back home each week, and when they did, many of them seemed determined to get out and enjoy themselves.

'I think someone's plopped some gin in the fruit punch,' Arthur mused as he started twirling Minnie about.

I'm being twirled about, she thought excitedly and found herself simply going with the flow. Without the aid of drink, she found herself utterly relaxing as Arthur led her in the dance. She picked up his moves easily and felt unabashed in mirroring his extravagant gestures. She secretly blessed the private hours she had spent in the scullery with the radio on, practising on her own. How she'd longed for a moment like this during all those endless hours, dancing on her own on the hard tiles.

Years afterwards, she would think of this as a turning point. It was the very moment – for good or bad – that Arthur let her into his world. The door was opened a tiny crack the second he'd impulsively asked her out for that Saturday night. Almost straight away, that odd couple realised that they adored being in each other's company. They danced up a storm inside a bubble of their own pleasure, grinning and laughing into each other's faces.

Oh, would that I could stay dancing all my life to this wonderful jazz, Minnie thought fleetingly as there came a pause between numbers and a girl singer in an emerald-green dress got up on stage. *Why can't I just stay dancing forever?* Minnie wondered.

'Oh, help, here we go,' chortled Arthur. 'Just listen to this.'

He was nodding in the direction of the girl on the stage. Minnie vaguely recognised her in her heavy make-up and bright costume. 'Isn't that Lily Johnson from the butcher's on Fowler Street?' she frowned.

'Fancies herself as a singer,' Arthur said, nudging her. 'Have a listen.'

It was an old Cole Porter song. For a moment, Minnie had bother identifying it, because Lily was mangling the words, the tempo, the melody; everything. 'Good God,' Minnie said. 'She's just . . . shouting it!'

It was 'Let's Do It', she realised, and as she realised, Arthur swept her up to dance again. The band was still good, even if the vocals were ropey.

What gave her the confidence to get up there and sing like that? Minnie wondered, wanting to laugh. Was it because she came from that criminal family? Did people think they'd be beaten up if they laughed her off the stage? Lily was known for having rough uncles and brothers who protected her and defended the honour of her family's notorious name. Surely that gave her all the confidence she ever needed.

'She looks like the Wicked Witch of the West in all that green,' she told Arthur and he hooted appreciatively.

'Look,' he said. 'Would you mind if I left you for a moment?'

He was so polite. 'Of course not,' she said, and drifted off to the punch bowl and the dainty little glasses, helping herself happily as Arthur went off. She assumed he went to use the lav or to get some air outside.

'Minnie!' someone called, and she was glad to see Bella Franchino there, looking beautiful and elegant as ever. She was standing with her red-haired boyfriend . . . Jonas, was he called? Oh, help. Wasn't he one of the mad Johnsons, too? Minnie seemed to recall that there'd been some gossip about the surviving Franchino girl running about with a member of the criminal fraternity.

'Eeeh, is that your sister up on the stage?' Minnie asked the handsome fella.

'Aye, it is indeed,' Jonas grinned, sipping what turned out to be rather strong punch.

'She's got a powerful set of lungs on her, that girl,' Minnie commented and Bella laughed at this.

'Are you out with Arthur?' Bella asked her. 'We could see you dancing. My, you're not shy, are you?'

'Oh no. Do you mean we looked daft?' Minnie gasped. She could feel her bravado about to crumble in the face of Bella's criticism. Bella was so composed and sweet. She would never stamp and shout and get all sweaty on the dance floor, Minnie was quite sure.

'No, no.' Bella was vehement, seeing that she'd made Minnie self-conscious. 'Not at all. You two looked as if you were having an absolute whale of a time.'

'We were.' Minnie grinned.

'You were dancing – the pair of you – like there was no one else in the room. I sort of envy that . . . kind of forgetting there's anyone looking on. The two of you were in a world of your own.'

Minnie beamed. 'Arthur is a great dancer.'

'I know,' said Bella. 'But, do you know, I think you're a match for him. You know, I never knew that you two were such good pals?'

'We aren't really,' Minnie shrugged. 'I never really knew him well until this week. But we just sort of chime in with each other, do you know what I mean? We get along. We laugh at the same things. And it turns out we can dance together, too.'

Bella's eyes twinkled and she smiled at the girl from number fifteen Frederick Street. By, it was good to see her with some colour in her cheeks. She was a canny lass, and she always had a friendly word for everyone. It would be smashing to see her fixed up with a nice fella, wouldn't it?

Except . . . Bella knew Arthur all too well. She had lived with him and his sister for several months after the bombing of the Franchino home and the loss of all her family. Oh, Arthur and Mavis had been a loyal, wonderful, loving new family to Bella and she would forever be in their debt. They were like extra siblings to her, but for that reason she knew rather more about their inner lives than she really wanted to. Bella knew all about Arthur's foibles and proclivities. Why, she knew things about him that he probably didn't realise she knew. Bella was a watchful and clever person. She was loyal and discreet, but she wasn't blind to the failings of those she loved.

'Just don't get hurt,' she found herself warning the excited Minnie that night. 'Promise me?'

'I'm not going to be hurt,' Minnie laughed. 'I'm not daft. And I've only come out for a bit of a dance. Arthur's not interested in me. Not at all. Are you kidding? No way.'

They laughed then, and looked back at the stage, where the noisy Lily Johnson was being replaced at the microphone by a surprise guest singer. Minnie and Bella gasped to see that Arthur had managed to inveigle himself up onto the stage. He had shed his jacket and unbuttoned his waistcoat. He was smiling at the whole audience like he had the lot of them in the palm of his hand.

'This is for Minnie!' he called out with a wave and counted the band in for an impromptu extra number.

It was Cab Calloway's 'Minnie the Moocher', which he sang with hugely entertaining relish. Effortlessly, he got the crowd at the Albert Hall joining in and singing along with all the call-and-response bits. Minnie squashed her flaming-red face between her hands and hooted with mirth. A red-hot hootchie-cootchie, indeed! Oh, she'd murder him when he came down from that stage.

Ah, but she loved it all, though. She adored every minute of it, and everyone looking round to see that she was the girl he was singing to. She lapped up the attention and squealed with glee.

*

That was the night that everything changed for Minnie Minton – or Minnie the Moocher, as Arthur started calling her on their chilly walk back to the Sixteen Streets that night. The sea mist was so chilly, it made their sweat-soaked clothes stick to their worn-out bodies.

'You're walking in the wrong direction, Arthur,' she told him, when she realised.

'I'm seeing you all the way home,' he told her firmly, sounding just a little bit drunk.

'You're a proper gentleman,' she told him, linking his arm in hers.

'There's nothing proper about me,' he said, and a hint of self-pity came out in his voice. 'I'm an improper gentleman, that's what I am.'

'There's nothing improper about you.' She wouldn't have any criticism of him. He was amazing in her eyes. He was dazzling.

'Ah, Minnie,' he told her. 'I knew we were going to be good pals. Even ages ago, when you were just the girl at the chip shop. I always thought – there's something special about that girl. She's worth getting to know.'

Minnie's heart rose in her chest like a full moon and it felt like it was about to burst. 'I can't believe that you'd think I was special. Me!' She shook her head laughing. 'Why, you're the one who stands out, man. Everyone looks at you. You're special. You're talented.'

He shrugged like it all meant nothing to him. 'Aye, I know. I know, pet. But you've caught my eye. And that's strange, you know?'

'Strange?' she frowned, slowing down. 'Why's it strange? Because I'm strange?'

'Yes. You're strange. We're both strange. We both stand out a mile. We're not like any of the rest round here, Minnie the Moocher.'

'Aren't we? What's wrong with us? Why aren't we the same?'

He danced her out into the middle of the empty street and whirled her about in the frosty air. 'Because our lives are going to be different, Minnie. Our lives will be different to everyone else's.'

Chapter Thirty-One

By the time that Junie and her small family were settled back with her mother at number twenty-one, Junie was pregnant again. They spent Christmas that year celebrating happily and anticipating new arrivals. 'Twins,' Junie told her mother gleefully, as soon as she knew.

Well, Cathy was delighted by everything these days. Her life had definitely taken a turn for the better. Her house was completely chock-a-block with family, and she couldn't have been happier. That Christmas was noisy and busy and she could barely catch her breath between looking after everyone at home and keeping the Robin Hood going. She even invited Derek's parents and sister over to share Christmas dinner, which they did. Unfortunately, relations with Betty were still quite frosty. She still resented the young family deserting her.

Ivy was just about old enough to enjoy Christmas and to be made a fuss of. The person she seemed happiest with was her Uncle Bob – Cathy's fancy man, as Junie insisted on calling the affable pot man. He was so affable he didn't mind the bairn clinging to him and calling his name, and he didn't mind the ironic jibes of Junie Minton.

Cathy was just glad that there were no more dramas. The war was well over and, though its dreadful legacy still hung over the world in so many ways, things were gradually getting back to normal. She felt she could breathe a huge sigh of relief and start enjoying her life again.

That Christmas night, as her houseful of people lay about in a satiated, happy stupor, Cathy found herself thinking back to other years under this roof. She remembered gloomier, darker times when her old husband, Noel, had been alive. Also, she was careful to remember the happier times she had shared with him, when his elderly mother, Theresa, had still been there, back when Cathy was a young bride. Yes, it certainly wasn't all bad back then, but it had been hard. Life was all about finding a place where you could fit in and feel welcome. Life was – as far as Cathy was concerned – all about making that place and role work out as best you could. And she had tried. God knew, but she had tried her best. Now, perhaps this happy, contented household was her just reward for all those years of holding everything together.

Why, even the sometimes spiky and difficult Junie seemed contented this year. Maybe motherhood had made her milder? It had softened all the resentment in her young heart, Cathy thought, and she was glad of that.

At about seven o'clock on Christmas night, they waved the Mintons back off to their home down the street. Minnie was still wearing the paper hat from her cracker. She was off to meet her friend, Arthur, and the Minton parents were going to church. They'd all stirred themselves out of their blurry tiredness to brave the frost. Cathy, too, had to get herself roused and ready to open up the Robin Hood for her regulars for just an hour or two.

'Thank you, Mum,' Junie told her earnestly, and Cathy's heart glowed at her daughter's words. 'Let me and Derek do all the cleaning up in the scullery and the front room. You put your feet up.'

Well. Cathy could barely credit it. She went off to sit in the parlour with her granddaughter. Gentle Bob passed her over with a warm smile and then he put on his cap. 'I'll be off to see me Mam and all that lot,' he mumbled, and slipped out of the house.

When Derek was well underway with the dishes, Junie sat down opposite her mam. 'I thought I'd tell you. We've got our name down for a nice little house on a new estate that's going to be going up. We'll be the first in line, the council say.'

Cathy stared at her. 'What, already? When did you do this?'

'Soon as we knew it was happening. You have to jump in quick with these things, before it's too late.'

'But . . . aren't you happy here?'

'Yes, of course . . . Well, we don't want to get too much under yours and Bob's feet . . .'

'You aren't. And there'll be more room when I've got old Noel's attic bolthole cleared out at last . . .'

At the mention of the old man's attic retreat, Junie gave a noticeable shudder. The awful memory came back to her unbidden, of how that old crookback had cornered her up there so many years ago. It was the very night he had died. He had been proposing all kinds of things to her. Junie hated to think about it now. He was going to swindle Cathy, and betray her. Why, he had even proposed unmentionable things to his own stepdaughter. He had deserved – hadn't he? – to wind up falling down those rickety stairs to the very bottom. Junie could still see his twisted, ominously still figure lying there.

Horrible thoughts. She shook her bonny head to clear them from her mind. 'No, no, Mam, you don't have to make extra room for us. We'll have our own home. Next year. This time next year, we'll be settled into our own place on the new estate by the Nook.'

'You'll be miles away,' Cathy moaned, hating the softness in her voice. Softness and dismay. She was welling up with disappointment.

'Well, look how far away I was when I lived in Manchester,' Junie laughed. 'You weren't so bothered then, were you?'

'Of course I was. I missed you dreadfully.'

'Well, never mind,' Junie shrugged. 'It's all decided now.'

Cathy hugged the quiet bairn to her chest. 'But how will you furnish a whole house? What are you going to sit on and lie on? You can't afford—'

Junie interrupted her. 'I've some money put by ready for all of that.'

'But . . .'

'We have to do it, Mam, we're going to be a proper little family. It's going to be a new world. It's going to be a bright, new, clean house with large windows and – if we're lucky – a view of the sea over the White Leas. It's our chance, don't you see? We can get away from these dark and dingy little streets.'

Cathy hardly knew what to say to that. Her heart flared in annoyance, but, truly, she knew what her daughter meant. You could scrub your net curtains and your windows and your front doorstep as much as you liked. You could keep your little home immaculate inside. But it was still a poky house in a terrace down by the docks, where the clouds of smoke went up from the chimneys and rubbed soot on every brick and every pane of glass. It was still dark and shadowy on even the sunniest days. Yes, her daughter was right to be keen to get away to somewhere brighter and lighter and new.

'We won't be so far away, you know,' Junie said. 'It's just a short ride on the tram.'

Cathy spent the evenings of the rest of that festive season behind the bar of her pub. Aunty Martha played the piano when she was in, jollying everyone alone. The Women's Table filled up with the usual faces and the women grumbled about their menfolk and laughed together about the daft things their kids got up to.

It was a time for sighing with relief that people were home and safe and there were no big dramas going on. *Come on, Cathy urged herself. Be happy, be content. Why, it could be months before they get their house on the new estate and leave you alone.*

She wouldn't be completely alone, even then. She'd still have Bob.

'You're thinking about Junie and them,' he told her when he came up from the pub cellar, wiping his large hands with a rag.

'I think part of it is that it makes me feel so old,' she laughed. 'They're having a fresh start. I feel so old and clapped out.'

Bob went to her and took his beloved in his arms. She thrilled all over again — just as she always did — to be in Bob's arms. Nowadays, it was all right to do this where just anyone could see. At the start, it had been so clandestine and furtive. Now, even Bob's overprotective mother, Ma Ada, accepted their relationship. Cathy was something like ten years his senior and no one round here even thought twice about their mismatch. They were just glad they were both happy.

'You will never be old,' Bob told her. 'You're not the type.'

She laughed at him and buried her face in his neck. She loved to nuzzle the soft skin above his collarbone, where she could feel his strong pulse beating through the skin like tom-tom drums and there was a lovely scent that was just his alone. He was her Bob: simple and straightforward, and it anguished him so much when she wasn't completely happy. He had trouble figuring out the complexities of other people's emotions and it upset him to see Cathy stewing over her worries. 'It's all right, love,' she told him. 'I won't be sad about them moving away. They're right. They need the space and their own life, away from me.'

Later, when she sat at the Women's Table with Ma Ada and Winnie, Cathy found herself wondering idly where Junie had got the money she claimed to have put by for furniture. She'd never mentioned having a nest egg before. Why, it wasn't so long since she was pleading destitution . . .

Cathy sighed. She had to give up being suspicious of her daughter and her motives. Junie's wild and spiteful years were at an end. She was happy and content and there were no more secrets and resentments anymore.

Betty Minton came up to sit with them, nursing a pint of stout. She was red in the face and reeking of chip fat as usual. 'Happy New Year, lasses,' she told them all. She nodded in the direction of old Winnie, who could be relied upon for a prophecy or two at this time of year. 'Have you seen anything in the tea leaves, Winnie love? What have you seen coming our way in the future?'

To everyone's shock, Winnie looked up at Betty Minton with a haggard expression. Her wild white hair seemed as if it was standing up in shock. Her eyes fixed on the fish bar owner's and her mouth moved soundlessly.

'Winnie, are you all right, pet?' Ma Ada cried. 'I've never seen her like this. I think she's having a stroke.'

Winnie stood up and her stool tipped backwards onto the floor. Her friends gathered round her, ready to catch her when she crumpled to the ground. She stood there frozen, however, her face in a rictus of fear.

It turned out that Winnie was – after a lifetime of chicanery and nonsense – having a genuine prognostication at last.

'*Death!*' she cried in a hollow and dreadful voice. 'Death is coming to your house.'

Everyone looked at Betty Minton.

'Hadaway, Winnie,' she growled. 'That's not funny. That's a bliddy awful thing to say to someone.'

'No, no, I mean it,' said Winnie, as she gradually returned to herself and had to be helped back into her seat. 'It's true. I can see it plain as anything. The angel of death is standing over you, Betty. Like a miasma, plain as anything. Believe me, hinny, Death is coming to your house.'

Chapter Thirty-Two

Derek wanted to make sure that his sister was all right.

'Pardon?' she asked.

'It's all been very fast, this,' he told her gruffly. The two of them were taking a brisk walk around the top of the town, early in the new year. They were up by the Roman remains, where great hunks of worn, ancient stone stuck out of the dirty slush and frost. From here, there was a marvellous view of the sweeping bay and the rooftops of South Shields.

'What's been fast?' she frowned.

'Life, all of it,' he shrugged. 'For both you and me, in recent months.'

'Oh,' Minnie said. 'Well, your life has changed more than mine has. You're a married man with all these responsibilities and even more bairns on the way. And Junie. You've got a lot on your plate, our Derek.'

'And don't I know it,' he mumbled. 'But I'm thinking about you, and this Arthur fella. You've never run around with someone like him before. This is a big change for you.'

Minnie laughed at him. 'I'm hardly running around with him. We've just had a few nights out. He's a new friend, who just happens to be a fella.'

'He's a funny fella . . .'

'He's hilarious,' Minnie grinned. 'Sometimes he makes me laugh so much I start crying. I've never laughed like that in ages.'

'I mean funny peculiar,' Derek said tersely, striding on ahead in his long coat. It was a dark lambswool coat she had found for him, rummaging in the stock of the market stall run by her friend Susan. It had been Minnie's Christmas present to him, and Derek was very proud of it and the figure he cut with its black astrakhan collar. 'I see him at work, remember, and I see how he carries on all the time. The messing on – it never stops, and the kinds of jokes he makes. It's like . . . like he's up on the stage all the time, like he's already famous. I find it hard to describe . . .'

'He's like a force of nature,' Minnie smiled. 'And when I'm with him, he makes me see how pointless it is to be shy and how hopeless it is, sticking to the sidelines. He makes me feel brave, Derek. Do you know how I mean?'

Derek didn't, really. He just knew that Arthur made off-colour jokes in a loud, braying voice, and flirted with everyone in a hundred-yard radius. 'I don't want you to get hurt, sis. You're a bit of an innocent, really . . .'

Minnie pulled a face. 'Derek Minton, you're being a right softy, you are.'

'I don't want Arthur messing you about. He's much more worldly than you are . . .'

'Maybe,' she said.

They walked around the dark, dingy old Victorian school and the tall houses of this part of the town. The wind from the sea was brutal here, and it felt as if there was more snow on the way.

'I'll be all right,' Minnie told him. 'I'm just having a nice time with a new friend.'

'Promise me it won't go further than that,' he said.

'What do you mean?' She frowned at the idea of promising anything.

'Don't go saying yes to him if he proposes.'

'Proposes. Don't be daft.' She laughed at this and shook her head, but, secretly, Minnie had been getting her hopes up just recently. It was crazy and daft and quite impossible, but in the middle of the night, she had been dreaming of the strangest ideas.

Why shouldn't we be happy? Why shouldn't we be an odd couple? What's it got to do with anyone else?

'You worry too much,' she told her grumbling brother. 'You should put your energy into worrying about Junie. She's enough to keep anyone busy.'

After their brisk walk together, the two of them went down the steep streets to Ocean Road, where the misty windows and glowing lights of Franchino's beckoned them in. They ordered coffee and that croaky-voiced Mavis brought it to their table.

'Chilly enough for you out there?' she bellowed. She was having bother with her hearing aid again.

'It's bitter,' said Minnie. 'But that coffee looks nice and hot.'

The two of them sat while the waitress clip-clopped back and forth, shouting at the top of her voice.

'I reckon this place is going downhill,' Derek opined.

'It's fine,' said Minnie. 'Bella's got a lot on, running it by herself.'

Derek didn't look quite at home here, crammed into the dainty booth. He was used to places that were a bit more basic and down-to-earth. That was her brother all over, she thought. Down-to-earth, no frills. There was no side to him, no hidden ulterior motives or anything. He just struggled with his thoughts and always tried to say exactly what was on his mind. It was funny, really, that he should end up with someone whose thinking was as minxy and complex as Junie's was.

And to think, at one time, Minnie had followed Junie about, all adoringly, just like a lost puppy. It was hard to imagine, now. It must have aggravated Junie so much, looking back. Fancy being the object of such schoolgirl longings. Because that's all they had been, really. Minnie understood that now. Such a crush, like the one she had once had on Junie, it was just a natural part of growing up. She was grateful that Junie hadn't turned on her and smashed her feelings. She could have, oh yes indeed. Junie could be as fierce as that stiff north wind they had braved on their walk today. But, instead, she had been relatively gentle with Minnie. Minnie could see that, now that she was looking back at their years of friendship.

Minnie felt like she understood so much more about human relationships and everything now. Why, she was getting to be old enough and ugly enough, wasn't she?

'Honestly, Derek, everything is good,' she assured her fretful brother. 'I'm going to be just as happy as you and Junie are. You'll see.'

He sipped his frothy coffee, but he still looked concerned. Arthur Kendricks was far too flashy, he thought. Minnie was dazzled by him, that's what it was.

'Come and see my mother,' Arthur urged her when it was his day off.

Minnie's jaw dropped. 'Your mother?' she gasped. 'I thought you and Mavis were orphans?'

But now that she thought about it, wasn't there some other story? It had gone round in a whisper, several years ago. Minnie could remember her mother and Ma Ada and others discussing it all at the Women's Table. Hushed voices and squawks of amazement. Then there was some posh old bird at the Robin Hood, wasn't there? A fancy old dame with frosted hair and expensive clothes, at some celebration one time? She'd been something to do with Arthur and Mavis . . . What was the story again?

Minnie found it hard to keep track of all the secret, scandalous stories of her neighbours. They twisted and tangled around like tramlines, all over the town.

'She's my adoptive mother, really,' Arthur told her, with a shrug. 'She bought us!'

Minnie stopped in her tracks. The two of them had taken the tram all the way along the coastal road and walked a little further on. They were almost as far along as Sunderland by now. 'Bought you . . . ?!'

Arthur grinned at her, with his silk-lined coat flaring out around him and his greased-back hair coming untucked. 'Aye, that's right. For there's no varnishing the truth of it. She bought us from the bloody wicked Johnson clan. Old Ma Johnson used to do a roaring trade in lost bairns and orphans in the old days. Me and our Mavis were picked up off the streets and we were sold off to this wife who lived in a grand house by the sea. Elizabeth Kendricks.'

Something clicked in Minnie's memory. 'I remember hearing something about this now . . .'

'Ha!' Arthur tossed his head and carried on walking briskly along the coastal path. 'Aye, we'd have been the gossip of the Sixteen Streets for a while. I heard that old Elizabeth turned up at Mavis and Sam's wedding uninvited and all hell broke loose in the church. Mavis wasn't at all happy to have our adoptive mother back in her life . . .'

'Why was that?' Minnie tried to keep up with his long strides. 'What had she done?'

'Ah, it was all very complicated,' Arthur sighed. 'But, really, after all these years and looking back, I don't think that our second mammy meant anything bad. She never meant us any harm, not really. She bought us like big dolls, really. We were just like playthings to her. She was prepared to lavish us with love and everything we wanted, but she could hardly believe it when we turned out to have ideas of our own. And we answered back to her, too. She thought we were proper guttersnipes . . . and we were, an' all.'

Minnie gasped. 'She's still alive, is she? And is that where you're taking me? Is that where we're going today?'

'Yes, we are,' he nodded firmly. 'It's time I showed my face and said hello to the old woman. She deserves that much. She was good to us, in her own way.'

'I see . . .' Minnie slowed down and felt a nervous dread coming over her. She wasn't sure why. She didn't feel dressed well enough to go visiting the fancy home of some posh old woman who had once bought her bairns off the black market. Minnie didn't feel at all equipped to deal with such an encounter today. Why, she'd had no warning at all. 'Do we have to do it now? Can't we just go home again? Look at me, I'm just in my ordinary clothes. I can't go getting introduced to someone special looking like this . . .'

Arthur swung round and surveyed her quite earnestly. 'Yes, you can. You look fine. You're just you. She should take you how she finds you.'

Minnie wasn't sure whether this was a compliment or not. It didn't sound much like one, and it wasn't very reassuring, either.

'Elizabeth always needed lessons in accepting people just how they were,' Arthur observed. 'She was obsessed with moulding them into what she wanted, so everyone and everything was bent to her will. It was all surface appearances with her. Quite shallow, really. No, it will do her some good, Minnie – to be introduced to someone as real as you are.'

Minnie blinked. 'As real as I am? Is that what I am?'

'Oh yes, you're the realest person I know.'

'And that's good, is it?'

'Of course.' He laughed. 'The world is full of people who put on airs, who never say what they mean. They're all slippery customers. But you, Minnie Minton, you're wonderfully real.' He grinned at her and grabbed her cold hand in his. 'Now, come along and meet my mum.'

They came to a pause at some tall gates in front of a large house right by the sea. It was in dire need of a lick of paint, Minnie thought. But what a place it was. It really was fit for a queen.

Chapter Thirty-Three

Minnie had never felt so out of place in all her life.

As they sat before the roaring fire in the room Mrs Kendricks kept calling her 'drawing room', Minnie was shooting Arthur anguished glances. 'Let's get out of here,' her eyes kept telling him, 'I feel so bliddy uncomfortable.'

Arthur was quite aware of what she was trying to say, but he didn't take a blind bit of notice. He carried on sipping his tea from a porcelain cup, looking around at the opulent room and grinning at the old woman on the settee opposite.

By, they were in a palace, Minnie thought. You'd never have known from the dowdy outside that this big old place was like this indoors. It was like a stately home or somewhere the queen might live if she kept a residence in South Shields.

The owner of the property was watching them very carefully, her own tea cooling on the antique coffee table between them. She was very smartly dressed in an outfit that seemed to come from a period after the previous war, with its high neck and puffy sleeves. She had a watchful, hawk-like expression on her skinny old face. She might have been old, but her eyes were sharp and bright still.

'So, Arthur,' she said at last in a voice like desiccated leaves. 'I'm glad to see you all in one piece and safely home. Thank you for letting me know you had returned from your war duties.'

Arthur nodded graciously and Minnie gasped. Safely home. Why, it was simply ages since he had returned from Burma. Was this the first time he had come to see his adoptive mother in person since then?

'It can't have been easy out there,' Mrs Kendricks said. She looked like something was paining her, or that she had something huge and weighty on her mind. With a flash of inspiration, Minnie realised that this was to do with her holding her feelings inside. The woman was all racing emotions and upset inside, Minnie could tell, but she was doing everything she could to preserve a calm and cool exterior. What a strange thing to do, Minnie thought. What was the point of that?

'It was something I'll never forget,' Arthur told the old woman, sounding just as cool and distant in his tone as she did. 'I've never known discomfort and misery like it. I saw some dreadful things. Monstrous brutality and wickedness. But I've never had friends like that either. Comrades that I lost. Some who survived. And I learned so much.' He shrugged. 'I became a man.'

Elizabeth Kendricks nodded approvingly. 'You look very well, son. And what about Mavis? She's not been to see me in an age, either.'

'She and Sam are doing well. You know she lost her bairn.'

Elizabeth nodded sorrowfully. 'The Lord giveth and he taketh away.'

'Quite,' said Arthur. 'And so they're trying for another one, apparently. They are happy, despite everything, in the little house that you bought for me and her.'

The old woman looked like she thought buying a house for someone was nothing, a mere frippery. 'Life is returning to normal,' she said. 'Except for here. Things are frozen here, in my house. Worse than that. They are falling apart.'

'The old house looks like it could do with some maintenance, and a lick of paint . . .' he suggested.

She pulled a face. 'I've not quite summoned up the energy to keep it all in one piece. A bomb landed, you know? A short way along the cliffs. It blew in my lovely conservatory. It just all flew away like a shower of fairy dust, leaving a great big hole in the side of the house. All the staff went, too. They all left me to take up duties elsewhere.' She looked at Arthur with great self-pity in her pale eyes. 'I have been alone and lonely for so long, Arthur.'

To Minnie's astonishment, Arthur didn't jump in to say things that would make her feel better. He didn't rush to make promises, or apologise for leaving her on her own. He simply nodded quietly and reached for a dainty cake from the plate in front of him. They were rather stale, as Minnie had already discovered, as if they had been in a tin somewhere for much too long.

After their stilted tea in the drawing room, Elizabeth Kendricks led them on a small tour of her house. She walked stiffly, with the aid of a cane, and Minnie thought she could see a minute sign of concern in Arthur's face as he watched the old woman lead them from room to room.

The house, as they explored it, was in a worse state than they had both thought. The drawing room was the best preserved of all the rooms. The rest were all in a shabby, distressed state, made blurry with dust and cobwebs.

'You'll have to forgive me for not tidying for your visit,' Elizabeth said. 'You've rather caught me on the hop.'

'That's all right,' Arthur said. 'It's your house. You can live how you want.'

'Yes,' she agreed sadly. 'I've no one to think of, have I?'

Minnie looked at the two of them and couldn't believe how strange they were with each other. Was this how rich and fancy people carried on? They were like people who'd barely met before. Minnie tried to imagine what it would be like seeing her own mam, years after a falling-out. They'd be weeping and wailing and yelling at each other. They'd be pulling out each other's hair and then they'd be falling into each other's arms. But these two . . . it was as if they barely had any emotions at all.

Upstairs, they surveyed the bedrooms. Arthur's and Mavis's rooms were preserved just as they had been when they had left, as children. Toys and expensive clothes were displayed as if it was a kind of museum. Arthur went over to stroke the face of a doll his sister had loved so much and had been so upset to leave behind. 'So long ago,' he murmured.

Elizabeth agreed. 'So long ago, and a lot of water under the bridge. All the bad feeling is washed away, I hope . . .?'

'Oh, yes, in my case, certainly,' he nodded. 'I don't have any bitter feelings about the past. Mavis is a different story, of course. She feels things very strongly. She's a tightly wound-up mass of furious feelings about almost everything.'

'She was never as attached to me as you were,' Elizabeth sighed. 'You were my little angel, Arthur. You were the favourite, even though it was wrong of me to have a favourite. You were adorable and so loving when you were little. Mavis was rather harder to love.'

There was a rush of mixed feelings playing across Arthur's face. He looked both triumphant and annoyed at the same time. 'You should have loved us both as much as each other. You were our mother.'

Elizabeth smiled. 'You both ran away and left me. You broke my heart.'

'It needed breaking,' he told her. 'It was made of china, your heart. All you cared about was possessions and being fancy. We were just more belongings to you. We were something for you to show off.'

The old woman sat down heavily in a painted wickerwork chair. It barely creaked beneath her slight weight. 'You, perhaps, were worth showing off. You were my pride and joy – why, your voice was like a miracle. Yes, I was so proud of you when you sang for my friends. But Mavis? No, I wasn't very proud of her. I tried to dress her up and kept her clean. But she was no kind of ornament, was she?' Elizabeth gave a strange, rasping laugh.

Poor Mavis, Minnie was thinking, her heart going out to the pale, thin girl. Fancy being treated like that from being a bairn. Always left out, always the inferior one. Why, no wonder she had run away from this place and preferred living on the streets.

With a jolt, Minnie realised that Elizabeth Kendricks was staring at her. Minnie put a hand up to fluff her close-cropped curls. *Why didn't I put on a dab of make-up? A nicer frock? Why couldn't Arthur have told me we were visiting here this afternoon? I feel such a dowdy mare, cowering under the complacent gaze of this old wifey.*

'Now, you must tell me about your companion, Arthur,' Elizabeth said.

'She's my best friend,' said Arthur.

'A special friend?'

'Perhaps.'

'I see.' She glared at Minnie. 'Come closer, would you, dear?'

The light coming through the unscrubbed windows was clear and silvery. It was a stunning view from this bedroom: a vast stretch of sea and sky. Fancy growing up here and seeing this view every day. Minnie flinched at all the exposed brightness of afternoon sky. She moved towards the old woman, feeling like she was about to reach out with her arthritic claw and scratch her.

'Minnie lives on Frederick Street,' Arthur told his adoptive mother. 'Quite close to where Mavis's husband, Sam, grew up.'

'N-next door,' Minnie said. 'The Farleys are next door to us Mintons.'

A shadow of dismay crossed the old woman's face. 'Is that a fact?'

Arthur smirked. 'Oh yes. And Minnie often works in her mother's business with her.'

'Business, eh?' asked Elizabeth.

Arthur enunciated very carefully, 'Swetty Betty's Fish Bar at the top of Frederick Street.'

Elizabeth couldn't help but show the disgust she felt. 'What a vulgar name.'

Arthur hadn't finished yet. 'Minnie also works as a barmaid at the Robin Hood public house. And on Saturdays she works on a junk stall in the marketplace.'

Minnie stood there having her life laid out for the old woman to comment on. She felt helpless and humiliated by the relish in Arthur's tone.

Elizabeth looked supercilious as she said, 'What a very busy young woman you must be.'

Minnie didn't know what to say. All she could do was agree. 'I am, yes. But I like being busy.'

'Well, that's good,' said Elizabeth. 'Arthur, would you help me up? This chair is rather low and, as you can see, I have become somewhat enfeebled . . .'

'You're not feeble,' he said encouragingly, helping her back to her feet.

'Shall we have more tea?' Elizabeth said brightly.

'I particularly wanted you to meet Minnie today,' Arthur said.

'Oh yes?' The old woman looked ditheringly about her, as if she was eager to leave the room. She tapped the dusty carpet with her cane impatiently. 'Why's that?'

'Because we have fallen in love with each other,' Arthur said abruptly. 'And I want to marry her. I don't want to be like Mavis and leave you out of everything. I want to tell you everything that's going on. This is Minnie and I want her to be my wife.'

Elizabeth Kendricks's whole body convulsed with shock and she had to sit down on the end of the bed. 'What . . .?'

Minnie almost fell down in a dead faint. 'What? You've never even asked me.'

Arthur looked very solemn. He wasn't trying to be funny. None of this was a joke. 'Well, I'm asking you now. In front of the only mother I still have. Minnie Minton, will you be my wife?'

'Oh . . . Christ!' Minnie burst out, in a way that would have shocked her mother. 'Why couldn't you have warned me?'

Arthur shrugged. 'I didn't know when the right moment would fall. But it's now. It's definitely right now. I'll give you a wonderful life, Minnie. You see if I don't.'

By now, the old woman was panting and whinnying down her long, pointed nose like a horse that had just run a steeplechase. 'No, no . . .' she was moaning.

'All of this,' Arthur told Minnie, taking in the whole dilapidated house with one sweeping gesture of his hand. 'All of this will be yours. What do you say, Minnie, love? Say yes.'

Chapter Thirty-Four

At first, it seemed as if no one was going to believe her.

'Are you sure, our Minnie?' asked her mam the next morning. The two of them were having toast and Minnie stared as her mother scraped beef dripping on her burnt black crust. 'Might you not have misheard or got the wrong end of the stick? You know you can be quite fanciful at times.'

Later in the day, her dad was concerned that she wasn't about to get hurt. 'And he said this in front of this posh wifey, did he? The woman who brought him up? Why, I think he was just putting her on, man. He was winding her up. It's just some cruel joke at your expense.' Harry folded up his *Gazette* and gave her a sternly loving look. 'Pay no more heed to him, our Minnie. Don't let him make a fool of you.'

Her brother Derek heard about it that following night, when she was pouring him a pint of warm mild at the bar of the Robin Hood. 'I'll punch his lights out, that little creep,' he growled. 'Has he upset you, pet? He's toying with your affections, y'knaa. That's what it is.'

But it was all true. All of it. Minnie wanted to burst out and tell them. Everything Arthur had said and done in front of his adoptive mother was all for real and she knew it. She had seen his face and heard the tone of his voice. He who was never serious was deadly earnest in that moment. He fully intended to make Minnie his wife. The pair of them were good together, after all. He said it to Elizabeth Kendricks and he said it again, after they had left her dowdy mansion and were back on the tram going home. He sat there in his best long coat and a silk tie and he looked very pleased with himself all the way back to Ocean Road.

'So what do you think of that, Minnie Minton?' he had asked her. 'What do you think of my romantic proposal?'

She had been quite honest with him. 'I'm absolutely flabbergasted,' she'd said. 'But yes. Yes, let's do it. Let's do it all.'

'Really?' he'd beamed at her. 'You went dead quiet there. I thought you'd been struck dumb. I thought for a second you were going to refuse me.'

Minnie had grinned broadly. 'Let's get married.'

She had surprised herself, really. All the way home on the tram, her mind was racing faster than the metal wheels on the rails below. Had Arthur really said the things he had? Some of it was like a dream. Wandering around that old woman's house, listening to the pair of them discuss the past. In a way, it was like Minnie hadn't even been there with them. The old mother and son could have carried on talking and Minnie could have turned around and walked home again, all the way back, and she felt like they wouldn't have even been any the wiser. But then, then came the shock. Suddenly, Arthur was on about marrying her. He was telling Elizabeth that Minnie was the woman he loved.

It was all a load of old rubbish. That's what all her family thought. What else were they supposed to think? Anything that had to do with Arthur was just a daft joke surely. He was just some funny fella. The whole thing about him knocking about with their Minnie was a great big joke to him and she was going to get hurt at the end of it. All of the Mintons were in agreement about this.

Minnie wanted to shake every member of her family by the shoulders and ask them, 'Why won't you take me seriously?' But they wouldn't. Not about this. Arthur wasn't to be trusted and somehow Minnie had been taken under his spell. Couldn't they see it was real? It might not seem as such to them, but Minnie knew it was real. It felt real. They might not be like everyone else, but that didn't make them any less real.

'I was right never to trust him,' Derek said at the bar. 'I knew there was something off about him. Seriously, I'll thump him for you.'

Minnie laughed in exasperation. 'I don't want you to thump him. And I'm surprised to hear the way you talk about him, our Derek, what with the way he got you your new job and all. Why, without Arthur, you'd still be sweating yourself to death at the biscuit factory.'

'Aye, maybe,' grumbled Derek, who hated to feel beholden to anyone, especially funny blokes who were messing his sister about.

'It's all fine,' Minnie reassured him. 'Everything is wonderful. You'll see.'

But neither Derek nor anyone else looked convinced by Minnie's news.

The next day, she went to see Junie, who was thoroughly enjoying her pregnancy and taking advantage of her soft-hearted mother. She lay in a nest of cushions in the back parlour with a pile of cinema magazines and a bag of biscuit misshapes.

'Eeeh, you've gone huge!' Minnie gasped, staring at her belly.

'Remember your manners,' Junie warned her. 'You're supposed to say I look radiant.'

'You look radiant . . . and huge!' Minnie burst out.

Junie laughed at her. 'I feel like a walrus lying here. Look at my swollen ankles.'

'Poor you.'

Minnie made them both tea and couldn't wait to get sat down comfortably beside her recumbent friend to regale her with the news.

'You don't know already, do you?'

'Know what? I've not seen anyone today. Your mother's been by to take Ivy for a few hours, but that's it. No one tells me anything.'

'Arthur's asked me to be his wife.'

Junie spat out her tea on the embroidered cushions. 'You what, pet?'

Minnie drew herself up and sipped her cup daintily. 'Yes, it's true. It happened when we went to visit his well-to-do mother who adopted him, Elizabeth. She lives in this big house nearly all the way out to Sunderland. Well, my bloomin' eyes were coming out of my head, Junie. The place is in a bit of a state, really. She's had no staff since the war was on, and so it's all gone to rack and ruin, Arthur says. It was opulent when he was a bairn, he reckons. And we'll soon have it back to being how it was. It'll all be marvellous again and . . .'

Junie waved her hands about to quieten Minnie down for a second. 'Look, shut up, Minnie. Slow down. What are you talking about?'

Minnie was still gabbling. 'Well, it might be a bit odd at first, while Arthur's trying to get going with his career. He'll have to go on tour and that, all round the country, with shows and what-have-you. He's explained it all to me. What he really wants, you see, is a proper home base here in South Shields. He wants a proper family life . . .'

Junie's pale eyes were huge, glaring at Minnie. 'You're saying that he's asked you to marry him?'

'Out of the blue. It was as much of a shock to me as it is to you. And right in front of Mrs Kendricks, too. Well, the old woman just about had kittens. She was coughing and spluttering and gasping. It would have been funny, if it hadn't been so deadly serious.'

'Serious,' Junie repeated. 'You're actually going to marry him?'

'It won't be a fancy do. Probably something like yours, at the town hall, with just a couple of witnesses to get the official bit done. Then, perhaps when we've saved some money, we'll go on a bit of a honeymoon somewhere and splash out . . .'

Junie sat up straighter, putting down her cup and saucer and pushing her heap of film magazines to the floor. 'But you can't marry . . . Not him . . .'

Oh dear, Minnie thought. *Here we go again. Another one refusing to think I'm entitled to the ordinary happiness that everyone else seems to get.* 'And why's that?'

Junie's voice hardened. 'Are you daft? Are you blind? Because he's a great big nancy, that's why! Are you really so innocent, Minnie Minton?'

A nancy? No, it was a horrible word. She couldn't stand the sound of it. It was a dreadful thing to say about someone, too. It meant incriminating someone. Tarring them with a dreadful accusation. Fellas could go to prison for having things like that said about them. If you had thoughts like that, you had to keep them quiet. Junie knew that it was better to say nothing.

Minnie's mind swerved around the possibility that what Junie said, and what everyone else hinted at, could be true. Arthur was just someone who loved to make everyone laugh. He was like someone off the films or the music hall stage. If sometimes he was a bit womanish or fairyish, then that was all just part of his act, wasn't it? It hardly meant anything, did it?

Minnie wasn't as innocent as they all seemed to think she was. There was something different about her Arthur, of course there was. But it was stardust. It was star quality. It was simply magic that was clinging to him, that's what it was. People liked to say nasty things and drag other people down. They saw someone who trailed stardust and magic in their wake and they had to say nasty things about them.

Minnie very deliberately closed her mind to all the nasty speculation, including her own darker thoughts about Arthur. From now on, he was her Arthur and she was going to marry him. She was going to live in that grand palace of his mother's by the sea and she was going to turn it back into a glorious home again.

'What about your mother?' she asked him, one night as they walked the chilly streets, dreaming up their shared future. 'Won't she mind us both moving in?'

Arthur was amused by Minnie's qualms. 'Ah, lovely Minnie. So concerned about the feelings of others.'

'But it's her home. She's been mistress there for decades, you said. Maybe she won't take kindly to the girl from the local fish shop and boozer moving in?'

'You don't understand,' Arthur told her firmly. 'Old Elizabeth has begged me and my sister for years and years to move back in with her. She craves our company. She made a huge mistake – a whole load of huge mistakes – years ago and she lost the pair of us. She wanted to keep us like little dolls, like possessions, like perfect little children she had adopted. Then she wanted to separate us. She wanted to keep one but not the other. Well, we weren't having that, of course. So we took our fate into our own hands, me and my sister. We ran away to find our own lives, and we never looked back. Elizabeth Kendricks has wept and moaned and worn herself into a shadow of the woman she was, longing to have us back under her roof. Don't you see? My promising to move back is the best thing that's happened to her in twenty years.'

'But me as well,' Minnie said. 'She's getting me as well, remember. Maybe she won't be as chuffed about that . . .?'

'Oh, she will,' Arthur promised. 'Just you wait and see.'

Minnie wondered about the family she was getting herself into. It all sounded a bit dramatic and strange. Her heart went out to the two orphan children in the past and how they had refused to be separated.

They walked down Ocean Road, looking at all the lit-up windows of the pubs and the houses in the frosty, misty night. It was all a wonderful novelty still, to see lit windows without blackout curtains. It felt like a luxury to walk about and never hear the dreadful moaning of an air-raid siren and suddenly have to run for shelter. It felt smashing to simply walk where you wanted, holding onto the arm of a man who said he loved you. A man who you admired and felt enthralled by. She wasn't sure if this was love. Maybe it wasn't, maybe it was. Minnie couldn't really tell. But she was excited and it was like life was happening to her at last.

Chapter Thirty-Five

It was a shocking cold winter, and it was as much as they could all do to keep going through the snow and frozen days. Junie's pregnancy seemed to go on for a hundred years and she felt trapped inside the house, hardly daring to go out on the slippery pavements.

'Oh, I wish I'd never bothered,' she moaned. 'I wish we'd just stuck with the one.'

'You won't be saying that when the twins come,' her husband smiled at her.

'What if they never do come?' she wailed. 'What if I just keep on getting bigger and bigger . . .?'

Her mother Cathy was a great help to them both, taking over the task of looking after their Ivy, running the whole house about them, as well as the Robin Hood over the road. As she advanced into her middle years, Cathy was finding herself busier than she had ever been in her whole life. Oh, but how she loved it. How she loved being needed and right in the centre of things. She wasn't only a mammy, she was a nanna, too – and she doted on Ivy, her first angelic grandchild. That winter, she loved to dress the bairn up in all her beautifully handmade woollens and to take her for long walks around the park and the hills of town to get her out of Junie's hair.

Junie sat by the warmth of the range and penned regular letters to the council housing office. As the months went on, her dreams of having her own home grew more fervent and desperate. She felt like she would scream if she had to think of living for many more months in these dark streets. Winter's short days were really getting to her. She looked out of the white lace curtains of the back parlour and saw only a small, pearly patch of sky, and that was soon dark by the middle of the afternoon. She was longing for light and space and openness, and just a hint of a sea breeze.

'You can't say all of this!' Derek gasped in shock one day when he read one of the letters she was about to post to the man in the council office.

'Why not?'

'Because it's all lies. The things you say about your mother – she'd be horrified if she knew what you were saying to strangers, man.'

Junie shrugged her shoulders. 'I need to lay it on thick, don't I? That way, we stand a better chance of getting what we want and where we want to be.' She looked at her husband like he was a bit thick. He was certainly guileless. It would never occur to him to exaggerate things a bit in order to get what he wanted.

'Aye, but you can't go saying that she shouts at you and hits you. You can't go saying that she makes your life a misery.'

Junie looked at him blankly. 'Why ever not?'

'Because it's not true, man. Your bliddy mother's been a saint. She does everything for you. For both of us. You can't go saying these dreadful things about the poor old wife.'

Junie explained to him very patiently. 'Yes, she's been nice and helpful in the real world, of course. But that's different to the world that I have to create in order to get what I want. What would the council do if I told them that we're living very comfortably with my mother, eh? Nowt, that's what. We'd be flamin' stuck here forever.'

Grumbling, Derek left her to her letter-writing. She sat in her nightdress and quilted matinee jacket, working her way through the fancy stationery set that the unwitting Cathy had bought her for Christmas.

Derek disliked the subterfuge and the lying, but he had to admit that he too had dreams about the day when they would have a house of their own on the estate by the cliffs. It would be the beginning of a whole new, wonderful life for the young family. They would be away from the Sixteen Streets altogether, which was something he had never imagined. Like everyone else he knew, he had pictured himself living out all his life within these red-bricked walls. Junie had given him the spark of inspiration and the idea of leaving for somewhere better. Not all that far away, perhaps, just a couple of short miles, but it was far away enough.

The future felt like it was going to be brighter for the small but rapidly expanding family. They were going places now.

'Eeh, but your mam misses you being at home, you and Junie and the bairn.' His dad was sitting with him at the Robin Hood and he looked more doleful than Derek had seen him in ages.

'There'd have been no room, Da'.' Derek supped his pint of mild and looked pained. 'Also, she's writing to the council and saying that Cathy's beltin' her and making our lives miserable. Would you want her saying that about Mam?'

'Why's she saying that? It's never true, is it?'

'Of course not. She says it's strategic. It's just bending the truth a bit so that she gets her own way.'

Harry looked more hangdog than ever. 'She's a clever lass, your one. But I don't hold with lying like that. 'Specially not to the council and all that. It'll end in bother if she doesn't watch out.'

'You know Junie. She doesn't care. As long as she gets her own way.'

'Aye, she's a proper little madam, that one.'

They drank in quiet for a little while, content to rest at the end of the day in each other's slightly melancholic company. All around them, the public saloon was bustling and noisy. At the Women's Table, Mavis Farley was gabbling away with her cronies, yelling at the top of her voice as usual.

'And what's happening with our Minnie and her marriage plans?' Derek asked, with a humorous lilt in his voice. Like many of the others around Minnie, he strongly suspected that these matrimonial plans of hers would surely come to naught. Everyone could see what kind of fella her Arthur was. No one had ever been in any kind of a doubt. But she was all moony and daft about him these days. She was thriving on his attention and it was wonderful. That funny fella had really turned her head.

'It's all gone a bit quiet on that front, thank God,' said Harry. 'It's been a few days since she last mentioned him. He's been off in Newcastle, trying to get into all this theatre stuff he keeps going on about. I don't understand it all, to be honest. I try to keep out of it.'

'Theatre stuff, eh?' Derek mused. 'So he's still wanting to go on the stage, is he?'

'Why, aye, course he does. He's a proper bloody show-off.' Harry rolled his eyes. The times that Arthur had been visiting number fifteen Frederick Street, Harry had found him overpowering. He was too loud and over-familiar with everyone. He had made Betty whoop with laughter, of course, and that was a rare sight to see. Somehow he had the knack of activating her funny bone and she adored it when he was there among them. Betty treated him like visiting royalty. But to Harry Minton there was something off-putting about him.

Something that made him want to keep his distance . . . But if Betty adored him and Minnie was so daft about him, then Harry was determined to try to see the best in Arthur. He put his own instinctive feelings aside.

'Our Minnie's been working in that new shop, hasn't she?' Derek asked.

'Aye, she has.'

'That'll be keeping her mind off her fella being away in Newcastle.'

'Oh, it seems to be. She's very excited about it all. Mind, she's only on a trial run there. The oldest of those Chesney girls she doesn't get on with. She's a bit snooty and doesn't think our Minnie is good enough to work in her emporium.'

'Ha.' Derek shook his head. 'Emporium. Why, it's only a junk shop, isn't it?'

'Don't let our Minnie hear you say that,' his dad laughed. 'Why, to her it's wonderland. You should hear her talk about it. To hear her go on, you'd think it was the most fantastic place in all the world.'

'Minnie can be fanciful,' her brother admitted. 'She's changing, isn't she? It's like she's not quite our daft little Minnie anymore . . .'

Fancy goods. That's what they sold. That was the term that Faith Chesney used to describe the miscellaneous items that their emporium sold. Their stock included everything from ribbons to chinaware, a selection of stationery and books and a corner that the two older sisters described as 'Susan's bazaar'. This was where Susan displayed the best of the second-hand garments that she used to sell on her market stall.

The market stall was a thing of the past. No more standing about in the freezing cold all day. Now everyone was inside one freshly painted room, where everything was spick and span and just so. All the wooden fittings had been painted daffodil yellow, from a supply of strong-smelling paint that had been left over from the redecorating of the Wights biscuit factory offices. The girls' grandad, Horace Wight, had also gladly donated the wood and the carpenters' hours to help fit out their emporium with all the counters and cupboards they needed.

The three sisters knew that they would never have been able to make a go of running such an eccentric shop in a town like this without the money and indulgence of their grandfather. They were quite well aware of the privilege they had in being able to do so. Cognisance of this made them all the more determined to make it work. They had to prove to their grandad – and their highly sceptical father – that they could make Mary's Shop work out.

Faith – the oldest, sternest and most serious of the Chesney girls – put herself in charge of every aspect of the going concern. This included all the staffing arrangements. She had rather reluctantly given in to her youngest sister's campaign to have Minnie Minton brought in from the market stall to work in the shop. Neither Faith nor Hope were completely convinced that Minnie was a good or useful worker. It was their shared fondness for their baby sister that led them to letting her have her own way. Minnie Minton was the first good friend that Susan had ever really had of her own. It did even the sour-faced Faith good to hear the girls' laughter as they arranged the musty old clothes in their corner bazaar.

'Listen to the pair of them,' Hope was tutting one Monday morning that spring. 'Are they ever going to do any work?'

Faith shook her head indulgently. 'They spend more time playing dressing up than anything else. They're like two little lasses.'

Faith was tidying the hardback novels on the little shelf of new books she had ordered in. Then she was straightening the pots of new pencils and inhaling the wonderful scent of their cedarwood. She was brisk and businesslike, but she was enjoying playing at shops just as much as the noisier girls in their bazaar. Stern as she was, she was content to let the lasses enjoy themselves.

Hope wasn't looking quite as complacent. 'I do wish we hadn't let Susan bring all of her second-hand stock in here. It pongs a bit, doesn't it?'

There was a pungent reek of mothballs, it was true, and a musty smell of old wardrobes and other people's houses. Such was the nature of second-hand goods, though. Not everything could be pristine and sweet-smelling and new. Faith was rather interested in Susan's stock, as it happened. She liked to rummage for herself among the costume jewellery, old fur tippets, gloves and hats that Susan dragged in from the sales she attended. Serious-minded she might be, but Faith liked dolling herself up as much as her two sisters did. They all took this trait from their late mother, who used to dress the three of them up like little dolls when they were tiny. Their happiest memories of their mammy were all to do with pulling strange old musty costumes out of the trunks and cupboards at home. Well, if Susan wanted to create a similar, magical nook in their emporium, then so be it. It only seemed right.

But . . . was Minnie Minton really the right member of staff for them to be employing? She was – and here Faith and Hope had to agree – rather common. She was from the upper end of Frederick Street, higher up the hill and nearer to the pub. The sisters accepted the local wisdom that this was the rougher part of the Sixteen Streets, and Minnie Minton was not really their type at all.

Still, Susan was fond of her, and so they would give her a chance.

Today, however, it seemed that Minnie wouldn't even be working a full morning in their shop. Something happened to drag her away at ten-thirty, before the first tea break.

'What? What is it . . . ?' gasped the round-faced girl, emerging from the fusty bazaar at the back of the shop.

Her brother was standing there in the doorway, panting and puffing like he had just run all the way from Frederick Street. His face was red and shining with jubilation. 'You're to come home, Minnie. You're to come back home at once!'

Minnie's eyes bugged out as she realised straight away what had got their Derek so worked up.

'What is it?' squealed Susan, pulling on her own coat and hat and flinging Minnie hers.

'It's the bairns. The twins. They're coming!' Derek cried. 'Junie's started . . . you know. She's gone into labour and the midwife's with her right now. Ha'way, Minnie. They sent me to fetch you to give her moral support.'

'Junie wants me there with her, does she?' Minnie beamed. 'Oh, that's lovely.' Pulling on her coat, she whirled round to ask Faith, Hope and Susan: 'May I go?'

'Of course,' Susan shouted. 'And I'm coming with you, an' all.'

The two older sisters could only stand there speechless in their new emporium as the three youngsters ran out of there, gabbling excitedly all the way.

Chapter Thirty-Six

It was a week before Arthur stirred himself to go and visit the new babies.

He arrived with a great show of enthusiasm, showering gifts on mother and babies. He did his usual thing of gathering all the attention to himself and making it all about him, Derek observed. Of course, Junie and Cathy and Minnie and Betty lapped all of this nonsense up. They squealed like someone famous was popping in to coo over the babies. They carried on as if they should be glad that he had bothered to step over the threshold of number twenty-one to peer into the crib.

Derek wasn't quite so taken in by Arthur. He glared at the over-enthusiastic, overdressed fool. What did he look like? He was all done up in an Ulster coat like Sherlock Holmes, and he had a hat on with a feather in it like Robin bliddy Hood. He was beyond eccentric these days, and it embarrassed Derek to be associated with him.

'Ah, look at the small darlings,' Arthur sighed into the crib. His slightly pointed nose gave him an odd, witch-like appearance as he watched over the two quiet bairns. They were swaddled up in soft new blankets: pink for Theresa, blue for Noel. They were very calm and self-possessed, these babies, even with great big faces looming over them and booming voices all around them. 'Junie, they are just perfect. You've done a marvellous job, here.'

Junie was exhausted still, even all these days later. But she sat in her night things by the warm, accepting all these compliments and looking radiant. She really did look radiant, Derek thought, with a rush of grateful love. How clever she was. Look what she had given him. Named for relations long gone and about which Junie had mixed feelings, but she was just as much a slave to tradition as everyone round here: Theresa and Noel the babies were to be called and that was the end of it.

Derek held their first bairn, Ivy, in his arms and marvelled at this whole large family that had sprang magically into being around them both.

'I hereby declare that you're all going to have a wonderfully happy life,' Arthur told them, grinning. He was playing to the hilt his role of visiting fairy godmother. 'You deserve every happiness, you lot.'

Cathy came bustling in from the scullery with a fresh pot of tea. 'Arthur, will you stay for a bite of supper? It's just a bit of rabbit stew, but we can stretch it out for you?'

He laughed. 'I'm not sure I want to have a stretched bunny on my conscience.' Then he remembered a nursery rhyme from when he was very small. Unbidden, a tear crept into his eye as he thought of his long-vanished mammy singing to him: 'Bye, Baby Bunting, Daddy's gone a-hunting . . .' He started reciting the rhyme, loudly now, for the benefit of the whole room. 'Gone to fetch a rabbit skin . . . to wrap poor Baby Bunting in . . .'

'So will you stay for your supper?' Junie asked him. She had dropped all of her suspicions and reservations about the man. He had brought her a beautiful painted silk scarf and splendid gifts for the babies. Perhaps she could learn to accept him as a part of her extended family after all . . .?

Arthur touched her hand, and then Minnie's, and blew them all kisses as he retreated to the doorway. 'I'm sorry, my darlings, but no. I must go to work. I've got rehearsals.'

'Rehearsals for what . . .?' Junie wanted to know.

'It's my big chance,' he said, trying to make fun of himself, but failing. All at once, they could all see how important this was to him. He was facing his greatest chance at last.

Days passed and there were a few pointedly murmured comments about how it was fine for some people to sweep in with gifts, make a noisy fuss and then rush out again. How, at the same time, others had to do all the routine, boring and messy jobs, like feeding and cleaning up. Minnie frowned when she heard these mutterings and tried to defend her fiancé.

'He's very busy. He's going through all these auditions in Newcastle. Arthur says it's make-or-break time for him right now.'

'Must be nice for him.' Junie pulled a face. She was in a proper grumpy mood that day. Breastfeeding both twins was proving to be exhausting. She had cracked nipples and a sore head from all their yammering. 'Oh yes, they're lovely and quiet when they have visitors. When it's just me doing everything, they turn into monsters.'

Minnie shook her head ruefully. As if Junie was ever left to do everything alone. She was so well looked after by Cathy. It was Cathy who looked like she was being run ragged.

'What will happen if he gets this job?' Cathy asked Minnie. 'What will it mean for you? Will you see even less of your Arthur?'

Minnie couldn't help smiling at his being called 'her' Arthur. This still made her glow: the idea of someone so irrepressible and wonderful somehow belonging to her. 'Oh, well . . . we've talked about it a bit . . . and yes. It would mean us being apart for a fair bit. It's a repertory company, you see.'

'What's that when it's at home?' Cathy asked.

'Well, that's just it . . . he'd rarely be at home,' Minnie sighed. 'He'd be on the road, you see, going from town to town. It would be a touring company, travelling all over the country, doing play after play. It sounds just exhausting to me . . .'

'It sounds horrible,' Junie gasped, trying to imagine all the work and the upheaval. 'And, what's more, it would be horrible for you. What would you do? Follow them around the place like some kind of camp follower?'

'No, of course not. I'd just get on with things here, same as usual.' She didn't sound all that enthused about the prospect. 'It's his big chance, you see. This is just what they have to do, actors and that.'

'Sounds like a funny do to me,' Cathy said. 'The two of you have only just . . . you know, got together and . . . pledged your troth.'

Junie cracked out laughing, startling both babies at her breast. 'Pledged your troth. Mam, you sound so old-fashioned.'

'Well, you know what I mean. Minnie was so pleased to have a lad of her own, at last. Going out to dances and whatnot. What good is that if he's gallivanting all over the flamin' country?'

'It's just for a while,' Minnie moaned. She felt like she was pacifying the disquieting voices in her own head. 'While he gets established in that world and learns his trade . . .'

Junie snorted. 'Yes, I imagine he'll learn quite a bit about his trade.'

'What does that mean?' Cathy shot at her, alert for Junie's snide tongue. She had been gentle and sweet since the births, but now there were signs of her usual sarcastic self returning.

'Well, I just think Minnie should watch out for herself. This thing with Arthur . . . well, it's all very well. It's been fun for her to show off about going round town with him. Going to dances and whatnot. It's brought her out of her shell a little, but let's be honest. They're not *really* suited, are they?'

Minnie rose out of her seat, suddenly flushed red with feeling. She couldn't help herself hissing at her oldest friend: 'You don't know anything, lady. What would you ever know about *real* feelings?'

Both Junie and Cathy were staring at her in shock as the moon-faced girl pulled on her woolly hat and scarf. 'Minnie . . .! Junie never meant anything by that . . .!'

'Yes, she did,' Minnie snapped. She glared at Junie. 'You've got absolutely everything. You've got our Derek devoted to you. You've got the most wonderful babies. You've got everything in the world you'll ever need. You are surrounded by love, you silly, selfish cow. And yet still – *still!* – you have to begrudge other people their chances of happiness.'

Then, all at once, Minnie was gone. The front door slammed loudly at her heels.

'Well. She didn't even kiss the babies goodbye,' gasped Junie.

'She's really upset,' Cathy observed.

'She was always a bit highly strung,' sighed Junie. 'And prone to jealously. She'll get over it. Now, Mam, take the bairns off of me, would you? The little beggars have sucked me dry and I'm thoroughly knackered. I need to sleep.'

'All right, pet,' Cathy said, swooping in gratefully to take the babies. 'You get your rest. I'll look after these precious bunnies.'

Minnie stomped down the hill, to the end of Frederick Street. The freezing wind made the tears on her face sting. At the bottom of the street, she was relieved to see a familiar face.

'Minnie, are you all right, love?' Susan Chesney was horrified to see her workmate looking so upset in the street. 'What's up? Nothing's happened to the babies, has it?'

Minnie let her diminutive friend reach up to embrace her. 'No, no, it's nothing like that . . .' She found herself sobbing into the shoulder of Susan's outsized sheepskin coat. 'I shouldn't make a show of myself in the street like this.'

'You just let it all out,' Susan chuckled. 'You clearly need a good cry.'

Minnie found herself wailing. Standing in the middle of Frederick Street in daylight. Wailing her head off. And it was like she didn't even care.

'It isn't to do with Arthur, is it?' Susan asked.

'No, not really . . .' Minnie puffed and panted. Then she was off again. She was crying so hard that her guts were starting to ache. She broke away from Susan's cloying embrace.

'Let's get you indoors and make you a cup of tea or something . . .'

'I don't want a bloody cup of tea . . .' she muttered miserably. 'Sorry, I don't mean to be rude . . .'

'What *do* you want, then? What can I do to help you?' Susan was very earnest and well meaning. She stared up into Minnie's contorted bright red face and said: 'I'm your friend, Minnie. I hope you'll let me help.'

'It's all right,' Minnie sobbed. 'I'll be all right . . .'

'I'm not sure you will. You're in no state to be out. Come into our house and calm down . . .'

Minnie turned away from her. She looked up the hill of Frederick Street, to the lofty end under the burnished heavens where she had lived all her life with her family, and the pub and the fish shop where she worked all her days. Then she looked back down the hill at the biscuit factory gates and the towers and the hulking brutal shapes of the ships in the dockyards. This was the extent of her whole, entire world. She had been bound in by these things all her life, eking out her life in the shadows of these dowdy terraced houses.

'I just need . . . *more*,' she muttered to herself.

'What's that, pet . . .?' asked Susan, concerned that her friend was going crackers.

'I want . . . *more* than I've got,' Minnie said in a quiet, determined voice. 'I deserve more love. I want more love. I want to be a person who is loved.' She covered her face with both hands. 'Oh God, that sounds so stupid. I think I'm losing my mind.'

'No, no,' Susan said. 'You're right. You *do* deserve to be loved. Of course you do. You're a wonderful person, Minnie. You deserve everything.'

This made Minnie cry all the harder. 'Then why don't I feel loved? Why do I feel so lonely? I feel lonely even before he's gone away from me. Why is that, Susan? Why is that . . .?'

Chapter Thirty-Seven

There was a leaving do for Arthur a few weeks later, held at the house he shared with Mavis. 'What's the point of cleaning and tidying before we throw a party?' Mavis squawked, astonished by her Sam's suggestion that they prepare to welcome folk. 'They'll just mess it all up again.'

'Good point,' Sam mouthed at her, ruefully amused by his young wife's skewed logic as usual. Mavis was a law unto herself, and he wouldn't have her any other way.

'By, we're all going to miss Arthur, aren't we?' Mavis shouted. 'We've only just got used to him being around . . .'

It had hit Mavis very hard, being separated from her dashing, charismatic brother when he went and signed up for ENSA. All her life, she had depended upon him: back when they were homeless and on the streets, and then when they'd been adopted by that queer Mrs Kendricks in the big house. Mavis's large, sad eyes had always followed her brother about, taking her cue from everything he said and did. It was fair to say that she worshipped the very ground he walked on.

'Ah, he'll be back regularly,' Sam tried to jolly her along. 'And when he's in these plays, he'll come back to Sunderland and Newcastle occasionally, to play the fancy theatres. Why, then we'll be able to go and see him and you can say: "That's my big brother up there." You'll be so proud.'

'Aye, I guess that's right,' Mavis sighed noisily. She started making sandwiches for the party, absent-mindedly chewing on pieces of the nice ham as she worked. 'I know it's important that he does this. He knows what he wants to do with his life. But isn't it a shame about Minnie? It looked as if, for a time there, they were going to be an item.'

Sam raised an eyebrow. 'Do you think? I never thought that was a real romance. They're just pals, aren't they? Arthur's not the type for romance. He never was.'

The pair of them let the matter drop. Sam hunted through all the kitchen cupboards for mismatched glassware to put out ready for their guests.

That evening, the little house filled up with miscellaneous friends. Bella Franchino and her fella were among the earliest. There was a surprise appearance by Lily Johnson and her beau from the butcher's shop, who was so mild-mannered that no one could ever remember his name. Irene and Tom arrived from Frederick Street, glad to be relieved of their bairns for the night. With them came Beryl and Minnie from next door to them. The latter was dolled up in an outfit she had borrowed from Junie, who sent her apologies.

'You look nice,' Mavis bellowed at Minnie. 'Are you slimmer or something?'

Minnie nodded and shrugged. Yes, she had lost a whole stone in a month, mostly through unhappily fretting and laying off the battered cod. She had adjusted a dressy wine-red cast-off with wide shoulders that made Junie look like Joan Crawford. Minnie felt more like Flash Gordon's nemesis, Ming the Merciless, wearing it, but never mind. It was nice to make an effort.

Soon, the house was teeming with guests, all come to bid Arthur adieu. 'I don't know half these people,' Minnie muttered to Irene as they helped themselves in the kitchen to brown ale and stotty cakes with ham.

'Arthur's got a lot a pals from all over the place,' Irene smiled. 'He's so familiar with everyone. He makes friends everywhere.'

'Yes . . .' Minnie said, munching on a sandwich. 'You know what? I think this ham might be off.'

'Well, you're the same, Minnie,' Irene told her. 'You make friends with everyone, too. You're friendly and not too shy. Not like I am. Why, it was you who introduced yourself to me through the privy wall, wasn't it? You just can't help yourself being friendly all the time.'

'It's good to be friendly,' Minnie shrugged. Her mind was only half on what Irene was saying, however. She was wondering where Arthur himself had got to. She had glimpsed him only briefly during the party, when he'd kissed her on the cheek in the hallway and greeted her noisily. Since then, he had been gadding about with everyone else and she'd never clapped eyes on him.

'Shall we go and sit in the main room?' Irene asked brightly, abandoning her ham sandwich. 'We don't want everyone thinking we're hiding in the kitchen . . .'

Minnie didn't much enjoy that party at the messy house. There were few places to sit that weren't littered with used plates or even discarded clothing. The music consisted of the same three or four gramophone records played over and over, and she had no great love for George Formby at the best of times.

Soon, even Irene drifted away from her to be with her fella Tom, and the pair of them were departing early for Frederick Street. 'Work tomorrow,' she heard them apologise, but they looked relieved to be leaving this increasingly raucous party.

Why don't I leave with them? Minnie wondered unhappily. *They're going my way. They live next door to me. I should catch the last tram with them and Beryl, shouldn't I?* But she never did. She felt like she'd only just arrived and had barely seen Arthur yet. She'd fastened herself into this stiff, uncomfortable outfit and she was going to make the most of it.

In the best room, Lily Johnson was up on her feet, murdering popular songs again, though everyone seemed to be enjoying her singing. There was something so harsh and off-key about her voice, especially in the close confines of a normal-sized room. To Minnie, she sounded like an old crow up on the telegraph wires, shouting obscenities to the sky. 'There'll be bluebirds over . . . the White Cliffs of Marsden . . .' she sang and made the drunken party guests laugh.

Minnie wandered out through the scullery into the backyard, listlessly searching for her fiancé. Surely he was going to spend at least some of the evening with her?

Eeh, but she hated how silly and dependent she sounded. Since when was she the kind to run about after the attentions of some fella? Never, that's when. But Arthur had done something to her. He had changed the very way that she behaved. And he had seen to it that she was going to miss him with her whole heart.

In the ginnel out back, there were dusky orange cigarette ends weaving about and low, rumbling voices. Ah, it was two blokes out there, chatting and smoking companionably. Minnie surged forward to bum a fag, but then something held her back. Some instinct kicked in. She had no idea why. She stopped in her tracks and crept soundlessly to conceal herself in the shadowy lee of the wall.

But who was it there? Who was she eavesdropping on?

Arthur and Sam. Arthur was speaking quietly. There was no act, no showing off. Had she ever heard him talk like this before? He sounded so serious. So unlike his everyday self.

A strange thought hit her, even before she could make out what he was talking about: maybe this *was* his everyday self?

This quiet, mumbly, sighing person, smoking in the dark with Sam?

'We're going to miss you being in the house,' Sam was saying. 'Messing everything up. Using all the hot water. Staying up all night. Causing dramas . . .'

Sweet Sam, Minnie thought. He was the youngest and the friendliest of all the Farley boys. The handsomest too, she thought. Ma Ada's blonde boy. How on earth dowdy, rasping, daft Mavis had nabbed him, no one was ever quite sure.

Arthur was chuckling, then he was taking a long draw on his Woodbine. He let out the smoke in a series of elegant rings, sending them floating up into the darkness. 'Ah, Sam. It's been good. You've been good to let me stay back here.'

'It was your home before it was ever mine,' Sam protested. 'You know you always have a place here. If things don't work out on the road, in the theatre and stuff . . . you know you can always come back here. There'll always be a bed for you at ours.'

There was a pause then. A strange silence between the two men. It wasn't an awkward pause, with them both looking for what to say next to fill up the gap. No, Minnie thought. It was a tender silence. It was a soft, small moment in which both men understood each other perfectly. Minnie was left on the sidelines, puzzling it out.

'It's not been awkward for you, then?' Arthur asked, more quietly.

'Mavis is an innocent, she always was,' Sam sighed. 'You know that. She's the sweetest, most wonderful lass. She doesn't know anything, though. Not about fellas. Not about you and me or anything.'

'And that's the way it must stay,' Arthur said, with a hint of steel in his voice. 'If she ever lost her faith in me, my sister would lose her mind. It would break her heart. You must never, ever break her heart.'

'Of course, Arthur . . .' Sam jumped to reassure him. 'Of course I'd never do that.'

'You just see that you protect my sister the best you can. You look after her, Sam. I'm trusting you in my absence.'

'I . . . understand, Arthur.'

'Eeeh, Sam, lad. What complicated lives we've got, eh?'

'Do you think so?' Sam asked brightly. The weaving light of his cigarette briefly illumined his grinning face. 'I've always found everything quite straightforward. I don't like complicated things, on the whole.'

'Ha. Is that true, daft lad?' Arthur asked lazily, fondly. 'Come here. Before we go back in and see the drunken dregs of that party. Give us a kiss, man.'

'Aww, Arthur, man,' Sam laughed, and moved closer. 'I can't believe it. Burma was bad enough. The bloody Far East. But now . . . going to London. Why, that's like you're really leaving us behind . . .'

'Shut up, man,' Arthur said gruffly. 'Kiss me, come here.'

And then there was stifled quiet for a few moments. Minnie was frozen with her back against the rough stone wall. She listened to their muffled, grunting, animal noises. She felt her gorge rising in her throat and started to silently panic. *No, no, not here. Don't let me spew up right here and now. Not in front of them. Oh God. Oh God. Imagine the shame. The . . . the horror of . . .* Her mind was reeling. She was drunker than she'd thought.

All she could think as she stood there, trapped, was that Junie had been right. Every foul thing she had ever said. Every awful idea she had planted into Minnie's head. Arthur was a nancy. Arthur was a fairy. And so was bliddy Sam. They were doing it right here. Right outside the back of Mavis's house. They were kissing each other and they were hiding round the back. Two blokes. Together.

Minnie's bloke. It was Minnie's bloke.

The two men broke away from each other. Silently, they chucked away their finished cigarettes and turned back to the house.

Minnie tried to move. She tried to slip back into the shadows. She tried to hide.

But all her muscles were locked solid. She just stood there.

'Minnie!' Arthur cried. 'What the devil are you doing here, out in the cold?'

How guilty he looked. And so did Sam. From their faces in the milky light of the scullery window, she could tell that they both knew that they might have been rumbled.

'What is it? Why are you looking like that?' Sam asked her.

'I saw you. And heard you. I bloody saw the pair of you,' she mumbled.

'Minnie, Minnie, wait . . .' Arthur stepped forward to grab her.

But Minnie wouldn't be grabbed. She darted back indoors, away from him.

Everything was ruined. They all knew it.

Chapter Thirty-Eight

Well, of course Junie got her own way when it came to the house on the new estate. Somehow, she always did manage to get exactly what she wanted, and her letter-writing campaign to the council offices paid off sooner than even she had expected.

'I just kept telling them that I've got three bairns, all babies, and that we're crammed like sardines in tomato sauce round my mother's house. I said that she drinks like a fish and gets handy with her fists because of all the noise and mess. Next thing, with a little persistence, they're offering me keys to my own place.'

Minnie shook her head at her, tutting. 'You're terrible, Junie. You'd do anything to get your own way.'

'Too right I would.'

Junie was back to her usual, fiery self these days. Her success with the housing office was her crowning triumph. She was getting her own house at last. She was going to be queen of her own palace, after years – as she saw it – of being tolerated as a cuckoo in the nest.

The two women were sitting in the front of the battered old van owned by the Chesney girls. The sisters had inherited it from their lovely old Granda, to run around town in, picking up their wares for the emporium. It still had the Wights Biscuits logo emblazoned on the sides, chipped and fading away with the years. Susan had very kindly offered to run Junie and Minnie back and forth with a few loads of Junie's belongings from Cathy's house.

'It's very kind of you, this, Susan,' Junie told her.

'That's quite all right,' Susan beamed at her, wrestling with the steering wheel and the clunky gears. The old engine growled at her and seemed to moan in protest. The back of the van was crammed with heavy wooden furniture that Cathy had donated to the young couple for their first home: good dining-room chairs and an old armchair from the sitting room. There was a mattress in there, and antique quilts made by Theresa Sturrock twenty years ago.

'Really, I wanted to tell my mother we didn't want all this old stuff,' Junie sighed. 'I'd rather live in an empty new place and gradually fill it up with things we actually like. But I think she felt the need to offer us this gubbins.' She shrugged. 'I suppose it'll all come in useful. But I hate the thought of crowding out my new home from the off.'

Susan tried to jolly her along. 'From what I saw, it was all quality goods. Antiques. Be worth a few bob.'

'Of course, you're the expert, aren't you?' Junie turned to look at the girl at the wheel. 'You and your sisters know all about the value of everything, don't you?' Junie was sounding just a bit haughty as she said this. She was letting slip her annoyance that the Chesney girls had chosen Minnie to work in their precious emporium and not her. Still, Junie had no intention of working now. She had three small bairns and a house to get shipshape. She had quite enough on her plate.

'This is really good of you, Susan,' Minnie told her friend as they approached the new estate by the cliffs of Marsden Bay.

'Oh, I had a day off and I was at a loose end,' shrugged Susan happily. 'What was I going to do, leave you to drag all this old stuff up the hill by yourselves?'

Minnie found herself smiling at her friend's warmth and easy humour. It was such a relief to bask in her company. Even the daft headscarf she'd tied round her head, looking like a comic cleaning lady, was designed to make Minnie smile. 'You look like the girl off the posters in the war,' Minnie said. 'With the headscarf and the sleeves rolled up and the dungarees. That's who you remind me of.'

'Good.' Susan grinned. 'That's just who I want to be.'

Junie sat up straighter, excitedly, as they entered the boundary of the new housing estate. She jangled the freshly minted keys in both hands, nervously. All Minnie could see were mounds of black, churned-up mud in messy hillocks and areas blocked off by little posts and makeshift fences. Only a handful of new houses had been finished. They were square, compact dwellings on the brow of the hill, sharply outlined against the bright spring sky. 'There we are,' Junie said. 'Home.'

The house was in the middle of a row of five. When the van pulled up outside, Junie was out the door and running up the path before the engine even stopped. She held the front door key out in front of her with an air of great determination.

'It's a pity Derek had to work today,' Minnie said. 'He'd have loved this.'

'He could have carried you over the threshold.' Susan smiled.

Junie scowled, as if she wouldn't have been bothered with such sentimental nonsense. 'I just want to get in and see that everything is tidy enough and the lights work and everything . . .'

'It's a shame your mam couldn't be here, too,' Minnie said, as Junie fumbled impatiently with the lock. Cathy was back at Frederick Street, minding the bairns, of course.

'She'll be here soon enough,' Junie said. 'Knowing her, we won't be able to keep her away from this place. Ah. There we are.' All at once, the front door swung open on a darkened interior. The bare hallway smelled very strongly of drying plaster and putty from the windows. The boards underfoot were pale bare wood, thick with plaster dust. 'Hmm, it's a bit messy in here . . .' Junie said, eyes narrowed as she explored, room to room. 'It's dark, as well, isn't it? I thought it would get more daylight in the afternoon . . .'

Susan and Minnie stood in the kitchenette and gazed around at the new fittings. 'Oh, it's wonderful, Junie. Look at these cupboards. And a brand-new oven, look. No more fussing with the flamin' range and everything. Look at this – a gas hob and an eye-level grill. It's like luxury, pet.'

Grudgingly, Junie had to admit that the kitchen was pretty nice. She tried out the taps and the water seemed to be running properly. 'I'll figure out how the water heater works later. It all seems quite complicated.'

'Ooh, let's look at the bathroom,' Susan shouted. 'I can't wait to see it. You're so lucky, Junie. No more sitting out in the cold on the privy for you . . .'

They trooped upstairs to stare solemnly at the bathroom, with its deep, luxurious bath and its spotless white toilet and sink. 'Oh, just look!' Minnie said. 'I can't wait to have a go on all of these.'

Junie laughed at her. 'Well, you're welcome any time. Now, come on. Let's get a fire going in the front room, shall we? And we'll get the place warmed through. Then we've got all that van to unload . . .'

It took the rest of the afternoon to get everything into Junie's new house. What had seemed like an awful lot of stuff didn't go very far in terms of filling up the new place. It still looked very bare inside when the three lasses were finished. The old rugs and chairs that Cathy had donated looked rather shabby and worn in the stark light from the bare bulbs. Junie looked disappointed all of a sudden. 'We'll buy brand new things as we go along,' she told herself. 'When we can afford them . . .'

After his shift on the trams was over, Derek came racing over from the depot. He could hardly wait to see his wife in the new place. He came tumbling through the door and his eyes were wide. Minnie's brother looked so excited, she laughed delightedly at the sight of him. It was like he was a little lad on Christmas morning.

'Just look at this place,' he grinned as he warmed himself by the blazing fireplace. 'This is the life, isn't it? Can you believe it, Junie? This is ours. This is where we live now. Oh, I can't wait to get the bairns up here and in their own room. They're so lucky. They'll never remember living anywhere but this wonderful house.' He took Junie in his arms and kissed her tenderly. 'We're so lucky, do you realise that? We've come through it all, and here we are. Living in a place like this, with all our lives before us. And our kiddies. They'll be happy and they'll have better air and more space than we ever did . . .'

Junie kissed him and hardly liked to point out that she had grown up on a farm in Northumberland, with plenty of air and space, thank you very much. But it didn't seem like the moment to go contradicting him. She had never seen her young husband so happy and excited. The two of them clung to each other in the chilly, half-bare house.

Minnie and Susan were starting to feel a bit surplus to requirements.

'Erm, why don't we get back to the Sixteen Streets, Minnie? I need to deliver this van back to my sisters . . . they'll be wondering where I am . . .' Susan grasped Minnie's arm, prompting her.

Minnie shook herself out of her reverie. 'Yes, all right. You're right. I've got to help Ma at the fish shop tonight. Oh help.

Is that the time? I'm due there in half an hour. Junie? Junie, are you listening? We have to go now.'

'Hm?' Junie stopped kissing Derek and blinked at her two assistants. 'Oh, I thought you'd help me make up the bed. It needs putting together and—'

'We have to go,' Minnie told her. 'I've got work and Susan has things to do, too.'

'Oh, all right,' said Junie, relinquishing them. She gave them both a brief hug. 'Thank you both so, so much for all your help today. I know I can be snappy sometimes, but that's just me being nervous that things won't work out. But today . . . everything has turned out fine. And you two have been wonderful friends to me. Thank you.'

Derek beamed at them. 'Aye, thanks lasses.'

Then, all at once, Minnie and Susan were back in the rattletrap old van and taking off down the new street again as the sunlight started to fade over the sea.

'They're so lucky,' Minnie said. 'Starting out on life like that, together . . .'

Susan turned to look at her. 'You'll have your moment too, hinny. You'll be happy, as well.'

'Will I?' Minnie asked, and Susan realised she had never seen her friend look so downcast in all the time that she had known her.

'You and your Arthur. You'll be in your own place once day. You'll be settled . . .' Susan tried to jolly her along with the things she thought she wanted to hear.

Minnie shook her head. 'No, he's gone. He's left me forever. That's all over now. I was a fool for ever thinking it might be something real.'

Susan gasped. 'But . . . why? Whatever happened?'

Minnie didn't feel like telling her all the details. 'It's all too shameful, really. But it's finished with and that's an end to it. It was a pipe dream I had for a little while and I was an idiot for believing any of it at all. Now I just have to count my blessings.'

The painted biscuit van trundled along the coastal road and back to the Sixteen Streets as Minnie tried her best to count out her blessings. 'I've got my mam and my dad and we've more space at home now with Derek moving out. Everyone's in good health and we have enough of everything we need. There's no flamin' bombs dropping on us anymore. And I have my work at the pub and the fish bar . . . and I have my job at Mary's Shop. I'm very proud of that. My life is as good as I can expect it to be.'

Susan grinned at her from under that absurd knotted headscarf she had been wearing all day. 'And you have me as well, Minnie. I'm your friend, remember? I'll always be your pal, you know. I'll always be there, just for you.'

Chapter Thirty-Nine

It was a couple of nights later before Minnie and Derek's mam and dad went up to visit the new house. They dressed up in their Sunday best on a Thursday night, and Betty wrapped a mammoth parcel of fish suppers in reams of newspaper and pulled it along behind her in her shopping basket on wheels.

'But it's quite a way to walk, isn't it?' she gasped, as they paused at the bottom of Ocean Road. She looked at Harry in the fading light of the evening and he looked worn out already. 'The fish and chips will be freezing.'

'Junie can put them in her new oven and warm them,' Harry said, wincing. He was clutching his knees, stooped over. Betty's heart went out to him, he looked so winded. He probably hadn't walked so far in years. Also, she could now see how shabby his old brown suit looked. It was from well before the war and looked it.

'We should have caught the tram or got a lift like our Minnie did the other day. What were we thinking about, walking all the way there?'

'We're old and more clapped out than we like to think,' Harry chuckled, straightening up with an effort and taking her arm.

'There, are you all right to go on, hinny?' she asked him tenderly. Most people never saw how sweet the two of them were with each other. Not even their kids saw them rubbing along as gently as they did. When others were around, they liked to play up to the image they had of Betty being the boisterous, bullyish fishwife and Harry being her meek husband who'd do anything for a quiet life. The reality was much more harmonious than that.

They ambled along the coastal road, appreciating the fresh air from the sea and the cooling breeze. 'Soon be the warmer, lighter nights,' Harry observed. 'They'll be rolling away the barbed wire from the beaches. The summer should see us all back to normal,' he smiled. 'Can you imagine it, Betty? If it was just like it used to be? I can hardly remember. But what if the summer was like it was, back in the twenties?'

She gripped his arm and agreed that, yes, it would be marvellous if they could roll back time and have things just as they were before the war broke out. Yes, if only it was as simple as that, it would all be wonderful.

'I know it can't be as easy as that,' Harry smiled at her, knowing just what she was thinking. 'But just taking up the barbed wire and letting folk enjoy the beaches again. Clearing up the bomb damage and the last of the bombs and the anti-aircraft guns. If all that stuff was gone, out of sight, we could start feeling something like normal again.'

'Aye, we could,' Betty said, surprised by the intensity of feeling in him. 'Wouldn't it be smashing to sit on the beach with the sun going down? That's what I'm picturing.'

'Oh yes,' he said. 'Champion.'

Derek's parents arrived at last at the new house, having negotiated their way through the black mud of the maze-like streets. By then, it was dark and the smudgy yellow street lights had come on. After the years of blackout, even the street lights merited comment and praise. 'They make where we live seem so dingy and dark,' Betty said, staring up at the sodium glare of the electric lamps.

'Aye,' agreed Harry, but he found this semi-built estate quite a bleak and unwelcoming place. Already, he was longing to return back to the familiar confines of the Sixteen Streets. It beggared him, but he could never understand why anyone ever wanted to move away from family and hearth. His and Betty's two older sons, Raymond and Martin, had been a recent disappointment in that regard. They had hardly been back from the war two minutes before they took off again, off to live lives of their own in the south.

Why didn't folk want to stick together anymore? Harry's own side of the family had a Bible that went back to the middle of the nineteen-hundreds, with everyone living in the shadow of the Shields docks. Now, that was proper family. That was proper belonging, wasn't it? Who'd ever feel that they belonged to a place like this, that had just been fields a year ago?

Junie greeted them on the doorstep, all done up in one of her famous smart costumes. She had her figure back already, and she'd had her hair set nicely at a place down on the Nook. Now she was taking their hands and kissing them on the cheek, so graciously, like she was lady of the manor. 'You're so welcome,' she beamed at her parents-in-law, and then sniffed the air suspiciously. 'What can I smell?'

'We brought six fish suppers in my basket,' Betty told her proudly. 'We thought we'd bring a contribution to the house-warming.'

A flash of irritation crossed Junie's face. 'You shouldn't have bothered. We have some nibbles out on the new sideboard. My mother has been baking . . . We have canapés.'

'Canapés, eh?' Harry said, shrugging off his jacket and hanging it with Betty's coat on the special hooks in the hall. 'That's fancy. Only the best for the people round here, eh?'

In the living room, Cathy Sturrock was sitting up holding the two new babies in her arms. She was all done up, of course, Betty observed. Mutton dressed as lamb, as usual. But then she dispelled the uncharitable thoughts. Cathy was a good woman and had always been nice to her. But look how at home she seemed here in the new house. Look how she had settled herself in already, sat by the sideboard beside the fancy nibbles she'd apparently baked. 'Hello there, Cathy,' said Betty stiffly. 'You've got your hands full there, I see.'

Derek was at the fireplace, looking every inch like the man of the house, Betty was pleased to see. Junie had made him get all dressed up in his best suit and even a tie. All dressed up like lord of the manor in his own home.

'Derek, I've brought fish suppers for us all, but I don't think your Junie's keen.'

Derek kissed his mother's cheek. 'Ah, you needn't have brought anything, Mam, but it's kind of you. Look, let me get you a sherry. And Da', will you have a brown ale?'

Soon, they were sitting round the edges of the new living room, some on the comfortable seats, others on wooden chairs dragged over from the dining area.

'Well, this is nice,' said Harry. 'I'm trying one of the canapés, did you call them?' He munched on something flaky and creamy inside. 'Very nice.'

Cathy beamed at his compliment and, for the first time, Harry noticed that she had her young fella sitting with her. That Bob Farley, her pot man. He was silent as anything, staring at the faded rug on the floor and holding Ivy on his lap.

'It's a shame our Minnie couldn't be here tonight,' sighed Betty. She had also bitten into one of Cathy's canapés and wrapped the remainder in her handkerchief. 'But she's got the pub to look after.'

'She's a good lass,' Cathy piped up. 'I'd never be able to go anywhere without her. I don't know what I'd do without your Minnie.'

They all murmured appreciatively about the absent Minnie. 'Such a good lass,' Junie agreed. 'She was the first friend I made when I first came to Frederick Street, you know. I was only sixteen and I really wasn't in the friendliest mood at the time. I was so scared and defensive, really. And your Minnie saw right through all of that and barged right up to me and demanded my friendship. That's what she was like.'

Everyone looked surprised at Junie's candour. It was true, Betty thought. When Junie had first arrived among them, she had been a proper snooty little madam. She had made her mother's life a misery. Now, it seemed, everything was sorted between them, and everyone was content.

Mind, Minnie wasn't content, was she? Minnie seemed unhappier than everyone these days. Without even thinking, Betty sighed heavily and said, 'I wish our Minnie could be happy, though. She's walking around with this great weight on her shoulders these days.'

'Aye, aye,' everyone agreed.

'It's since Arthur went off to find fame and fortune,' Derek pointed out. 'That's what it is. That lad led her a merry dance. I think he got her hopes up.'

'But our Minnie's never been one to get her head turned,' said Harry. 'She's allus been so sensible and down-to-earth.'

'She wasn't immune to Arthur, though,' Junie said. 'I was watching her, all the way through that strange courtship. It was like she was under that funny fella's spell . . .'

'Ah well,' said Cathy. 'It'll all sort itself out. She won't be upset for long. It was never going to happen, was it? Let's face it. They weren't suited. He isn't the type, obviously, for settling down . . .'

'Aye,' they all agreed, and the conversation petered out.

Betty patted her knees to get their attention. 'Do you think those fish suppers will have warmed through by now? Shall I go and dish them out?'

'Oh, yes!' came the hungry chorus.

Junie looked slightly piqued at the thought of them all eating chips and battered cod in her new front room.

It was quiet at the Robin Hood that night, thank goodness.

Minnie went about her routine tasks. She could have run this bar in her sleep, which was just as well, because lately her mind wasn't on anything much at all. She couldn't concentrate on anything. At night, she dreamed she was out dancing. She was in Arthur's arms and they were dancing up a storm to the band at the Alhambra – a place he had only taken her to once but which had left an indelible print on her.

Arthur had given her a glimpse of a life of glamour and excitement. With him, she saw and did things that she had never expected to. It was like being in a film, going out with him. She never thought she would be so daft as to expect to live like that, and she never thought she would miss such things when it all came to an end. But there it was. She missed him, and she missed her more exciting life.

There was nothing more to be said about it.

But then Minnie received a strange surprise that evening. At about the same time that the rest of her family were sitting down with fish suppers in newspaper on their laps, a visitor came calling at the Robin Hood. She was a woman who knew her way to Frederick Street and the warmly glowing lights of the pub. She had been here before and, back then, she had stood out just as much as she did tonight.

The visitor was wearing a fur coat and expensive shoes. She was dressed up as if she was attending a Buckingham Palace garden party. When she stepped tentatively into the saloon bar, everyone's eyes were on her.

'Mrs Kendricks . . .!' Minnie gasped, astonished to see Arthur's adoptive mother here.

'Ah, you're here, good,' the old woman looked relieved to clap eyes on Minnie. 'Oh, my dear, you must help me.'

'Help you?' The good-hearted Minnie came scuttling out from behind the bar. The old wifey looked like she needed propping up. Had she been drinking? There was a hint of something sweet and strong on her fluting breath. 'Whatever's the matter?' Minnie led her over to the Women's Table, where old Ma Ada, Winnie and friends were agog at this new development.

'It's Arthur, my dear,' Elizabeth Kendricks sighed and seemed as if she was on the point of tears. 'I think he is making the most terrible mistake. And I think he must have broken your heart, just the same as he once broke mine.'

Minnie stared at the old woman and took a deep breath. 'Let me get you a drink,' she said, and readied herself for a heart-to-heart by the fire.

Chapter Forty

During the course of that summer, Minnie saw Elizabeth Kendricks several times. Mostly, she took the tram along the seafront and visited her at home. It never ceased to be a thrill to Minnie, stepping up to those tall gates and entering the private world beyond. The gardens might have been neglected and become tangled with roots and dead leaf mulch, but it was still a special place to visit. She loved to sit in the glorious sunlight of the conservatory with its patched-up windows, taking tea with the old lady.

Elizabeth, too, seemed delighted to have company. On the days that Minnie was coming to visit, she would dress up in her nicest clothes and struggle with her now-arthritic hands to load up a silver tea tray in preparation for her guest.

What did they talk about? What did they have in common? Oh, so many things, it turned out. First and foremost, there was Arthur, who they both cared about so passionately. As the weeks and months of his absence went by, Minnie was startled to find herself caring even more about him. She missed him terribly and wasn't sure that her long teatime chats with Elizabeth were making her feel better or worse about him.

'If you could have seen him back then,' Elizabeth sighed shiveringly. 'I'd dress him up like a little Indian prince, or something out of the Thousand and One Tales. All my friends in their fancy houses would swoon when he opened his mouth to sing. He really was something, Minnie. You could tell that he was going to be famous, even back then.'

'I wish I could have seen him,' Minnie smiled. Arthur had mentioned once or twice that, as a kid, he'd had a kind of career as a singer at parties at big houses in Sunderland and Newcastle. He had described the satin and silk outfits his benefactress had given him and the brilliant glamour of the houses they had visited. Minnie had assumed that he was mostly just tale-spinning, in that wildly inventive way of his. Now it was turning out to be true, all of it. 'No wonder he craves the attention, and being up on the stage . . .'

They were eating rather crumbly, dry fairy cakes. Minnie was pretending to enjoy them, but they were quite horrible, really. She wondered how long they had sat in the pantry, waiting for an occasion like this.

'Oh, don't get me wrong.' Elizabeth beetled her brows and looked perplexed. 'When I said that he's making a horrible mistake, I don't mean going on that stage and touring the country and going to London and all that. Oh, indeed not – I think he should go everywhere that his talents lead him. He should go all out and follow that star of his to the ends of the earth . . .' Then she looked directly at Minnie, fixing her with those sharp, birdlike eyes of hers. 'No, the mistake he is making is to do with you, my dear.'

Minnie started coughing up her desiccated sponge cake. 'Me? How do you mean . . .?'

'I think he has rather let you down,' Elizabeth said sadly. 'I think he led you a way up the garden path and then he let you drop. If that's not mixing my metaphors too horribly.'

Minnie wasn't sure what she meant by metaphors, but she felt too embarrassed to start talking about all of this. She was still haunted and perplexed by what she had seen and heard that night at the back of Sam and Mavis's house. She had tortured herself by playing the scene through her head again and again. She kept seeing them and listening in on them: Arthur and Sam kind of kissing and canoodling in a way that a lass would with a lad. It was the kind of carry-on that she and Arthur had never gone in for, even after a hot, happy night out dancing. She thought that was because he respected her too much.

Oh, how she'd tortured herself with all of this since he'd left town. She'd ended up thinking that it was all because of her. It was her who was faulty, somehow, she who was in the wrong. Didn't he used to call them both odd bods? Odd ones out? He was a queer – that's what they called them, wasn't it? And his assumption was that Minnie was one too.

But she wasn't, was she? There'd been that time, of course, years ago. She'd been so confused. She'd thought she loved Junie. She had kissed her. They had lay in Junie's bed and they had kissed each other deeply and passionately and neither of them had mentioned it again, although Minnie had longed to. At that time – when they were nobbut bairns, really – she had wanted nothing more than to spend the rest of her life kissing and being kissed by Junie like that. Her mind had raced and her heart and glowed like the biscuit factory ovens whenever she'd been anywhere near Junie.

But all those feelings had gone now, hadn't they? She had grown up and seen that Junie was happy with their Derek, and everything was as it should be. Minnie wasn't a queer. She wasn't any kind of queer at all.

But Arthur most definitely was. She could see that now.

Perhaps Elizabeth didn't know about any of this. She'd not heard the folk of the town sniggering behind his back and calling him funny names. All these things Minnie had been content to ignore – until she had seen evidence with her own eyes. Young Sam, locked in Arthur's arms, looking like he belonged there.

Oh, the world was strange and much more upsetting than Minnie had ever imagined.

She sipped the last of her cool tea and smiled sadly at Elizabeth Kendricks.

'Is there really no hope that you two might start courting again?' The old woman sounded beseeching, like it was all down to Minnie's choice. 'You both seem so suited. I thought . . . I had thought . . . that there might be a wedding in the offing . . .'

Minnie allowed herself the indulgence of picturing herself living here, in Elizabeth's marvellous home. What would all her family and pals say about that, then? Surely Arthur was the old woman's heir and if Minnie married him . . . well . . .! She could just picture herself being lady of the manor here. Was that a bad thought? Was she being greedy and sly? Maybe she was. But she could put her back into getting this place cleaned up and repaired. She could clean all the dusty panes of glass in the conservatory, that's how she'd start. She'd rip down all the musty curtains and get them steeping in hot water. She'd scrub the whole place through and see what repairs needed doing. Why, her hands were itching, even as she sat there, full of fantasies. She was longing to get to work on making the place wonderful again. She would restore the big house, all for Arthur's sake. And how pleased the old woman would be, to step aside and let Minnie be mistress of the place . . .

Minnie shook her head to clear it of these seductive ideas. No, she was being wicked. She was looking at this place with envious, desirous eyes.

She told the woman who had brought him up: 'Arthur isn't going to marry me, or any other woman. He's not the marrying type, as they say.'

Elizabeth's mouth hardened. 'That's nonsense.'

'I'm afraid it's true.'

'He will, you'll see. You've no right to think that he'll never be happy. Why would you say that? Just because he's decided he's gone off you?'

Minnie felt stung. She felt like the old woman was turning on her. She'd twisted her around in a cloying web of suggestion and now she was stinging her with her words and turning nasty. 'I . . . We were never really a normal couple . . .' Minnie said. 'His mind is elsewhere all the time. I was just a diversion for a little while.'

Elizabeth hunched over the coffee table and looked upset. 'You must realise that Arthur is a very special person. The woman who he marries will have to be very understanding and she will be very special, too. And her reward will be a wonderful life. I had thought . . . I had hoped that that woman could be you, my dear.'

'I-I'm sorry,' Minnie said, getting up from her chair. 'But I don't think I can . . .'

Moments later, a defeated-looking Elizabeth showed Minnie to the door. It was time to catch the tram back to the poky confines of Minnie's life in the Sixteen Streets.

'It feels rather as if we have quarrelled today,' Elizabeth frowned. She touched Minnie's blushing face with her clawed hand. 'But we haven't really quarrelled, have we? We haven't really even disagreed. Why, we both love our Arthur deeply and we both want to see him happy. We both believe that you are the person he should be with, and that you should live here.'

'I . . .' Minnie opened her mouth to speak, but the old woman shushed her.

'So we agree on the principal things. Now we just have to find a way to make them happen, don't we?' A new energy seemed to take over the mistress of the house then. 'I'm a woman who likes to get her own way, you know.'

Feeling oddly as if she had been recruited for some kind of secret mission in a movie, Minnie said goodbye and left the big house to catch her tram. She was in a daze all the way home. What was Elizabeth promising to do? What did Minnie want her to do? What did Minnie really want from all of this?

And then she thought about dancing with Arthur, and laughing with him, and feeling safe from all the gossip and snide nonsense that everyone muttered behind both their backs when she was with him. *Yes, we're both outsiders and misfits*, she thought. *Maybe we should really be together and living in the big house. Why, then we'd show them all. Oh, wouldn't we just show them all.*

She hopped off the tram on Fowler Street and thought about popping into Mary's Shop to see if Susan was finishing her shift. Then they could walk up to Frederick Street together. Maybe Minnie could even pick her younger, cleverer, more sophisticated friend's brains about this whole perplexing business. She had never really talked about her feelings for Arthur with Susan, and she wasn't even sure why. It was like she kept the two friends in separate compartments.

Just as she turned to the gaily painted frontage of the sisters' fancy goods shop, there suddenly came the loudest noise that Minnie had heard since the end of the war. It was the loudest bang that anyone in town had heard since the last of the air raids. In the late afternoon of a lovely summer's day, quite some time after everyone had become used to the war being over and gone, there was an explosion. A huge explosion that rocked the whole town. A bomb had gone off about half a mile from where Minnie was standing on Fowler Street, but she could feel the ground shake underfoot and she went stone deaf for a full minute after the bang.

She turned and saw the column of dirty brownish black smoke rising up somewhere beyond the tall shingled rooftops.

Somewhere beyond the market hall. There were screams and yells and she saw people staggering about with shock in the street. They were gobsmacked and panicking, just as she was. The three Chesney sisters came hurrying out of their shop.

'It's a bomb!' Minnie cried out and her voice sounded weird in her own ears. 'A bloody bomb's gone off, somewhere over that way. Look – the smoke's going up from somewhere by the . . . by the . . . by . . .'

It was the tram depot. They were going to learn pretty soon that it was the tram depot that had gone up in the explosion. An unexploded bomb had lain in the ruins of the house next to the tram depot ever since a certain night in October 1941. It had lay there peacefully, quietly, for all this time and just this moment, on this afternoon, it had chosen to go off, blowing up the depot, the trams, the drivers and all the clippies who happened to be taking their break at that very hour. By the time Minnie, Susan and others got to the site, there was hardly anything left to see.

Chapter Forty-One

There was nobody left.

The explosion had been so fierce that the whole tram depot had been blown to smithereens, along with everyone inside it. That had included two drivers, four of the clippies, one manager and – at best guess – seven passengers. It had been a slow day, and a sunny one, and many of the people who might normally have caught the tram at the main depot had elected to walk and take the fresh air instead. They would be thanking their lucky stars over this for the rest of their lives. Nobody who had been under the draughty eaves of the old iron building had stood the slightest chance.

Minnie and Susan could only get so close to the bomb site. Almost as soon as it happened, there were fire brigade fellas and the old ARP warden back in control. They were cordoning off the area and waving people back, making it all secure and warning people off with the threat of a thick ear. It was still dangerous. No one knew exactly what had happened. Perhaps it was still hazardous. Who knew if another hidden bomb was about to go off?

Minnie drew as close as she could to the makeshift barriers. She felt like all her clothes, her hair and face, and her mouth and nose were coated and filled with black soot and brick dust. The air was thick and glaucous all around them, with the sunlight shining through the filthy clouds. She felt Susan reach for her hand and squeeze it tight, which came as a great comfort to her.

'He might not have been there, he might have been out somewhere else on his round . . .' She kept repeating it to herself, like a hopeful mantra. Surely Derek was still out, driving his tram so happily, so easily, unaware of this terrible thing that had happened. How he'd loved his driving. He had passed with flying colours. He had swapped his jobs so easily, with hardly any fuss at all. Minnie had grown used to the sight of him in his shirtsleeves and his cap at a jaunty angle on his thick, dark hair. Her brother – the tram driver.

'We don't know anything yet,' Susan told her.

But Minnie did. Hoping so fiercely against hope; trying her best to damp down the fear in her chest that hammered at her like tom-toms: she knew it was no good. Deep down, she knew he was dead. It was a strange, desolate feeling. She had always been so close to her lovely, gruff brother. The bond between them was deep. And now, today, it was gone. It was neatly severed. It was an instant absence just as palpable as those moments when her hearing had gone, blown out by the noise of the blast. But her hearing had gradually returned in the panicky moments that had followed. Her sense of dreadful loss remained. Derek had gone. She just knew it.

When the news reached Frederick Street, Betty Minton had a screaming attack. She stood in her hallway and couldn't get control of herself. No one had ever seen her like this. Not even her husband, who didn't know what to do. He thought she had lost her mind on the spot, hearing that her son was blown to bits.

Harry's own reaction to the impossible news was delayed by shock at his wife's shrieking. She hadn't even screamed like this in childbirth, he thought crazily. She had been up in the back bedroom here, in this very house, all those years ago, giving birth to Derek. She had been ripped open, the midwife said, and there were bucketfuls of blood going up the walls as the fierce young lad fought his way out of her. Yes, there had been screams that day and they had turned Harry pale as he sat downstairs, listening and terrified. But this noise, today, from his beloved wife, was so much worse.

He felt like she was never going to stop.

All over South Shields that summer's evening, there was appalled chatter about the awful thing that had transpired. A bomb. A leftover bomb. Some thought it had been lodged there inside the derelict building beside the depot for up to five years. It had lay there, wedged in a hollow wall, resting benignly like a hidden canker, just biding its time.

Bob Farley, the pot man at the Robin Hood, turned out to know a thing or two about this sort of affair. That night, at the bar, he was explaining all this business to do with the acid inside the workings of the incendiary device. He had learned about this during his own war years. It would eat through the workings gradually, so gradually, and even though the bomb might stay there quite still for years, there was this slow, corrosive drip, drip, drip inside. Eventually, the acid would reach the trigger mechanism. And off the bomb would go, just when nobody was expecting it. When people hadn't even known there was a bomb still there.

Listening to this, Cathy Sturrock shivered. The acid her fella had described – it sounded just like the roil of bilious acid in her own stomach tonight. She felt crippled by it. She felt waves of nausea going through her as she pulled pints for her regulars.

'Shouldn't you be with your daughter, Cathy?' Ada Farley asked her, frowning. 'She'll be needing her mammy tonight, surely? If it's really her fella who . . . you know . . .'

Cathy nodded tightly, biting her lip, annoyed at the suggestion of criticism from Ma Ada. 'I've only popped in here for half an hour to help out Bob. I've been over at Junie's already and the doctor's been in. He's sedated her and she went out like a light. She won't wake up till tomorrow. It's the best way.'

'What about the bairns, though?' Ma Ada asked, supping her milk stout. 'Who's got them?'

'They're over at mine,' Cathy told her. 'We brought them back here and Minnie Minton's feeding them right now. I'll go back in a minute.'

'Eeeh, Minnie will be so upset an' all,' Ada sighed. 'To lose her lovely brother like that. The pair of them were so close always. And you say that you've left poor Junie alone in her new house? All the way across town? Won't that be awful for her? Waking up alone and realising what's happened?'

'Yes, yes, it will,' Cathy nodded, close to tears herself, at the very thought. 'I'm going to sleep over there tonight, to be there when she wakes. Minnie will have the babies. Her mother's gone hysterical apparently, so she's no use to anyone tonight.'

'I'm not surprised,' Ada said darkly. 'I remember when the news about our Tony arrived. About him going down on that ship. I felt my legs give way underneath me. I couldn't take it all in.'

Bob patted her podgy hand as it trembled on the wooden bar. He still felt the loss of his oldest brother keenly, too.

Ma Ada went on, 'But at least that was in wartime. At least I could even kind of understand that. There was slaughter and horror everywhere and at least it was in the cause of the war. But this . . . today, this is just senseless. If it really was just some leftover bomb . . . it's just too cruel and pointless, isn't it?'

'It is indeed,' Cathy said. She was silent then, thinking about how she had sat with Junie. The news had already reached her daughter. Even though Junie knew her husband's timetable and she knew that at the precise time the bomb had gone off he had been finished with his shift and he would have been preparing to leave the depot and come home . . . she was still hoping against hope. 'He wasn't there, he wasn't there . . . he had left already . . . he was on his way home . . . I'm sure of it. He can't have been there, Mam. He can't, can he? He just can't be dead . . .'

Cathy had held her daughter's head against her breast and rocked her gently. 'I know, I know . . .' she had kept crooning.

Derek never returned from work. With each passing hour that evening, it became clearer that he was never coming back. Of course he had been at the depot, right after his shift had finished. He would have been slurping tea, eating the corned beef sandwich Junie had put in his bait box that morning. He would have been looking at the racing pages of the *Gazette* and then: boom.

At least – Cathy thought – he would have known nothing about it. One minute there, the next minute gone.

The doctor had come to inject her daughter with something to make her sleep. 'But the babies, the babies . . .' Junie had moaned, and her mother had reassured her that Ivy, Noel and Theresa would be just fine in her care. She had put her daughter to bed and spirited her babies back to Frederick Street.

'How terrible it all is,' Ma Ada said. 'We thought we'd seen the last of it. We thought we were scot-free. But death is still here among us.' She shook her head sorrowfully. 'Pop another half in this glass, would you, pet?'

Numbly, Cathy served her and wouldn't take any money for it.

'Ah, let's drink to the poor bloke, shall we?' Ada sighed. 'I mind when he was just a little tyke, the same age as my lads. Somewhere between my Bob and Sam, he came. They all grew up in the back lane and the front street here together. Like a bundle of puppies, they all were. At one time, all the kids were young together on Frederick Street – it was so noisy. All that seems like a hundred years ago, now.'

'Aye, it does, Ma,' Bob smiled.

'Bob, will you look after your mam and the rest of the bar?' Cathy asked him. 'I'd best slip home and see how Minnie's doing with the babies. She's got that Susan helping her, but she's not used to bairns. They'll be a handful . . .'

Bob nodded. Of course he could look after the bar. It wasn't so busy tonight. Just a few of the regulars, talking in hushed voices about the terrible thing that had happened. The shockwaves would be going out from that bomb for years to come.

Cathy nipped out and Ma Ada sat hunched at the bar, tutting and muttering to herself about the pity of it all. 'To think, as well, that they'd just set themselves up in that fancy new house. Three bairns, as well. All of them babies still. What's Junie supposed to do now? She's stuck out there on that new estate, away from her family and all the people who know her. What a time for this to happen. Just when they were setting out on this new life of theirs. Why, they thought they'd got away. They thought they were on easy street, didn't they?' The old woman was letting her fatalistic mood get the better of her. It was just as well there was no one but Bob to hear her maundering on like this. 'It just goes to show,' Ma Ada moaned. 'It all just goes to show.'

Chapter Forty-Two

She kept seeing him wherever she went.

Not that Junie went very many places in the weeks after Derek died. Mostly, she stayed inside her new house on the new estate with her three bairns. If she'd had curtains up in every window, she'd have drawn them to stop the light getting in. She retreated into a distant and quiet place as she tried to reckon on the fact that her husband had gone forever.

But whenever she went out of doors, on the occasions that she had to, she kept catching glimpses of Derek.

She went to her mother's, she saw him in the street. She walked through the town centre with Cathy and there he was, coming out of the railway station. Down Ocean Road, she could have sworn that was him going into that pub. All these men that she saw out of the corner of her eye were the spitting image of her dead husband. They had his dark, tousled hair, his broad back in that donkey jacket of his. They had his rolling gait and the way he kept his head down as he walked along. Derek seemed to be everywhere.

'I'm losing my mind,' she confided to her mother.

'No, you're not, hinny,' Cathy whispered to her, holding her close. 'All these things are natural. You're longing to see him, of course you are. And so your mind plays tricks on you. It's like seeing faces in the flames. You're coming to terms with him being gone forever.'

'Oh, Mam . . .' Junie sobbed. 'I can't bear it. I can't go on, I don't think. It's just so cruel and hopeless. What's the point? We thought we had everything . . .'

'You did have everything, and you had a wonderful life with him, short as it was,' Cathy told her. 'But you can't give up, now, pet. You've got to be strong. You've got them bairns of yours to look after. You can't let them down. What would Derek say? He'd tell you that you've got to get on with life, without him, for their sake.'

'I know that, I know . . .' Junie replied testily.

In those days after Derek's death, Cathy had never felt so close to her daughter, as she coached her through the business of carrying on. It was a terrible thing to be brought together by. She almost felt ashamed, relishing her daughter's reliance on her.

'I don't know how I'd have managed with the bairns, without your help,' Junie told her. Cathy had been dressing and feeding them all and washing all their things in her scullery. Junie had followed her babies back to Frederick Street, to live at number twenty-one. It was just easier that way.

'I've had a lot of help from Minnie,' Cathy pointed out. 'That poor lass would do anything for you.'

'Aye, she would, I know,' Junie said. 'Eeeh, but what am I going to do next, Mam? How'm I ever gonna support us all? What am I going to do, left with three kiddies and a new house?'

The weight of the future was pressing down on Junie. They hadn't even had a service yet to mark Derek's death and already she was dreading the difficult years to come.

Minnie, meanwhile, was exhausted. Between her three jobs – at the fish bar, the pub and the shop – her time was filled quite enough. But now she had pledged to help with the babies as much as she was needed, and so much of her spare time was taken up confirm through stinking nappies and turning them through the mangle. She fed babies and sang to them and saw them off to sleep. She sat watchfully and waited while Junie sat in a dumb stupor, trying to take in the fact that Derek was gone.

There was nothing to show for his loss, that was the thing. There was no body to bury, and so the funeral they held eventually was a strange affair, with a box they all knew was empty and the priest's words echoing hollowly in the chilly air of St Jude's. There was a letter from the tram company, all solemn on fancy headed notepaper, and there were several pages in the *Shields Gazette*. There was even a piece in the Newcastle paper, mostly about the dangers of unexploded bombs. All of these things were cut out and pasted in a scrapbook that Junie could later show the bairns when they grew up: 'These are all about your daddy, who you were too young to know. These are so you'll remember him and keep him in your hearts. He'd have liked that: to be remembered by you.'

The three bairns didn't understand a word of any of this. Of course they didn't. They wouldn't understand any of it for years and years. For the moment, they were dressed up in lacy woollens and taken to the church as Father Michael intoned over the empty box and the full congregation sang the old, reassuring songs. Only Junie didn't sing the hymns, and she didn't say 'amen' at the end of the priest's prayers like she was supposed to. She had no faith in God. She hadn't for years and years, as it happened. But now, because of what had become of Derek, she found herself actively turning against him. What kind of God could do this?

'It was a senseless waste,' Harry Minton said. He was in his Sunday best, looking more dapper than he had in a long time. He stood at his hearth and tapped out his pipe on the brickwork with a heartfelt sigh.

'There's nothing more to be said about it than that,' said Tom Farley from next door. 'It's just one of those things. One of those terrible things.' He was the most settled and sensible of the boys from next door. He had known their Derek all his life and he was a welcome visitor at number fifteen. Tom had come with his Norfolk wife, Irene, to see that all was as well as could be expected next door.

'Sit down, the pair of you. Our Betty's just gone to wash her face, make herself look decent.'

'She doesn't have to go to any effort on our account . . .' Irene began.

Harry waved his hand and went to put the kettle on. He fussed with the teapot and the cups in a clumsy fashion, unused to messing about with all this womanish stuff. He counted teaspoons of loose tea into the pot, frowningly. 'She wants to make herself up for visitors. It's very good of you to come.'

It was more than a week since that service they had all attended at St Jude's. Since they had all stood on a bright sunny day watching an empty box being lowered into the earth. The whole thing had struck Harry as absurd, but it had been what Junie had declared she wanted, so there it was. 'She wants somewhere with a gravestone to mark who he was,' Cathy had explained to Derek's parents. 'So in later years she can take the babies there and show them.'

So they had all stumped up to pay for the empty grave. To Harry – never one for religion or elaborate shows of grief or sentiment – the whole thing seemed a bit of a waste. The money could be much better spent on feeding and dressing those bairns. They would soon need every penny they could get, without Derek's wages coming in . . .

'Ahh, there you are. Thanks for coming round.' Betty Minton tottered into the room, looking scrubbed and tired. The skin around her eyes was red and sore-looking and her hair was in a net because she hadn't bothered washing it. The most shocking thing about her to both Irene's and Tom's eyes was all the weight she had lost. The poor woman's brown crêpe dress was hanging off her. In a matter of weeks, she must have lost more than two stone.

'Drink your tea I've made for you,' Harry told her. 'Look, Irene's brought some biscuits.'

'They're not misshapes, either,' Irene said, presenting Betty with a fancy tin box of Wights Biscuits. It was a running joke locally about the broken misshapes coming cheap. These ones were a special treat, but even though she nodded appreciatively, Betty couldn't take a single bite.

'I've not been able to take a thing, Harry will tell you. Ever since we heard the news. And I can't set foot in the fish shop. Just the smell of the cooking fat turns my stomach. Our poor Minnie's been having to do all the work without me. She's had her young pal Susan in helping her, but she's been run ragged, poor lass.'

'Minnie is a marvel,' Irene smiled, sipping the weak tea that Harry had made for them.

'Minnie has taken it all hard as well, of course,' said Harry. 'Well, you know how close she and Derek were. Especially when they were little. They were two peas in a pod.' Alarmingly, the old man looked like he was about to cry. Irene and Tom tensed up until the moment passed and he regained control of himself.

'Look, if there's anything at all we can do . . .' Irene said.

Both bereft parents nodded at her. 'But what can you do?' said Betty despairingly. 'What is there to be done?'

'There's the bairns to be looked after and brought up,' Harry said.

'Yes, I'm sure the whole of Frederick Street will rally round and help Junie out with all of that, with seeing to them,' said

Irene firmly. 'Why, they'll want for nothing. And they'll have all the love and closeness they could ever want.'

Betty looked up, with a hard, sceptical look on her face. 'Oh, have you not heard then, hinny?' She shook her head. 'Junie says she's sticking in that lonely house of hers. She's going to take them back there. That cold, square, queer house on that half-finished estate. She says it's their home and she won't abandon it. I tried telling her – you'll be better off here, where everyone knows you. Where everyone can help. But she won't hear a word of it. She's stopping right there.'

Irene and Tom felt relieved to get away from the grieving parents, and then they felt guilty for feeling so. 'Shall we get a drink at the Robin Hood?' he asked her and she nodded.

'I need one,' she said. 'It's knocked me sick, seeing them like that. Betty and Harry were always so full of life. Almost like funny music hall characters, going on daft and all that. They've had all the stuffing knocked out of them.'

Tom took his wife's arm and led her to the pub at the top of Frederick Street. She gripped him tightly.

'I can't fathom what Junie must be going through,' she said. 'If I ever lost you, I don't know what I'd do. To be left alone with the bairns . . . I don't think I'd be able to cope . . .'

Tom patted her hand. 'You'd manage splendidly, I'm sure. But you don't have to worry about that, pet. I'm not going anywhere. And this street has already had its fair share of bad fortune. You know, I don't think lightning can strike twice . . .'

Irene glanced fearfully at the darkening sky. 'Oh, Tom . . . don't say things like that. Never . . . never tempt fate . . .'

Chapter Forty-Three

In the autumn, Arthur came home with a kitbag full of dirty washing, utterly exhausted from doing more than twelve shows a week. He'd been living in sometimes insalubrious digs in seaside towns all over the country and scrubbing out his socks and smalls in filthy sinks.

'I've had my eyes opened in more ways than one, I can tell you,' he declared to anyone who would listen back in South Shields. 'The life of a thespian isn't a very glamorous one by any means. I've lived with animals. Filthy beasts. And every night I'd have to jump on whatever stage it was and sing and act my heart out. Ohh, but it's been wonderful, Minnie. I wouldn't have missed a second of it.'

There were still traces of theatrical panstick make-up around his face that he hadn't managed to wash off, his beard was growing through and his hair was lank and greasy. He was beaming at her as he stood at the fish bar at the top of Frederick Street, soon after closing on a cool Friday night. He had come running up the hill to look for her as soon as his train had arrived in Shields. 'Are you glad to see me, then?' he grinned wolfishly.

He was a sight for sore eyes, all right. Minnie hadn't seen anyone look so happy in ages. The past few weeks had been mournful, dreadful ones around her house. Her mother was still in her trance of grief and still losing weight. The heavy wattles of flesh had disappeared from her face and she seemed to take up less than half the space that she used to. Her dad was treading on eggshells the whole time, terrified of saying the wrong thing. Minnie could see that he wanted to urge his poor wife to carry on living, to stop dwelling on her loss, terrible though it was. He was scared that she was going to drive herself into an early grave, and Minnie felt the same.

Tonight, Minnie was manning Swetty Betty's single-handedly, working automatically at the fryer and the till. The early queue had died down and the skies were turning lilac and gold over the harbour. She could see the colours in the top of the fish-shop windows and it felt like her soul cried out for that bit of colour and beauty.

Then, all at once, Arthur was standing there at her silver counter, with no warning whatsoever.

'How long are you home for?' she asked him. Really, she should have put down her work and dashed round the counter to hug him. But there was nothing wrong with playing slightly harder to get, she thought. He had run out on her. Why should she appear slavish and daft all the time?

'Just a couple of weeks till we're off again on the next round of shows. A murder thing and then we start rehearsals for the pantomime.'

Minnie couldn't help herself perking up at this, 'Ooh, a pantomime.'

He laughed excitedly, like a great daft bairn. 'I've always wanted to be in a pantomime. And get this – I'm Buttons. It's the biggest part I've ever had.' He pulled a comic, salacious face at his own double entendre.

'That's wonderful, Arthur. I'm very glad for you.' Minnie tried to make herself sound less excited than she actually felt.

She was punishing him, she thought, by not dancing to his merry tune. Not right away.

'We're doing it here, first, Minnie. We're playing South Shields first. And you'll get to see me in panto. What about that?'

Later that evening when all the fish and chips were gone and she'd cleaned up the place and turned out the lights, Minnie walked with him down the hill. They took one of their nocturnal walks around the streets, just as they had earlier in the year. *Back when I thought we were courting*, Minnie thought to herself sadly. *Courting, indeed.*

'I was so, so sorry to hear about Derek,' said Arthur. At last, he brought the subject up of everyone's terrible loss. So far, Arthur had been so full of himself and his show-business career, he gave the impression that he hadn't even thought about Derek at all. 'I know you loved your brother so much,' he went on. 'This must be a horrible time for you and your family.'

Minnie nodded and felt gratified that he'd actually thought about them. 'It's not been easy.'

'I-I would have come back, if I could . . . but, as you know, I was right down south, on the coast. There was no one to stand in for me, of course. It's a bare-bones company. They'd have sacked me if I'd gone off. Even if I'd said it was compassionate leave . . .'

Minnie could understand. But if he'd even just come for the service, that would have been something. She had lived through weeks, waiting for the door to swing open and for Arthur to step dramatically into the room. He would have made everything seem . . . not all right, exactly. But his presence would have been a relief. He was so big and noisy that it was like he could ward off anything bad or nasty. 'Thank you for the letter you sent us,' Minnie said, 'that was very nice. Very thoughtful.'

'It was the least I could do, but it was all I could do . . .'

Oh, how her mother and father had exclaimed over his beautiful penmanship, and the elegance of his sentiments. He had expressed his sorrow for Derek's loss really beautifully and her parents had nodded in appreciation over those sheets of blue onion-skin paper. 'They'll want to see you, to say thank you. Everyone will want to see you, now that you're back,' Minnie said.

'I wanted to see you first,' he told her. 'I . . . wanted to say sorry for your loss, in person. Derek was a lovely fella. And I felt a bit guilty, too.'

She glanced at him sharply. 'Guilty? What for?'

'I got him that job with the trams, didn't I? I spoke up for him. Why, without me, he'd still be safely working at the flamin' biscuit factory.'

'Oh, Arthur . . . no one has even thought about that for a single second. It was Derek himself who was so mad keen to become a tram driver. It was his choice. He was just where he wanted to be.'

Arthur pulled a face. 'I suppose so. It still feels strange. And I lost others, you know . . . other people I knew, from the trams. I heard that Tilda Grant was one of the clippies who died.'

'Yes, she was.'

'And I can't help feeling . . . that I might have been there, too. The chances were, if I was still working there, I'd have been killed as well.'

Minnie felt all of the blood run out of her face. She went cold inside. 'I hadn't even thought of that. Oh God, don't say that, Arthur, man. Everything's bad enough as it is.'

They truncated their walk around town and went to sit in a booth at Franchino's ice-cream parlour. Minnie stepped back as Arthur's sister, Mavis, grabbed him and gabbled away nosily. 'Eeeh, look at you! Buggerlugs! What are you doing here? Why did you never say you were coming home, you beggar?'

All the coffee drinkers paused to watch this tender reunion.

'I thought I'd surprise you,' Arthur mouthed at her, making sure she was picking up his words. 'I'm home for a few weeks, lovey.'

'Oh, smashing.' Mavis clasped her chest, her eyes misting up. 'Sam will be that pleased. We've both missed you, hinny. We've missed you something rotten.'

Listening to this, Minnie felt a stab of envy when she thought about Arthur and Sam together and that moment she thought she had observed. She had witnessed a strange, intimate scene between two very old friends. She shouldn't have stayed there to listen, trying to figure it out. It was nothing to do with her. It was her who had been in the wrong: that was the conclusion she had come to, eventually, as the weeks had gone by. It had been nothing to do with her at all, and she was best off forgetting all about it.

But what if she had really seen what she thought she saw? What would that mean? And what would it mean for her? Something jumped around in Minnie's heart: it felt like a strange dislocation, like she had suffered a sudden injury or hurt. Could such strange things really be? Such tender things? And what might it really mean for her own life? Her thoughts kept galloping away with her. Days and days went by and she kept thinking about them.

'Eeeh, let me bring you coffee and ice cream,' Mavis shooed them both into a corner booth where they could sit behind the privacy of frosted glass and shining mirrors.

'I'm glad that nothing much changes round here,' Arthur said, as they stirred the foam of their frothy coffee round their pale blue cups.

'Things do change,' Minnie sighed. 'Sometimes they're quite slow, other times it's all changed about in a flash. I feel like a different person to who I was in the war.'

'Do you?' He smiled at her warmly, staring straight at her, holding her gaze. She felt parched all at once and wanted to sip her coffee, but now she felt hypnotised by him. 'To me, you always seem like the same wonderful Minnie Minton.'

'I'm not so wonderful,' she frowned. And maybe that was the big change in her? Up until the past year or so, she had felt better about herself. She hadn't felt disappointed, like she seemed to all the time these days. She hadn't been cast off yet. The thing was, she had had her hopes raised up, and sometimes that was the cruellest thing that could happen to a person. Especially to one who was used to sitting on the sidelines, not expecting much out of life. It was quite impossible to express these ideas to Arthur tonight. How did you explain what it felt like to sit in the shadows to someone who was used to striding out into the limelight? He would think she was a fool.

'I think you're smashing,' he told her, and started eating his ice cream.

'Oh, I . . .' Minnie began hesitantly. But why should she be hesitant? She hadn't done anything wrong. 'I've been to see your . . . Elizabeth. Mrs Kendricks. I've been up to her house a couple of times to have tea with her.'

Arthur raised his plucked eyebrows. 'Have you, indeed?'

'She's a lonely soul. We seem to get on. She came down to the Robin Hood in person to see me. That's what started it. We've become . . . you'd almost say we've become friends.'

Arthur shrugged. 'Stranger things have happened.'

'That house . . .' Minnie sighed. 'It's falling down around her ears. She's got such lovely things there. She's been showing me. All of her treasures. And she showed me the little fancy outfits she bought for you to put on your shows when you were a bairn. You must have looked a picture.'

'I must have,' Arthur said sadly, and spooned up the melting gelato. 'That house . . . I wonder what she'll do about it. I wonder . . . if it'll ever have folk living in it again.'

'You're all she's got, you and Mavis . . .'

'Mavis wouldn't go and live there. That place gives Mavis the horrors. She thinks our adoptive mother is a witch.'

'Elizabeth . . . thinks you were wrong to break up with me,' said Minnie boldly. Her own outspokenness surprised her.

It surprised Arthur, too. 'Break up with you? Is that what I did?'

'Yes, you did,' Minnie burst out. 'Off you went. Nothing more was said. After you'd said . . . let's get married and all that. Odd bods fitting together and all that. But then you let it all drop . . .'

He looked pained. 'I just . . . went away. I had to go away on this tour. You knew that. But my feelings for you never, ever changed, Minnie.'

Anger flared up in her and her round face went red. 'I severely doubt that you ever had feelings for me, Arthur Kendricks. Not real ones. Just pretend ones.' She squinched her eyes tight shut to prevent herself from crying. 'I feel like you've been stringing me along and making fun out of me.'

'No . . .!' Arthur shouted out dramatically. Then he glanced about sheepishly and lowered his tone. 'I'd never willingly hurt you, Minnie. I love you. Maybe I'm not your average kind of bloke. Maybe it's not love that anyone else would recognise, but it comes from my heart and I'd never willingly run out on you or hurt you.'

'But you did!' she accused. 'That's exactly what you *did* do. You ran out on me.'

He took a heavy breath and bit his lip. This next thing was something he had hoped he wouldn't have to say. 'It was Derek. It was Derek who warned me off you. He told me that you deserved better than me. He told me to get right out of your life and to leave you alone.'

'*What* . . .?' Minnie sat there looking like he'd slapped her. '*Derek* said that?'

'I didn't want to tell you, but I've got no choice. I'd never have run out on you, Minnie. I think we should get married. I always did. Two lonely funny souls like us . . . I thought we could keep each other safe from the world. I still think we're the best thing that ever happened to each other and I think that your Derek was wrong.'

She was flummoxed. 'Derek told you to dump me?'

'Forget that now. Just forget it all and . . .'

Minnie's head was spinning, though. She sat in the corner booth and felt like she was on a fairground ride. What now? Where did all of this leave her now? Was it love she felt or was it just feeling sick and betrayed and hopelessly confused? Their being together would keep them safe from the world, Arthur had said. Yes, that was so very appealing as a thought. They could hide both their odd selves away from the world. Together they might look normal.

Chapter Forty-Four

The autumn winds came rushing along the seafront, bringing hints of the winter to come. 'The sea looks absolutely freezing, doesn't it?' Junie said, staring at the far distance and the frosted whitecaps coming all the way from Norway. She and her bairns were swaddled up against the cold, taking a brisk walk around their new neighbourhood. The twins were in the ancient black pram and her mother was pushing Ivy in her little chair. Cathy was feeling the cold in her aching bones, or so she claimed. She was slowing them all down. Junie wanted to be home in her little palace.

'You need to think more practically about things, our Junie,' her mother was admonishing her. 'I feel like you're burying your head in the sand.'

'What?' It was hard to hear what her mother was going on about, with both of them wearing headscarves and the wind whipping around them. 'What are you trying to say to me?' She couldn't keep that edge of anger and bitterness out of her voice. Try as she might, it seemed that everything she said these days sounded like she was furious at the world. Well, she had every right to be, didn't she?

'Living all the way out here . . . it doesn't make sense. Away from all your loved ones, who can help you and the bairns.'

'It's not that far,' Junie muttered. 'It's about half an hour door to door.'

'Aye,' Cathy conceded. 'But that's not the same as having you and the kiddies on the same street as me, is it? Or under the same roof. Don't you see how I'll worry about you all? Even when you went over the street to live with the Mintons, at least you were still within spitting distance . . .'

They were going over all this again and again until Junie was pig sick of it all. No, she didn't want to move back in with her mother, or, for that matter, Derek's parents. Her autonomy and her own home felt to her like hard-won things. They were the prize she had been fixed on for so long. She was damned if she was going to give them up now.

'But the bairns,' Cathy went on. 'What are you going to do about them? If you have to get a job to support yourself?'

Junie sneered at her mother. 'What do you mean, "if"? Why, of course I have to get a job. I have to get all the work I can to keep us going. You know that.'

'Well, of course, and I'll do everything I can to babysit. You know that. I can have them during the day, you know I don't mind. I love the bones of my grandbairns. But it does make it harder, that you're all the way out here . . .'

Junie was walking more briskly, her head held high as she pushed the second-hand pram. Her mother hobbled slightly on her painful knees. All those years standing at the bar had wrecked her joints, she realised. It felt as if they made noises like snapping twigs as she tried to keep up with her angry daughter. 'It's the house that me and Derek wanted together. It's our home. He didn't get to have it for long, but it's still his. It would feel wrong to give it back to the council for some other family to live in. Don't you see that, Mam?'

Cathy had to admit that she could see some warped logic in what Junie was saying. 'But Derek's never coming back, hinny. You do understand that, don't you?'

Junie turned to her mam and gave her such a strange, piercing look it made Cathy's heart freeze in her chest. She looked so anguished and hurt, but at the same time, there was something in her expression that made it seem that she had been caught out. Yes, caught out. Like caught out in a lie she was telling herself, or a futile dream she was entertaining.

As they turned back off the coastal road and into the lane to the estate, she confided to her mam, 'Oh, it's mad . . . but I kept seeing him everywhere. I was hallucinating him wherever I went. I'd catch a glimpse of someone who stood like him, or who walked like him . . . I'd run up to fellas in the street, hoping that when they turned round they would somehow, magically, turn out to be Derek. I thought I was going mad.'

'Ahh, lass,' Cathy said, linking arms with her, which was awkward when they were pushing both a pram and a pushchair. She had to give up the attempt at closeness after a few steps. 'Bless your heart. The mind can play funny tricks on you, especially when you're grieving.'

'Yes, but also during the first few weeks . . . there was this other thing. I'd sit up alone at night . . . I'd wait for everyone to go home and leave me alone. And people were so good to me. You were so good to me. But I longed to be alone. I'd sit there in that house and I'd wait. Because I just knew . . . I had this feeling that Derek was going to come back to me.'

Cathy drew in her breath sharply. 'What? Like in spirit form?'

Junie shook her head. 'No, no, nothing like that. We never believed in rubbish like that. No, I thought I would hear his key in the door. I thought I'd hear him come up the hall. Well, you remember how heavy he was on his feet, stomping about. Then I thought he'd walk into our new front room and he'd say, "Eeeh, what's all the bliddy tears about, our lass? Why are you looking like that at me?" And then I'd have to explain: "But we all think you're dead. We all thought you'd been blown to smithereens in the tram depot." Then he would gather me up in those huge arms of his and kiss me and say, "No, no, that was all a mistake. That was all a daft mistake. I'm still alive, Junie. I'm right here with you and I'm still alive."'

Cathy listened in dismay as Junie led them through the winding, empty streets where all the new family houses were going to be built. 'Oh, Junie. That's awful.'

Junie had tears running down her face. She paused to take out a hanky and her house keys before pushing the pram again. 'It wasn't awful. It was lovely. It was so him. He was exactly like him. I just knew it was going to happen like this. If I sat there alone, quietly, in the night. He would walk in again. Some day. I just had to sit there and be ready.' Now they were up the garden path and Junie was unlocking the front door. 'Well, weeks went by. I was holding my breath. I was keeping this whole thing secret from all of you. I'd even catch myself thinking: won't they be surprised when they find out that me and Derek have this secret from them all? Maybe they'll be mad at us. But then they'll be so glad to find out that it's all been a terrible mistake.'

Her mam helped her carry the heavy, clunky old pram over the doorstep. The babies were starting to grizzle, eager for their feed. In her pushchair, Ivy was as contentedly quiet as she always was. 'Ahh, pet.'

'Anyhow,' Junie paused in the dark hallway before snapping the lights on. 'It was all made-up rubbish, of course. It didn't matter how many nights I sat up waiting. He hasn't come back, has he? Not yet, anyway.'

'Shall we pop by and see her?'
'What time is it? What do you think?'
'It's on the way back home. It's not much of a detour.'

'We could hop off at the next stop, then . . .'

'You know what she's like. If we don't tell her, she'll kick up a fuss. Why was she the last to know . . . She hates being left out.'

'Ha'way then.' Arthur jumped off the tram at the stop and helped Minnie down. He carried on like the trams were still his province. When he was on board one of them, he showed off like mad, chatting with everyone and carrying on daft. Sometimes his forwardness with strangers made Minnie feel a mite embarrassed. He loved to get the old women giggling, and acted like it was a triumph when he cracked people up.

Tonight, it was dark as they left the tram early and headed off to knock on Junie's door.

'She might not appreciate us stopping by, if she's got the bairns to sleep . . .' Minnie worried.

'Ah, she'll be glad of the company. This estate of hers is a lonely old place, isn't it?' Arthur was frowning at the dark ploughed earth and the handful of council houses on the horizon.

'Well, she seems to like it here,' Minnie shrugged.

'I can't wait to tell her, can you?' Arthur grinned at her.

'Aye,' said Minnie.

She knocked at the door and it was answered by a blinking, surprised-looking Junie. 'What are you two doing here at this time?'

'We've been out at Seahouses seeing my guardian,' Arthur said, using the posh word that sounded so impressive to Minnie. She wondered how much it must hurt Elizabeth's feelings that Arthur had never really called her his mam.

'Oh, have you indeed?' Junie asked and let them into the house. In the living room, they discovered that Cathy was there, and that all three bairns were still up, getting their feeds.

'It looks like action stations here,' Minnie said. 'We'll not bother you for long.'

'I'll make some tea,' said Cathy, getting up with Ivy clinging to her.

'We've had gallons of tea already,' Arthur said. 'We've sat with Elizabeth Kendricks all afternoon. Maybe a tot of something stronger would be good. Then we could have a toast.'

'A toast, eh?' asked Junie, narrowing her eyes at the pair of them. She had a baby over each shoulder and looked like she had no patience whatsoever. 'What's the toast to be about, eh?'

'It's what we went to tell Elizabeth this afternoon. Straight after we told my mam and dad, as well,' Minnie explained solemnly. 'You see . . . it's me and Arthur. We're going to get married. And we're moving into Elizabeth's house. Can you believe it? We're going to live in her great big house.'

Junie simply stared at her oldest friend. 'You're going to do *what . . .?*'

Chapter Forty-Five

For once, everyone at the Women's Table was in agreement. It didn't happen often. But as they sat around in front of the fire that particular night, they all agreed that the forthcoming wedding between Minnie Minton and Arthur Kendricks was a marvellous thing.

'Why, aye,' Ma Ada nodded firmly, well into her third half-pint of stout. Tonight was an unusual night, with more of her friends in attendance, more matters in hand to discuss, and therefore more drinks to be carefully eked out. 'That daft Minnie deserves a bit of good luck. Her family's had a rough time of it. Why shouldn't the lass be happy? She's allus been a plain little thing . . . but by, she's blooming with happiness lately.'

Ma Ada was apt to become noisily sentimental when in her cups, and they all knew it. On the stool beside her, the wildly white-haired prognosticator Winnie was nodding sagely. 'Aye, and I saw all the bad fortune and disaster coming, didn't I? I warned them, didn't I? But no one can really be prepared . . .'

Bella Franchino – who, since her own family tragedy, had become very alert to superstitious things – asked her: 'And what do you see in the future now, Winnie?'

The old travelling woman was gratified by the attention she was getting. Lately – after a run of successful predictions - she was receiving a bit more respect. After years of being ridiculed, Winnie was actually being listened to. 'I see a lot of happiness about,' she said, sounding almost disappointed. 'I don't anticipate many major disasters. This business of the wedding is a good one and Minnie is going to take to her life in yon big house like a duck to water.' She stared at Bella with her ice-blue eyes. 'And this venture of yours, with the ice-cream kiosks on the seafront. That's going to be a big hit, come next summer.'

They all laughed at this.

Irene Farley looked delighted for Bella. 'Well, there you are, pet. You can't ask for better than that. The seal of approval from mystical Winnie.' Irene had become quite inured to the old woman's rambling predictions over the years. 'Won't it be lovely to be down on the sands in the summer all day, selling ices and making coffee?'

'Remember, I've promised you a kiosk of your own,' Bella told Irene.

'And me?' piped up Mavis huskily. 'I'm a loyal employee, too. Will I get my own ice-cream stand to run on me own?'

'Errmm,' said Bella. 'We'll see. Perhaps you'll be better off helping Irene?' She knew all too well that Mavis was hopeless at handling money, and even though she said her hearing was just about normal nowadays, it wasn't at all.

Luckily, Mavis didn't push the point and her flighty thoughts were back with the impending wedding. 'Eeeh, wait till you see what our Arthur's got himself for the day. He's only wearing white, isn't he? He's got an ivory linen suit lined up for himself, from a theatrical costumier in Newcastle who he's pals with.'

The women all hooted with mirth at this. 'Whoever heard of the fella wearing white to his wedding?' laughed Ma Ada.

'He'll look lovely,' sighed Mavis. Everyone knew that her brother could never do wrong in her eyes.

They were joined by landlady Cathy, who seemed absolutely worn out tonight. In recent weeks, she had been looking her age, and it was no wonder. What with all the dashing back and forth between Junie's house and here that she was doing. The biggest surprise tonight was that she hadn't even done her hair. Her luscious red locks were tied up in a ponytail, as if she hadn't had time for anything more elaborate. She sat with the girls and sipped a dry sherry, taking advantage of a lull at the bar. 'Now then, lasses. What's all the merriment about?'

'Ah, just wedding talk,' Bella shrugged.

Cathy felt a little left out of it all. Was everyone tactfully keeping away from the subject in her presence because of her daughter's bereavement? That was daft, if they were. Hadn't Minnie also been bereaved? Cathy spoke up: 'I must say, I'm glad that this wedding is happening. We all need cheering up. Especially the Mintons. I've not seen her mother in ages. I've knocked on the door and she didn't want visitors. The fish bar's been shut for weeks now . . .'

'Don't I know it,' Winnie burst out. 'I've had to walk all the way to the Nook for my supper.'

'Hopefully, Minnie's happiness will help Betty get back to her normal self . . .' Cathy worried.

'The shock of sudden loss like that,' Bella began. 'It . . . can take a while . . .'

'Yes, of course – you know more about that than most,' Cathy murmured. 'But look at you, Bella. Since your terrible loss and family tragedy, you've come into your own. You're a credit to your mam and dad. You've stood on your own two feet and made them proud.'

Winnie slurped her pint. 'Well, apart from when you go running around with one of them Johnson lads. I happen to know that your deceased parents aren't quite so chuffed about that . . .'

Everyone glared at the ever-tactless Winnie.

Cathy swerved the subject back to the wedding: 'I hear that you're doing the reception for Minnie and Arthur down at Franchino's?'

Bella nodded shyly. 'Yes . . . I hope you won't mind, Cathy?'

'Me? Why should I mind?'

'Well, I know that you usually have receptions here and it's the done thing in this street. And I know that Minnie has worked here at the Robin Hood for so long that it's like she's one of your own family. But I offered this as my gift to them. It's the best thing I can do for them. They've both been good friends to me . . .'

'Of course.' Cathy smiled at her. She loved the fact that Bella was so open-hearted and delightfully straightforward. Why, she reminded Cathy of Bella's own mother, Sofia, in that regard. She had her same beauty and her openness. There was no other side to Bella. There was nothing sly or self-serving to her. 'As a matter of fact, I'm just as glad. If I had one more thing to do, I'd have the screaming hysterics. If Minnie had asked me to do the party here, I'd have felt obliged to say yes . . . but I really haven't got the time or the energy . . .'

All of Cathy's friends at the Women's Table looked at her, quite concerned then. It was true that Cathy looked very pale and drawn. They had assumed she was just run ragged by that daughter of hers and the grandbairns. But what if it was more? What if she was sick?

Ma Ada and Winnie exchanged a significant glance. They would have to keep a watchful eye on their landlady friend.

Minnie was surprised to find that things had changed in Junie's house in only the week or so since she had last been here.

'Ooh, lovely curtains,' Minnie gasped, hurrying over to touch the rich, wine-coloured brocade. 'Why, pet, these must have cost you a fortune.'

Junie was scowling on the sofa with the bairns laid out on the cushions beside her, all squalling and boisterously hungry. 'Not as expensive as you might think. But I needed something to put up at the windows, didn't I? I needed some privacy. There are new folk down the road; there are new people moving into these houses all the time, as soon as the houses are finished. I don't want them all looking in through my bare windows and spying on me, do I?'

Minnie looked at her friend worriedly. She was sounding harried and shrill. 'Hey, now . . . I didn't mean anything by it, hinny. I was hardly judging you, was I?'

Junie glared at her. 'I know what you and all the others say. You've always said it about me. There goes that Junie, all dolled up to the nines. She likes shopping in the fancy places, doesn't she? She's never liked to have second best. Well, it's true. I won't wear rags and now I've got my own home I want it to be as nice as it can be. I deserve that much, don't I? Or do I have to sit in a hovel and wear widow's weeds all the time, eh?'

'Junie, no one's ever said anything like that,' Minnie said, feeling flustered and hating to upset her friend. 'All I did was comment on your lovely new curtains.'

'Yes, well, you can comment on the dear new settee as well, if you like. And the bliddy cushions. 'Cause they're all new as well, and they come from the big shop. They cost a pretty penny, too.' Junie was defiant and strident.

'What?' Minnie went over to sit on the pouffe beside her and helped give the bottles to the bairns. 'But I thought you were struggling for money? You said you'd have to get jobs as soon as you could leave the bairns with a sitter . . .'

They sat listening to the bairns pulling and sucking on the rubber teats of the bottles and gulping the warm milk so eagerly. It was a sound that always cheered Minnie and made her want to laugh: they always sounded so busy and keen.

Then Junie said, quite craftily: 'I had some cash socked away. I never told anyone about it. I suppose . . . it was stolen, really. But the one I stole it from deserved to have it taken from them. They deserved it, right? And after all my tragedy, I deserve a little happiness, don't I?'

Minnie was alarmed. 'Y-you stole money . . .?'

'Oh . . .' Junie shrugged. 'The people who it rightly belonged to . . . well, they're all dead now anyway. It would be too late to return it to them.' She gave a brittle laugh. 'And I know better than anyone, don't I? That you can't bring people back from the dead. So . . . I just figured . . . I should just blow all that money I had hidden away. I should just spend it all now, on making this place into a palace for myself. And it *is*, isn't it, Minnie? It's a real palace, isn't it? It's a lovely home now, isn't it?'

Minnie smiled at her friend, wishing that she would calm down a bit. She was letting Junie get away with things yet again, she knew. She had stolen money, and Minnie had an idea where the money had come from. But it was all a long time ago and, yes, the people were gone. Time was moving on. She'd rather see Junie happy now. That was important. Minnie would just have to turn a blind eye again. 'Aye, pet, it's really lovely. Them curtains are the fanciest I've ever seen. They'll keep out the draughts and the eyes of the world, all right . . .'

'That's what I thought,' Junie nodded.

'But what will you do for money now? That nest egg could have lasted you a while . . .'

Junie's face hardened. 'I'm not afraid of hard work.'

Chapter Forty-Six

When it came to the actual wedding at St Jude's – rapidly but lavishly organised – Junie put her foot down.

'I'm sorry, I can't be Minnie's chief bridesmaid. I just can't. How do you think that would make *me* feel?'

It was only days before the actual event and the denizens of Frederick Street were full of excitement. It felt like one of the few outright, whole-hearted celebrations they had been able to share since VE Day. There were some who viewed the coming union of the comic Arthur with the ungainly Minnie as an incongruous – even laughable – spectacle. But even those folk were keen to don their best bib and tucker and polish up their shiniest shoes to step into church to witness the affair. All the stops were being pulled out and everyone was preparing to sing hymns until the old church's rafters shook. Then, as word had it, there was to be a proper feast at Franchino's.

Even Mr Chesney was being dragged along by his daughters, and their elderly grandfather, Mr Wight, would be making an appearance. It seemed, as far as Cathy Sturrock could see, that everyone who was anyone in the Sixteen Streets would be paying their compliments to the bride- and the groom-to-be.

'Well, I don't have to if I don't want to,' said her daughter snappishly, snuggled into her plush cushions on her new settee.

'Everyone knows how I'm fixed here with all the babies to see to. No one would mind me missing a wedding.'

'Wrong,' Cathy told her flatly. 'Of course they will miss you. Minnie especially. You two have been friends forever and people will be thinking there's been some terrible falling-out.'

'No, they won't, Mother,' Junie sighed. 'And it's got nothing to do with anyone else, either. Look, I just don't have the energy for all of this. It's hardly any time at all since Derek was killed. I'm a widow. I'm in mourning, here. Don't you think people will understand?'

Her mother was looking at Junie's new pink satin housecoat and the burgundy velveteen of her new three-piece suite. Her mouth squinched up in a judgemental, ironic expression. 'I'm sure people have every sympathy for what's happened to you, Junie. Derek's loss was a terrible, dreadful thing and everyone's hearts broke for him and for you.'

'There you go, then,' Junie said, with satisfaction. 'So no one would expect me to go through the torture of someone else's lovely, lavish wedding, would they?' She leaned forward to pick up her tea. She had china teacups and saucers out for her mam. 'I never got a lavish wedding, did I?' she said, pitifully.

Cathy gasped at this. 'Eeeh, our Junie . . . that's never what this is about, is it?'

'What?' Junie frowned. Her mother was reacting wrongly. She should be wrapped round Junie's finger by now and doing what she wanted. Instead, she was shouting out and her raised voice was going to wake the bairns if she kept it up like this.

'You're jealous. You're jealous of your poor friend. Poor bloody Minnie, who's never had a lucky break in her whole flamin' life. She gets a bit of luck. She gets a shot at happiness. And how do you react? You put your dainty little foot down. You won't even go to her wedding. You won't give the poor little cow your blessing.'

Junie looked down. She flushed with anger and shame. Her mother had seen straight through her, as usual. 'That's nonsense. What a thing to think.' Still she tried to brazen it out, sipping her tea and avoiding her mother's shrewd eye. 'How could I be jealous of Minnie?'

'Because even if they might look like a funny match on the face of it, her and Arthur really do feel something for each other. They deserve as much chance of happiness as anyone else.'

At this, Junie was surprised to experience a gut-wrenching blast of true, indignant feeling. She had been play-acting and exaggerating and manipulating people for so long, it came as a shock to her when her insides rose up in genuine fury at her mother's words. She felt sick as she raged back: 'And what about *me*? My happiness? I was more in love with Derek than them two are with each other. They're just playing at it like bairns. They can't be in love. Not like I was. Not like me and Derek were!'

Cathy was out of her chair and beside her daughter in a flash. She folded her up in her thick arms, patting and stroking her as she sobbed. She, too, was alarmed by this sudden rush of genuine emotion in the girl. She was all too aware – much more aware than Junie knew – of how often the tears and the tempers were put on. But this was all real. She was still grieving, of course she was. But she was letting her sadness make her spiteful, and that, to Cathy, was a shame. 'There, there, pet. Come on, think again. Come to Minnie's wedding. We can get the bairns there, too. We'll all be there. You can dance at Minnie's wedding and wish the pair of them well . . .'

Junie kept shaking her head miserably, even locked as she was in her mother's embrace. 'No, no, I can't. I feel like . . . I feel like they're . . . mocking me. It's like they're taunting me . . . by being so happy . . . by having this whole do . . . when I'm left on my own like this . . .'

'Ah, pet,' her mother rocked her in her capable arms on the new settee. 'Now that's a dreadful thing to think. Other people's happiness doesn't come at your expense. We're not in debt to each other like that. Everyone's lives just go on in their own ways. We're all up and down at different times . . .'

But Junie was hardly listening. The floodgates had really opened up now. She wept on her mother like she never had before. 'I really miss him so much, Mam . . .'

Cathy comforted her. It was quite simple, comforting her, and she was happy that she could do so. In truth, Cathy had longed for this moment ever since she had first been reunited with her lost daughter. How sad it had to be like this, after such an awful loss . . . but still she was glad the two of them were close. *At last, at last*, she thought, and hugged her daughter closer.

The night before the wedding, bride and groom decamped to their families' homes and spent an evening apart. There was a small, not too raucous celebration at Mavis and Sam's house, where Arthur and his good fortune were toasted by a small number of friends. Bella brought Jonas for an hour or two, even though they still had work to do readying the ice-cream parlour for tomorrow's reception.

They drank rum and brandy and all the other spirits from the sideboard in the cluttered living room and beamed at each other sloppily. They made sentimental speeches in each other's honour and there was much singing.

'I mustn't get too drunk tonight,' Arthur beamed at them. 'I'm getting married in the morning . . .'

'Too late,' Sam cried out and topped up his glass with a poisonous-looking liqueur that had been in the cabinet since before the war.

'You have to be on your best behaviour tomorrow, you bugger!' Mavis warned him. 'This will be the biggest day of

Minnie's life. If it's anything like *my* day was . . .' And here Mavis went off into a private reverie about the happiest day in her own life, not so long ago, and also at St Jude's. She blinked her eyes open as she remembered one of the few factors that had marred her day of days. 'Is Mrs Kendricks coming?'

Arthur didn't like the way she referred to their adoptive mother in this formal tone. The breach between them would never be healed, it seemed. They would never find the footing that Arthur and Elizabeth had established. It seemed a pity to him that his sister couldn't accept the old woman's excuses about the past and simply move on. Elizabeth would love to be a part of Mavis and Sam's life. She wasn't as snooty and as snobby as she seemed. Arthur knew – just as Minnie had realised – that Elizabeth was dreadfully lonely. She had suffered enough already for her insensitivity and her onetime belief that her fortune could buy her anything at all, even people.

'Ah, Mavis,' Arthur held her face in his hands and enunciated carefully so she could follow his words. 'Our adoptive mother will be there, and you must greet her warmly. She is a part of our lives again now. And, as you know, Minnie and I will be living at her house from now on. When I am away working, that's where Minnie will be.'

This was news to Bella Franchino, who gasped to hear it. 'You mean . . . Minnie is going to leave Frederick Street behind?'

'Oh yes, indeed,' grinned Arthur. 'Actually, she's rather relishing the thought of living at the big house . . .'

It was all news to Minnie's mam and dad, too, and delivered in an offhand way by Minnie on the night before her wedding.

The three of them were sitting up in the parlour, and Betty was helping her daughter with some final work on the wedding dress they had put together so quickly. It had all come from second-hand panels of silk and oddments and scraps from the Chesney girls' shop. Really, it was a magpie affair, with pieces snitched from here and there. Minnie was rather proud of that fact and adored the way the dress looked on her. She had never had a figure before – not like this.

'I'm an hourglass. I've a proper curved shape,' she gasped, and her mother smiled at her delight. She and her daughter and her husband had all shed pounds since Derek's death.

'Eeeh, what would our lad say, if he could see you getting ready for your big day?' Harry grinned. 'He'd be so proud of you.'

Minnie wasn't quite so sure. She believed what Arthur had told her: that he'd been warned off courting her by her beloved brother. Mistaken and wrong-headed, Derek had muscled in and tried to interfere with her happiness. It left a sour taste in her mouth that she was trying to ignore. The truth was, if Derek was still here, he might have been kicking up a ruckus about Minnie's fast-approaching ceremony.

They drank tea and they sewed. There were seed pearls and satin bows and all kinds of whatnots still to be added to the dress. Susan had nipped up the street with another bagful of them this afternoon. She had been slipping choice bits of frippery from the fancy emporium, right from under her sisters' noses. 'They won't miss a few bits,' Susan had grinned, from under her shapeless, floppy hat. 'Please consider all these pieces for your gown as my contribution to the day . . . and please know that you have all my love and best wishes, Minnie.' She had smiled sadly on the doorstep of number fifteen.

Minnie had been puzzled by her sweet, sad expression. 'Won't you come in? We're just spending the evening quietly in the parlour, sewing and—'

'I won't intrude,' Susan Chesney had shaken her head and backed away along the cobbled street. 'I'll see you tomorrow in the church.' Then she was gone.

And now the last few pearls and beads and bows she had brought were almost all fixed in place. Thankfully, talk had turned from Minnie's deceased brother to where she was going to live.

'We haven't discussed this properly yet,' her mother said, looking anxious. 'Your father and I have talked about it and, of course, we would love you both to be here. There's enough space. We have the room now, and . . .'

Minnie shook her head sadly. 'Mam, Mam . . . I won't be living here. I'll be moving out.'

Betty had to sit down with shock. 'You'll what?' Then she clutched her chest. 'You're not going after him in this ridiculous search for fame, are you? You're not going down south? You're never going . . . to that *London*?'

Minnie smiled and shook her head. 'No, no. Not that far. No fear.'

'Well, that's something,' Harry mumbled, standing by the fire and looking worried.

Betty glared at her daughter. 'Well then, where is it that you think you're going to be living as a married woman, my girl?'

Minnie said, quite simply: 'I'm going to be living in the big house. That's where I'm going to be.'

Chapter Forty-Seven

This time, at this wedding, Elizabeth Kendricks felt welcome at St Jude's. Thank goodness.

This time, she sat right at the front, one of the few people on the groom's side of the church. She was in all of her finery: fur and feathers and cashmere. She wore layers and layers of clothing because the place was so draughty and cold. Still, her heart glowed with happiness and that spread a kind of inner warmth through her whole body. It didn't go quite as far as her numb, empurpled fingers as they gripped her hymn book, but you couldn't have everything.

It was all worth it, just to see her beloved boy getting married. It was even worth being down in this part of the town, in the dreadful slums. It was appalling, actually. They were right beneath the shadows of the cranes and ships. This church was so cold because it was never in the sunlight. Its ancient stones were perpetually chilled by the darkness, the poverty and the hopelessness that existed all around it. That's what Elizabeth Kendricks imagined, anyhow.

But still, these were the people that her beloved son had chosen to live among. Both he and his far less loyal sister, Mavis, had chosen this life for themselves, among this type. It was as if something deeply abiding, deep inside them had reverted to type the moment they had chosen, as children, to run away from the comfortable home that Elizabeth had provided them with. They ran back at once to the heartland of the peasants they truly belonged to.

Surreptitiously, the old woman looked around the rest of the congregation and was amazed and appalled by the ragtag rabble who had trooped out. She almost felt ashamed to be among them. All of them had made an effort with their dress, she had to concede, but their poverty was still so strikingly evident. Why, it seemed that most of the clothes people were wearing dated back to well before the war. They had brushed the coal dust and creases out of their old suits and frocks and donned them, hoping that they would do. Elizabeth's heart ached for these poor, brave people. She was appalled by them and their salty, coarse talk, but she pitied them all as well.

Arthur caught her eye as he went to stand up at the front with his best man, Sam. He grinned and nodded at his adoptive mother. It was an acknowledgement and a thank you, she realised. He was thanking her for everything she had ever done for him. As well he might. She had instilled in him his belief in himself. She had given him the confidence and the wherewithal to escape the circumstances of his birth, yes. Her Arthur was going to go far, and it would be partly – even mostly – down to her.

His being married was a good thing. It was a steadying thing. It would look good to the outside world, to see that he had a normal married life.

And, while he was away living his life in show business, Elizabeth would have a companion, a friend and a housemaid. Yes, Minnie would surely willingly become all those things. Everything was working out very nicely indeed.

At that moment, Aunty Martha sat up straighter at the organ, pressing down on the pedals with all her might and striking up the wedding march. Here came Minnie herself, at a stately pace, held proudly on the arm of that smiling, rather slow-witted father of hers. She had slimmed down – mercifully – and was wearing a bizarre confection of lace and silk and silver beading. Evidently home-made and the work of many hands. Elizabeth had to give it to these people – they were pragmatic. They could turn their hands to anything and make something out of nothing. Look at the raw materials this strange, moon-faced girl had been given to start out with. Not very promising, really. But she was willing to work and persevere, and there was something docile and sweet about her nature that Elizabeth found appealing. And so she had been given an opportunity to better herself. It was very gratifying to be a small part in the betterment of Minnie Minton. Minnie Kendricks, as she must now be called.

Now here was Arthur, immaculate in his own ivory outfit, welcoming his intended at the altar. There was such joy in his face that Elizabeth was almost taken aback. Why, the lad had genuine feeling for this girl, after all. She could see it in his brilliant eyes, in the clear light of the church. Was it really love like a man felt for his bride? Old-fashioned romantic love? Well, would Elizabeth even have recognised such a thing if she ever saw it? Like the peasants round here, she was pragmatic, too. She knew that matches had to be made and marriages had to be lived through. Sometimes they were conveniences and subterfuges. Sometimes they were one thing to one partner, and something else again to the other. Here, she started thinking about her own husband from long ago, as the priest began intoning and slurring his welcoming words . . .

Ah, but it was over in a flash.

Before she even knew it, Minnie was back outside the front of St Jude's in the frosty air, standing between her lovely new husband and her chief bridesmaid, Irene Farley.

'Eeeh, that went like a dream,' Irene said to her, patting her back as they readied themselves for photographs. It was all a palaver with the man from the expensive shop on Fowler Street. He had all his equipment ready, plus an elaborate set of flashes and a strange umbrella, but he seemed a dithery, indecisive sort who didn't quite know what he was about.

'Well, nothing's gone wrong . . . so far,' Minnie gasped, shivering through her thin dress.

'Nothing will,' Irene reassured her. 'Plus, the most important part is done with now. You've both said your vows in the church and you've signed the special book. That's it now, you're hitched. You're stuck with that daft bloke forever.'

There was a wave of laughter then, and they realised that Arthur was doing what he always did when there was an opportunity or a hitch in the proceedings. He was making everyone laugh. He was taking the mick out of the hapless photographer, who only grew more ham-fisted and nervous the more that Arthur drew attention to him. 'Come on, mate,' Arthur urged him. 'Or we'll be having to go back in for the funerals of some of these old buggers. Some of them don't have very much time left.'

Minnie blushed as he called out and jollied everyone along. She linked arms with him in the middle of their assembled guests and glowed with pride at his noisy nonsense. She could feel herself growing quieter as he grew louder. It almost felt like a relief. *Now I am allowed to be quieter and to retreat into myself a little. I don't have to be brave, confident Minnie, always on my own. Now I can rely on someone brasher and more boisterous than I could ever be.*

'All these people all dressed up for your wedding, Minnie,' Arthur whispered into her ear as the camera at last started flashing and the moments were preserved. 'Isn't that wonderful? They're here to be with us, and to celebrate *us*.'

It did feel wonderful, after all, to realise that people had trooped out today for their sake. All her life, Minnie had been used to feeling like the girl on the edge of things. She would always be on the sidelines and never getting noticed. Well, not today, it seemed. Today, she was standing right in the limelight with her man. They were both standing right in the middle of the picture.

'This whole group of people,' she said to him, once the photos were taken and the group started to break apart. 'We are everyone who has survived. We are the ones who came through the war years . . . and we are *still* here.'

Arthur tried to kiss her through her billowing veil. 'Yes, my love . . . we're still here. We are the survivors!'

The reception at Franchino's was civilised at first. Lovely music was playing and there was ice cream and coffee for everyone. There weren't quite enough places for everyone to sit and soon the glass windows and partitions were misting up with condensation. Then the big band jazz records came out and a larger space was cleared for dancing. From somewhere, there appeared bottles of spirits and beer, courtesy of Cathy and Bob from the Robin Hood. There were also a couple of bottles of lethal limoncello that Bella had concocted from her beloved Nonna's ancient recipe.

Minnie danced all evening long with her new husband. They were the first ones up, encouraging everyone to forget their inhibitions and just dance. Then they were almost the last ones standing, come midnight, when everyone in their Sunday best was looking a sight more damp, depleted and dishevelled.

The oldies sat in the booths at the back of the ice-cream parlour, conserving their energy and sipping their drinks.

'We've made another Women's Table here, in another home,' Ma Ada cackled, as she took note of the women's faces around her at the back of the room.

'We have indeed,' said her friend Winnie, looking even more witch-like than ever in the bizarre purple outfit she had chosen for herself at the Chesney girls' emporium. 'Wherever we sit, it's the Women's Table, and from where we sit, we can see everything.'

Beside them sat the mother of the bride, Betty Minton, who was feeling very small and unsure of herself today. Several times she had tried to give herself a talking-to: 'Look, buck up your ideas, woman. This is one of those days you should remember all your life. Your little lass is getting hitched. Now, you should be delighted, shouldn't you?'

She had tried her very best to look as happy as could be. She had applauded and sung and cried out her congratulations with all her heart. But inside her best clothes, her heart was breaking. She couldn't make herself forget the fact that Derek wasn't here to see his sister wed. Harry had told her: 'Put it out of your mind for the day. Concentrate on our Minnie's happiness, can't you?' And she was shocked by how callous that had sounded. How could she put her dead lad to one side? How cruel was that? How horrible was that? It would feel like a betrayal.

Mind, Harry seemed to be managing all right. There he was, on the makeshift dance floor, jigging about with the rest of them. What was that playing? Minnie the Moocher or some nonsense. Cab Calloway, someone said. Harry seemed to be having a rare old time, stripped to his shirtsleeves and hopping around.

Oh, but I'm sounding so bitter and nasty, Betty thought. *I mustn't, I simply mustn't let grief turn me into a sour person like that. She had seen it happen to others . . .*

At that moment, she felt a cold hand on her arm. She realised that Elizabeth Kendricks was leaning in to speak with her. That snooty old dame – what relation was she to her now? She supposed they were both bonded forever over the union of their children. Well, she looked a bit fancy and hoity-toity, but Betty was prepared to give the old bird a chance.

'You won't miss Minnie, then?' she was asking, raising her voice above the level of the music.

'What's that?'

'When they move in with me,' Elizabeth went on. 'You won't miss her living with you.'

'Well, of course I will,' Betty shot back. 'What do you think? Our bliddy house is going to be empty. Empty.' The sudden force of her feelings surprised Betty. They burst out of her, and next thing she knew, her eyes were wet and her pulse was pumping at her exposed throat. 'We used to have a full house. You could never get moved. We took in other people's bairns when they needed us. We had a house that was teeming. Our older sons fled the nest. Derek is dead. Minnie is leaving us. And now . . . now there's no one. Just us.'

Elizabeth nodded sagely. 'Yes, I'm quite used to living in a lonely house. It can be a terrible thing.'

Betty glared at her. The old woman was looking very pleased with herself. Why shouldn't she? Her sort always got just what they wanted. 'Now I've got no one to work at the fish bar with me,' Betty said. 'I might have to close up shop.'

Elizabeth smiled wanly. She couldn't imagine anything more horrid than working in all that steam and grease. It had completely ruined Betty's complexion, it was obvious, and poor Minnie had been going the same way. But not anymore. Now she had been rescued from all of that. 'You will be so proud of your daughter,' the old woman said. 'I'm going to make it my business to see that she turns into a proper lady.'

Betty's eyes widened. 'You're going to turn our Minnie into a proper lady, are you?'

'When she lives under my roof with me, it will be inevitable.'

'And . . . that's what she wants, is it?'

'Oh yes,' said Elizabeth. 'She does indeed. She wants to be a credit to Arthur, you see. He's going places in his career and she wants to be able to blend in and mix with all the top people he will meet. She wants to better herself, you see. And that's good, isn't it?'

Betty felt her heart breaking inside of her. She couldn't let it show though. Not for one second. She couldn't let this old bitch see all that hurting.

Elizabeth went on: 'Don't worry, my dear. I can see that you're nervous for her. I will guide her. I promise. I will see to it that your daughter is worthy of my Arthur. And she will be. With a little work, I am sure she will be fine.'

Chapter Forty-Eight

The kiosk stood just a short distance from the fairground's edge, at the top of the golden sands. 'It's the perfect placement,' Bella Franchino had enthused at the start of the season. 'You'll be right where all the kids pass by, to and from the beach. And you're only a few yards for all the old grannies playing bingo and the amusements to come toddling out when they need refreshments. You'll do a roaring trade.'

Well, clever Bella had been right, of course. Now it was late in the summer heatwave and Irene had been run off her feet for days on end. More or less ably assisted by Mavis Farley, she had piped ice cream onto cones and into paper dishes and sold it by the tonne. She had brewed up paper cups of frothy coffee by the hundred, it seemed like, as well as little cups of diluted orange. It was said that there was no money about these days, still so relatively soon after the war, but it seemed like people had enough to spend on refreshments when they needed to. And under the bright, spangling sun of late July that year, they certainly needed refreshment.

'Eeeh, isn't it lovely?' Mavis sighed loudly, leaning on the glass walls of the kiosk during a rare lull in custom. She was dreamily smoking a cigarette and gazing into the spotless blue sky. 'Can you even remember what it was like when we couldn't get down on the beach? When it was all roped off and covered in barbed wire? When we thought the bloomin' Germans were gonna come storming up the sands any day?'

Aye, as it happened, Irene could remember exactly what all that had felt like. It hadn't been so long ago. She had lay in bed terrified at such a prospect, especially after she had become a mammy. She used to lie with her heart racing, wondering just what kind of a world she had elected to bring her bairns into. One with bombs, barbed wire and the threat of imminent invasion.

But now the whole world was at peace again, or so they said. And that was the way it was to stay. The most important thing was to get back to normal and to remind everyone of what normality felt like – and that included enjoying themselves in the summer, when the weather was as glorious as this, especially.

'We've been very lucky,' Irene said. 'To be here and well and able to enjoy life. After everything. After so many didn't make it this far.'

'Aye, you're right, uh-huh,' Mavis noisily agreed, smacking her lips on the freebie ice cone Irene had given her. 'So many weren't lucky like us, were they?'

For just an instant, Irene felt her heart twinge and her eyes begin to prickle with tears. She had thought her Tom had returned from his war duties safe and well. These days, she wasn't quite so sure. The way he was coughing lately . . . well, he'd always coughed. His whole family smoked Woodbines, of course . . . but this was different. He was up in the night, sitting hunched forward in the bed, waking her up with all of his heaving noise. 'W-what's the matter? Tom?' She was frightened when he couldn't catch enough breath to answer her. His whole slender body would be shaking. This occurred night after night and she was trying to get him to seek help;

to get his chest listened to by the doctor. It couldn't be right, could it? Irene knew that it just had to have something to do with him being up in those planes. He had described to her the flames, the smoke, the hot burning fumes. She was convinced that he had been breathing in substances that had done him some lasting damage . . . and together they had sat awake through the night, trying to calm his breath and his racing heart.

She shook her head to clear it of these discomforting thoughts. He was a grown man and she couldn't force him to go to the hospital, could she? He belonged to a world of men who ignored anything that was wrong with them, and simply tried to soldier on. *I'll have to convince him*, Irene thought determinedly. *He's got two bairns and an adopted one, and he's got me as well. He needs to be fit and well and to stay with us . . .*

'You've gone off into a dream,' Mavis was shouting at her. 'Irene, man. You're in a trance.'

She blinked at Mavis's raucous noise and smiled. 'Oh. Sorry . . .' She reeled slightly, seeing sunspots. 'I was staring straight at the sun there . . .'

'You're so serious-looking, Irene,' Mavis joshed her. 'Look, pet – we're about to have visitors. Ahhh, look at the bairns.'

Irene looked across to see Cathy Sturrock approaching with all three of her daughter's bairns in tow. She had Noel and Theresa in a double pushchair – a funny-looking contraption that looked clumsy to push – and she was holding Ivy by the hand. Ivy was being very solemn and grown-up, walking beside her Nanna, and holding her wooden bucket and spade. Cathy, meanwhile, was looking flustered and hot and like she regretted walking all the way down here from Frederick Street in the broiling heat of midday. 'Hallo, lasses,' she called to them. 'We've come for some ices to cool us down.'

Irene happily obliged, and Cathy wouldn't dream of taking them off her for free. 'Let me get my purse out . . .' She fished around in her old leather handbag as the two bairns in the chair slobbered all over their ice creams and Ivy delicately picked at hers.

'Babysitting today, then?' bellowed Mavis, with her usual quickness of wit. She fussed over the three toddlers, desperate to hold them, to gather them up, just as she always was with anyone's kids. All three of Junie's children stared at her warily. She was much too noisy and kissy for their liking.

'Aye, I've got them all today, all night and most of tomorrow, too,' Cathy told the lasses. 'So I'm glad the sun's out so we can get out, get some air and kill some time . . .'

'You look shattered,' Irene told the landlady. 'They must be running you ragged.'

'Ah well, not really. They're just little . . . and I'm old. I'm feeling my age, aren't I? That's what it is.'

'You're not old,' Irene reassured her, spooning the sugar into her frothy coffee. Mind, having said that, Cathy certainly was looking her age in the bright sunlight today. She had widened considerably and become more thick-set. Her hair was streaked with silver and her usual glamorous make-up was reduced to just two quick spots of rouge and a dab of lipstick. It seemed to Irene that Cathy wasn't quite looking after herself these days.

'It's my poor daughter who I'm worried about,' Cathy confided to the ice-cream kiosk girls. 'She's going to drive herself into an early grave.'

'What?' gasped Mavis, alarmed by the sound of this.

'She's working herself too hard,' Cathy said. 'She's got jobs here and jobs there. She picks up every hour that she can. At the biscuit factory, then she's out cleaning. She's got at least three different cleaning jobs that I know of, and they're all over town, so she's dashing between them all the time. She's always in her pinny, carrying a bucket of cleaning supplies. She's never home these days. She never sees her bairns.'

'Ahh, that's a shame . . .' Mavis said, chucking the chins of the two babies as she crouched beside them. 'They're such lovely babbies, too.'

'I've warned her,' sighed Cathy. 'You'll miss out on them growing up. They'll be walking and at school before long. It all happens in a flash . . . I tell her: I missed out on her crucial years through no doing of my own, and it's the biggest regret of my life. I'd do anything to turn back time. But she's spending all her time scrubbing other people's houses out . . .'

'Oh dear,' Irene said. 'Is she really that needy for the money that she has to be out working all the time? Surely there has to be a balance?'

Cathy looked sceptical. 'Well, I don't know about all her financial affairs. I've said I can help out more, but she won't take any more from me. Mind, not that I'm rolling in it just now . . .'

'None of us are,' Irene agreed. 'But it's a shame if she makes herself ill with working. She could drive herself over the edge . . .'

'That's what I've warned her. But when did that lass ever listen to me?' Cathy sipped her coffee. 'I think she's in debt, that's what it is. All them fancy things she bought for her new house, after she moved up there with Derek? Well, she went in for expensive carpets and chairs, didn't she, after he died? It was like as if to cheer herself up. As if things like that can make up for such a loss.'

'Eeeh, they can't,' Mavis cried.

'Well, I think it was all on the never-never,' Cathy said. 'I've tried to talk about it with her, but she won't tell me. I think she's forking out all her money for this daft furniture that she hardly gets time to sit on. She's barely in that house of hers for more than two hours at a time. That flamin' palace of hers. She should just have stayed at my house . . .'

Cathy was getting herself aerated and the oldest child, Ivy, was taking note. She slid her hand into her grandma's grasp to reassure her.

'These bairns will grow up without hardly knowing who their mammy is,' Cathy sighed heavily. 'So what's the use of that?'

'Maybe one of us could have a word with Junie,' Irene mused. 'Someone she'll listen to, perhaps. They could tell her to accept more help, or help her look at her finances . . .'

'Who, though?' Cathy frowned. 'Who's she even close to, anymore?'

Irene clicked her fingers. 'What about Minnie? Those two were always so close.'

Cathy gave a bleak little laugh. '*Her*? Well, there's an irony. Because you'll never guess where our Junie has just started work this week . . .'

'Where?'

'Up at the big house itself. Now she's cleaning Lady Muck's castle by the sea.'

Chapter Forty-Nine

'Lady Muck' was what Junie and other friends called the old posh lady, Elizabeth Kendricks. They tended not to do it front of Minnie, her new daughter-in-law, however. Minnie had chosen her own destiny and thrown in her lot with Arthur's adoptive mother, incongruous as that seemed to everyone from the Sixteen Streets who knew her. It was hard to reconcile the idea of that flush-faced, friendly girl behind the counter of the fish bar with the idea of a lady in a big house by the sea.

But here she was. Waking up each morning in a room that overlooked the rolling waves and the beautiful beach. She was feeling luxurious and almost relaxed, waking up in such surroundings each day. There was no busy work for her to rush off to do, no family or friends to contend with, no noise as she stepped out of the door into the world outside. Minnie had never known such a quiet and peaceful time.

Arthur was away, of course. He hadn't been around much all year. In fact, with their first wedding anniversary approaching this autumn, it would be a wonder if he spent more than three weeks in the company of his wife during that whole first year. But such was the life of a travelling player, and of someone setting off on his journey on the show-business ladder. Minnie had never been under any illusions about what that life would be like.

Ever since *Cinderella* had finished in the frozen, endless days of January, Arthur had been away, seeking his fortune. He was her very own Dick Whittington, sending occasional gossip-filled letters and postcards from seaside resorts all around the country.

She had nothing to complain about, she knew. The life she was living had been very precisely described to her by Arthur: she had been warned. 'Mostly you'll be here for Elizabeth, with Elizabeth, being her companion and looking after the house. It will be your place, really, and you can make it all your own . . .'

The idea of an easier life had been very tempting, of course. No more dashing from job to job as she had done for as long as she could remember. But by . . . she did miss seeing everyone she knew. Working at Mary's Shop, or at Swetty Betty's, or at the Robin Hood, it had kept her in touch with everyone who was important to her. She had been abreast of all the developments, all the gossip. The work and making a living had been almost incidental to being in the midst of that great rush and deluge of living everyday life along with everyone else.

Living out here, in this decaying carbuncle of a house on the beach, she was separate from everyone she had ever known.

I've been a fool, Minnie realised, several weeks into her self-imposed exile in the Kendricks house.

And yes, it *was* a decaying carbuncle. Oh, she had been very impressed with it to begin with. The very first time she had come here, she had been so impressed. It was like somewhere the queen would live, she had thought. However, familiarity had brought a touch of contempt. The pipes were leaky and fractured. The primitive electrics would fail at the slightest thing and plunge the house into darkness. Windows were broken and the sea winds would creep in through a thousand hidden cracks in the masonry. The ceilings groaned at night as if about to give up the ghost and collapse.

Elizabeth Kendricks hadn't maintained her house. It had an air of dereliction that had kept pace with her own decline exactly. At some point before the war, she had given up looking after herself and her home at precisely the same moment.

Foolishly, Minnie had thought she could make a difference. Having moved in, she rolled up her sleeves and attempted to bring some pragmatism and hard work to bear on the mess and the chaos around her. She swept and mopped and polished. She soaked newspaper in white vinegar and tried to clean the accumulated muck off the remaining panes of glass in the conservatory. She put down poison for the rats and mice and borrowed two cats from her mother.

Elizabeth Kendricks sat in the draughty conservatory with a rug over her shoulders and watched all these efforts with mild, benign hope. 'I've rather let this place go to rack and ruin,' she pointed out, sipping her tea as she watched her daughter-in-law do all the work. She drank brandy in her tea from first thing in the morning. 'Bring me my special tea,' she asked Minnie, and through the day the proportions would alter, so that by four o'clock she was drinking almost completely neat brandy from her china cup.

For those initial weeks, Minnie threw herself gladly into all of these restorative tasks. It was almost a labour of love, the idea of bringing this place back to its one-time glory. She would fondly picture her beloved Arthur returning from a theatrical triumph for some time off between shows and being so surprised at the miracles she had wrought in his absence.

'Why . . . it looks exactly like it did when I was a bairn!' he would gasp, staring at the pale ice-cream colours of the big house. It would all be painted and lit up beautifully, like a beacon at the edge of the North Sea, calling him home to his mother and his devoted wife.

Still, there was a lot to do before it was anything like the beacon as Minnie imagined it. The task of getting everything shipshape and clean was losing its novelty and joy. By late summer, Minnie was becoming frustrated with herself and the tide of decay that was threatening to overtake everything. She was fed up with relatives and friends turning up to visit and finding her in her filthy old clothes, cleaning and scrubbing like Cinderella, while the old lady sat in the conservatory, playing the gracious hostess.

Minnie's mother had put it most succinctly: 'Is this what you wanted? Being that lazy old wifey's skivvy?'

Minnie had stared at her mother, furiously. 'No.'

'Well, that's what you are, lovely. I hate to break it to you. You've been a fool. She's got an unpaid servant running about the place. You cook and clean for her and I bet she's got you dressing her as well, hasn't she?'

Minnie had to admit that, yes, Elizabeth had come to rely more and more on her new daughter-in-law as the months had slipped past. There had been one or two falls, up in her lavish bedroom, and Minnie had been called upon to keep a closer eye on her and to hoick her out of her bath. None of these tasks were things that Minnie resented doing until her own mother was standing there, preparing to leave after an unsatisfactory visit, pointing out the obvious: 'You're her housemaid. That's what you are. And you're not even getting paid.'

Minnie watched her mother stump off down the drive that day and felt all her insides clench together with frustration and foolishness. When was her mother ever wrong about things? Minnie had wanted to refute her words and fight back, but she knew she was right.

I have been a fool, Minnie thought.

And then, next thing was, she found herself losing her temper with Elizabeth Kendricks.

'Oh, my dear, while you're up on your feet, would you mind fetching my shawl?' The requests would come in a mild, polite, rather helpless voice. 'Minnie darling, how about one of my special cups of tea?' Or, 'About time we had a fire lit in the drawing room, don't you think?' And Minnie would comply, gradually coming to see that no matter how politely or gently put, these requests were actually commands.

Then there would be the air of disapproval and the twist of the mouth when Minnie did something Elizabeth didn't care for. 'Tell me, my dear. Are we the sort of people who bring the milk bottle to the table? I don't think so.' Or, 'Don't we hang up our coats and outdoor things rather than leave them in the hall like this?'

Minnie bit her tongue, thinking: *She's old and she's used to living on her own and having her own way.* They would both have to get used to each other. Once Minnie allowed herself to retort with sarcasm, 'What did your last servant die of?'

'Typhoid, dear, it was very sad,' was all Elizabeth had to say to that.

Weeks and months went by and Minnie came to realise that she had made a mistake by coming to live here and, what was more: she was trapped.

'I am so glad that you and my adoptive mother are getting along so well,' Arthur wrote from Brighton that summer. 'It really means so much to me. You two are my best girls and it does my heart so much good to picture you, in my absence, living in this kind of seaside paradise together.'

If he could only see me, Minnie thought desperately when she read this particular missive. *Surely he'd be horrified to see how unhappy I am, and how Elizabeth treats me.* Oh, to the naked eye perhaps there was nothing to see. Nothing malign in the way she carried on, nothing bullying or overbearing. ('I think we're the kind of people who polish the silverware at least once a week, aren't we? Especially since it's in constant daily use. We don't like to sit down to tarnished silver, do we?') But somehow the old lady had chipped away at Minnie's sense of self and her confidence. By late summer, Minnie was a gibbering wreck, listening for the little bell that Elizabeth kept on her table and dashing to be at her side and to do her bidding.

'I need some help around this place,' Minnie told her mother-in-law eventually.

'Nonsense, dear,' Elizabeth snapped. 'It's not really a very grand house at all. It's perfectly manageable, I'm sure you'll find. When you're more used to the work, perhaps.'

Minnie sat opposite the old woman as she ate the breakfast Minnie had brought her. Soft-boiled egg and soldiers, brandy-laced tea. The old woman had golden yolk glistening on her chin and down the front of the satin nightie that Minnie had scrubbed by hand. All of Elizabeth's fine and expensive articles of apparel had to be scrubbed very carefully by hand, it turned out. Minnie suddenly decided that she had to stand up for herself. 'I need more help. We can afford to pay someone to come for a few hours each week.'

Elizabeth crunched on a finger of toast. 'Are we the sort of people who can simply throw money away needlessly, do you think?'

'It wouldn't be throwing money away,' Minnie protested.

'My dear, I think you mistake me for a much wealthier woman than I really am. Is that it? Did you think you were marrying into a fortune? Did you think you were going to live a life of luxury, moving in here with me?' Elizabeth threw back her head and laughed. It was a delicate, tinkling laugh. Minnie stared at her spindly, scrawny neck and felt a sudden impulse to throttle her. This darting urge frightened her and she squeezed her hands under her thighs in order to resist it.

'I don't want some easy life of luxury,' Minnie said. 'I never expected such a thing.'

'I should think not.' Elizabeth pursed her lips and started spooning up egg yolk again. 'This egg is rather raw, my dear. No, I should be very disappointed to find that my wonderful son had found himself a gold-digger . . .'

A gold-digger. Nothing could be further from the truth.

Minnie went off to spend the morning digging the front gardens. Turning the heavy, cloddy soil over with her spade felt good to her. These beds hadn't been tended to in years and the going was heavy and tough work. She loved the feeling of getting worn out as she worked and taking out all of her frustrations on the hard-packed earth.

'Hey, lady,' came a familiar voice from the front gate. 'Any chance of a cup of tea and a welcome from an old friend?'

It was Junie. Minnie hadn't seen her for weeks. She looked fit and well, in her work clothes and her hair tied up in a headscarf.

'I'm between jobs for an hour and I was going to go home to put my feet up. But then I thought . . . what about popping in to visit my old friend, Lady Muck?'

Minnie hugged her and led her happily into the house. 'Eeh, don't let Elizabeth hear you calling her that . . .'

Junie looked mischievous. 'I was calling *you* it, not her. You're the grand lady now.'

'Hardly . . .' Minnie said and led the way to the conservatory. Elizabeth had tottered off for her late-morning nap, and the breakfast things were still strewn everywhere, just as she had left them. Minnie could hear her mother-in-law's voice inside her head: 'Are we the sort of people who leave our dirty dishes lying around for visitors to see? I don't think we are, are we?'

Junie wrinkled her nose, taking in the mess and the smeared glass panes and the dying plants. 'This place is a dump,' she burst out. 'It's even worse than it was *before* you moved in.'

Minnie felt like crying. Suddenly she could see it all through her friend's eyes and she felt horribly ashamed and miserable. She could see herself, too, covered in mud and looking exhausted and unhappy.

'This is all wrong,' Junie said decisively. 'You, Minnie Minton, need my help.'

Chapter Fifty

Not even the formidable Elizabeth Kendricks could face up to Junie when she was determined. 'It stands to reason,' the young woman told her. 'Minnie is run off her feet and it's making her miserable. Can't you see that? And I need the extra hours of work.'

Mrs Kendricks grumbled a bit and pulled her face. She wasn't keen on Junie: there was something hard-faced about her. She couldn't be browbeaten and bullied like most people; it was obvious that she was tough as old boots. 'Well, all right, if you think so . . . but I'm not made of money. I can only pay the going rate . . .'

It wasn't even as much as that. Mrs Kendricks paid less than even the meanest of Junie's cleaning jobs, but at least it meant that Junie could be there in the house a couple of days a week. She could keep an eye on Minnie and see that she was all right. To her surprise, Junie had found that she cared deeply about her old friend. She couldn't help thinking: *What would I have done over the years without Minnie nearby? I've taken her devotion for granted.* Junie hadn't even realised she cared that much for her until she saw Minnie looking so fed up, trying to live in that mucky house with the old woman.

'I'll look after you,' she told Minnie. 'You'll see. I'll do it for Derek's sake. He would hate to see you having a rotten time.'

Junie's kindness almost brought Minnie to tears. On those first few days that Junie swept round the place, cleaning and tidying with great efficiency, Minnie followed her about, awkward and grateful.

It was hard to reconcile this hard-working Junie with the spoiled girl that Minnie had known for much of her life. This wasn't a vain and showy girl. It was one who knew how to roll up her sleeves and get on with things. Motherhood and widowhood had clearly changed Junie forever. A part of Minnie was delighted to see her change, but another part couldn't help wondering about the Junie of old. Wondering if she wasn't up to something, and after something . . .

One day towards the end of summer, the two of them took a break outside the conservatory, sitting in the sandy marram grass and looking out to sea. They smoked Woodbines and sighed at the sight of the rolling waves. 'It must make up for the misery of it all, living right by the sea like this,' Junie said.

'It's not all misery,' Minnie smiled. 'Not quite.'

'You can't lie to me, Minnie Minton,' Junie told her fiercely. 'You never bliddy could. It was a mistake you moving here and you know it. You're stuck in this mausoleum with that old cow and now you're too proud to admit how unhappy you are.'

'Oh, she's not so bad. She's just disappointed in life, and it's made her go a bit funny and loopy.'

Junie gave a bitter laugh. 'Ha. We can all say we've had our disappointments. We can all go a bit funny. But we just have to get on with things, don't we? We have to live our lives as best we can.'

Minnie looked away from her, into the endless, colourless waves of the North Sea. She dragged very deeply on her rough cigarette. 'The thing is, I tried so hard for so long. I threw myself into everything, doing as best I could. Helping Mam out, helping Cathy out. Working at the counter even though

I felt shy, and trying to join in with everyone, even though I knew I was the type to be left on the sidelines . . .'

Junie pulled a sceptical face, but she listened anyway, knowing that Minnie was wrestling with expressing her true feelings: they weren't easy for her to put into words.

'And then Arthur came along, and I thought – oh, I like being a part of this pair. I feel braver in the world, somehow. Now I can be seen by other people. And so I tried my very hardest at something else. I was his fiancée and I did my best to play the part. And so I ended up here . . .'

'Lady Muck,' Junie grinned, and stubbed out her fag in the deep sand.

'Aye . . . and I end up thinking, after all the effort I've put into everything . . . was any of it worth it? I mean, I feel like I've been trying to be someone that other people wanted me to be. The effort seems . . . Oh, I don't know. I don't know what I'm trying to say, really . . .'

Junie held her gaze and was about to say something when they were rudely interrupted by shouts from the open French windows. 'Oh, Minnie! Minnie, come quickly. Oh . . . where are you, girl? Where the devil have you got to?'

Elizabeth Kendricks sounded breathless and panicked. When Minnie and Junie traipsed down from the grassy hill to find her, she looked wildly excited, with her nightie blowing up around her. 'Girls! Girls, there's been such wonderful news.'

'News . . .?' Minnie asked, dashing to her.

'The telephone rang and there was no one there to answer it. So I got up and picked up the receiver and you'll never guess who was at the other end . . .?'

'Surprise us,' Junie snapped, rolling her eyes and picking up her bucket and mop.

'It was Arthur.' Elizabeth beamed. 'Arthur phoned.'

'Oh,' said Minnie. 'But . . . didn't he want to talk to me . . .?'

A flicker of irritation crossed the old woman's face. 'You weren't anywhere to be found. Besides, payphones are terribly expensive. Do you think he's made of money? Anyhow, listen to what he had to say . . .'

Minnie was eager to hear it. They bustled inside the conservatory and Elizabeth looked flushed and excited.

'He's coming home! He's coming to visit. Isn't that wonderful . . .?'

It was the following Monday, and Arthur was only going to be around for less than half a day.

'It turns out that he's en route to Scotland with this tour and he's managed to wangle a little time off on the journey. Just enough to stop by and see us . . .'

Junie looked highly sceptical about the whole business. 'Less than a day? Hardly worth bothering with. What's he going to do in half a day?'

Minnie shrugged. 'It's enough to see us, and to have a bite to eat . . .'

The two of them were in the kitchen at the big house, which was a lot cleaner and usable since Junie had started working there. Together, they were making pies and fancy little vol-au-vents to tempt Arthur's appetite when he stopped by.

'Everyone always makes a fuss of Arthur . . .' Junie muttered.

'It'll be worth it, even if he's only here for a few hours . . .' Minnie beamed. Personally, she couldn't wait to see him again. He had become a kind of mythical, made-up person in her head. It was like she could hardly remember what it was like to be with him.

In the event, he was rather late.

He rolled up at the front of the house in a taxicab he had paid to bring him all the way from Newcastle.

Elizabeth was scandalised by the sight of the shining, beetle-like cab. 'But that must have cost you a fortune.'

Arthur shrugged, pulling her close to kiss her on the forehead. She basked momentarily in his embrace. Then he was turning to look for Minnie, who was suddenly right by his side and throwing herself into his arms. 'Ahh, Minnie, pet,' he smiled, as if he was hugging a dog. Then he noticed Junie staring at him through narrowed eyes. 'My mother told me that you were working here now, Junie,' he said. 'It's nice to see you.'

Junie nodded, taking in his dandified appearance in one hostile glance. Those clothes he had on were clearly expensive. That jacket and trousers must have cost a pretty penny. His tie looked like something out of Liberty's. Surely he couldn't afford to dress like that on the money he got in a repertory company? All at once, Junie felt even more suspicious about Arthur than she usually did. Where was he getting all his money from? Maybe he had some rich old lady looking after him? Another one.

'Come inside, my dear,' Elizabeth told him. 'We have a delicious lunch all prepared for you.'

It turned out that Arthur had less than two hours before the car had to come and fetch him again, to take him back to the train station in Newcastle. Two hours. Minnie felt her hopes of seeing him on his own crumbling away. They were going to sit at the dining table and watch him eat and Elizabeth was going to fire questions at him and monopolise all of his attention. She just knew how it was going to be.

They sat at the polished table and Junie helped Minnie bring in the fruits of all their kitchen labours. The corned beef and onion pie had once been Arthur's favourite when he lived with his sister, but today he couldn't help turning up his nose at the sight of it. 'Oh dear, it's going back to wartime food,' he chuckled. 'This reminds me of making do with what we had. Ha ha!' He lifted up the pastry and sniffed the pie and pulled a face. 'Ah, did you make this, Minnie? Well, good try . . . though I don't think I'm all that peckish, really.'

Elizabeth tried to get him to eat some of the fancy pastry puffs she'd asked Minnie to make, but Arthur only nibbled at things, really. He'd become skinnier than ever. There was hardly a picking on him, and Minnie remarked on the fact.

'It's all the dancing,' he told her eagerly. 'They've always got me doing numbers and dancing, whatever the show is. Even Shakespeare. They recognise what I'm good at, you see. So I'm forever hoofing my way across the stage and, as you can tell, it's made me keep my figure.' He glanced pointedly at Minnie, who felt like she had ballooned in recent unhappy months. She crammed her mouth with mushroom vol-au-vent and smiled at him.

'I'd love to see your show,' she said.

'Well, maybe on the next leg of the tour,' he smiled. 'But not yet. I'm going to be away another six months on this one. All round Scotland and then down the North-West. Panto in Lytham St Anne's, this year.'

'Lytham St Anne's?' Minnie echoed. 'Where's that?'

It was a long way from home, was the answer. Near Blackpool.

'I'm never going to see you, am I?' she asked him.

'Now, now, dear,' Elizabeth berated her. 'You mustn't think only about yourself. How do you think it makes Arthur feel? Being away from his nearest and dearest so much? He must be simply riven with anguish at the very thought. Aren't you, my love? Aren't you disappointed at being away so much?'

Arthur simply beamed at the three of them. 'To be honest? I'm having the time of my life. I wouldn't have it any other way.'

Minnie suddenly felt close to tears and he noticed this. He grasped both her hands in his own.

'Though, of course, I miss you terribly. It does me good, though, to know that you are living here in the lap of luxury, in the care of my beloved mother. Why, that thought keeps me going through all the hard work and the lonely nights.'

This made Minnie feel the tiniest bit better.

Then it was time for the black cab to roll up at the front door, and they left the messy, mostly untouched meal on the table and hurried out to see him off.

'Why, it's just like waving you off to war again,' Elizabeth called out as he jumped into his cab.

'I will see you all again very soon,' he waved grandly from the back window, and then the car roared off down the drive, on its way back to Newcastle.

Junie turned to look at Minnie, who stood there on the gravel drive with a peculiar, lost expression on her face. 'Well, that's that,' Junie said, with a shrug.

Elizabeth led the way back indoors. 'That poor boy,' she muttered. 'He works so, so hard . . .'

Chapter Fifty-One

It was a chilly autumn morning, early on, and Junie had left her bairns in the care of her mother, Cathy. 'Eeeh, I've traipsed some miles for you these past few months,' Cathy tutted, looking absolutely shattered. 'Not that I mind, of course. It's lovely spending my day with the bairns . . .'

Junie looked less than delighted to be trekking out to Elizabeth Kendricks's house, where the old woman seemed to becoming more imperious and doolally by the day. And the house. That great, big white elephant of a palace on the shifting sands . . . well! It was becoming increasingly decrepit and dirty by the day. Whatever effort both Junie and Minnie could put into it, all was to no avail. The sea winds came rushing in and blew filthy dust and sand into every nook and cranny and loosened every shingle, every tile.

'The whole place is falling apart,' Junie opined gloomily that morning. 'It doesn't matter what we do. Those outside walls I painted in the summer – have you seen them? They look just as patchy and dingy as ever.'

Minnie privately thought that was because Junie had mixed the wrong kind of paint, but she wasn't about to criticise her when Junie was in this mood. Instead, she kept a wary distance as she watched Junie put together Elizabeth's usual breakfast tray and take it through to her in the conservatory.

'Ah, there you are, girls. Late!' the old woman snapped peevishly. They weren't late with her breakfast at all: she just liked having something to mither about. 'This tea's rather lukewarm,' she said, sipping her cup.

'That's because it's half brandy,' Junie told her.

'What's that?' Elizabeth frowned.

'Nothing,' Junie beamed at her. 'Do you want a top-up?'

Junie filled her cup several times as Elizabeth crunched up her toast, and Minnie noticed that she was pouring brandy each time, too. 'You'll get her drunk too early in the day,' she fretted.

Junie didn't care. 'Good. Maybe she'll sleep and then we'll get some peace.'

The two of them carried dishes back to the messy kitchen and scrubbed them in the deep sink. The water boiler wasn't working, so the sink was filled with greasy suds and Minnie had to keep heating the kettle.

'This whole place should be knocked down,' muttered Junie. 'Don't you think?'

'Don't say that,' Minnie said. 'It's Elizabeth's home . . .'

'That old bag,' grunted Junie. She plunged her hands into the dirty water with a grimace. 'Do you know, when I think about all those bombs falling on the town during the raids, and when I think about the bombs left unexploded, like the one that got our poor Derek . . .' She shook her head tearfully and scraped the hair away from her face. 'I wish those bombs had fallen on all these old places. They're falling down anyway. Why couldn't the bombs have smashed them all up. Like this horrible old house and this old woman.'

Minnie was horrified at her. 'Junie, that's awful. You oughtn't to say wicked things like that.'

'Why not?' Junie snarled. She picked the cups and saucers one at a time out of the greasy water and shook them. 'Look at this old rubbish.' With a sudden impulse, she dashed one of Elizabeth's favourite teacups onto the tiled floor. It shattered loudly and she looked satisfied. 'Here, you smash one as well, Minnie.'

'No,' Minnie gasped. 'Junie, you're being—'

'Being what? Terrible? Horrible? Wicked? Well, *good*. Because that's how I feel.' With that, she smashed another dirty cup, and a saucer. 'This rotten dump. I wish it was all blown sky-high. And all those slums, too.'

'What slums?' Minnie frowned. 'Junie, what on earth are you talking about . . .?'

'The Sixteen Streets,' cried Junie. 'All of them. All those outdated slummy, rubbishy streets of houses. Everyone living in each other's pockets. Everyone doing just as they're told. Living their little lives and keeping their hopes and dreams and unhappiness hidden away.'

She was striding about the kitchen now, looking and sounding quite mad as far as Minnie was concerned. 'Junie, calm down . . . it isn't all bad . . .'

'I wish the bombs had destroyed all of it. Everything. All the past. And then we could all start again. We could start again, from scratch. And maybe we could all be on level pegging, eh? We could all have just the same and there'd be no one feeling that they were better than anyone else. No one like this snobby old bitch who owns this dump.'

'Junie . . .!' Minnie was starting to wonder if her friend had been on the brandy as well, this early in the morning. 'You're going off your head, man.'

'No, I'm not,' Junie said. 'I'm just sad and exhausted and I'm angry. That's what I am.'

Then, all at once, she was out of the kitchen and back in the conservatory. Minnie followed worriedly.

'Aye, you were right,' Junie said. 'The extra grog ration has knocked the old witch out. Good. That's us taking the morning off. No more work for us, Minnie.'

*

It was Junie's idea to crack open the cocktail cabinet under the stairs and then to dash up to the old woman's boudoir, where they dragged open her wardrobes to look at all the old frocks.

'Oh, I knew it was a treasure trove, but these are spectacular,' Junie gasped. She ran her work-sore hands through silk gowns of every colour. 'She must have been the belle of the ball on Tyneside in her day. That old cow down there, just imagine!'

'Let's not get them all out,' Minnie worried. 'She'll notice we've been among her things . . .'

'Oh, I don't care. She can't do anything to me.'

'She can sack you. You need the money, don't you?'

Junie paused midway through stripping off her work clothes. 'I can get cleaning work just about anywhere. Everywhere needs a good worker like me. Don't you see, Minnie? The reason I'm here, the reason I'm working for the old woman, is to keep an eye on *you* . . . I'm here to look after *you*, Minnie, love.'

'Oh!' said Minnie, who had suspected this, but loved to hear it spoken out loud. Junie was doing something selfless – just for her. It felt wonderful. After all their years of friendship, it filled her with a warm sense of accomplishment and love, just like the Apricot Schnapps was doing.

Soon, both women were trying on the most wonderful garments they could find in the depths of Elizabeth's dressing room. They lost all sense of time, or of how noisy they were being. They took turns parading up and down on the soft carpet, swishing their gowns about and draping furs over their shoulders.

'Arthur told me once that he did this,' Minnie was laughing, 'when he was a little boy. Him and Mavis came up here and they were messing about, just like bairns do. He was in one of Elizabeth's old frocks and she came and found him. She came bursting in here and frightened the life out of him.'

Junie was laughing too, and at the spectacle of the pair of them, dolled up to the nines in outdated clothes. 'He's never stopped dressing up, that one,' she cried. 'He's more of a lady than we'll ever be . . .'

This made Minnie laugh more than ever, but she hardly knew what she was laughing about. She wanted to laugh and cry at the same time. It was like everything was rising up in her breast all at once. All the feelings she had pushed down over the months. It was all mixed up inside of her: everything to do with Derek and Arthur and everything else. All the changes that had come to her poor life. Plus the fact that she was here, with her best friend, Junie, dressing up and carrying on and laughing about it all. It all seemed crazy and it was making her feel quite dizzy and sick.

'Oh, Junie Sturrock, I do love you,' she said.

Junie beamed at her. 'Aye, I know you do, hinny.'

And then there was a screeching cry from the doorway of the bedroom.

They both turned to see Elizabeth leaning in the door frame, looking confused and drunk. She was muttering incoherently. 'You *damned* little bitches,' she shouted at last. 'What the devil do you think you're doing in here . . . ?'

There was a horrible, silent moment when they stared back at her. They really had made a mess of her room. Gowns and wraps and silken under-things were strewn on every surface. *What have we done?* Minnie thought wildly. *Have we gone mad?*

'Get out, get out, get out . . .!' Elizabeth shouted, her voice getting higher and louder, like an air-raid siren.

Junie laughed in her face. 'Don't worry. We will!'

'You! You're hopeless. What kind of help have you been? You're *sacked*.'

'Good!' Junie cried.

'Elizabeth . . .' Minnie began, intent on mollifying her.

'And you can have your cards, as well. You're sacked, too,' Elizabeth screeched.

'Y-you can't sack me . . . I'm your daughter-in-law!'

'Yes, I can,' Elizabeth shouted. 'Get out. Get out. Get out of here!'

Junie and Minnie looked at each other.

Then they took off, together, at a run.

Without looking back, they ran down the curving staircase and out of the front door. They raced over the sandy hills and through the stiff grass to the beach. They left the big house and the old woman far behind them.

'She sacked me!' Minnie whooped. 'That old woman sacked me as her daughter-in-law.' For some reason, she found this hilariously funny and halfway down the beach she had to bend over with a stitch. But she couldn't stop laughing. 'She's thrown me out.'

'You're best off without her,' Junie told her. 'That old place was doing your head in.' She took out the bottle of brandy she'd snatched on the way out and passed it to her friend.

'But what now?' Minnie asked, looking up and down the empty beach. 'Where do I even go now? And how do I live . . .?'

Junie grabbed hold of her arm. 'Come and live with me, in my lovely house. Come and live with me and the bairns. There's all the space we need and we'd love to have you there. Come on, Minnie. Come and live in our place with us. Wouldn't we be happy? We'd be happy as anything, don't you think?'

Minnie looked at Junie and her eyes widened at the thought of them living in the same place together with all her bairns. 'Yes, I think you're right,' she said. 'I think we could be very happy indeed.'

Chapter Fifty-Two

Cathy's party at the Robin Hood was on the twenty-eighth of December, slap bang between Christmas and New Year. It was becoming traditional, that all her regulars and most local punters would spend the whole of that evening getting pie-eyed at her expense. She would spend a whole day baking sweet and savoury party food and laying it out on the tables ready for the hordes to descend. It was Cathy's way of saying thank you to her fellow denizens of the Sixteen Streets for another year of keeping body and soul together.

This year, Ma Ada very generously offered to stay at home during the party and to look after all the bairns at number thirteen. There was quite a tribe to take care of. What with Irene and Tom's kiddies, and Megan's, and then there were Junie's babies, too. 'I'll have a little nursery at mine,' Ma Ada suggested. 'I'm too old and tired for parties nowadays. I'll stay home with all the bairns and everyone else can enjoy themselves.'

Well, she almost had a fight on her hands with Betty Minton from next door. 'If anyone is staying at home and doing the babysitting, it's going to be me,' she thundered crossly. 'I'm not big on enjoying myself these days. You might as well let me look after all the kiddies.'

It soon became a competition between the two Nannas, about who could be the most put upon and averse to parties.

'I don't care who you decide is looking after them,' Junie told them in the end. 'Just so long as it isn't me. I want a night off from bairns. I want to enjoy myself tonight.'

Typical Junie, they thought. Just as outspoken and self-centred as ever. Oh, but she looked a picture dolled up in a new frock ready for her Christmas party. The older women looked at her with joy and relief, seeing that some of her spirit had returned at last. Old Swetty Betty clasped her in her arms and said, 'If only our Derek could see you now. He'd say you were a right bobby-dazzler.'

Junie awkwardly hugged her mother-in-law back. She found it hard, the way that Betty would bring up Derek every opportunity she could. As if Junie needed reminding who she had been married to. Of course she would spend time, quite often, mourning lovely Derek, too . . . but time moved on. It had to. Life kept surging onwards, didn't it? You couldn't afford to spend too long looking backwards with regret or anger or pain. Junie had learned that much in this past couple of years: that life was for those who could keep looking and moving forward. If you looked backwards too much, then you were lost.

'Tell you what, *I'll* stay home and look after all the bairns,' suggested Harry Minton, looking determined all of a sudden.

'You?' Betty smiled.

'Why not? I'm a damned good babysitter.'

'You'll teach them all your rude songs again . . .'

In the event, the small nursery was run by Harry and Bob and Tom Farley, all of whom were more than happy to stay home for the night.

*

The Robin Hood was mostly dominated by women for Cathy's party that year. The Women's Table by the fireplace was overrun, and all at once every table had women at it.

'It's a bit bloomin' noisy in here,' Ma Ada complained.

'That'll be the singing . . .' her daughter-in-law, Beryl, smirked.

'Who the devil is that, braying away like that?' Ada asked. 'Oh, Lily Johnson . . .' The diminutive, raven-haired chanteuse was standing on a bar stool beside Aunty Martha's out-of-tune piano. She was belting out a brand-new song called 'Rudolf the Red-Nosed Reindeer' at the top of her voice. 'Why on earth do people encourage her?'

Winnie, Betty, Irene and Bella Franchino were also clustered about the Women's Table, tucking into ham and pease pudding stotties and talking about the year gone by. They had already reached the conclusion that it had been a dramatic and disturbing year, once more, and they would all settle for something more sedate and straightforward next year.

Psychic Winnie's eyes lit up at this mention of the future. 'Ah, well,' she began. 'You're asking for a more sedate time, are you? Well, let me tell you . . .!'

Ma Ada shushed her. 'I don't think we want to know too much in advance, do we, girls? Let's just take the future at our own pace, shall we? And deal with everything as it comes along . . .'

They all agreed and toasted each other in milk stout and pale ale.

'Here come your lasses,' Ma Ada told Betty, nodding at the door. Junie and Minnie were entering the saloon, all done up in their party frocks, having left the bairns at number thirteen with the already exhausted menfolk. 'Eeh, aren't they lucky to have each other? After everything – their friendship has been the making of them. It's saved them both from even more heartache.'

'Aye, well,' Betty nodded. 'It's working out so far . . . I just wish they lived closer to us lot in the Sixteen Streets. That estate of theirs . . . it's too modern. It's got no soul to it. No heart.'

'Oh, I think it's lovely, where they are,' Ma Ada smiled. 'That house is like a palace inside. Goodness knows how Junie could afford all that fancy furniture. Oh, I think it would be smashing to live somewhere like that. Your Minnie has certainly landed on her feet.'

Betty buried her discontent and mumbled into her glass. She'd have been much happier if Minnie had come back home. It had been a disturbing year, full of horrible upheavals. For some reason, Minnie was intent on staying away and living at Junie's house, where, it seemed to her mother, she was left to do all the housework by herself while Junie swanned around all her days in a quilted housecoat. Well, there was nothing Betty could say. You could never tell younger folk what to do, could you? It only ended up causing upset when you did . . .

There was kerfuffle then, as Mavis noisily arrived at their table, gabbling away with all the gossip from her less salubrious part of town. She also had a letter from her brother, Arthur, which had been enclosed with his somewhat gaudy Christmas card. 'What's that funny fella got to say for himself, eh?' Ma Ada smiled.

'Well!' Mavis said. 'As you know, he's appearing in Pantomime at Lytham St Anne's near Blackpool, and guess what? He's not Buttons this year – he's the dame. He's one of the ugly sisters and he's having a ball.'

'A female impersonator!' laughed Irene. 'Oh, I'd love to see him up there on that bloomin' stage.'

Mavis was nodding. 'Aye, aye, he says he's going to be the best in the business. Listen to this bit: "I have found my show-business calling, Mavis. I should have known what it was. To make a living in this world, it turns out that I have to don a fancy frock and a wig and pretend to be a lady. Oh, but I have been enjoying it, lovey. I feel like I'm free to do anything – I can be anyone at all when I'm up on that stage . . ."'

Mavis read out her little bit and all the ladies looked impressed.

'Well, good luck to him,' Ada Farley said.

'Aye, so long as he comes back for our Minnie,' said Betty. 'So long as he makes our Minnie happy.'

The other women all exchanged glances at this, thinking that Betty was kidding herself. It was well known that Minnie had fled Arthur's adoptive mother's house and left that whole life behind. She wasn't content to be the old woman's slave, and neither should she be. Arthur hadn't been home yet to try to pick up the pieces. He was by all accounts too busy dressing up as a lady somewhere near Blackpool.

'You should show Minnie your letter,' Betty told Mavis.

Over at the bar, Cathy was chatting away with her daughter Junie, and Minnie had fallen gladly into the arms of her friend and erstwhile workmate Susan. 'Eeh, I've not seen you in weeks, pet. How's Mary's Shop doing? How are your sisters?'

Susan was wearing one of her eccentric outfits put together from second-hand stock, including a cloche hat that must have been more than twenty years old. 'Well, my sisters are at each other's throats arguing, as usual. They can't seem to agree about anything to do with the shop. All the bother between them is driving my poor dad into an early grave.' She beamed at Minnie and told her: 'I wish you'd come back and work at our shop again. We used to have fun, didn't we? And when we worked on the market stall together, we used to have a great laugh.'

'Yes, we did,' Minnie smiled fondly, though when she thought of it, it all seemed like a hundred years ago. She did rather miss her busy life when she used to race between jobs at that ramshackle emporium on Westoe Road, and the fish bar and then back here to the Robin Hood. Why, Minnie had loved being in the thick of life and seeing everyone. Nowadays – though she loved her home with Junie and the bairns – it felt as if she hardly saw many people at all. Just Junie and the bairns. 'Well, maybe in the new year,' she said musingly. 'Maybe I can get some hours away from home, and come back to work with you at the emporium . . .'

Susan's eyes lit up at this. She had really missed her lovely friend.

Then Lily Johnson was mangling 'My Old Man Said Follow the Van', which was a favourite of the drinkers at the Robin Hood. Suddenly, everyone was up on their feet and joining in.

Cathy Sturrock took a pause from serving drinks at the bar and sighed happily. Now, this was what it was all about. All the difficulties and heartaches that the years might bring – and it seemed that no year was exempt from those things – they all came to a climax here, in this pub. At the year's end, everyone could gather here to say goodbye to their woes and look ahead to whatever might be coming next.

This evening was somehow both rowdy and peaceful all at once and Cathy was very glad of that fact. And she was glad to stand there, taking stock of her friends and relations all about her, and to still feel like the woman who everyone called the Queen of the Sixteen Streets. Cathy stood there in her green velvet frock and her red hair piled up beautifully just so and felt every inch their queen.

However, with Bob on babysitting duties, she had more lifting work to do than usual tonight, and that included fetching in a fresh barrel of ale from the back. 'Oh hell,' she cursed, surprised by how much beer the mostly female gathering was getting through tonight.

She was glad of the cool of the backyard of the pub, however, when she nipped out to fetch the barrel. The frosty air was welcome on her flushed face and she stood breathing it in for a moment or two.

Well, here I am, she thought. *Right at the very heart of my world*. Her thoughts drifted momentarily back to her one-time husband, old Noel Sturrock, who was once landlord here, and his kindly and ancient mother, Theresa. Back when Cathy was nothing but a runaway girl, they had taken her in and made her part of their lives here. Yes, Noel had treated her like dirt at times and her life had been a nightmare. She thought she would never be free of him. But in the end she had to admit that she was grateful to Noel and his mother, looking back. Her life here in the Sixteen Streets was just as good as it would have been anywhere. Cathy Sturrock had no regrets.

Here at the top of the hill, in the middle of the Sixteen Streets, she had been happy. Here where the air smelled of biscuit factory smoke and . . .

Hang on. Why could she smell biscuit factory smoke? It was the twenty-eighth of December. The furnaces and ovens and the chimneys were cold. There'd be no more smoke till the new year started.

Cathy hurriedly opened the gate and tumbled out into the cobbles of Frederick Street.

Oh no . . . *Oh no*.

There, down the hill, the factory buildings and chimneys were outlined brightly against the starry night sky. They were all engulfed in gold and scarlet flames.

It took a second or two for Cathy to find her voice. She jolted into action, hurried around to the front of the building and burst back into the saloon bar. She stared wild-eyed at the noisy, happy room and she knew she had to silence all the revellers to get their attention.

Cathy screamed at the top of her voice: *'The biscuit factory . . . it's on fire!'*

Acknowledgements

Thanks to Jeremy, my family and friends, agent Piers, editor Rhea, Snigdha and everyone at Orion.

Credits

Elsie Mason and Orion Fiction would like to thank everyone at Orion who worked on the publication of *The Loveless Child* in the UK.

Editorial
Rhea Kurien
Snigdha Koirala

Copyeditor
Alice Fewery

Proofreader
Jade Craddock

Audio
Paul Stark
Louise Richardson

Contracts
Dan Herron

Ellie Bowker
Oliver Chacón

Design
Charlotte Abrams-Simpson

Editorial Management
Charlie Panayiotou
Jane Hughes
Bartley Shaw

Finance
Jasdip Nandra
Sue Baker
Nick Gibson

Production
Ruth Sharvell

Sales
David Murphy
Esther Waters
Victoria Laws

Rachael Hum
Frances Doyle
Georgina Cutler

Operations
Jo Jacobs

Also by Elsie Mason

The Runaway Girl, the first in the Sixteen Streets series

1918. Fleeing from her past, Cathy Carmichael is new to the Sixteen Streets. She has nothing to her name, no plan and nowhere to go.

Cathy thinks she's struck gold when she runs into Mrs Sturrocks, an elderly lady who offers her a room at her boarding house. Her son, Noel, might be strange and sulky, but he gives her a job at the Robin Hood pub and before long, Cathy is thriving as the new barmaid.

The Sixteen Streets was only meant to be a temporary stop for Cathy... but could it become home instead?

The Forgotten Daughter, the second in the Sixteen Streets series

Tyneside, 1930s. Years after she first fled to South Shields, Cathy is known by everyone as the landlady of the Robin Hood pub. But Cathy has a secret from her life before - a daughter, June, whom she had to leave behind.
After all these years, can June accept her?

Cathy's friend Sofia faces her own dilemma. Encountering a man from her past, Sofia is given the opportunity to return to her hometown, Naples. It would mean escaping her own troubles in the Sixteen Streets... if only she dares take the chance.

Cathy and Sofia have worked hard to shed the sorrows of their youth. But maybe by revisiting the past, they can work towards a happier future...

The Biscuit Factory Girl Series

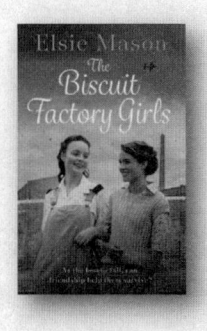

Newly married to dashing RAF officer, Tom, Irene Farley leaves behind her safe countryside life to move in with his family by the docks in South Shields. Little prepares her for the devastation the Jerry bombers have wreaked on the Sixteen Streets or that they should be living under her mother-in-law's roof, alongside Tom's three brothers and two wives!

Irene's only escape is her job at the local Wright's Biscuit factory packing up a little taste of home for the brave boys fighting for King and country across the channel. As the threat of war creeps ever closer to the Sixteen Streets, the biscuit factory girls bond together, because no one can get through this war alone . . .

Beryl was the first Farley clan bride, finding a home in the arms of loving, attentive, elder son Tony. Yet even now, wrapped in Tony's embrace, Beryl has never quite been able to forget the past she ran away from, nor the shocking family secret she tried to bury.

With Tony away fighting the Jerries alongside his brothers, it's up to Beryl and her sisters-in-law to keep the family afloat. Hard, gruelling work doesn't faze her, but the sudden arrival of a devastating letter does...

Will Beryl be able to hold her family together and face up to her past? Or will the war take away the one thing she holds most dear - the one person she never thought she deserved?

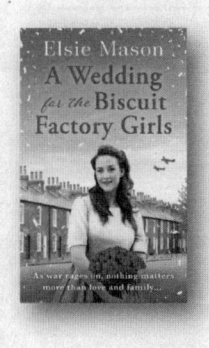

Her wedding day should have been the happiest day of Mavis Kendricks' life. Marrying handsome Sam, the youngest of the Farley boys, means joining the Farley clan, and there's nothing Mavis has ever wanted more than a family of her own. But the appearance of an unexpected guest ruins everything... and brings back painful memories Mavis would rather forget.

It's not long before the war-torn streets of South Shields are buzzing with rumours. One of the biscuit factory girls, funny little Mavis has always been a bit of a mystery. As far as anyone can remember, Mavis and her twin Arthur have been orphans. So who was the grand old lady at the wedding? How do the twins own their own house? And just what is Mavis hiding? On the Sixteen Streets, nothing stays a secret for long...